I0761617

The Girls Before

Also by Kate Alice Marshall

A Killing Cold
No One Can Know
What Lies in the Woods

We Won't All Survive
The Narrow
These Fleeting Shadows
Our Last Echoes
Rules for Vanishing
I Am Still Alive

Thirteens
Brackenbeast
Glassheart
Extra Normal

The Girls Before

A Novel

Kate Alice Marshall

PINE &
CEDAR
NEW YORK

This is a work of fiction. All the characters, organizations, and events portrayed in this novel are either products of the author's imagination or used fictitiously.

 Printed in the United States of America. For information, address Flatiron Books, 120 Broadway, New York, NY 10271. EU Representative: Macmillan Publishers Ireland Ltd., 1st Floor, The Liffey Trust Centre, 117–126 Sheriff Street Upper, Dublin 1, D01 YC43.

www.flatironbooks.com

Designed by Sue Walsh

Library of Congress Cataloging-in-Publication Data

Names: Marshall, Kate Alice, author.
Title: The girls before : a novel / Kate Alice Marshall.
Description: First edition. | New York : Pine & Ceder, 2026.
Identifiers: LCCN 2025027606 | ISBN 9781250343086 (hardcover) |
ISBN 9781250343093 (ebook)
Subjects: LCGFT: Thrillers (Fiction) | Novels | Fiction
Classification: LCC PS3613.A7746 G57 2026
LC record available at https://lccn.loc.gov/2025027606

First Edition: 2026

10 9 8 7 6 5 4 3 2 1

For those who are lost, and those who are searching

Part I

Above

Below

Below

I don't know how long I've been down here in the dark. Three days? Four? Maybe longer since the door at the top of the concrete steps (*twelve steps: the bottom one is cracked; it will try to catch your foot*) has opened. Since I last saw the rectangle of light and the shape that cancels it.

That's how I think of my captor: the shape, the shadow. Never a person, never a beast or a monster, not even really a *thing* but an event. There is an arrival and a departure. And in between—I blot it out, like the shape blots out the light.

Always it comes, and always it leaves, and always it comes again.

Until now.

I've never been alone down here for this long. Except that I'm not alone, not really. I'm never alone because the other girls are here.

They carved their names in the secret place—their names, their words, their warnings. Instructions passed from one dead girl to another in the hopes that one of us might survive. And with their names, I have conjured them, here in the dark where there is no difference between opening your eyes and closing them, between the waking and the nightmares. Their whispers are a gossamer sound, like insect wings being drawn over one another. Their shapes are gossamer, too, hallucinatory, flickering at the edge of the nothing that is my vision—glimpses of gleaming hair, pale limbs, bruised throats, and gaping wounds. I have no idea how they actually died, but I can never imagine them whole.

It's good that it's been so long since the door opened, one of the girls whispers.

Maybe it won't ever open again, another says.

A girl with sparks of auburn in her hair gives a hiss. *If the door doesn't open, the food will run out.*

So what?

So she'll die.

I know they aren't real. My mind has invented them to stave off the madness of a world without light, without any sound but my own breathing, the horrible beating of my own heart.

These are the things that are real: A wooden bed frame. A thin mattress, stained, occupied by things that scuttle over my limbs when I sleep. A cold chain, one end anchored to the wall, the other to the manacle around my ankle. The quarter circle the chain affords me: six steps to the corner, no more. The toilet, the plastic crate, the supplies inside it. The world beyond my fingertips: concrete walls, everything gray. Milk crates against one wall. A table, two chairs (I have been allowed to sit there, sometimes). A broom and dustpan in the corner (I have been instructed, sometimes, to use it). A light switch on the wall, far out of reach.

And the stairs. Twelve steps. The door at the top. If I am fast enough, someday. If I am strong enough, someday. If the chain is gone. Then I can climb them.

But the door has not opened, and the gossamer girl with cherry-gloss lips is right. The food is running out. Is almost gone. And the door has not opened.

In the pure black, a silvered hand brushes mine, and a dead girl whispers in my ear:

You are running out of time.

1

Above

We forget how eager the world is to swallow us up, how deep and hungry the wilderness remains. It's surprisingly, hauntingly easy to vanish.

At 3:23 a.m. Wednesday morning, Bryson Lee, age four, slipped out the back door of his family's vacation home. The motion-activated camera recorded Bryson as he walked across the short stretch of grass, looked back over his shoulder, and then continued on into the woods. The camera shut off.

It's been thirty-seven hours since then, and the weather is turning.

I pull off the road, angling for the canopies, emblazoned with the local Search and Rescue logo, that are serving as the command center for the search efforts. I haven't made it far up the gravel drive before I have to park on the grassy lip between road and trees.

Vehicles jam up the rest of the strip—everything from rusted pickup trucks to a shiny new Tesla getting its wheels baptized with their first splash of real dirt. Some of them I recognize as belonging to other volunteers with Search and Rescue. Others go with the locals who keep wandering up to the incident command post looking for a way to help or to gawk, neither of which is particularly useful. The last thing we need is dozens of untrained locals flooding the area, trampling evidence or getting lost themselves. Even less useful: the TV vans.

If all Bryson Lee needed was manpower and enthusiasm, his survival would be a done deal. But it takes more than that.

In the US, it's easy to get the impression that the wild has been overrun, hemmed in, tamed with trails and GPS and an omnipresent thrum of human activity. True isolation is nearly impossible to find, with a road only a few miles off no matter where you drop yourself, but a few miles is more than enough for a grown adult to vanish into. Much less a four-year-old boy in dinosaur pajamas. The area he headed into is hundreds of acres of wilderness bordered by privately owned land that's only a notch less dangerous for a kid his size.

We'll find him, I tell myself, as I have several times an hour for more than a day. Like every other time, I believe it. Whenever a search ends in tragedy, I wonder if it'll cure my hopeless optimism or break me entirely. But after ten years of weekends and evenings and every sick day I get devoted to SAR, I'm still a hopeful fool.

I scan the crowd as I grab my gear from the back seat. The biggest cluster of bodies is off to the left, centered around a man and a woman. The man has paired an expensive haircut with department store flannel, radiating the sort of engineered man-of-the-people look that suggests political ambitions—though Andrew Hill has steadfastly denied those rumors. His sister Melinda, on the other hand—crisp white blouse and navy blazer, her eyeliner immaculate and her dark hair offering not a wisp out of place—has never wanted anything else.

What the hell are they doing here?

"Back already?"

I offer a weary smile to Len as he approaches—whip-thin, soulful brown eyes, eyebrow split with a silvered scar. His deputy's uniform is decidedly rumpled; yesterday's five o'clock shadow is turning full scraggle. My instinct is to put my arms out, to hold on to him like I have so many times before, with his heartbeat thumping right in my ear, his knobby spine under my flattened palm. But he's working, and so am I.

"You know me," I say instead. I nod at the stack of flyers in his hands, each one featuring a picture of a beaming Bryson. "Flyer duty?"

"I've been handing them out all day," he says. I nod. Posting flyers is the standard task for untrained volunteers. Half of Franklin is probably papered with the things by now. "You look like crap, by the way. What are you running on?"

"About two hours of sleep and two gallons of coffee," I say, stifling a yawn. We're walking together now, heading for Tamara, a woman with the shape of a wine cork and the no-nonsense attitude of a union boss. She's heading up Operations, which means handing out assignments. Right now she's got her hands in her pockets, scowling at nothing in particular. "Where's your boss?" I ask Len. "Parked in front of the nearest news camera?"

"Nah, he's busy telling the county sheriff how well he runs this town." Franklin's so small Len is one of only two full-time deputies. Our police chief is exactly as competent as the job requires, and refusing to retire so his ex-wife doesn't get a cut of his pension, which leaves Len to do most of the heavy lifting. "The Hills are the ones getting the screen time."

"What are they even doing here?" I ask.

He raises an eyebrow. "It's their land."

"Seriously?" I'd missed that detail.

"They've been hovering all day," he says. "Making noise about getting us anything we need, all the resources in the world, et cetera. Trying to out-soundbite each other."

"Think she's going to run again?" I ask idly. Two stints in the House of Representatives ended abruptly when Melinda resigned to undergo treatment for breast cancer—prompting speculation about Andrew taking her place—but the cancer is gone, and Melinda has never once let her brother take something she views as hers.

"The answer to that question is on a long list of things I don't care even a little bit about," Len informs me. He gives me a sidelong look. "But you know them better than I do."

"I don't know them at all," I murmur, and at that moment, Andrew Hill looks straight at me. His head comes up; his shoulders stiffen. I wonder if he, too, is remembering the rumble of a truck engine. His hand tangled in copper hair. But, no—he would be thinking of a different encounter altogether. One that didn't reflect well on either of us.

But Andrew Hill doesn't matter. Bryson Lee does, and he's out there now, scared and alone and alive.

Tamara's voice brings my attention back to the present. "Good, there you are, Lucky," she says, using a nickname I've mostly grown not to hate. Len gives me a wave and fades back, returning to his task. Tamara turns her perpetual scowl on me. "I'm putting you with Rick's team. He's got the maps. You'll be bordering private land we don't have permission to enter, so stay in your area." Frustration is evident in her voice. We can only go on private property with the owner's permission, and it's shocking how often that isn't forthcoming.

"Got it," I say, nodding, and swivel my head until I catch sight of Rick. He's standing with two other volunteers. There are dozens of us crawling these woods right now.

"You sure you're good to go?" she asks me, gaze probing.

"One hundred percent," I assure her, though my limbs feel like lead and my eyes are gummy. She just grunts. If she hadn't forced me to go home for a few hours, I'd have been here straight through and she knows it.

I extract myself from her attention and hustle over to Rick. Rick's a slender guy, hair gone gray, eyes sharp. He's soft-spoken but a steady leader, which means Tamara sticks him with the newbies more often than he'd like. The other two volunteers with him are an older woman I've met a couple of times and a new guy who's probably twenty but looks about twelve and whose name exits my mind immediately.

Rick hands out assignments. The role of medic goes to the other woman; I'm unsurprised to be tasked with navigation. Sometimes I joke that the reason I'm so obsessed with the missing is my own seeming inability to get lost. It's nonsense, of course. It doesn't take a therapist to pinpoint what started me down this road. One girl. Not missing, not really, because to be missing you have to be missed.

She's just gone.

My eyes sweep left and right as we head to our assigned area, my gait steady but unhurried as we make our way down narrow footpaths through the underbrush. This close to the commotion, it's hard to imagine a kid wouldn't know which way to head for rescue, but you never know. Could be hurt. Could be scared out of his mind and not able to process what he's hearing. Kids this age tend to find a spot to sleep—I found a girl curled up in a sunbeam once, a couple of hours after she got separated from her family on a hike.

New Guy keeps pace with me. "Those parents must be losing their minds," he says. "I can't imagine."

"I don't think anyone can, really," I say. I don't spend a lot of time thinking about the families—not until the search is over. That pain and fear, even borrowed, is too overwhelming. I have to stay focused, keep myself in this honed-knife state, my belief untarnished. *We will find them. I will find them.*

And so often I do. To the point that it's a joke, a superstition. Tamara called me her lucky rabbit's foot, and it stuck around like a nickname. Almost turned into Bunny, but I managed to nip that in the bud.

"You don't think there was any foul play, do you?" he asks.

"As far as I know, there's no indication of that," I say. I don't point out that if there were, we'd be following very different procedures. A manhunt is for law enforcement, not SAR.

"But there was that other kid. Disappeared a few months ago, right? Could be a pattern," he continues, his eyes all shiny like this would be particularly exciting. A bird swoops overhead, chattering about its day.

"What other kid?" I ask, frowning.

"That girl. From Franklin? Mackenzie or Mindy or—"

"Meghan Vale," I say flatly. Of course I know about Meghan. Seventeen, a senior at Franklin High School, where I work as a counselor. I've seen her in the halls, though I don't have any particular memories of her—she's assigned to one of the other counselors. She's been gone for three months now. We were never called out to look for her. Last I heard, the assumption was she'd run away. "I don't see how that could be related."

"Not exactly the same type. Serial killers have types, right?" he asks.

"There's no indication there was anyone else involved." I try to make it clear with my tone that the conversation is over. Not that I'm terribly intimidating at my towering five feet, four inches, with a face that even in my thirties gets "cute" at best, in the same voice you'd use on a spaniel. At least I know how to growl.

"Still. People are talking. There have been other missing girls, you know."

I know. All of them he does and probably more. You could call it an obsession, maybe, but I think of it more as penance. The same reason I'm out here every weekend, after work, every time I have vacation days to spend. Because years ago, my best friend disappeared.

And I didn't even notice.

"Cut the chatter," Rick says. "We need to be listening, not talking."

New Guy ducks his head, mumbles something. I check the GPS, confirm we've reached our designated search area, and wait as Rick relays this back to Tamara. Then we're on the move again. We stick together on the path, pausing periodically to call out Bryson's name in unison and then listen for a response. This area's already been gone over once in the hasty search stage, those first few hours spent setting up the command post and doing an initial sweep. A lot of the time, it ends there.

Time bleeds, smears into monotony, the endless scanning for a footprint or scrap of cloth or dropped toy. Bryson's name echoes in the distance as well, other teams probing. The underbrush here is thick. It makes it hard to maneuver off the path. It'd slow a kid down, too. "He'd never have made it this far, would he?" New Guy says quietly. Rick calls out Bryson's name, and we all pause, listening.

He's out here.

I've got that feeling. The one that I've never talked about even to the others because it feels a step beyond luck, beyond intuition. More like mysticism. Because here's what I won't admit to the others: All those jokes and superstition—I believe them, at least a little. In a part of me that I can't logic out of it.

It's the part that says that there is an equation the universe wants me to balance. I could have saved a life and I didn't. And so now I have this penance, this purpose—but also an awareness.

I believe that I am meant to find these people; that the times I don't, it's because I have not been able to listen to this small voice inside me.

And that voice is saying that I am supposed to be here today.

The clouds are moving fast, filling in the gaps between the leaves and branches above, and as a shiver of wind blows past, the first cold pinprick of rain hits the back of my hand. I turn up the volume on my radio a tick, hoping for the word that he's been found—the too-loud volunteer, the matter-of-fact cop, Tamara's no-nonsense orders that bleed with heartfelt relief as she delivers the news.

Nothing yet.

There's a holler from my right. I look over in time to catch New Guy going down, arms upflung as he loses his footing. A quartet of starlings startles into flight. I swear under my breath and stride over, already certain by the way he's huffing and puffing and grabbing his ankle that we're done here. I flag our medic.

"I think I twisted it," he says as we approach. "It's not too bad." He grimaces.

Rick radios in as the kid strips off boot and sock. It doesn't, in fact, look serious, but the rictus expression on his face suggests it's bad enough.

"I'm fine," he insists. "I can keep going."

The last thing we need is him walking on a bad ankle and getting so messed up we have to divert resources to get him out of here. Rick tells him this, as gently as possible, and he hangs his head.

A quick flurry of conversation on the radio results in a plan. We've got a spare radio, so the other two will head back to CP while Rick and I join up with another group. Not ideal, but it happens, and all of us reassure the guilt-stricken young man as he toddles off. As they move away, Rick and I stand in a sudden moment of stillness.

Just before rain, when the mist of it is in the air but the clouds haven't yet let go, there is a furtive quiet to the woods. As if all the business of the wilderness is suddenly being conducted in urgent silence. The squirrels have stopped chuffing and scrambling; the birds sit expectant on their perches. The light gains a quality of gray that leaves the world half real at best.

I breathe in, scenting the damp. Too many hours already, and Bryson Lee is such a little boy, but there is no fear in me.

And in that silence, I hear something. So faint I can't be sure I heard it at all, but I tip my head, hold up a finger to keep Rick from speaking.

Nothing.

And then there it is again, a sound that could be anything. A bird, a squirrel. The sob of a lost and frightened child.

"What is it?" Rick asks.

"I don't know. I thought I heard crying," I say, frowning. I stare in the direction the sound came from. Three trees down, a red flag flutters on a branch. The GPS is clear. We're snug up against the property line we're not meant to cross, and the noise is coming from the wrong side of it. As if a child would notice that flag, or care what it meant. As if Bryson is any less likely to be in that square foot of woods than the one next to it.

Rick looks at me. I look at Rick. "Where's the property line, again?" he asks.

"Hard to say exactly," I reply. "Signal's pretty bad out here."

He nods. "Easy to get turned around."

Rain begins to patter against the leaves above, but hasn't yet reached the ground. There's no change in the air when we cross that invisible line, but I feel it on my skin just the same. We stop, listen. Move again.

"Bryson?" we call, voices hoarse after hours of use.

Nothing, and more nothing. No sign of a boy or anyone else out here.

Something pale lies in the dirt up ahead, too uniform to be something natural. I walk over toward it and kneel down to get a better look.

It's a string of six cheap white plastic beads. The cord is packed with dirt. It's been here for a while. Days, weeks. Could even be years, I suppose—the cord looks plasticky, immortal. I've seen it before. Not this one, but ones like it.

"What is it?" Rick asks, drawing close. "Something we should call in?"

If it's a clue, we don't touch it. We take a photo, call it in for instructions. But these beads have nothing to do with Bryson Lee. "Witch beads," I say. Rick gives me a blank look, and I remember he's not from here. "It's a local superstition."

I reach to touch the string of beads hanging from my pack. Six white beads on a leather cord, all but identical to the one on the ground. The tokens of Jenny Red-Hands, the witch of Franklin, doling out vengeance for wounded girls. *They're supposed to be teeth,* Janie told me. *The original ones were teeth, not beads.* I could never tell if she was making it up to mess with me. She left them on my windowsill that last night. I never found out why.

Girls still wear them now and then. The ones a little on the goth side, the ones with tarot cards and crystals on their dressers. But even the cheerleaders will sport them sometimes, after a bad breakup. A boy cheats and the girl's friends are all suddenly clipping white beads to their zippers like a warning.

And I can almost remember seeing them not so long ago. Swinging from the zipper pull of a black backpack covered in patches. The girl had red-gold hair, and for an instant, she reminded me so keenly of Janie that I almost said her name, but when she turned around, I didn't know her.

Meghan Vale, I think, but I can't be sure. I didn't know her then. She looked familiar when they showed her picture around, but that only meant that she was, in fact, a student at the school. I can't tell now if I'm conflating the memories. Still. How long have these beads been out here?

Three months? More? She could have left them here. She could have been here.

Jenny, Jenny, hands of red, I remember Janie chanting, but the rest of the rhyme escapes me.

I don't register the footsteps behind me until I hear the voice.

"What the hell do you think you're doing?" comes a growl.

I turn, apology and explanation on my lips—and find myself staring down the barrel of a gun.

2

Above

I lift my hands in the universal gesture for surrender, rising slowly to my feet. Rick reaches for his radio.

"Don't you move," the man barks. A fringe of salt-and-pepper hair sticks out from under a lumpy gray beanie. His pupils are flared, wary. Rick carefully holds his hands away from his sides, and I can see them shaking as we look at each other.

"I said, what the hell do you think you're doing?" the man with the gun demands again. He's a wiry man with a beard a few days past tame, cheeks spattered with what might be freckles or dirt. I try to focus on him and not the black barrel of the rifle currently trained on my chest.

"We're with Search and Rescue," I say calmly. "We're looking for—"

"This is private property, and you're trespassing," he says, cutting me off.

"I'm sorry. We must have missed the flag," I say, struggling to keep my voice level. His finger is on the trigger, not alongside it, and the look in his eyes says he's not opposed to the idea of pulling it.

"We'll leave immediately," Rick adds. His voice has a quaver to it. I'm distantly surprised to realize I'm not shaking at all. I can feel adrenaline like a chill through my body, but it's only making everything sharper, slower.

"You're not supposed to be here. I told them. I told them you weren't allowed," the man says, and comes forward a step. Rick stumbles back. The man tightens the butt of the rifle against his shoulder, bracing himself as if for a recoil. *He's going to shoot,* I think, and still fear refuses to come.

"Leave them alone, Bill," says a female voice, soft but authoritative. A woman is striding toward us, blond hair back in a no-nonsense ponytail, a sleeveless blouse showing off inked-up arms. There's something vaguely familiar about her—something around her eyes, or maybe her voice.

"They're trespassing. And so are you," the man says. "You don't own this land yet."

"We didn't mean—" I start, but she cuts me off.

"There's a kid missing, Bill," she says. "Four years old. Haven't you heard?"

"I heard," he says. "Doesn't have anything to do with me."

"Nobody's saying you had anything to do with it, the kid just ran off," she says. She squints, shades her eyes. My mouth is dry. I keep quiet. "How's your brother doing, Bill?"

He shifts, wets his lips. "Well enough."

"He's lucky he's got you looking out for his place," she notes. "But look. You and I both know he's not going to be happy if a bunch of cops tramp all over his land, which is what's going to happen if you pull that trigger. Or you let these nice people walk fifty feet back that way, and we all forget this happened."

Bill's jaw tenses. The rifle barrel lowers.

"You should get on home before you get yourself in trouble," she tells him. "I'll make sure they leave." He glares at her. "Bill. This isn't the kind of trouble Terry needs right now," she says firmly. Finally he grunts, and without another word, he wheels around, striding off back toward the road.

I let out a trembling breath of relief.

"Thanks," I say. Rick grabs his radio but doesn't call in yet. The way he's shaking, I'm not sure he could speak clearly just now.

"Not a problem," she says, her arms still crossed loosely. Without a gun in my face, I can get a better look at her. She's about my age, her skin lightly tanned, the suggestion of crow's-feet at the corners of her eyes. Spatters of color decorate the backs of her hands, her fingers, like she's been painting—a buttery yellow and a green the color of lichen. "I'm glad I saw him heading out here."

"Sorry, you're . . . ?" I say, feeling like I should know the answer, and then it clicks. "Emmie."

"Emily," she corrects. Emily Hill. The youngest of the Hill siblings. The last time I saw her, she was fourteen years old and wearing my sweater over her homecoming dress.

"This is Rick Lohman. And I'm Audrey. Audrey Dixon," I say. "I don't know if you remember me."

"Audrey. Of course I remember you," she says, some meaning snarled up between the syllables that I can't read.

"There was a sound," I say. "Out here. We need to—"

But Rick cuts me off. "Audrey," he says, and cranks up the volume on the radio, and a voice babbles, "Brown hair, blue dinosaur pajamas, him, he's all right, he's dirty, doesn't seem to be hurt," and it's like a rush of wind, all the tension leaving me at once. They found him. He's alive.

Rick laughs; Emily lets out a hissing breath between her teeth. I close my eyes. I've never been one to pray, but it's like prayer, this moment, feeling the world slide back toward the proper balance. I tilt my face up, thinking I hear the rain, thinking how strange it is that I don't feel it, and then I open my eyes and realize it's not rain I'm hearing at all.

I stand beneath the wide boughs of an oak tree. It surrounds me in soft shadow. The branch above me is thin, old, leafless. From it are hung strings of white beads—dozens and dozens of them, their cords gone gray and fraying with age. The wind stirs the trees. The beads click against the branches softly.

Only then does it start to rain.

Back at CP, we debrief. Rick and I report in about our encounter, but we're spared a chewing-out for now. It's a temporary reprieve, I know, and I'm not looking forward to Tamara's infamous tongue-lashing.

"The lucky charm strikes again!" Paul Matsuda declares as we mill about in the aftermath. Matsuda's five foot six and every bit of it muscle, the kind of guy who's pushing seventy and still scaling cliffs that make me woozy just to look at. He credits his health to a vegan lifestyle and freakishly cheerful attitude. Shadow and Pebble, his dogs, sit next to him with their tongues lolling in happy exhaustion.

"I'm not a lucky charm," I protest.

"Whatever. When you're working, we get happy endings," he says, jabbing a finger in my direction. "It's scientific fact."

"It's confirmation bias. I want a statistical analysis," I grump at him.

"Whatever you say, Lucky," Matsuda declares. He slaps me on the shoulder. "Drinks tomorrow, okay?"

I dip my chin. "We'll see."

"Yeah, yeah, that's what you always say," Matsuda tells me, and ambles off, dogs trotting at his heels. This is the deal: they invite me, I pretend I might show up, they pretend to be surprised when I don't.

I leave the debrief feeling battered, trading nods and smiles with the others. I should feel relieved, but that hum in my bones hasn't faded. The muscles between my shoulder blades remain tensed, my senses still straining. *There's something out here. You haven't found it yet,* they tell me, but that's impossible. Bryson is on his way to the hospital, safe in the arms of his parents. It's over.

I keep hearing the rattle of beads in the pattering of rain. I take the string of witch beads from my pack and run my fingers over it.

I need to see you, Janie said, the last time I heard her voice. *I need to tell you something.* She'd sounded strange. Out of breath and on the verge of laughter—or tears. I'd wondered if she was on something. I told her not to call me again, and hung up the phone.

And when, later that night, she came to my window the way she always used to do and knocked and called my name, I pretended not to hear. I never even turned over to look.

I found the beads on the windowsill the next day. I never saw Janie again.

"Witch beads," Emily Hill says. I startle; I didn't hear her approach. She nods at the beads in my hand. "Gifts for Jenny Red-Hands, right?" A smile ghosts across her lips, lingering a moment at the corner of her mouth.

"You know the story?" I ask, and then I realize that of course she does—Janie told it to her. To her, and to me, and to Andrew Hill, on homecoming night all those years ago. I'm struck again by the depth of her eyes, a gold veil over the green, and something in them that brings me right back to that night, the fire and the story and the small figure disappearing in the gloom as my bus pulled away.

She laughs. The sound is less amused than rueful, hemlock-bitter. "The witch in the woods who helps wronged women. I think there's a new version every few years. Our town's own Bloody Mary. I've always liked the idea."

"What idea is that?"

"That there's some kind of power out there that gives a shit what happens to girls," she says. "So the kid's really okay?"

"They told us he's cold, hungry, and very unhappy, but nothing worse than scrapes and cuts," I say. "It sounds like he got scared and went into an old root cellar to hide. It wasn't marked on any maps."

"There's lots of stuff like that out there," Emily says with a shrug. "We used to find them all the time."

"Hopefully there's not too much trouble with us being out of bounds," I say probingly. "Bill seemed like the sort of guy to hold a grudge."

"There won't be," Emily says, with more certainty than I'd expect. "Andrew and Melinda will make sure. Don't worry. And speak of the devil . . ."

Andrew Hill is approaching, his hands swinging freely at his sides in a way that makes his gait more purposeful. The years have hardened his already angular face. You could call it handsome, but it's always been an uncomfortable kind of beauty to me, with those blue eyes so pale they seem almost colorless. "Emily," he says as he joins us. He lifts a hand lightly to her elbow, a quick protective touch. "I thought you were going to stay at the house." He can't quite keep the frown from his lips.

"Well. I didn't," she says. He regards her for a moment, and then seems to decide to let the matter go. His attention swings my way instead.

"Audrey, right?" he says. As if he doesn't know. "Good to see you again."

"Is it?" He stares at me; his sister snorts a laugh.

Andrew scowls. "I only meant it's been a long time. Almost twenty years, isn't it?"

Less than that, but clearly we're pretending *that* particular interlude didn't happen. "More or less," I say.

"Audrey was a friend of Janie's," he says to Emily. Part of me is surprised he said her name out loud. They'd broken up long before that last night, the knocking on my window. Their break had been cleaner than ours, but I knew Janie—you couldn't just walk away from her. She always left herself scratched on your skin somehow.

"Yes. I remember," Emily says with evident annoyance.

Andrew clears his throat. "Well. If you'll excuse us. Melinda wants a word," he says, directing the last to Emily.

"Am I in trouble?" she asks, a joke that isn't quite a joke.

"Just some logistics to work out," Andrew says. He puts a hand on her arm, less protective and more demanding this time. He nods to me. "Thank you for your service." He moves off, guiding Emily along with him.

"Nice to see you, Audrey," she says over her shoulder. I offer a nod in return, and watch a beat longer as she and Andrew recede.

Len ambles up to my shoulder, watching after them. "So," he says pointedly. "We being nice to Hills now?"

"The nice ones," I reply.

He gives me a look. "No such thing." Len is the only person on the planet other than Andrew and me who knows what a colossal idiot I was one night in college.

I shrug and fold my arms, chewing my lip in thought. "Did you ever really meet Emily? She seems . . . fine."

"I honestly don't remember," Len says. "She didn't hang around much, did she?"

I rub the back of my neck. I try not to think about my teenage years. Janie haunts too many of those memories. "I never really saw her after sophomore year that I can remember."

"Did she even go to FH?" Len says, frowning. "I think I remember something about her being homeschooled."

"Maybe." I clear my throat. "Hey, Len. Do you know anything about Meghan Vale? What's going on with her case?"

He looks startled by the change of subject, but considers, scratching his chin. "There isn't really one, as far as I know. She was fighting with her parents. Told people she was going to run away. Did. At least that's what it looks like. Why?"

"Do you know if she had witch beads?" I ask.

"Those weird charm things you girls used to try to scare the menfolk with? No idea," he says. "Is that still a thing?"

"Not as much as it used to be," I say. "I found some in the woods. I wondered if they belonged to her."

"Meghan Vale isn't in the woods, Audrey," Len says, with a hint of gentleness in his voice. "She's in Seattle or LA or somewhere, or already on her way back home."

I scrape my hair back, let out a breath. "Yeah. Probably."

"You want to come over tonight? Kenny's making lasagna."

"I'm good."

"You love lasagna," Len says in a singsong voice. "Come on. Don't spend the night alone in your apartment staring at pictures of dead people."

"They're not necessarily dead," I say. "Besides, I'm not alone. Barry will be there."

Len sighs, but he doesn't argue. "I've got to go. Take care of yourself, okay?"

"Cross my heart," I say. I trace an *X* over my chest, and I flee before he can call me on it. It used to be, Len and I took care of each other. These days, he's got Kenny and a therapist. It leaves me feeling like I'm failing to keep up my end of the bargain.

I glance back toward the house. It's a low, sprawling building, extensions tacked on at uncomfortable angles. The trees cloistered around it leave little sunlight, but garden pots proliferate in the shade, hosting snaking vines and bursts of purple and scarlet flowers. At the corner of the house, Emily Hill stands talking to her brother and sister.

Arguing with them, rather. Her arms are crossed, her head bowed, as Melinda speaks to her with short, animated gestures. I can hear the blunt edge of her tone but not the words. Emily's pose speaks surrender, but even from this distance, I read rebellion in the set of her shoulders. Then Andrew raises a hand, cutting Melinda off.

Whatever they're arguing about, it's none of my business. I get myself signed out properly and cleared to leave, and then I get in my car and maneuver my way around to point in the right direction, leaving the Hills and their land in my rearview.

I wait for the feeling of release and relief. Bryson Lee is alive, is safe. But that feeling doesn't come.

Everything in me calls instead to turn back.

But it's nonsense. I'm not a lucky charm, and I'm not some sage of the missing. Today was a good day. I should leave it at that.

I pull out onto the main road, and ignore the whispers urging me to stay.

3

Below

I count the food again. Tuna and salmon and chicken in little plastic packets, packs of crackers, a jar of peanut butter scraped clean. It's not much. Two days' worth, I think. Three if I stretch it.

It'll take a lot longer than that to starve, won't it? People last for weeks. Months, even. But I'm already weak, and it won't be the hunger that kills me.

The water has stopped running.

I have what's in the toilet and two bottles more, and then I'm done. How long can you last without water? Two days? Three? Not more than that, I think.

"I don't know what to do. I don't know what to do," I whisper.

Listen.

The word is like the sound of a sharp stone scraping over wood. The other gossamer girls shift and flutter at the edge of my vision—my lack of vision, really—but this one sits next to me on the bed.

"I'm running out of time."

But you have more than you've ever had. Listen.

"Then tell me."

But the girl is gone (was never there). How can I listen if there's no one to speak? Except, of course, they did speak. They left their words for me to find.

I lie down on the floor, moving my ankle carefully to keep the chain from tangling me. I work my body under the bed, and my practiced fingers find the small flashlight hidden between the mattress and the slatted frame.

Fifteen seconds. That's all I allow myself, because I don't know how long the batteries will last, and once they're gone, the dark will truly own me. The flashlight is a gift from one of the others. So is the warning about the batteries. One warning of many, scratched into the wood with the sharp edge of a rock (too small, too dull to break skin; not a weapon, not salvation, not yet) or scrawled with a dull pencil lost before I ever entered this place.

Don't waste battery
Don't use name
Save food
Toilet = water

I don't know which of the girls first wrote the words. I think there must have been others who were here before the words began, or who never found them. Those who slipped silently into the dark. But some have left their mark.

At the center of the middle slat, not drawn but carved with some unknown implement, are five lines, gathered together at the base: a thumb, four crude fingers. The wood along each spindly digit is stained dark with thumbprints of blood. I've added my own, but I wasn't the first.

My name is Amanda.
My name is Madison.

They've left their own memorials, clustered around the carving. Did they know that they were going to die when they wrote their names? Did they still think they might escape, might break the chain, might make it up twelve cruel steps, might claw their way into the light again? Or did they only leave their names when they realized it would be all that was left of them?

My name is Stranger.

I run my fingers over the words. They are the truest here. I am a stranger to myself, to anyone who knew me. What I have become down here is not who I was, and will never be again. That, too, is real.

I crab my fingers over the boards, searching for the words I need among these secrets passed from tomb to tomb. Voices babble in my head. *Made a knife from can lid.* There are never cans anymore, only those sealed pouches of food.

The messages warned me I would get one attempt at escape. *If you get caught once you get to live.* I used mine foolishly—running for the door in one of the rare moments when the manacle was removed from around my ankle. I didn't even make it to the bottom of the stairs before a hand caught my hair and yanked me back with vicious efficiency.

Punishment followed. Punishment, but not death.

You'll know better now.

The girls before chronicled their attempts. They were caught fashioning tools, cobbling together makeshift weapons, picking the padlock that holds the chain around our ankle. They were cleverer than me. I'm too ashamed to add my own failure to the list. What could I say? *Be faster. Be smarter. Be better than me.*

I'm going to try again, one message reads. I know it was her last. I know, from the shape of her words, that her name was Madison. And I am certain she knew she was going to die. They all did. There's no other reason to leave those messages, except for the girl who came next, and the one after that. The girl who scratched *checks toilet tank, don't hide things there* had to know her words would only be read after she had died.

THE CHAIN IS FIRST.

The words are bigger, bold, in the center of the slat. I splay my fingers under them. Yes. I've been thinking about the stairs, the door, the food, and the light, but I need to start smaller. If I can't get the chain off, nothing else matters.

DON'T GET CAUGHT.

I breathe out. Almost laugh. Because all the girls before have tried and failed, but I have something they didn't. The same thing that's killing me.

Time.

Because the door hasn't opened. Which means that maybe it won't open at all.

Maybe I don't need to worry about being caught.

If I try and it opens again, I'll die. But if I do nothing and it stays closed, I'll die anyway. Slowly.

I have to take the risk.

So many avenues of escape have been cut off because any attempt would be discovered. But if things don't need to be kept whole or hidden, there is so much more I can try.

And if the light comes again, if I'm discovered—

Then I will die quickly and become gossamer. And either way, I will be free.

4

Above

By the next morning, everyone at Franklin High has heard about Bryson Lee's miraculous rescue, and the front office is buzzing with it. Thankfully, interest in my role fades rapidly when my colleagues realize I wasn't actually part of the team that found him, and by lunchtime, the drop-ins to my office for gossip have stopped completely. Which is good, since taking time off for the search has left me a pile of tasks that include managing a helicopter parent who won't stop calling about her son, despite the fact that he's doing perfectly fine, and three others who won't pick up the phone despite the fact that their kids won't be graduating if they don't get their acts together.

As I make calls, I scroll through Instagram on my phone. The school network blocks it, of course, so I'm going rogue and eating up data to snoop on my students. Three in particular. Meghan Vale's friends.

I've got no real reason to think the beads have anything to do with Meghan. I don't even know if she ever had any or had heard the story—it's much less popular than it was when I was a student, after all. But her name is lodged in my head. Last night, I found everything I could about her disappearance, which was basically nothing. Not so much as a local article. The most substantive reporting was a post in a Facebook group for Franklin High parents.

Meghan Vale was last seen on the night of January 17 by her father, who reported that she took dinner into her room and didn't come back out. Which was, by the sound of it, far from atypical or alarming. According to the comments on the Facebook post (admittedly not an unimpeachable source), she'd been threatening to run away for a while. Some of her belongings were missing. It really looked like she'd followed through on her threats. She was only a few months off from eighteen. Not a prime candidate for an extensive police investigation.

Meghan herself didn't have much of an online presence. Not rare, exactly, but unusual in my experience. Half the social issues I deal with are actually social *media* issues, with online arguments spilling into the halls. Until the school banned phones entirely last year, kids would keep them in a death grip in case the social hierarchy updated via app during class. It could be downright dangerous to be friendly to a newly exiled former queen bee after a second-period regime change conducted entirely on Snapchat.

But Meghan seemed to lurk at the edges of that ecosystem. She has accounts, the same moody selfie uploaded to each, but didn't post much. Her Instagram is private, though, which made me wonder if it was her actual digital home base. She has the usual fleet of courtesy followers. Over the course of the evening, I managed to find three with whom she actually interacted with some regularity.

Alison Parker, Theresa Abbott, and Chloe Brittain. Alison Parker's feed is mostly earnestly terrible poetry that reminds me all too keenly of my own adolescent attempts. Theresa Abbott favors selfies with her cat. Chloe Brittain actually has a few photos of the three of them—and one or two that include Meghan. Meghan was a member of the group, but a peripheral one. I search the photos for witch beads, but there are none on display.

Theresa Abbott and Chloe Brittain are on my roster, but I haven't spoken much to them, which means they're part of the vast middle of the pack—the kids who aren't flailing so badly that they need lots of extra support but aren't distinguishing themselves enough to draw positive attention, either. I try to remember what I know about them, but I just have an impression of dyed hair and disinterest.

I'm midway through leaving my thirtieth message on a parent's voicemail with the desk phone and scrolling through Theresa Abbott's feed when there's a polite knock on the doorframe, and our new social studies teacher, Dev Khanna, pokes his head in with a little wave. He balances rugged features and a thick black beard—just starting to show a peppering of gray—with fashion sense borrowed from stodgy college professors. All his jackets have elbow patches, and he owns more than one pocket square. It works for him.

I quickly power off my phone and hold up a finger. "—several options to make up those credits, but we need to begin as soon as possible. Thank you, and you can reach me here during school hours or by email at any time." I hang up, and then drop my head in my hands and groan.

"Having a stimulating day as a valued member of the public schooling apparatus, are we?" Dev asks, with sincere if exaggerated sympathy. As well as being new, Dev is one of the younger teachers at a school where most of the humanities department is determined to die with a dry-erase marker clamped in one wrinkled hand. We've formed an instant bond over our cultural references coming from the same decade.

"Some days I feel like I'm making at least a little bit of a difference. This hasn't been one of them," I say.

"Would a burrito of frankly terrifying size help at all?" He holds up a familiar paper bag. "Chicken, pinto beans, all the fixings, as spicy as they're legally allowed to make it, if I remember your order correctly."

"Are you trying to bribe me? You should be aware that I have literally no power or influence," I say.

"Yes, I am trying to bribe you, but we can discuss that after you've eaten the burrito and thus become indebted to me for life," he says.

I chuckle. "Well, you are a hero. I forgot my lunch. I was going to have to eat in the cafeteria."

"You always forget your lunch after you've been off rescuing children and kittens or whatever it is you do," he says.

I raise an eyebrow. "How would you know that? You've been here like two weeks."

"Four months!"

"Hadn't noticed." I smirk at him. He puts a hand to his heart, wounded. I wave him into a chair, and we divvy up salsa and piles of napkins.

"I heard you were out there," he says. "Want to talk about it?"

"Not really," I say honestly. I pick at the foil on my burrito. "It's . . . private. Kind of. I don't like the attention."

"Then I won't ask," Dev says, and though I can see the curiosity in his eyes, he doesn't press.

I roll a piece of foil into a little ball on the desk. "I did get a gun pointed at me," I say.

"Holy shit. What? Are you okay?" he asks immediately, freezing in the act of uncapping a tiny container of salsa.

"Still breathing. Probably need therapy, but who has the time?" I say blithely, and bite into my burrito. My mouth fills with the delectable taste of cheap street food. "Things just taste better when they come out of a truck," I note around a full mouth.

"And you have sour cream on your cheek," he says, holding out a flimsy square of paper napkin.

"Thanks." I wipe away the offending cream and consider Dev. He started midyear, but he *did* overlap with Meghan by a few weeks. "Random question. Did you have Meghan Vale in any of your classes?"

"Meghan? Yeah, third period," he says. "Poor girl."

"Why do you say that? Was something going on?" I ask.

"Must have been, right? If she ran away, I mean."

"And you think she did?"

He pauses, looking at me like he's trying to figure out what my angle is. "Meghan was only in my class for a few weeks. She was always pretty quiet. Decent student, when she showed up. Good grades, when she bothered to turn things in. She was artistic. Had a real eye for photography. I told her she should talk to Mr. Christiansen about entering the art show. She's not one of yours, though, is she? Alphabetically speaking."

Most of the students are divvied up based on the first letter of their last name. I'm the custodian to the first third of the alphabet, which Dev clearly knows. I brush past the subject. "One more question. Did you ever see her with witch beads?" I ask.

"What now?" he asks, clearly baffled.

"Oh, right. You're new," I say.

"A stranger. An interloper in your lands," he confirms.

"It would be a short string of beads. Usually just the cheap ones from craft stores. White. Six of them."

"Wait, this is that weird girl-cult thing," Dev says, snapping his fingers and pointing at me. "Jenny something."

"Red-Hands," I supply. "So you have heard of it."

"I listened to the podcast," he says. I stare at him blankly. "It was about the only thing I'd heard about Franklin before I moved here. This podcast I listen to did an episode about the story, trying to track down the origins and the way it's shaped the town, that kind of thing."

"What podcast was this?" I ask.

"*The Darker Half*? It's mostly a true crime show, but they were doing a Halloween episode. It's good, if you're into true crime. Which I am, more than I should probably admit. But it's one of those shows that makes you feel deep and intellectual instead of just ghoulish. Though to be clear, I listen to both," Dev says, then dips his head to get a better angle on his burrito.

I jot the name down in my notebook. "I think it started when I was a kid," I say, sitting back in my chair. "I mean, the story is that Jenny's been around since the 1800s, but I'm pretty sure she's a modern invention."

"But does that make her any less real?" Dev says, ticking a finger toward me. "Sorry, force of habit. We do a unit on urban legends as cultural record."

"Are you asking if there's really a witch out in the woods who will take a payment in teeth and/or plastic beads to wreak vengeance on cheating boyfriends?" I ask.

"No, I'm asking if you think there's real power in a town's shared mythology including a witch in the woods who holds abusive men accountable," Dev shoots back.

I raise an eyebrow. "You're forgetting the part where she takes a liking to some girls, and they're never seen again."

Dev looks considering. "That's the nature of vengeance, isn't it? Sometimes you're the one who gets burned," he says.

"I bet you're a good teacher," I tell him, chin propped on my hand.

"How else would I have earned my way to these vaunted halls?" He cleans his fingers on a napkin and folds his hands, elbows on the arms of his chair as he examines me. "So, what, you think that Meghan Vale was a devotee of Jenny Red-Hands?" Skepticism and curiosity mingle in his voice.

"I'm not sure. I don't have anything to suggest it, it's just . . ." I almost tell him about the beads I found, but on the verge of saying it aloud, it all sounds ridiculous.

He *hmms*. "What about you? Ever wander out into the Franklin Nature Preserve with a string of beads?" he asks.

"Never had cause," I say with a thin smile. "But I know someone who did." I don't elaborate, and he doesn't press. Instead, he clears his throat and looks serious.

"So. About that bribe I mentioned," he says.

"Yes?" I prompt.

"Today. Is Friday," he says with some difficulty.

"I'd heard that," I say gravely.

"Tomorrow, therefore, would be Saturday," he goes on. "And I was thinking perhaps you might want to get coffee. Or tea, if you don't drink coffee. Or a beer, if you'd rather do an evening thing, or if you're free midday, then . . . sandwiches?" The last word stretches out uncertainly.

I lean back in my chair, battling back a wave of panic and trying for a friendly tone. "Dev, are you asking me to hang out, or are you asking me on a date?"

"Either. Both? I would genuinely be delighted to have you as a friend but also, yes, if you are so inclined, I would be similarly, you know, inclined," he says. He runs a hand through his hair.

"Dev, I . . ." I trail off helplessly.

"Like I said, genuinely happy with the friendship-hang option. Eager, even. Forget the other thing." He shakes his hands in a *never mind* gesture.

"It's not that." I swallow against a too-dry mouth. What am I supposed to say? *Yes, I'd love to, but I always manage to screw things up, so it's a terrible idea?* Dev is attractive. Gorgeous, if we're being honest, and funny, and easy to be around, and if I were anywhere near functional, I would be an idiot to turn him down. But I know how this goes.

I say no, and it's awkward. We stop talking so often. The friendship fades, and it's uncomfortable, sure, but it doesn't reach the level of pain. Or I say yes, and down the line, sooner or later, I screw things up. And then it isn't an awkward fade; it's a break, a wound, a snapped bone improperly set.

"I'm not . . . not interested," I say. "It's just . . ."

"You have a lot going on," he supplies. "Bad timing. I get it. No worries."

I like you too much to go out with you, I don't say, because it sounds like one of those ridiculous lines people come up with to try to make rejection sting less. But it's true. I don't have enough friendships to risk destroying this one. "Maybe another time," I say.

When? When is the right time? Len asks me, and I don't want to tell him the answer is *When I find her.*

"Another time," Dev agrees. "I'll hold you to that. For the hang-out. Not . . ."

I smile, try to make it genuine. "I really would like that."

"I'm taking you at your word," Dev says. He slaps the arms of his chair. "Now I have to go convince twenty-five teenagers that the 1950s are relevant to their lives."

"Sounds daunting."

"Actually, it's one of the easier ones. The problem is wading through all the essays on 'Joe McCarthy: American Canceler,'" he tells me. "See you Monday, Audrey."

I clear the remains of our lunch from the desk, wrapping up the leftovers for dinner. I'm done with my calls, at least the ones that have any chance of being productive. I chew my lip. And then, before I can think better of it, I pull up Chloe Brittain's schedule and dial the number for her next-period classroom.

Fifteen minutes later, Chloe is hunched in the chair across from me, her ankles crossed awkwardly under. She looks up at me from under dark bangs—they look like she cut them herself. "Am I in trouble or something?" she asks.

I fold my hands on the table. "Not at all, Chloe," I say. "I just wanted to check in with you. I know that it's been a difficult few months."

She blinks slowly, uncomprehending. "It has?"

"Because of Meghan."

"Oh." She looks down. Her hands grip the sides of the chair. She wants to be anywhere but here, but that's hardly unusual for my visitors. "Yeah. I guess."

"How are you feeling?"

"Good," she says, and then her face draws together like she's realized this isn't the best answer when your friend is missing. "Okay, I guess? Um, I mean . . ."

It strikes me that Chloe may not be the brightest girl in the world. Her gaze flops nervously around the room, and she releases her death grip on the chair, only to tug on her lower lip, which sports a piercing, the hole ringed with scaly dry skin. I look over at her records, displayed on my screen. B student, barely, but her attendance is solid. No real extracurriculars. I picked her of the three because, in all the photos that included Meghan, she was standing next to Chloe, and Chloe was the only one who ever responded to Meghan's comments on her posts.

"Were you two very close?" I ask, my voice free of judgment.

"N-not really," she says, guilt rusting at the edge of her words. "We were friends? But not, like, really good friends? We hung out sometimes."

"Can you tell me what she was—what she's like?" I ask, catching my slipup just in time. She doesn't seem to notice.

"She's weird, I guess? Not in, like, a bad way," she hastens to add. "But she's into really morbid stuff? And she's like . . ." She drops her voice. "A witch. I think. Like, it's called Wicca?"

"I'm familiar," I say, smiling. "What do her parents think of that?"

"Her dad does *not* like it. But I don't think he likes anything she does. She's always complaining about him," Chloe says. Now that she's talking more, she's lodged solidly in present tense. I decide that's a good sign. Chloe, at least, doesn't think her friend is dead.

No mention of the mom, I note. Dead or absent? "Did she tell you she wanted to run away?"

Chloe's shoulders go up in the first half of a shrug and can't seem to find their way back down. "She said she was going to run away to live in a bog."

I stifle a small laugh, and I think suddenly of Janie crooking her fingers at a classmate, telling him she was going to put a curse on him to make his dick fall off. We got detention for that one.

"But no specific plans? Real ones, I mean, not bog-related."

"No? Not that she mentioned, but we didn't usually talk about that kind of thing. We mostly talked about TV and stuff. There's this old show we were really into? *Teen Wolf*?"

I consider whether it's time to start looking into retirement homes and applying for AARP membership. "I heard she was artistic. She liked photography?"

"Oh, yeah," she says, nodding. "Her Insta is really, like, dark but pretty, you know?"

"Could you show me?" I ask, hoping I sound casual.

The guileless Chloe doesn't ask why I would possibly need to see a missing girl's Instagram account—she just pulls her phone out, then freezes. "Wait. Am I going to get in trouble for taking my phone out during school hours?"

"You have my permission," I assure her. She visibly relaxes, taps away at the screen, and then hands the phone over.

Meghan Vale's Instagram is a marked departure from her friends'. No personal photos here at all, no tortured poetry—just black-and-white photos, the contrast pumped up until the shadows devour any nuance of gray. There are photos of flowers, candles, what looks like a cat's skull balanced on the top of a fence post, branches framing an empty sky.

And then more branches, but these ones are closer together. They're cast in darkness, making the pale shapes that dangle from them almost glow.

It's the same tree. The same beads hanging from its branch.

She was there.

I click through. The date is January 5—roughly two weeks before she was last seen. *I took a walk through the woods. It felt like someone was watching me. I think I know who it was.*

My mouth is dry. My mind's eye fills with the deep black of the photographs, skewed into the shape of a pit—a hole—the barrel of a gun. She was out there, in a place she shouldn't have been. Land that belonged to a man adamant that it not be searched, not even to save the life of a little boy.

"Um, Ms. Dixon? Can I have my phone back?" Chloe asks.

"Of course." I hand it over. "Chloe, let me know if you need anything, okay? Anything at all. Or if you just want to talk."

"About Meghan?" she asks, that brow-crumpling confusion back.

"About anything you like."

"Yeah, okay," she says. She gathers her backpack, pulling it against her protectively. At the doorway, she pauses. "She wasn't happy. And she said she was going to run away, but I didn't think she meant it. And . . . she would have said goodbye."

She's gone then, leaving me with the afterimage of branches and bare sky.

She would have said goodbye. The words echo in my mind.

They don't always, I want to tell her. Or they say it so many times that it stops being real. They leave so many times that you stop believing they might not come back, until one day you realize how long it's been, and how quiet. By then, it's too late. The last day you could have done something is already a fading memory, and you're left grasping at the empty space where the person you loved once stood, and only then, for a fleeting moment, will you suddenly know the words that would have made them stay.

5

Above

Janie Martin made a practice of disappearing. At first, I thought it was because of me. Something I'd done, something I'd said, some way in which I wasn't a good enough friend to the half-wild girl who crawled in through my window at night and made games of trading secrets. But she made a practice of appearing, too—her entrances considered and crafted.

She arrived in a burst of winter air, wearing her hair in two neat braids, spots of red high on her cheeks from the cold. She wore a thin blue cardigan, little protection against the December wind, as she strode into my parents' store, where I was sitting behind the register doing homework.

I looked up as she slapped two crisp twenty-dollar bills on the counter. "I need silver," she said.

"Silver?" I echoed, confused.

"Anything silver will do. It's for melting down into bullets. I have a werewolf problem, you see," she said, and at my utterly blank look, she burst into laughter. "Just kidding. A pack of Camels, please. Beer in the back?"

Later I'd realize, of course, that the werewolf story was her attempt to throw me off so I wouldn't realize how absurd it was that a twelve-year-old was buying cigarettes and beer. It worked. I'd rung her up and watched her go before I realized quite what had happened.

The next time I saw her was in class after the holidays. The first-period teacher introduced her as our new classmate, Janie Martin, and sat her next to me.

"How are the werewolves?" I asked, trying to be clever.

She arched an eyebrow at me. "No full moon right now. It's vampires you need to be worried about this time of the month. Luckily, silver works on them, too. Or maybe not so lucky, since you didn't seem to have any."

"My name is Audrey," I told her, sticking out my hand.

"January," she said. "The roster says Janie, but my *full* name is January, because I was born in a snowstorm and because I have an extra invisible eye that can see directly behind me." A beat, in which she took in my lack of understanding. "It's a reference to Janus. The god? Don't they teach you anything in schools these days?" She let out a dramatic sigh and turned to face forward. It was the second time I'd disappointed her. And the second time she'd lied to me.

It would be months before I realized the story about her name was a lie—it was Janie on her birth certificate, had never been anything else—and years yet before I started to think about just how often she made sure to let me know I didn't measure up.

"You have no imagination," she would lament. Or "You're very nearly fun sometimes, Oddity, you know that?" That was her name for me. I was never certain if it was fond or mocking. I think sometimes she wasn't sure, either.

The first time she disappeared, she did it in plain view. Very suddenly, instead of spending every lunch period with me, she installed herself at a table across the cafeteria with a crowd of boys I'd never seen her talking to before. When I made my way over, she declared, "Oh, Oddity. You wouldn't like it here," and set her books on the only empty seat beside her. Stunned, I sulked away.

My exile lasted a week and a half. And then she was back, and it was like it had never happened. "I need a break from you sometimes, Oddity. It's no big deal, don't be a baby about it."

The next time, I showed up to her house for a planned visit and no one was home. She returned weeks later with a tan and stories of meeting boys at the beach and chided me for being worried. "You couldn't entertain yourself for two minutes?" she asked, rolling her eyes.

"You didn't tell me you were leaving."

"Didn't I? Huh." A shrug, and that was that.

Later, of course, I'd learn that she hadn't known she was leaving, either. That her father had done a stint in county jail, and she had been bundled off unceremoniously to stay with her maternal aunt, since her mother couldn't—or wouldn't—take her.

It went on like that. Three years of Janie-called-January rushing in and out of my life based on her whims and the strange weather of her home life, next to which my own was dull and steady. She was the one who would be the heroine of a story, I was sure; I would be the boring friend she left behind by chapter two. Maybe I left her for good so that she couldn't do it first.

By the time she vanished, I'd given up on her. I'm not going to make that mistake again now.

"I'm not saying anything except that she was on that property, and maybe it's worth looking into," I say, juggling my purse and keys as I make my way up the walk, phone clamped between my shoulder and ear.

"Based on an Instagram post and some beads," Len replies.

"Based on photographic evidence," I retort. "She was there. Two weeks before she went missing. She wrote that she thought someone was watching her." I fit my key into the lock. "What do you know about that guy, anyway? Bill something?"

"William Butler," he says. "I know he lodged a complaint that members of SAR trespassed on his land yesterday."

"That was an accident."

"I can tell when you're lying," Len says. "Anyway, you got lucky. Melinda Hill called fifteen minutes later, and suddenly there's no complaint anymore."

"We found the kid, didn't we?" I ask.

"And I would have done the same thing in your place, but we both know this is part of a pattern."

I grit my teeth. "What pattern is that?"

"You putting yourself at risk any chance you get because you're stubborn and obsessive and have very little regard for your own safety," Len says, snappish.

I let the silence hold a moment. "So you'll look into Meghan?"

He lets out a long-suffering sigh. "I'll see what I can do, Audrey, on one condition."

"Anything."

"Have a conversation this weekend. Face-to-face. Don't spend the whole weekend holed up alone."

"I'm not alone. And I talk to Barry all the time," I say.

"Do I really need to specify that Barry doesn't count?" Len asks as the door swings open. Barry is waiting on the other side, tail thumping gently against the ground.

"He heard that. He's very hurt," I tell Len. He sighs again. "Look, I promise. Just find out what you can."

"Deal. But, Audrey . . . you aren't a detective. This girl's not one of yours. Just let us do our jobs, and you do yours, okay?" Len asks.

"Okay," I agree, not meaning it for a moment. Which he knows, but still he lets me go. I end the call, drop the phone onto the credenza by the door, and turn to the oh-so-patient Barry. "Thanks for waiting, Barry."

With those words, over a hundred pounds of pit bull–mastiff–moose hybrid are unleashed at my midsection. Barry—blue gray, a head like a concrete block, ninety percent muscle and ten percent slobber—flings himself into me at the speed of sound, his back end gyrating as his tail fails to adequately express his joy at my return. I drop to my knees, mostly for the added stability, and scrub my hands over his muscled flanks, making all the requisite cooing noises. He finally flops onto his back, waving the white flag of his belly for me to scratch.

"Oh, buddy. I have had a *day*," I tell him. He huffs understanding.

Barry was the deal I made with Len. If I was going to be going out solo hiking and taking long walks alone at night, I had to get a dog. The biggest, fiercest one I could find. I ended up with Barry, whose scarred muzzle suggested a tragic past. Joke's on Len: Barry loves everyone. He'd give Ted Bundy the garage door code in exchange for belly rubs, but at least he looks scary.

My phone buzzes. I pick it up long enough to check the notifications. The group chat is pinging back and forth with plans to meet up for post-deployment drinks at Wolf's, the best mediocre tavern in Franklin. We come from all over the county, but Franklin has proved a convenient middle ground, making my absence all the more conspicuous.

I mute the thread and put the phone face down. "What do you think tonight? Popcorn and a movie?" I ask Barry.

He quirks his head, his look skeptical.

"No, really. Let's watch a movie," I say. "I'll just look at something on my laptop first."

Twenty minutes later, Barry is curled up next to me on the couch, delicately nibbling individual popcorn kernels from my fingers while I scroll on my laptop. There is, in fact, a movie playing. I haven't paid attention to a single line of dialogue yet. I have the file open on my computer that I'm only allowed to open once a week, because that proves that Len is wrong, and I'm not obsessed.

Len calls them my dead friends. And some of them—maybe even most of them—must be, logically and statistically speaking. They're the names and faces of the missing I've collected over the years. Most of them are fairly local. A few are from farther afield and caught my eye for some reason. It's part of my penance—remembering them. Looking for them. I know the odds of ever finding someone from my list are near zero, and yet still I look through my collected files regularly, committing their details to memory. Someday I will walk down the street, and Mikaela Dawson will be walking the other way, eight years older; I will follow Barry off trail and find the bones of Nicholas Tarbor wrapped in the tattered remnants of his rain shell.

Janie is the first. She was never officially reported missing, but I've created my own case file. There's little to go on. Janie left Franklin when she was seventeen. By that time, we hadn't been friends for two years. No one, including me, did anything to try to bring her home. I've tracked her path from the first few months, found people she met along the way as she bounced around the country. A girl who let her crash on her couch, a man who went on a few dates with her, a bass player who took a photo with her at a concert. It was a brief window when she was easy to find, if anyone bothered to look. But we never did.

All the people she had twined around her, intoxicated by her presence, and not one of us tracked her down while we still could. I wonder how many others breathed a sigh of relief when she took off that summer before senior year and promised she'd never come back to our dead-end town.

But she *did* come back. Just once. Just that one night, as far as I can tell, five years after she left, long after the trail goes cold. First the phone call, and then rocks at my window and her voice crooning my name.

Or maybe I dreamed it. There have been times when I wondered if I did. No one else saw her. No one else spoke to her, that they'll admit. But it wasn't a dream. She was here.

And then she was nowhere.

The photo I linger on isn't the last one I've found of her—hair loose and messy, turned to pure fiery red in the sun, sitting on the sidewalk in an unknown city. I look instead at the last photo of the two of us in our homecoming dresses—hers bright green, clinging to her hips, mine blue and poorly fitted to my squarish torso. I might as well not be there at all, the way the camera focuses in on her, the hand propped just so on her hip, the knowing smile.

She's wearing a bracelet, a thick silver thing with a chunk of turquoise at its center. In the later photos, it's gone. Replaced with black cord and six white beads. I don't know when she started wearing it. And whether there was someone in particular she was thinking of when she did.

My phone chimes. A text from Dev with a link to the podcast episode he mentioned. I thank him and follow the link. Barry lets out a tiny, pathetic whine and looks up at me, eyes pools of pure tragedy.

"Should we take a walk?" I ask him. He scrambles off the couch.

As I get on a coat and Barry's leash and harness, I download the podcast episode. I never have the patience for these things. The guy's voice is deep and melodic, but by the time I'm past the intro, I've sped it up until he sounds like he's had way too much caffeine.

"When my producer suggested this story for our Halloween episode, I was skeptical. I'm not exactly a believer in the supernatural, and I have a firm rule about not doing ghost episodes. But when I looked into the story of Jenny Red-Hands and the town of Franklin, I found real people, real events. I found a mythology that has grown up around them, and sometimes consumed them. It's been a source of empowerment for young women, but it's also become a scapegoat, one that has been used at times to downplay real crimes."

I'm surprised by my instant reaction—anger. No, I don't believe Jenny Red-Hands is real, but what is this? A hot take about how our story of female vengeance is actually bad? I walk with my head down, legs pumping. Barry trots along beside me without a care in the world, used to my moody speed-walking. If there's something he truly wants to stop and sniff, he knows that all he has to do is plant his feet and there's nothing I can do about it.

"Let's begin with what exactly the story of Jenny Red-Hands is—which is a harder question to answer than you might think. The most popular version goes something like this: In the 1800s, a young woman—the titular Jenny—was wronged in some way. Assaulted, abandoned, betrayed. In all versions, Jenny tries to get justice, but is discredited. Instead, the perpetrators claim that she is a witch. The town is ready to execute Jenny, but when they arrive to find her, she's fled into the woods. It isn't long before she's seen again—her hands gloved in blood, standing at the edge of the woods. The body of her victim, or victims, was found soon after. The story claims she took teeth as trophies and vanished into the wilderness, but that when a woman was suffering at the hands of a man, she could go beseech Jenny for aid, searching for the sign of a red handprint. Supplicants would leave her offerings of white beads to represent the teeth she'd taken, and carve the names of the men who wronged them into a tree. Vengeance was sure to come to them. But sometimes, Jenny took a liking to the young women who came to her for help. Those girls would vanish—killed by Jenny, or maybe spirited away to somewhere they would forever be safe from the violence of men."

In the original, they were teeth, Janie told me. I had always wondered if she made that up, but here it is, reported as fact.

"There are many elements of the story that changed depending on who I heard it from. For instance, the teeth—I heard it five times, but only from people who had attended Franklin High School around the mid-aughts. In other versions, the beads were actually pearls, gathered up from a broken necklace after the initial assault. In still others, they had no explanation at all."

I laugh suddenly. Those would be exactly the years that Janie attended high school. Maybe she'd heard it from someone else . . . but no. Janie told that story. It's hers. I have no doubt.

The host dispenses with the other details and origins of the story quickly; it's clear he's not that interested in its particulars, given its obvious lack of historical veracity. The story originated in the early 2000s online, in a series of breathlessly serious websites and forum posts. Every "fact" they referenced was a complete fabrication. There was no Jenny in all of Franklin's history that might have matched—or Jennifer or Jessica or Janet.

Or Janie, I think. Barry pauses to inspect a bed of flowers and leave his contribution to the aroma. I've been letting him choose the direction, and unsurprisingly, he's been leading us toward the coffee shop downtown that stocks dog treats behind the counter.

"I don't think they're even open," I warn him. He sneezes in disgust.

The podcast has moved on. Moving from ghost stories into sociology—the way that the Jenny Red-Hands story has shaped the discussion of violence against women in Franklin. And soon my anger at the host has no choice but to fade, because he has a point. The real stories of women—and men, for that matter—who have suffered in Franklin have been co-opted as part of the Jenny Red-Hands myth. A young woman disappeared and was later found dead, but in the meantime, the school buzzed with the idea that Jenny had taken her, an idea that prompted more laughter than concern. *Go tell Jenny*, more than one woman recalled being instructed, while no one real would listen.

But mostly, she's been a rallying cry. A little bit of power for the young and voiceless to claw back.

We've come to the coffee shop. As expected, it's closed. Barry sits on the mat out front and lets out a mournful whimper.

"We can't just wait. They don't open until the morning," I tell him. He does not respect my logical explanation.

A burst of laughter sounds from nearby, followed by a familiar voice. My head whips around. Of course. The team are out carousing, less than a block away—I can just see the back of Matsuda's head, out on the pub patio. Luckily, I'm currently hidden by a thick wall of potted plants.

"We gotta go," I say to Barry, tugging at him. He reluctantly follows me. I pick up my pace. It's not like I'm actively trying to avoid my colleagues—despite the fact that yes, right now I'm all but running away from them. We have plenty of camaraderie when we're training or working. But I don't do happy hours, don't do the heavy drinking and loud conversation. It's the same reason I don't talk about my SAR work at school. There is a sacredness to it, and something shameful, too, inflected by old guilt.

I have my head down, hoping not to get spotted, when I come around the corner, which is why I don't see Emily Hill stepping out onto the street until I've nearly smacked into her. She catches me by the shoulders to prevent a collision, pivoting to let my momentum carry me past her.

"Whoa!" she says. Her grip on my arms is firm, strength in her fingers. For an instant, we're frozen there, face-to-face, close enough for me to see every tiny freckle on her cheeks, the smallest whisker of a scar along the bridge of her nose.

"Sorry," I stammer, instinctively choking up on the leash to keep Barry snug against my thigh—but he's correctly assessed the threat, or lack of one, and stays put. I pull my earbuds out of my ears guiltily. "I wasn't looking where I was going."

"No harm done," she says. She puts her hands in her sweatshirt pockets, backing up a step to put a more comfortable distance between us. "Urgent errand?"

"Just walking the dog," I say, gesturing to Barry. He pants, exhibiting the vastness of his jaws.

"He's gorgeous," she says. Barry's tail thumps the ground.

"He certainly thinks so."

She flashes a smile as she turns to close the door she came out of. The business next door is a vacuum repair shop, but the door opens on a steep staircase. She tugs it firmly shut and locks it. "It's my studio," she says at my curious look. "I do most of my painting at home, but sometimes I need more space. Or just to get out of the house."

"You paint?" I ask.

"Now and then," she replies.

We both hover, like neither of us is sure how to end the conversation. "You know, I feel like I should apologize," I say.

She raises an eyebrow. "Why's that?"

"For ditching you, I mean," I say.

"Ditching me?" Understanding blooms. "You mean homecoming." I nod. She gives a little laugh. "We were kids."

"Still."

She considers me. "Do you mind if I walk with you for a little bit?" she asks.

Surprised, I blink. "No. I guess not," I say. Barry is already anxious to get moving, so I start again, and she falls in beside me. She walks with her head high, attention around her. Wary in a way I've never gotten the trick of, despite the steady diet of horror stories I nourish myself on.

"I was thinking about that night, actually," she says as we walk.

We'd meant to go together, Janie and I, neither one of us having a date—I hadn't been asked; she'd made a show of turning down three boys in our grade—but somehow, we'd ended up in Andrew Hill's truck instead. Andrew and Janie in the front, me and Emmie in the back. Emmie was a grade below us, dressed in a girlish blue frock. She had enormous eyes, I remember, and a shaky smile. I didn't know her well—she usually kept to the shadow of her more gregarious twin, Liam. Andrew was a senior that year. And a star. And you didn't get in cars with boys, but his little sister was with him, so how bad could it be?

We drove to the old lot where the Franklin Shopping Center had been torn down, after the big mall was built in the town over. The crust of pulverized beer bottles and stubble of abandoned cigarettes was proof of just how often it was used for gatherings like this. Half the football team was there, along with a gaggle of female hangers-on, a random assortment of students, and a few guys who looked too old to be in high school.

Parts of that night are a blur, but moments flicker into focus—"Aren't we going to the dance?" I asked, arms crossed tight over me. I'd saved up my allowance for weeks to buy this dress—off the bargain rack at JCPenney, admittedly.

"Only babies go to school dances," someone said.

"Yeah, Oddity. Babies," Janie echoed with a smirk.

And then there was the smeared light of the fire and my one taste of beer staining my whole tongue with a flavor that made me want to retch. A girl pulling a boy away from the fire, winking when she caught me looking. Andrew holding court, reenacting the highlights of his greatest plays with an empty bottle as a stand-in for a ball.

Emmie and Janie sitting shoulder to shoulder, between us the skittering flames of the small fire.

"Don't we look like sisters?" Janie had asked. An innocent question, except that nothing was innocent with Janie, and that day she was mad at me, and *we* were the ones who were supposed to be sisters. But she was right. Two peas in a pod, my mother would have said. Milky complexions, the hint of freckles on their cheeks, matching red hair—Emmie's a touch more golden, Janie's a deeper orange. I heard those words and my stomach pinched, knowing they were directed at me. It was Andrew who got angry.

"You don't look anything alike. Come over here."

They went off together then, and the others had somehow drifted away as well, leaving me alone with Emmie. We'd talked, I think, though I can't remember about what. I do remember the truck engine starting up. Realizing what it meant. The truck peeled out of the lot, dust kicking up behind it. Andrew saw us in the mirror and didn't slow down, his hand threaded in Janie's hair, her head on his shoulder. One of his buddies threw a water bottle out the back window. It didn't hit either of us, but the message was clear.

"It's my fault we got left behind in the first place," Emily says now, and the present regains its footing.

"How's that?" I ask, startled.

"Andrew was pissed that Melinda made him bring me along. I was his date. He was humiliated," she says, sounding almost satisfied.

"I had no idea," I say. I look away. "But it wasn't just you. Janie and I were fighting that day. Every day, really, for a while, but that week it was intense."

"What were you fighting about?" she asks, without any apparent embarrassment at being so probing.

I shrug. "I think I was finally realizing that I didn't just want to do what she said. And always be the ugly, boring friend who made her look better in comparison," I say, and regret it immediately, like I've betrayed her all over again. Even with Len, I'm careful not to say these things, and he knows what it was like. He knows what *I* was like, the year after my friendship with Janie ended.

"Is that how you thought of yourself?" she asks. "It's not really how I remember you."

"Oh? And how do you remember me?" It's a little bit shocking to be remembered at all. It startled me every time someone knew my name, even with a school the size of Franklin High.

"I remember that you talked to me like I was worth talking to. You gave me your sweater and asked me about myself," she says. "You cared. Not many people do."

"I left you," I say. We'd walked from the lot to the bus stop. We'd gotten there as the bus was pulling up, and I'd gotten on. I hesitated, wondering if I should ask her to come with me, or make sure she had a way to get home. But I'd just left her there. I went home and hid in my room and cried, and then I forgot all about Emmie Hill, because then Janie was knocking on my window (the almost-last time), and getting ditched at the lot was no longer the most memorable thing about the evening.

"You let me keep the sweater," Emily says.

"How did you get home?"

"I walked."

"That's a hell of a walk."

She shrugs. "I wasn't about to call my dad. He didn't want me going in the first place. I had to beg, and then Melinda was the one who actually talked him into it."

"Are you and she close?"

She hesitates. It's a complicated silence, full of thorns, and I regret asking immediately.

"I'm sorry, I shouldn't pry," I say.

"It's just one of those things," she says.

Maybe I know what she means. I have one sibling—older brother, Camden. He and my parents have always gotten along amazingly well. They go on vacations together with him and his wife and his two kids, have a family chat I'm only nominally a part of, get together for dinner every other week. He loves baseball, like

Dad does; his wife loves gardening, like Mom. I've always been the odd one out. A little too strange, a little too quiet, a little too sad for their perfect family life.

"What about Liam?" I asked. Her twin brother. He'd been the darling of the drama club, for good reason. I'd worked stage crew my senior year when he was strutting around as Mercutio. Anyone could see his talent and his energy on the stage. Not many got to glimpse the way he collapsed in on himself as soon as he thought no one was looking, as if exhausted by the performance of everyday survival. I remember the way he would stare at the wall, emptied out, until it was time to go back onstage again, and he suddenly came back to life. "Is he still acting?"

"Not for a long time," she says, words clipped. "Not since his last relapse."

I blanch. "I'm sorry. I didn't know." I'm making a disaster of this.

"You shouldn't apologize for things that aren't your fault," she tells me.

"Bad habit of mine."

"I prefer not to apologize for anything," she says. "It's much more fun."

We've come to the corner where I have to turn to get back to my neighborhood. Barry has the loose-legged walk that means he's had his fill and is ready to return to his spot on the couch.

"I should let you get home," Emily says.

"Wait," I say. "Before you go—do you know a girl named Meghan Vale?"

She seems to consider. "It doesn't sound familiar."

"She was in your woods," I say. "Or your neighbor's, rather. She took a photo of the witch beads—they were hanging from a tree. Where we found Bryson."

"You mean, where you almost got shot," she says.

"Yeah." I flush. "The thing is, she's missing. The police think she ran away, but if she was out there, maybe Bill . . ."

She shakes her head. "Bill is paranoid, ornery, and entirely too obsessed with guns. But I don't think he'd actually shoot a girl, if that's what you're asking."

"Not even in the dark, if all he saw was an intruder?" I ask.

Her brow furrows. "When did this girl go missing?"

"Mid-January."

"Wouldn't have been Bill, then. He's just been watching the place for his brother now and then."

"Who's the brother?"

"Terry Butler," she says. "He's in the hospital right now. Heart trouble, I think."

"What's he like?" I ask, not backing down.

"He's . . . not a good man," she says carefully. "Bill's got a survivalist streak, but Terry makes it his life. He's always sure the apocalypse is two weeks away, max, and that he's the only one smart enough to survive it." She thumbs her lip. "She was out there. You're sure?"

"I'm sure."

She looks away, lost in thought. When she speaks again, her voice is distant. "Your friend Janie. She told us the Jenny Red-Hands story that night, didn't she?"

I nod. She'd made it into a performance. Made it, somehow, into flirtation. Threatening to take the teeth out of Andrew's mouth as she tapped her finger against his lips.

"It wasn't the usual version," she said.

I think back. I'd been tuning Janie out at that point of the evening, but memory stirs.

"Everyone knows the story," Andrew had said. "The scary witch does bad things to bad men, ooooh." His buddies guffawed. Janie bristled.

"That's not the real story," she'd said, drawing herself up. "The girls don't all come back, you know. The ones who stray into the woods to beg Jenny's favor." The firelight cast a golden glow across her skin as she curled her fingers as if beckoning Andrew toward her. "They make their offerings and carve her mark and pray she comes, but they ought to pray she doesn't. Because it was monstrous, what happened to her, and it made her into a monster. They carved every soft and gentle part of her away. So if you come to her and your heart is cold and sharp as steel, she'll grant your vengeance. But if she sees that you still have any of that softness, any of that gentleness—" She was standing right in front of Andrew now, her fingertips trailing up his shirt, and suddenly she flexed her fingers, digging her nails in. "She'll rip your heart out."

Her eyes reflected the light of the fire, wild and bright. Andrew caught her wrist.

"You'd be safe, then," he said, and Janie broke into laughter, head tipped back, until he pulled her into his lap.

I looked away then. I don't remember what happened next.

"I'd forgotten that," I say. I look to the side, old feelings roiling. "No one else is looking for her."

"Meghan, you mean," she says softly.

"Of course," I say, not sure I'm telling the truth.

She nods slowly. "Come by my place tomorrow. If Bill isn't there, I can take you out to look around. You know where it is?"

"Yeah," I say. I pass the long driveway all the time, heading out toward the wilderness area to hike. "And thank you. I know there probably isn't anything to find, but . . ."

"But you have to try," she says, understanding. She reaches out to scratch Barry between the ears, and then she walks away without another word. She takes the corner wide. So she can see who's coming, I think, and I notice again the way her eyes drink in every pocket of shadow.

What made her so careful? I wonder. Not, I think, lurid stories of murder piped in through earbuds. There's something personal about the coiled tension in her body.

The Hills were all in the public eye, one way or another. Melinda with her political career, Andrew with football and then the foundation, and Liam with his acting career—there was a big stir in town when he was cast on *City Rescue* as the soulful-eyed Kyle, paramedic by day and street racer by night. But there's never been a whisper from the youngest Hill. I think of the girl I walked with all those years ago. How quietly she spoke. As if she assumed no one would listen.

I didn't know then what I know now. Wouldn't learn that lesson for years yet—what happens when no one is paying attention. How quickly someone can vanish, even when they're standing right in front of you.

I start up the podcast again, trying to banish the sound of Emily's voice. And my pulse suddenly speeds up.

"At Franklin High School, the story of Jenny Red-Hands is alive and well. I asked a number of students about the most recent iterations of the story, and what it means to them," the host says, and then the audio changes—background chatter, a bird chirping.

"This is Meghan, a student at Franklin High. Meghan, why don't you tell us about your experience of Jenny Red-Hands?" the host asks, and then a young woman's voice speaks.

"I know Jenny Red-Hands is real," Meghan Vale says. "Because I've seen her."

6

Below

My fingers are raw, my palms lashed with abrasions, but I have pried free the lowermost slat of the bed—a slender length of brittle wood. Rather than nails, long staples jut out of the ends. It's almost nothing. And it's everything. Because it's proof of what I can do, and it's a declaration.

I can't turn back now.

What can she even do with that? the girls ask.

Too flimsy to be a weapon.

It won't break the chain.

It's nothing.

Useless.

She'll die down here.

They're a chorus of insects, wing-buzz chatter, flitting shapes. Some are more distinct than others. The girl with round eyes, the one with glasses (broken, bent), the one who holds her hand over her throat at all times. These are the ones who wrote the messages. They're more real to me, easier to imagine into being. But there are others. I can't count them—they're only quicksilver shapes that merge and split and watch soundlessly. I can't give them voices unless I have their words, after all. I can't know how many might have never left their mark.

I wonder where they've gone, the girls who came before. Buried deep or left in the open for flies to crawl across their staring eyes.

Stay focused. The girl sits next to me, head high, unafraid—nothing to ever be afraid of again.

"I don't want to die," I say.

Is that the truth?

"It was supposed to be my choice."

And that makes it different.

"Of course it does."

The gossamer girl lowers her chin a fraction, acknowledging the point. *Think it through. What do you have?*

A length of wood. Pine, probably. No real weight to it. Only the pricks of the staples at the end, little strength to them.

What do you have that you didn't before?

I imagine the layout of the room. The sweep of the chain. The toilet. Beyond my reach, the chairs. The table. They're outside the range of the chain; they're a privilege to be earned. The farthest stretch of my fingertips won't graze them, but now—now I have reach. Maybe I can snag them, pull them toward me. The chairs, definitely. Maybe even the table.

They're cheap aluminum things. Hollow legs, flimsy surfaces. They won't be strong enough to chip away at concrete, to break a chain.

But they're more than I have now.

Good, the gossamer girl says, satisfied.

I wonder if I'm going crazy. They seem more real than ever, these ghosts of my invention. The first time they appeared, they were only a shiver in the air and a yearning not to be alone, my mind fixed on those scattered words. I shaped them bit by bit in my imagination, but I can't tell the difference anymore between what I see and what I wish I could see. My eyes have been starved of light too long for reality to matter.

Think, the gossamer girl says, or I say to myself (is there a difference?).

What do I have? A length of wood; some strength yet; an improbable desire, after all this time, to survive. A bed, my breath, enough food for another few days, enough water for less than that.

Water—the water in the toilet tank, which means the toilet, too. The top of the tank is covered with a flimsy plastic lid taken from a storage box, ill-fitting, and even if the original ceramic had been there, I don't think it would have been strong enough to break the chain, strong enough to do anything but shatter (but the pieces might have been sharp, might have been useful). But the toilet isn't just the toilet. It's the mechanisms inside. It's the pipes, and it's the bolts driven down deep into the concrete slab to hold it in place.

I kneel down next to the toilet, running my fingers over the cold porcelain. I follow its contours to the base, and there I find the rusted lumps of the bolts and nut heads. My fingers find no purchase on them. I'll never get a grip tight enough to turn them, but I can tell they're substantial.

There are places where the chain is weak. Links waiting to break. If they're long enough, strong enough, those bolts might be enough leverage for the task.

She's fooling herself, one of the girls says, contemptuous. Her scorn ripples over my skin.

Maybe I am. But I'm done waiting in the dark.

The chatter of the girls is near constant. A voice slips in among them, and I don't notice that rather than the distant, dry echoing of the girls, this voice is muffled to softness. It comes not from the alcoves of my own mind but from beyond the walls of the room, beyond the stairs and the door. I register it only when it's gone, the sound of it lingering like a question never to be answered.

By the time I'm sure of what I heard, I've already convinced myself that it was only my imagination.

7

Above

At eight o'clock, I head out the door. It's a solid two hours after I would have preferred to leave, but I doubt Emily would appreciate me showing up at the crack of dawn.

I fill a Kong toy with peanut butter for Barry and promise him we'll go hiking later, and then slip out the door while he stares accusingly after me. He'd be good company, but if Bill *is* out there with his rifle, I'm not going to risk him being willing to shoot a dog.

Along the way, I pass the patch of dirt on the shoulder where a bus stop once stood. I track the miles past it, imagining how long it would have taken a fourteen-year-old girl and how much her feet would hurt at the end of it, crammed into kitten heels.

By the end of the Hills' drive, I can practically feel the ache in my own soles. I know without being told that she would have walked to the side of the drive here so the gravel wouldn't crunch. There are wheel ruts there this morning, marks chewed into the grass and weeds by our tires only two days ago. The search for Bryson Lee has left no evidence behind but these, campsite rules observed to the last biodegradable coffee cup. I pull all the way up to the house. It sits back among the trees, shaded and shielded, a dappling of light crowning the moss on its eaves. A wind chime of hammered copper spins lazily over the porch; a wreath of colored glass adorns a fence post. Small creatures of twisted wire, each almost but not quite an identifiable species, peer from beneath the broad leaves of potted plants or crouch with an air of polite skepticism under fern fronds.

I step onto the porch. A half-dead moth clutches the doorframe above the bell, so I knock instead and wait. The rain, which began to fall softly during the drive, patters against the roof. Even in a quiet town like Franklin, this kind of silence is rare.

There's no answer at first. I knock again, check my phone—though I never gave her my number, so I don't know why I'd think there might be a message there—and ring the bell, making silent apology to the gray moth. The chime is muffled on the other side of the door, but it summons movement at last. Quick footsteps and then the clack of a dead bolt, and Emily opens the door with a distant expression. She looks at me for a moment like she can't imagine who I am or what I'm doing there, and then she blinks.

"Audrey," she says. "I'm sorry. I was . . . I got distracted." I don't have to ask what she was doing. She wears a pair of paint-splattered overalls over a thin white T-shirt. The paint is like an archaeological dig, history stratified into layers. She favors earthy colors, the more muted greens of winter or late summer, blues made humble by tones of gray. A pale streak the color of bone still shines wetly on her wrist, obscuring part of the tattoo that twines from her wrist to the crook of her elbow: black ink blurred to blue, tracing the intricate shapes of a moth and ferns and various fungi. Her hair is up in a messy ponytail, darker roots beginning to show at the base of the blond.

"I realized we never said when we'd meet up," I say, letting her off the hook. "If you're not available—"

"No, I am," she assures me. "Let's get going." She doesn't wait for a response, just grabs a coat from a hook by the door and shoves her feet into a pair of rubber boots. The coat hangs loosely over her small frame. "Did you bring Barry?"

"Not today," I say.

"I thought he might be trained," she says, half a question.

"Like for Search and Rescue?" I ask. At her nod, I smile. "Sort of. As in, he's trained for trailing and cadaver work, but he gets too excited by all the volunteers. He'd rather go check them all out than find the subject, so he got demoted to bodyguard."

"He seems like too much of a marshmallow for that," she notes.

"You're not wrong," I say with a laugh.

She hums a little and sweeps her hair back behind her ears, still more than half lost in other thoughts.

"You should see Matsuda's dogs, though—Paul Matsuda, he's one of our senior volunteers. They're incredible," I say, but she only hums a response, her gaze tracking over the woods.

"You want to start where you saw the beads?"

"That seems like the best plan, don't you think?"

She nods. Some part of me is oddly wounded by her distraction. Was, I realize, grateful for her interest last night. Now she seems preoccupied, her eyes focused on the canvas she's been forced to abandon instead of the trees before her.

"Promise we're not going to get shot at?" I ask as we walk.

She steps over a fallen log without breaking stride. "Bill left last night. He hasn't been back."

"You're sure?"

"I would have seen the headlights," she notes. "You have to take our driveway up to the other house."

"You couldn't have slept through it?" I ask.

"I didn't sleep," she confesses. She clears her throat. "How did you get into it? Volunteering?" I can't tell if she's interested or just trying to be polite. There's an edge to her today that wasn't there yesterday, a nerviness.

"I just answered an ad," I say. "We're always looking for more volunteers."

"I guess what I was wondering is why," she clarifies.

"Ah." I look down as I step over a root, taking the excuse to break eye contact. "Janie, really."

"Oh. Of course." She looks chagrined.

I clear my throat. "Did you know her?"

"Not really." The rain is picking up, but remains more mist than droplets.

"She dated your brother."

She shrugs. "For a few weeks. We only really met a couple times."

"Sometimes I think no one knew her," I say, and she halts, expression gentling. "Meghan reminds me of her, a little."

"How so?" She cocks her head, curious.

"I don't know, exactly. They're both . . . peculiar, I guess. And gone." My lips twist in half a mirthless smile.

"Do you know where she went?" Emily asks, and her voice is soft now, cautious.

I shake my head. "She just left." I think of knuckles tapping at glass and a voice I tried not to hear. What might have happened if I opened that window?

"Do you think something happened to her?"

"I don't know," I admit. "Maybe she just went to live a new life. I know she wanted to. But . . ."

"But the world isn't that kind," Emily finishes for me.

"Sometimes it is," I say. "For every tragedy, there's someone found."

Her jaw tenses briefly. "The scales don't balance out like that." She tilts her head to the right. "We're here."

The red marker hangs limply from the tree. I follow Emily past it, walking the scant few steps to the tree where the beads hang. In the rain, without the tension of the search, the distance seems shorter and the display in the trees less ominous. A few scraggly strings of cheap beads stuck there by a bored teenager, nothing more.

"You think Meghan was here?" Emily asks.

"She took photos," I say.

She squints up at the beads. "Do you think she's the one that put them here?"

"I don't know. Maybe." I try to imagine it both ways—hiking out here to tie up offerings, or stumbling across them. Each feels true in its own way.

I look up at the tree. There must be three dozen strands of beads. They look old—cords grayed and fraying. Meghan didn't leave these here. Not recently, at least. These have been here for years.

We're near the rear edge of Terry Butler's property; there are trails that snake all over the place, in from the public land and the Hills' acres. "What exactly are you looking for?" Emily asks.

"I'm not sure. Nothing. Anything," I say, and she nods like this makes sense.

I don't need to tell her that Meghan Vale has been gone for months. The odds of finding any trace of her are slim, as are the chances that this little tableau has anything to do with where she is now.

"Do you know where that cellar was? The place they found Bryson?" I ask.

"Yeah. Up this way," she says. She sets out northward. It's not long before we're off the Butler property, and despite Emily's reassurances, I relax a bit at that. It was the team Rick and I were supposed to join that found Bryson, in the end. We were so close to him. A short hike later, Emily pauses to get the lay of the land and then directs us to a hillock.

Calling the hole she points to a root cellar is generous. It's barely wide enough for a grown man to fit down, with the remnants of a crude and long-rotted door framing the uneven, muddy steps down. Wooden beams have been shoved into the earth to provide the semblance of structure, but it's far from trustworthy. I crouch and peer down, shining my flashlight inside, and I can just make out a low-ceilinged room supported partially by the thick root structure of the tree beside it. The whole thing is maybe four feet by five feet, with nothing but an ancient wooden apple crate for decor.

Bryson must have been terrified if this place looked like a safer option than staying out in the open. There's no sign that anyone else has been out here. Certainly not Meghan Vale.

"Did Terry build this?" I ask after I extract myself, wiping mud from my arm. "Some kind of survivalist thing?"

"Could be," Emily says. She stands with her foot braced against a tree root. She's gone without a hood, and the rain slicks her hair against her brow and cheeks, drips from the tip of her nose. "I don't think we're going to find anything out here, Audrey," she says apologetically, but my eyes track up past her shoulder to the trunk of the tree. There, at shoulder level, someone has gouged rough lines in the bark. Five lines, splayed, drawing together to a single point, the last one shorter than the rest.

Like a crude rendering of a hand—and around the marks, something has been dabbed. Blood, I think, but of course it isn't—blood would have turned brown out here. It's paint, smeared roughly around the shape.

I walk toward Emily. Her brows draw together, and then she startles as I reach out, fit my hand over the carved mark. I've never seen a mark like this. It isn't part of the story, but isn't that what the story *is*? Something each of us tells, changes, makes our own. It isn't real, so it can be real to each of us the way we want it to be.

"She was here," I say, and the words are more certain than I possibly can be.

"Are you sure?"

I scrape at the paint with the edge of my fingernail. A bit of it flakes off. "This isn't fresh, but it isn't years old, either," I note. I turn to Emily. "Someone hurt her. That's what this means. Doesn't it? If she was calling on Jenny Red-Hands."

"Do you think she still had a gentle heart?" Emily asks, and there's something rough in her voice. Her hands hang loose at her sides, her gaze fixed unerringly on me.

"That isn't funny," I say.

"No," she agrees. Her head tilts. "You aren't going to find what you're looking for out here, Audrey. It's been too long, if she was ever here at all."

"We should keep looking," I insist.

"For what?" she asks flatly, and I flinch.

"I don't know. I just—there's something here. There has to be."

Her expression shifts, softens. She shakes her head a little, loosing drops of rain. "It's cold. It's wet. Come have some coffee," she suggests. "If there's a trail out here, it went cold a long time ago. This isn't where you need to be looking."

I want to argue, but she's right. Wherever Meghan Vale went, I won't find her by traipsing around in the trees. I need to find out why she was so fascinated with the story of Jenny Red-Hands.

I dip my head in surrender. We walk in silence back to the house. We shed our muddy coats and boots at the door, and Emily offers me a towel for my dripping hair.

Everything about the house feels old and out of date—the wood-paneled walls, the coral carpet, the musty smell of it. It reminds me nonspecifically of my grandparents, though I can't quite place why. Maybe just the sense that I am welcome, but only reluctantly welcome.

Most of the surfaces have some kind of potted plant on them. Succulents clustered on the mantel, a peace lily spreading its wings by the front window, spider plants making a tangle of the coffee table. Books are abandoned precariously at the edges of surfaces, as if set down in the middle of reading and never picked up again. The bookmarks sticking out of them are eclectic—envelopes and scraps of paper and pens and bobby pins.

There are no photographs on any of the walls, but paintings hang here and there. Nature paintings, mostly—not landscapes, but collage-like paintings of mushrooms growing from logs, the blue folds of a stream, and a decaying leaf; or else the pebbled back of a toad, an acorn cap, a twist of bark. Pieces brought together into a cohesive but surreal whole.

I'm examining one when Emily returns from the kitchen, two mugs in hand. She passes one over to me and follows my gaze. The painting in front of me is a view of a hillside—a scrape of grass and rocks giving way to thickly wooded slope, which spills into a tumble of wilderness beyond. A rust-brown rock protrudes at the bottom frame, the edge flat and worn. I know it well.

"Eden Crest, right?" I ask. She hums an affirmative. "I go up there all the time," I say, turning back to look at it. "We used to sit up there and pretend we were going to run away into the woods. Walk right through and be totally different people on the other side."

"'We'?"

"Janie and me," I clarify, and she nods thoughtfully.

"I can see that. Sitting there, it feels like you could just start walking and vanish," Emily says.

"You probably could," I say. She gives me a questioning look. "You'd be surprised how easy it is to disappear."

"Like Meghan Vale?" Emily asks.

But she isn't who I'm thinking of. I clear my throat a little. "Is it yours?" I ask. "The painting, I mean." At her nod, my eyebrows raise in appreciation. "I never asked what you do for a living."

"This," she says, ticking her chin toward the painting. "I sell them now and then. It's not much, but I don't need much."

"I'm impressed," I say. "I was never artistic enough to amount to anything, but I always wanted to be."

"It's all a matter of practice," she demurs.

"Not all of it," I counter. "I don't have the eye. Or the creative spirit."

"Who told you that?" she asks, quietly probing.

I flush, because the answer is Janie. Janie, showing off her own top marks in art class. Looking over my own sketchbook with a careless disinterest. *You know,* she said, *you have the diligence to learn the technical skills in a way I can't. That's the tragedy of art. That busy bee, worker attitude and talent are so rarely found in the same person.*

She was the talent, of course. She never let me doubt that.

"Tell me about her," Emily says.

"That's hard."

"Why?" she asks. She wanders over to the couch and settles onto it, sitting cross-legged. I take up a perch on the opposite end.

"Janie was my best friend," I say. "But I didn't like her very much." The words feel disloyal, even after all this time, but Emily's expression holds no judgment. The mug warms my palms. The coffee smells strong, tastes thick and bitter. I drink deeply. "We were friends for three years."

"Not that long," Emily notes.

"An eternity when you're twelve."

She makes a soft noise, understanding. "Why did you stop being friends?"

"Homecoming," I say.

"Because she ditched you?"

"No. Because of what happened after," I say. I'd been asleep for hours when Janie showed up. That night, I let her in. She crawled through the window stinking of alcohol, laughing at the look on my face.

"You're so *boring*," she'd complained. Called me uptight, a baby, all the things I was afraid I was. "Live a little," she told me. I asked her what she'd done with Andrew Hill, what they'd gotten up to, and she piled her hair on top of her head, wiggled her shoulders suggestively. "Wouldn't you like to know?"

No, I decided, I wouldn't. I'd turned away, told her to go. Instead, she flopped onto my bed, her dress hiking up around her thighs and falling off her shoulder. Makeup made smoky rings around her eyes. "You wouldn't even know what to do if a boy kissed you," she teased.

"I don't even want to," I'd made the mistake of telling her.

"Oh my gosh, Oddity, are you a lesbian? Are you in love with me? Do you want to kiss me?" Eyes big and a smirk on her lips. "Oddity. You're in love with me, aren't you?"

I don't know why that was the last wound I was willing to suffer. Maybe because I wasn't sure she was wrong. Or maybe it was only the smugness. That ugly smile, that hideous laugh. I screamed at her to get out. I told her that I never wanted to talk to her again.

"You'll come crawling back. You always do," she said before she left.

But I didn't. She wouldn't stoop to making amends, ever. Normally I was the one who tried to fix things, and then she would act like she'd forgotten about the whole thing. But this time, I didn't bend. And then it had been a month and then two, and I sank deeper and deeper into a depression but never broke. Never begged. By the next fall, life had rearranged itself. I'd met Len. I'd stopped thinking about Janie every second of every day.

And then, suddenly, she was gone altogether.

I tell Emily some of this. Bits and pieces, the parts that I can hold without scouring my skin with their touch.

"She sounds awful," Emily says.

"She was." I sigh. "And she wasn't. You have to understand, her life was hard, and she was young."

"Is that an excuse?"

"She deserved a chance to change," I say, and Emily has no rebuttal to that. I look down at the rapidly cooling coffee. "I fantasize sometimes that one day I'll find her, and she'll be different. That she'll have grown into some new thing. Still wild, but gentle, too. Someone who can wield her sharp edges only when she means to. I wouldn't have to talk to her. I wouldn't have to tell a soul where she was, if she didn't want me to. But I'd know."

"And if you can't find her, Meghan Vale will do." It feels like an insult. It feels like being called out, but she's so calm about it.

I stare at her, unable to summon up an answer.

"I never really had friends," Emily says, shifting her weight. "I could never get the hang of it. Keeping people around long enough."

"You weren't in school, were you? After that year," I say.

"My father decided it was better to homeschool me," she says. "He thought he could handle my particular needs better than the government. He would have pulled Liam and Andrew, too, except Andrew had football and Liam had theater. So it was just me and Dad."

I look at her uncertainly. "How was that?"

"Formative," she says with a hook of a smile I can't read at all.

The air thrums with the intensity of her, for all that she is relaxed and loose-limbed there on the couch.

My mother once called me a cup, easy to fill. Said I let others spill into me. Like Janie. Like Emily, I think, and how she seeps into every available molecule of the air. Yes—at another time in my life, I think Emily would be a person who would spill into me so completely it would feel for a while as if there were no difference.

It's only then that I realize that during our conversation, I've failed to register the sound of tires on gravel.

The front door opens. Melinda Hill freezes in the doorway. She's in jeans and a loose teal blouse, a day-off outfit. Her hair is in a braid over one shoulder. She's not wearing makeup—probably the first time I've seen her without it. The effect is startling, like a figure on a poster suddenly stepping onto the street.

Her gaze flicks quickly to me, to Emily, back to me. "What is she doing here?" she asks, looking at me without addressing me.

"Having coffee. Would you like some?" Emily replies mildly.

Melinda's eyes track to the coats dripping dry on the rack, the muddy boots by the door. "You were out," she says.

"There's a girl missing. Audrey's looking for her," Emily explains. "She was on Terry's land, apparently."

Melinda's head whips back around. "You were on *Terry's* land?"

"Is that a problem?" Emily looks entirely too innocent, sipping her coffee.

"We don't need any more problems with that man," Melinda says. She presses a fingertip to the point between her eyes, shutting them briefly like she's fighting off a headache. "You need to stop antagonizing him. You're going to get yourself killed."

"He's violent?" I ask.

Melinda fixes me with a flat look. "When I was a teenager, he tried to shoot my dog because she 'made too much noise.' And that was when I was standing right next to her. So yes, I'd say he's violent."

"Jesus," I say. "I'm sorry."

"Terry's not here. He's in the hospital, and he's probably going to die there," Emily says, blunt and disconnected. "And Bill isn't here, either, so you can calm down."

Melinda looks like she wants to say something, but she only clenches her jaw. "You should go," she says to me.

"She's my guest. This is my house," Emily says. There's tension in the air between them, a power struggle I can't begin to fathom.

I rise. "I probably should be getting home anyway," I say. "Thank you for showing me around."

"Come back anytime," Emily says, but the remark seems more directed at her sister than me.

"Let me walk you to your car," Melinda says. Emily rises, takes my mug from me wordlessly, and ghosts her way into the kitchen. I gather up my things, shoving my feet into my boots.

It's only a few steps to the car, but Melinda keeps her word and comes with me. I open the driver's side door, but she still stands there, like she's trying to decide whether to say something. She looks back over her shoulder. Emily stands at the kitchen window, looking not at us but at the trees beyond. Melinda sighs.

"I'm sorry, Audrey, this isn't exactly how I'd prefer to run into you again," Melinda says. "I haven't really seen you since . . ."

"Since you dropped an unconscious teenager on my doorstep," I say dryly.

She winces. "I didn't handle that situation well."

"I don't think any of us could say it was our finest hour," I reply. I still have no idea why Janie gave Melinda *my* address when the eldest Hill found her at a party eight shots in and pooled in the corner of the couch while Andrew partied in the next room. Their short-lived fling was long over, but I guess Melinda still felt some sense of responsibility for her.

"She told me to bring her here. What do you want me to do?" Melinda had asked, car still running on the street. My parents were out of town. Janie's dad wasn't, and I knew she'd be in deep shit if she went home like this.

"Bring her in."

We put her in my bed. I stayed up, making sure she was okay. Left aspirin and a bottle of water next to her bed and left before she woke up. I didn't come back until the afternoon. She was gone. She didn't even leave a note. That was three months after we'd stopped talking. Still more than a year before she ran away.

Sometimes I imagine the version of our lives where I stayed. Helped her sober up. Had a heart-to-heart. We would have fixed what was broken, and she would have stayed my friend and stayed in Franklin, and maybe—

But we only would have fought again. It wouldn't have changed anything.

Melinda's lips compress. "You should be careful with Emily," she says, as if this is a natural continuation of the conversation.

"Careful? How so?" I ask, struggling to sound casual. The whole situation has me on edge. The tension in the air is palpable, and I don't understand why.

"Emily has lived a very sheltered life," she says, clearly picking her words with deliberation.

"She was pulled out of school, she said."

Melinda hesitates. "Yes, well. Things weren't always . . . She's always had some problems. And being isolated out here didn't exactly help matters. She can't really cope in the real world. Sometimes she does or says things that people find . . . alarming."

"All right," I say slowly.

She rakes her hair back from her face. "She's not . . . I don't want to sound like I'm insulting her. I just don't want anyone to get hurt. You or her."

"We were just talking. How would we get hurt?" I ask.

She considers me for a long moment. "I'm sorry," she says at last. "I shouldn't be butting in. I just worry about her."

"It's fine," I assure her, though I still don't quite understand what she's getting at.

She reaches into her purse and pulls out a business card. "Listen.

This is my number and email. Please, just . . . call me if you notice anything off," she says, holding my gaze. "With Emily, I mean."

"Off how?" I ask.

She shakes her head and turns away. Her footsteps crunch on the gravel as she makes her way back to the house and shuts the door behind her. A moment later, Emily vanishes from the window. I wait a minute more, straining for any sign of argument, but the house is quiet.

I get in my car and drive toward home.

8

Below

I heard a voice. But I hear voices all the time, and none of them are real, so how is this one different?

I should have called out—should have screamed or struck something, made noise however I could, but instead, I've just been frozen here, huddled on the ground. For once, the dark is quiet around me, and empty. As if the intrusion of the voice made reality snap back into place. My hands shake. I strain to see the others, but I've lost the trick of it.

"Focus," I whisper to myself. With one fingertip, I trace words on the cool skin of my forearm. *Don't cry.* One of the first rules. It should have been hard to follow, but I've always been good at giving people what they want. I haven't cried in weeks. Months, maybe. I'm not sure I even can anymore.

Amid all the instructions written beneath the bed, there are no words of comfort or affirmation. None of the girls before me have been foolish enough to write anything as laughable as *It will be all right.* They were smarter than that, and so am I. I don't need to hope; I need to act.

Before, survival meant making myself into another person. Playing a part. I was good at it. Better than some of the others, I think, because by the time I found their words, I had already learned my rules well. What to say, who to be. When to smile and when to flinch, when a soft voice would spare me pain and when I had to be forceful.

Now survival means something entirely different.

Focus. Think. These are the words I would write if I thought another girl would come after me. But there won't be. Not if the door has truly stopped opening. One way or another, I'm the last, and every hope of every girl finds its end with me.

The voice is gone. The chain remains. It's time to get back to work.

Pulling a chair over is easy. I hook the leg with my pried-off board. The chair scrapes across the floor, and then it's in my hands. I spare a few seconds of battery, training the flashlight at the bottom of the chair. I've gotten lucky. The legs simply screw in place, and they're loose enough I can turn them with my fingers. A few minutes of careful work later, I have two of the legs free and in my hands.

The edges of the legs are squared. They fit against the flat sides of the nut threaded onto the toilet bolt. I can do this.

Focus.

It's something I've always lacked. Impulsive, my dad called me. Right around the time I gave myself a haircut with cheap scissors, hacksaw bangs, a disaster that made me look feral, made me grin. *You never think, you just do,* he said. Like everything he did was logical. Like I didn't see the absolute anger in his eyes, as if he never wept drunkenly and begged for forgiveness for all his screwups, for every raised fist.

I'm so sorry, I can't help myself. He disgusts me. He always has.

I've never been anything but a liability to him. When Mom was around, that was one thing. But once she was gone, everything changed.

That's not the life I want to go back to. Not that, and nothing like it. I'll make myself anew.

A caterpillar destroys itself into a slurry and builds itself again, not one part repeated. I'll emerge into the light and spread wings that gleam like oil slicks. I'll walk down the road and no one will know me. Not my friends, not my father, not a soul.

But first I have to survive. And then I'll live—

I'll live—
I'll live—

And all the gossamer girls will boil out, take flight, and they'll be a storm in the sky. They will be lightning.

I set my makeshift tool into place and begin to work.

9

Above

I leave Emily's with my mind swirling, my thoughts thick with darkness. The car is suffocating on the drive, and at home the walls are too close.

At the house, I dash off a message to Len, asking if he's found anything yet about Meghan. I get back a reminder that it's his day off and to cool my heels, along with an invitation to board game night with Kenny.

I like Kenny. He's a biologist, teaches at the college. He's whip-smart and sweet and can talk your ear off for three hours about bird facts, and he likes me, which is not a given. He also has a tendency to treat me like a wounded fledgling that needs to be gently put in a quiet dark box and provided a steady supply of food. Right now, I'm not in the mood to be doted on.

I pass on the invite and spend the next few hours banging around the house. I send some emails, try to find anything more on Meghan—a complete dead end—and scrub the bathroom. Earbuds in, I start my podcast back at the beginning, listen to a man explain women's anger to me, explain how all that rage and hurt was poured into the mold of a folktale and emerged with hands dipped in blood.

It's never been vengeance that I want. *Anger* isn't the right word for the heat in my chest. At times like these, I need to move, to *do* something. I want to be out with the team, but my phone is silent. No tourists determined to wander off-trail to give purpose to this trapped feeling in my chest.

No hint of where Meghan Vale might have gone, no way to look for her.

I'm no investigator. I've only ever searched for someone through the physical medium of the world. My own five senses, a perimeter, progress assessed by distance covered. My only tool is my own body, and I might fail, but I know what to do. This, though—peering not through underbrush but the strange web of how people move around each other, the murk of the past, the way that we collide with people, prey on them, become entangled with them—these things, I've never really understood.

As afternoon shadows lengthen and I haven't clawed my way free of the gloom, I throw my pack in the car, whistle for Barry, and head back out.

The audio system kicks on automatically. On the podcast, a folk band sings a mediocre ballad about Jenny Red-Hands, giving her a faithless husband and a cleaver. The basis of this Jenny, the host tells me, is real, but was incorporated into the story long after it had already started being passed around. I wonder how many women have had their faces and their names stolen and handed off to our invented monster. As much as Jenny is a way of giving us power, it's a way of taking it, too. The real woman is forgotten, and so is her anger; Jenny consumes it, and Jenny, not real, can be dismissed.

I stop at a familiar trailhead. I park away from the road, out of sight. The lot is fairly full now, but even later, when it thins out, no one driving by will be able to spot my car from the road. I tell myself I'm just here for a hike, to let the movement drum through me and chase this trapped feeling away, but I know I'm lying to myself.

"Let's go," I tell Barry. He hops out and lets me clip his lead to his harness, dress him up in his oversized yellow rain slicker. Before we leave, I use the scrap of signal here to schedule an email, and then I strap on my pack and get moving.

There are a few easy loops and one longer trek here. I take the long trail that winds up the hillside. The elevation gain deters the more casual hikers, though a few families with kids scramble past me in mud-spattered rain gear. I keep close to the side of the trail and keep my body between them and Barry, who knows to weld himself to my thigh when we're passing. The point of Barry is to be intimidating, so I can't exactly blame people for getting skittish around him when he could fit their kid's whole head in his jaws.

An untrained Aussie barks and lunges as we pass. Barry doesn't so much as twitch. When I got him, he was a disaster. Too big and too wild to even walk on a leash, and after weeks of work, I was beginning to think he was untrainable. Matsuda gave me the number of a trainer—a giant Norwegian man who was constantly surrounded by a pack of dogs of every conceivable breed, all of them eerily calm and alert. He asked me to let Barry stay with him for a month. At the end of it, he held my hand in both of his and said, "My work is done. This dog, he is beautiful, and precious, and he will be always loyal to you."

He's proven right on all counts so far.

My legs are burning by the time I reach the top of the hill. It's not much to look at—you emerge from the woods to a bald hump of earth that's always reminded me of a scabbed knee sticking out of a pair of shorts. There's a flat boulder that seems made to sit on. It offers the perfect view of the hillside sweeping away to the flatter land beyond. There are no official trails down the back side of the hill, but you can trace the path with your eye—down the flank, among the trees, across the creek. A mile before you hit a road, miles more along it to reach the highway. And from there, you could go anywhere.

I can't imagine a place that feels more open than this. There is nowhere less constrained. Even the pull of gravity urges you only toward freedom.

We used to sit up here, Janie and me, before everything that went wrong. She would cross her legs and point in one direction or another, and invent the lives we would have over there. They had absolutely no relation to reality, of course. She didn't care which towns were eclipsed by her pointing finger, where the roads really led. We would be queens there; we would join a rock band over there; follow the bend in the creek and we'd travel the country in a van.

If we just started walking now, we'd get there, she would say, and I pretended not to hear the hunger in her voice.

The rain hasn't let up. Barry doesn't mind, nose to the wind, eyes half closed. The rain against the hood of my jacket makes a cocoon of sound around me, and I sink into it.

Meghan's voice plays in my ears. The podcast, looping again. How many times have I listened to it now? Enough that I can almost imagine I remember the sound of her voice. But she was invisible to me. Not one of mine to tend.

She says she saw the witch. What does that mean? A woman in the woods? Like Emily, in her witch's cottage of a house. But a woman in paint-splattered overalls would hardly be mistaken for a murderous witch.

Melinda said Emily was—what word did she use? *Unstable?*

I hunch forward, watching the movement of the clouds. A lone man arrives, stands ten feet from me to appreciate the same gray vista. After a while, he departs, our momentary fellowship broken.

The sun is setting. The cloud cover affords no blaze of color, only a gradual gathering of the dark. The rain has let up, though, and by the time twilight recedes, the stars have emerged. It might as well have been night all along, behind those clouds. I've been alone for a long time now.

"We should go," I tell Barry, but we don't. He sits against my legs. After a while, I get out a towel, lay it down for him. It's cold, but I have the right gear, and Barry's stayed dry, is suited for lower temperatures than these. I'll stay another hour, I tell myself; one hour, and then we'll go.

Up here, in these moments—after everyone else is sensibly gone, everyone home who knows how to find it—I can hear that hum the clearest. The sound and sensation that isn't real, can't be real, but that I have utter faith in nonetheless. The one that draws me to where I need to be.

Lucky.

I've done the math. I'm no luckier, no more successful, than anyone else on the team. I've disproved myself thoroughly, and yet I still chase it.

Where are you? I ask silently. Not just Meghan Vale, but all of them. All the way back to Janie. I imagine her with her hair cut short, her cherubic face gone thinner with age, sitting at the table across from a man with a kind smile, planning their day. I imagine her at a bus stop, a cigarette clamped between her lips, skin pitted from years of hard living. I imagine her buried shallow in a field with worms in her rib cage, and they all feel true.

Where are you?

There's nothing but the hum. The call onward. *Keep looking.*

But I don't know how. And I am less and less sure, each time I follow that sound, that I will find my way back again.

By the time the sun rises, the sky is clear, the morning chilly but not cold. I ache in ways that I know will make me pay later. Barry thumps his tail as I gather our things. He's used to this. Part of me wonders if he knows why I come out here, and why he comes with me.

On the way back down the trail, I pass just one hiker, an older woman with a walking stick and a baseball cap, who gives me a bright greeting as we edge past each other on the trail. With Barry's rain gear in my bag, we probably look like just another pair of early risers.

Down at the base of the trail, I cancel the email I had scheduled, the one I always set telling Len where I've gone. He hates that I do this. Camping is one thing. This is something else, and we both know it. That dream I have, of walking far enough that I find them—all the missing, all at once—it's a feeling I never shake. It feels like *lost* is a place as much as a state of being, that maybe someday I can pierce the threshold.

That's why Barry comes with me. Because I am afraid that one day, on my own, I wouldn't turn back. I would follow the hum and let myself become unmoored, unfound. But I would never do that to Barry. He keeps me tethered, because I have to bring him home.

When I turn onto my street, my heart sinks. Len's car is in the driveway. I pull in next to him, putting on my most innocent expression. He glowers at me from the porch.

"Where have you been?" he says.

"Early-morning hike," I say.

"Right." He doesn't believe me for a second. He sighs, closes his eyes briefly. "You have to stop doing this."

I open the door to let Barry out. He bounds over and jams his head against Len's stomach, demanding attention. Len is very practiced at providing it without interrupting the effort of glaring at me. "I'm fine. You don't need to worry about me."

"Bullshit."

I walk past Len, unlock the door. "I know how to take care of myself."

"That doesn't mean you do it," Len counters. He follows me inside as I strip off my hiking gear. "Is this about Meghan Vale?"

"No," I say. He makes a skeptical sound. "Maybe." It's rarely about one specific person. When there's someone to look for, there's something to *do*. It's the times in between that trouble me. "Did you find anything? About Meghan, I mean."

"I know what you mean. And no, not really," Len says. He half sits on the back of the couch, arms crossed. "Everything looks like a typical runaway. She packed a bag. She'd told people she wanted to leave. She stole a couple hundred bucks her dad had stashed away, and she left in the middle of the night. No sign of struggle, no sign that she had trouble with anyone other than her dad. We looked at him, but he only had half an hour unaccounted for between talking to a neighbor and leaving for his night shift. We followed up and put out the word, but she's turned eighteen since then, so even if we did find her, we couldn't make her go home."

"Meaning no one's looking for her."

"We aren't," Len concedes.

I bite back the thing I want to say, which isn't fair or kind. "If you were, what would you do?"

"You mean, how would we investigate?" Len asks. I nod. He scratches his jaw, considering. "Given that it looks like she took off under her own steam, I'd start with organizations that help people in her position. Aid groups, shelters. We'd check bus stations, that kind of thing. Ask around about places she might have mentioned."

"And if she didn't leave on her own?"

"Audrey."

"She was out in those woods," I say. "If you searched them—"

"I'm not going to get a warrant to search based on, what, some beads that you don't even know for sure were hers?" Len says.

"She took a photo."

"Weeks before she left," Len points out.

"It means she was on Terry Butler's land. Have you talked to him?" I press.

"No. And neither should you," he says warningly. He rubs the back of his head. "I know you want to find this girl, Audrey. But it's not going to happen. There just isn't a trail. And . . ." He stops himself.

"And what?"

"And she isn't Janie," he finishes reluctantly.

I huff a breath and stalk past him. Barry follows, nails clicking. Len sighs in my wake. "Audrey."

I ignore him, busying myself with getting out Barry's breakfast. My anger is the crack of a bent stick breaking, deep in my chest. I count breaths waiting for it to fade.

"I know you don't like it when I talk about her," Len says. "I didn't know her, fine, whatever. But I know what she did to you, and what she's still doing to you."

"She's not doing anything to me. I haven't seen her in over a decade, how could she?" I ask.

"She broke your heart," Len says. He's right, of course, and he knows better than anyone. By the end of the school year after that disastrous homecoming, I'd stopped going to school. Stopped eating or going out. I slept most of the day. My parents decided that what I needed was fresh air and moral guidance, so they sent me to a two-month camp for "struggling youth," a term that was so ill-defined it encompassed every kind of trouble a teen could get into. Drugs, bad grades, depression, the wrong boyfriend. The general ethos was that any ill could be cured by learning to build survival shelters and identify edible plants.

In Len's case, his parents were starting to suspect he might be gay, and thought that exposure to manly skills like building a fire might somehow turn him heterosexual. Strangely, it didn't work.

Over the course of two months, I discovered that I loved the outdoors as much as he hated it and that friendship did not mean making yourself small enough to fit into the limited space someone else permitted you. By the end of the next year, Len was living at our house after his parents threw him out. We lived together in college, and I was his "best man" at his wedding. We've always been there to save each other, Len and I.

Except he doesn't need it anymore.

"I want you to come over tonight," Len says, with more force this time. I don't tell him that saving each other only works if it's mutual. That I can't be a drain on him; if I have nothing to give, I can't take anything in return.

"I can't," I say.

"Why? Are you planning to go out again?" Len asks.

I put a hand on my hip. "No, actually, I have a date," I lie on impulse.

His eyebrows spring up. "With who?" he demands.

"Dev Khanna," I say, digging my hole deeper with impressive rapidity.

"Hot social studies teacher Dev Khanna?" Len's tone is begrudgingly approving.

"He asked me out on Friday." A pulse of panic is starting up in my chest. I'm already regretting the lie, but I can't back out now.

"And you said yes." He's always been able to see through my bullshit.

"Why not? He's cute."

"And stable and nice, so. Just wondering how quickly you're going to drive him off," Len says.

"Hey," I say warningly.

"You can't deny that you have a track record. You make self-sabotage an art form."

"I'm turning over a new leaf."

"Well. Good for you, then," he says, still skeptical. "You'll have to tell me how it goes."

"Right. I will," I agree, kicking myself silently. Now I'm going to have to report back.

"And, Audrey, let the Meghan Vale thing go. I know you're worried about her, but there's nothing you can do. It's not your job, and it's not your place," Len says.

"It's your job, though," I shoot back. "Isn't it?"

He looks away, shaking his head in frustration. "Fine. Tell you what. Go on this date with Dev, and I'll take a look at the file. I can't promise anything, but I'll see if we overlooked anything. And *you* keep out of it. Deal?"

"Fine. It's a deal," I snap.

"Great," he says.

"Good." We glare at each other.

And then he sighs. Kisses me on the top of the head. "Barry, keep her out of trouble," he says, and then he's gone.

When the door closes behind him, I pick up my phone. I debate for a moment. I could tell him that Dev had to cancel. But he'd know I was lying, and we did make a deal. Instead, I pull up Dev's number and send him a text.

Still want to go out? I'm free tonight.

Would love to. Just to clarify,
by "go out . . ."

I bite my lip. Look at Barry. "What do you think?"
He wags his tail and whuffs.

Let's call it a date. See how that
hits us.

Fantastic.

There. Normal life. I can do normal life.
There is a hum in the air, so soft I might be imagining it. I have hours before I need to get ready.
I pull up the visiting hours information for the nearest hospital.

10

Above

We don't have many options in the area when it comes to hospitals. Unless Terry's gone far afield, I have about fifty-fifty odds of guessing right, and the coin flip comes up in my favor. The front desk offers me a mask and directs me to the intermediate care unit. When I explain to the disinterested woman at reception that I'm a concerned neighbor dropping by for a visit, she tells me to wait while they ask if he wants to see me. I take a seat against the wall, shifting in the uncomfortable chair.

A heavily pregnant nurse in purple scrubs gives me a speculative look as she passes, and stops to talk to the woman at the desk, who has a phone pressed to her ear. I hear the name "Butler," and the nurse's head whips around as she reconsiders me.

A moment later, the first woman beckons me up.

"He'll see you," she says. "Just sign in there."

The pregnant nurse raises her eyebrows. "You sure you want to see *him?*"

"Just trying to be a good neighbor," I offer cheerfully.

She snorts. "If I was that man's neighbor, I'd be moving in a big damn hurry," she says. She grabs a file off the desk and gives me a *better you than me* look as she departs. I finish signing in and get a terse "Room seven" by way of directions.

My shoes squeak on the tile. My breath feels hot beneath my mask. The door to room seven is half open. I knock on the doorframe tentatively.

"Come in," calls a hoarse voice. I slip inside and ease the door shut behind me.

Terry Butler lies propped up amid white sheets, a pale blue blanket laid over his frame. With all the wires and tubes attached to him, I would expect him to look frail, but despite the deathly pallor of his skin, he's a large man, and ropy with muscle. His white hair is long and thin, swept back from a liver-spotted brow that creases with something like amusement when he sees me.

"So nice of my neighbor to visit," he says, suppressing a cough. "Who the hell are you, really?"

I glance behind me.

"They can't hear us," he says. He waves me toward him. I step in hesitantly. His eyes are sharp and clear, even as he hacks into his fist.

"My name is Audrey Dixon," I say, my mouth dry. I stop two feet from the end of the bed. I've got no desire to come any closer.

"Is that supposed to mean something to me?"

"No," I say. This is about as far as I'd planned. "I—I work with Search and Rescue. I'm looking into the disappearance of a teenage girl. Meghan Vale."

He leans forward and makes a show of swiveling his head around the room. "Doesn't seem to be here, sweetheart," he says. "But feel free to look around."

I flush and grit my teeth. "I have reason to believe she might have been on your property."

"Trespassing, you mean." He scratches at a scaly patch of skin along the collar of his gown. His fingernails are thick and cracked, the skin beneath them bluish. He coughs again, the racking cough of a failing heart.

"Did you see her?" I ask, leveling out my voice, trying to sound official.

He works his lips. "Hand me my water," he says. He lifts a finger toward the cup on the table beside the bed. Reluctantly, I draw closer. He smells sour. Smells like sickness past the point of a cure. He watches me intently, with a gaze that slips beneath the skin. I hand him the water without letting his hand touch mine and retreat half a step.

He drinks. Sits back.

"Was Meghan Vale on your land?" I ask.

He purses his lips. "No one has respect for private property anymore," he says. "It's mine. I own it. Those bastards might have taken everything else, but I'll be damned if they take my last thirty acres before I'm maggot food."

"Bastards?" I ask. "The Hills, you mean?"

"Didn't mind the father. Knew how to mind his own business. It's why I rented to him in the first place. Those kids, though—those girls—he should have kept them in line."

"I didn't realize the Hills were renters," I said. "I thought they owned the land."

"They do now," he says. "Vultures, the lot of them."

"Mr. Butler, Meghan—" I begin, but he's undeterred.

"He came to me after the wife died. Mason did, the father. Said, 'Terry, I need a safe place to raise my family. Away from the world's problems.' Wickedness, he called it. A man takes care of his family. And I needed the help, so I let him stay. Plenty of room for both of us. Didn't even mind the kids roaming around. All I asked was that they respect the boundaries I set and leave me in peace."

"And keep their dog from barking too much," I can't help but interject.

He makes a sound that might be a grunt or a laugh. "That mutt? You've been talking to Melinda. She's never let that go. That dog was a menace. A killer. It went after the animals every chance it got. Only one thing to do when a dog gets a taste for blood."

"Shoot it?" I say flatly.

"It was a warning shot," he scoffs.

A killer. A memory stirs.

I was at the vet. Our cat Pumpkin was dying. Or rather, not dying so much as about to die. A cancer in his gut that would kill him sooner or later but hadn't yet. My parents didn't want him to suffer. Better to go a few months early and happy, they said, but truthfully Pumpkin had not been happy a day in his life, angry at the world and everyone in it. The kind of creature who thrived on his own misery. Still, I loved him; sometimes I wonder if he's the one who taught me that love is devotion to someone despite their disinterest, and despite the marks they leave on your skin.

I was in the waiting room because my mother wouldn't let me go into the room. She supposed, wrongly, that I would be more disturbed by witnessing death than by knowing that it was occurring invisibly, just out of sight. I was sitting on my hands, eyes fixed on the linoleum tiles, when a boy burst in. He was younger than me—twelve to my fourteen, if I'm doing the math right. He clutched a shoebox in both arms, which he placed on the countertop. He was crying so hard the receptionist could barely understand him.

A rabbit, I heard. His sister's. It had been in a dog's mouth—could she help it?

The receptionist looked in the box, and her face went very still. Promises to do what they could were made, and then the box and its contents vanished into the back. The boy came and sat several seats down from me, swiping his nose with his sleeve.

"It's my fault," he said. "I didn't check the hutch before I let the dogs out."

"It's the dog's fault, isn't it?" I said. At the time, I thought this would make him feel better.

He fixed me with a look that made me afraid—not of him, but of something like a shadow behind him. "You can't blame an animal for doing what it's supposed to do."

I didn't know then why those words unsettled me so much when I knew he was right. But it was the way he said it. As if he was repeating what someone else had told him. As if there was another part to that lesson.

Man is an animal, too.

The door opened then. Andrew Hill, whom I did recognize. "Liam, what are you doing here?"

"It was hurt." He seemed to know this wasn't an adequate explanation. The receptionist emerged then, along with a vet in a white coat. "We can't pay," Andrew said immediately, but there wouldn't be a payment. The rabbit was dead when it arrived, which the vet attempted to explain kindly, but Andrew interrupted. They had to get home.

"Stop crying," I heard Andrew say as he dragged Liam toward the door. "You don't want Dad to see you like that."

There was anger in his voice, but urgency, too.

I saw Liam on the television screen years later, playing the bad-boy character in a leather jacket, and I thought of the boy crying over the soft body of an animal that should have been safe. When the headlines appeared later—drugs, arrest, overdose, rehab, repeat—part of me said, *Of course, of course,* because what is the world but a set of jaws?

Terry's still got his eyes narrowed at me. "The Hills have been spinning stories about me for years," he says. "While they steal my land bit by bit."

"How'd they manage that?" I ask.

He gives a phlegmy sniff. "Got behind on my taxes. Then the medical bills—didn't have a choice but to sell, and they were always there to buy it up."

"I'm not here to talk about the Hills," I remind him. I pull up Meghan's picture. "This is Meghan Vale. Are you sure you haven't seen her?"

He stares at the picture, and the corners of his mouth creep up in a smile that makes my gut clench. "Pretty little thing, isn't she?" he says. "She looks like trouble, that one."

I start to pull the phone back, but his hand shoots out. He grips my hand in his, holding it steady.

"And lost in the woods?" he asks, as if he is enjoying my discomfort. "How long has she been gone? You think she's all alone out there? How long do you think she can last?"

"Have you seen her or not?" I demand.

He works his lips, and his grip relents. "Could be," he says with some reluctance.

"'Could be'? What's that supposed to mean?"

"It means my eyesight isn't what it used to be. I saw someone. Could have been her. Too far off to be sure. I hollered at her and she scampered."

I raise my eyebrows. "Just hollered? You didn't fire a warning shot?"

"Not that I recall," he says with a halfway grin. He settles back into the pillows and closes his eyes. "Now I'd like you to go."

I stare at him. There is utter peace on his face. Could he look like that if he'd done something to Meghan?

I think he could. I think this man could slit someone's throat and stroll down the street with a smile.

But if he did something to Meghan, he's happy to take that secret to his grave—and he won't have long to wait.

11

Above

Dev and I meet at the only vaguely high-end restaurant in town. He's wearing a blazer over jeans; I've gone with a drapey purple top and my hair in messy curls, and next to him I feel underdressed.

We greet each other awkwardly on the sidewalk, not sure whether to hug or wave or something else entirely, and finally Dev laughs and gives me a polite one-armed hug. "You look great," he tells me.

"You always look great," I reply. "I had to step up my game. Usually the only thing on my face is mud."

Inside, the hostess asks us if we've made a reservation. We glance at each other, chuckle nervously. It hadn't occurred to me that we might need one, but she makes a face.

"You really should make a reservation," she says, and sighs heavily as she picks up two menus. "This way."

She leads us to a nearly empty side of the restaurant and seats us, and we look at each other in amused bafflement. We order a pair of cocktails off the menu—Dev's fruity, mine boozy—and then, abandoned, topple into jittery silence.

"So," Dev says at last. "Can I ask what changed your mind?"

I fold my hands on the tabletop loosely. "A friend forcefully reminded me that I have a tendency to isolate myself for no good reason."

"I see. And I'm better than nothing?" he asks, eyebrow raised. It's half a joke, half cautious inquiry.

"A lot better," I assure him. I fiddle with the edge of my napkin. "It's just—not easy for me to get close to people."

"Oh? How so?" he asks.

I grope for an explanation. "Friendly is great. Acquaintances, work buddies, all of that. And I have a few friends—Len, mostly—I've known forever. In between, though, that's hard. I have a history of panicking. Disappearing."

"I think I know what you mean," Dev says. "That point where you have to be vulnerable and show the parts of yourself you haven't carefully curated. It's terrifying."

"Exactly," I say.

"And that's why I prefer to just dive right in on a first date and start interrogating a woman about her attachment style and psychological foibles," Dev says, and I laugh.

"I don't mind," I promise.

"Let's try a lighter subject. At least before we get a drink in us," Dev says.

"All right," I say. "What brings you to Franklin? I don't think I've ever asked."

He winces. "Ah. Well, see, I was engaged."

"Oh, no," I say, eyes widening as I realize I've clearly stumbled on a subject that's not light at *all*.

"Long story short, she broke my heart. Or more like ripped it out of my chest, stomped on it a bit, and then squished it back into my shattered rib cage," Dev says with mordant humor. "We worked together, which made things especially painful. I decided I wanted a change of scenery, and Franklin was the only place hiring in a hurry midyear."

"I'm so sorry," I say.

"It's fine," he says, waving off my apology. "Actually, once I got done feeling like I'd been shanked with a sharpened toothbrush, I suddenly felt . . . really okay. We were together because of inertia. Got together in college, never had a definitive reason to split. It took getting betrayed for me to realize just how unhappy I'd been for a long time."

"So you're, what, looking for a rebound?" I say. "A bit of fun?" My tone is lightly teasing. He smiles, shakes his head.

"I wasted most of my adult life in a bad relationship. I'm looking to get it right this time," he says. Then, overly serious, "Again, no pressure."

I laugh. The drinks arrive. It gives me something to do with my hands, at least. It's easy to talk to Dev. It helps, of course, that we've been friendly for months. Not my usual pattern. People who actually know you are dangerous, after all. Harder to fool. Not that I can ever quite say what I'm trying to conceal—only that I have a bone-deep certainty that if someone sees into the deeper parts of me, they won't stay.

"And how about you?" Dev asks. "You grew up here. Did you ever think about leaving?"

I shrug. "Like you said. Inertia. I left for college, but I bounced back when I couldn't find a job right away. And then my best friend was here, my family was here, I found a job here . . . There wasn't a reason to leave."

"Not the same as a reason to stay," Dev says.

"No. It's not," I agree. I take a sip of my drink. It's rich and bitter. There's a joke in there somewhere, I think, but I can't quite get a hold of it.

"To inertia, then," Dev says, lifting his drink. "Since it's the reason we met."

"To inertia." I clink my glass against his, and for once, my mind isn't somewhere else, wandering down forest trails or city streets. I'm simply here, and there's nowhere I'd rather be.

The conversation strays and wanders down safe paths. We don't talk about vanished girls or heartbreak. The food is good, made better by the company, and we linger over a dessert neither of us particularly needs. At the end of the night, we put on our coats at the door, and Dev offers to accompany me to my car.

"I walked, actually," I tell him. "I live about half a mile from here."

"Then let me walk you home," he says, and I know him well enough to be sure there's no expectation hidden under that. He offers me his arm. I take it, and we don't hurry as we make our way out of the short strip of downtown into the surrounding tree-lined neighborhoods.

"Thank you for the escort," I say.

"Well, you don't have Cerberus here to defend you, so I'll have to do," Dev says.

I snort. "His name's Barry, actually. What's your cat's name?"

"What makes you think I have a cat?" he asks. I reach out and pluck an orange hair from his lapel, and he chuckles. "Ah. A keen deductive mind. I really need to get a lint lifter. His name's Skipper. Well, legally speaking, it's Norman, but my ex named him and I never thought it suited him. Your dog doesn't eat cats, does he?"

"He treats them with a mix of worship and terror."

"Perfect," Dev says, and clears his throat like he's realized we're jumping forward a bit, talking about pet compatibility. We've reached my driveway. I stop, stepping free of him. The air has just an edge of chill, enough to make you want to be near someone.

"This was wonderful," I say.

"I'm glad. I had a very good time," Dev says.

The drinks are still twining through me. I feel soft at the edges, and safe, and the streetlights on Dev's warm skin give it a glow I can't quite describe. I wonder if Emily would be able to paint that color, and the way the deep shadows make every plane of his face more beautiful. "Would you like to come in?" I ask.

I'm afraid he'll draw back. I'm afraid he'll say yes too quickly, too hungrily. Instead, he smiles. "I would very much like to come in. But I'm going to say no," he tells me. "Because I had a wonderful time tonight, and I've also had three drinks and so have you, and I don't want either of us wondering if this was a good idea in the morning."

"You're a true gentleman," I tell him, disappointed and relieved in equal measure.

"A self-interested gentleman. I told you, I'm not looking for something quick and fun," Dev says. He tucks his hands in his coat pockets. "I'd like to go out with you again."

"You know where to find me. If it still seems like a good idea in the morning," I say. "I'll see you at work?"

"I'll see you then." He leans in. His lips brush my cheek, and it is impossible, I think, that a kiss can be so chaste and still send this flood of warmth through me. He draws back, his dark eyes reflecting silvered light, and I want to draw him to me. To taste his lips and feel his touch, because I cannot remember the last time I felt like this—whole, and here, and wanted.

Then Barry woofs, the sound muffled through the window. I twist and find him with paws draped over the back of the couch, watching us with a chaperone's disapproving skepticism. I laugh and Dev echoes the sound.

"All yours, buddy," he calls. He's stepping back from me, hands in his pockets. "Good night, Audrey." There's enough reluctance in his voice that I can't even fool myself into thinking that he's just being polite, that he doesn't actually want to come in.

"Good night, Dev," I say. I walk up the drive to the door. He waits there, watching, until the door is shut and locked and I wave to him from the window. He raises his hand in a final farewell and then turns to walk back the way we came. Barry snuffles at me inquisitively.

"I think that went well," I say. "I think that went very, very well."

I'm smiling, I realize. I'm still smiling when I finally slip into bed, Barry settling with a sigh on the floor beside me. For a few hours, the wilderness has been at bay, and for the first time in a long time, I wonder if I should keep it that way. Let go of Meghan Vale and of Janie and of all the others, and live in this present moment. Be among the found, the never-lost, and not dwell in borrowed grief and fear and wondering.

But I can still hear it. The hum in the air, ever present.

I slip into dreams of the woods, of a figure running through them as I follow. Her hands are red and her hair is the color of blood, and the sound of her steps is the soft clicking of beads in the branches.

12

Above

Being in my thirties means three drinks isn't enough for a hangover, but I'm not exactly one hundred percent, either. By mid-morning, I'm limping by on terrible office coffee and sheer determination, when all I want to do is curl up and take a nap. I haven't seen Dev yet. My mind insists on concocting a parade of reasons he might have decided he hates me now, picking apart every verb I uttered at dinner for a misstep.

Instead, he appears at lunch, my order in hand. "I can't stay," he says. "But I thought you might be hungry, and slightly averse to the bright light of the outdoors."

"You're a prince among men," I tell him.

"That bodes well for my chances of a second date," he remarks.

"It does."

He sets the bag on the desk, and we make vague promises to check our schedules before he flees. I find myself smiling as I open my little cup of salsa—and try hard to keep my promise and not think at all of missing girls.

Tuesday night, Len finally drags me over for dinner. Kenny cooks, both Len and I having been declared menaces in the kitchen years before. Len cracks a beer for me and we clink bottles, sitting to either side of the dining room table. Len looks tired, which he usually does. Less from hard work and more from managing an increasingly cantankerous boss who should have retired a decade ago.

"How's work? Bust any international smuggling rings?" I ask him.

"Ha ha."

"Tell her about the raccoons," Kenny says, leaning in from the kitchen. He's wearing an apron that declares I LOVE TITS AND BOOBIES over an illustration of the relevant birds. Len got it for him early in their courtship as a gag gift, not realizing the depth of Kenny's commitment to a bit. Now, every time he wears it, Len heaves a regretful sigh.

"I am not going to—fine, they were breaking into trash cans. An old man thought they were Mexican cartel," Len says, rolling his eyes. "God, I need a new job."

"Take Chief Wagner's job, he's not using it," I suggest, which only elicits another groan. I roll the beer bottle between my hands, bite the corner of my lip. "So. About Meghan Vale's file."

Len gives me a warning look. "Audrey . . ."

"I promise I'm not obsessed. Just curious," I tell him. He doesn't look like he believes me.

"I pulled the file. There's not much in it you didn't already know," Len says. "Blake was the one who did most of the follow-up—talked to the dad and the friends and everything. Did you know it wasn't the first time she ran away?"

I shake my head. "I hadn't heard that."

"Couple years ago. She was gone for two weeks. Dad never bothered to report it," Len says. "Eventually, she showed up at the Hope's Hands shelter. They mediated contact with the father and Meghan agreed to go home. The family was offered counseling services, but they never showed."

A little jolt goes through me. Hope's Hands was founded by Elizabeth Hill, the siblings' mother. It was her life's work. Even after her death, it limped along, providing services to homeless and at-risk youth and young adults. Then it received two windfalls: Andrew's football money and Melinda's management skills. Since the end of her political career—or the pause in it, at least—Melinda has been running the place personally. "That's a weird coincidence, isn't it?"

"Is it?" Len asks, challenging me with a raised eyebrow.

"Just—she was on the Hills' land, and at their shelter."

"She's not there now. We've checked," Len says.

"Terry Butler saw her," I say. "He said he chased her off. But the look in his eyes—"

"When the hell did you talk to Terry Butler?" Len asks sharply.

My face flushes. "I dropped by the hospital. Just to ask him a couple questions."

"Jesus, Audrey. This obsession—"

"It's not an obsession," I insist.

Len heaves a sigh. "I'm just worried, that's all. And saying maybe it's not a complete coincidence that you're throwing yourself into this right as a cute guy starts showing some interest."

Kenny's head pops back out of the kitchen. "Are we talking about the date? You promised you wouldn't talk about it without me."

"Then sit your ass down and stop babying the lasagna. It's in the oven, it cooks, the end," Len says.

"I like to watch it bubble," Kenny says archly, but sweeps out of the kitchen with a glass of pinot in hand, joining us at the table. He crosses an ankle over his knee and regards me. "So. Spill."

"That's not actually what we were talking about," Len says. "We were *talking* about Audrey's unbroken streak of sabotaging every relationship she gets near."

"I do not," I object. "I haven't sabotaged my relationship with *you*."

"Mm. That's because you're trauma-bonded to each other. Different beast," Kenny says. "Len's right. You're a disaster. But Dev can fix you. I have faith."

I snort. "Seems like a lot to put on the guy."

"You don't need fixing," Len says, sounding frustrated. "You just need to stop pushing people away as soon as they get close."

"That's not what I'm doing."

"Not yet. But every time you get into a relationship, you start getting that look. Like you're desperately searching for an escape route."

I set my jaw. He's not wrong. Last time, it was Jordan, and it was a man who'd gone missing a county over, out on a hike. Searches turned up nothing, but I knew the area. I knew that if I kept varying my path, I'd find him eventually. And so every spare minute, I was out there with Barry.

We did find him, in the end. What was left of him. And when I got home, Jordan was already packed.

"It's not going to be like that this time," I tell Len.

"Prove it," he says.

"How?" I ask.

He takes a sip of his beer, locking eyes with me. "Go on another date with the hot teacher. And let me deal with Meghan Vale."

"I was already going to go on another date with Dev, so no problem," I say.

"And Meghan?"

I work my jaw, but relent. "I'll let you handle it," I say.

"Good," he says.

We extend our bottles and clink them. "Now can we please change the subject?"

The conversation shifts to biology department drama. Every once in a while, I catch Len watching me, worry and skepticism dark clouds in his eyes. I tell myself that I'm going to do as I promised. I'm going to enjoy myself with Dev, and I'm not going to go any deeper down this rabbit hole.

I believe it all the way up until I'm leaving. I get on my coat and head out to the sidewalk, and right then my phone chimes. It's an email. From the host of the *Darker Half* podcast, in reply to one I sent days ago and had almost forgotten.

I'd be happy to chat. I'm free tomorrow, if you'd like to give me a call.

13

Below

I'm lucky to have always been aware of my own flaws. How could I not be? Everyone's always been eager to list them. I'm impulsive and selfish. I'm a liar, lazy, disrespectful. I'm smart, but this is a waste given what I do with it.

My aunt told me I don't have any grit. If I try something and it doesn't work, I give up right away. She, by contrast, stayed married to a man who didn't love her for over a decade—because she didn't stop doing things just because they weren't working.

My aunt didn't like it when I made this little observation.

I think of her now, foundation caked on, blush too bright, voice scraped to ruin by thirty years of cigarettes. I clench my jaw and set my makeshift tool around the bolt and nut yet again. I've lost count of how many times I've tried this. It hasn't worked yet, but I'm close. The two chair legs grip the nut. There's a catch of engagement each time I twist, resistance I wouldn't feel if it wasn't doing *something.*

The makeshift wrench slips again, jerks free. I swear viciously. It's a habit I trained myself out of, the last few months. A punishable offense. There are many. Survival down here means mapping the boundaries of the role you're meant to fill. The name to answer to. The way to speak, sit, move, breathe. I'll never be her—whoever that girl really is—but I'm good at pretending.

I find the edges of the nut again. Test the tool. It's difficult to squeeze it tightly enough to get the grip I need, but it will work, has to work.

I turn. It slips. I fit it again. The legs are long and bump against my ankles where I crouch. My hair falls in front of my face, but there's no point in tucking it back. It's not like I can see better either way.

"Come on, come on, come on." It's the loudest I can stand to lift my voice. Even a normal volume is like a scream.

The tool slips. No—it turns, a stiff movement but movement nonetheless. Only an instant of progress before it leaps free again, but it's something, and I let out a soft cry of relief.

I tuck my tongue between my teeth as I try again, again, again, and now I've managed a quarter turn. It starts to come more easily then. I don't know how long I've been bent over working at it before it finally comes loose enough that I can wrap my shirt around my fingers and unscrew it by hand. Finally the nut pops loose and hits the ground, and I don't bother to try to find it—I've done it.

I laugh. Such a small victory. There's another washer on the other side and then I'll need to move the toilet and *then* I'll find out if the bolts in the concrete are long enough to provide the leverage I need—but I've done it, done *something*.

Eager, I move toward the other side of the toilet. I've grown used to the dark and the borders of my own body. Too used to it. Comfortable enough to get careless. The tool swings wide, catches against something with a plastic *pop*—the water bottle I set aside, the one I was drinking from earlier and didn't close all the way again.

I lunge for the sound. My hand strikes the wrong bottle. I grope in the dark, find the bottle lying on its side and tip it up, but my palm against the ground tells me I've spilled most of it.

Idiot. Idiot.

I pull the flashlight out of my waistband and turn it on. The toppled bottle is all but empty. I have only two others. All that's left after I drained the toilet.

How long does that leave me? A few days.

Not enough, not enough, I think.

The light flickers. I turn it off quickly, holding my breath. It can't fail now. It *can't*. I don't think I can do this in complete darkness.

I think for a moment the gossamer girls have returned, their voices a steady murmur around me. And then I realize the voice belongs to me, softly pleading. I sink to the ground and shut my eyes tight, and the words keep coming in a babbling flood.

"Please. Please help me. Please," I say, as I haven't allowed myself to say aloud in all this time.

Not even the dead are near enough to hear.

14

Above

At eleven, I put out my DO NOT DISTURB sign, lock the door, and dial the number the podcast guy gave me. The line picks up almost at once, a pleasant male voice with an edge of chronic weariness on the other end. "This is Ethan."

"Hi," I say, stammering. "It's—my name is Audrey Dixon."

"Hi," he echoes. "You wanted to talk about the Halloween episode, right? That was a fun one. Not our usual thing. You said it had to do with a missing girl?"

"Meghan Vale," I confirm. "You interviewed her, actually. On the episode."

"The girl who said she saw the witch," he says. "She's missing?"

"Probably a runaway," I say, which is only a little bit of a comfort and we both know it. "The thing is, no one's really looking for her."

"What's your connection?" he asks carefully.

"I don't really have one," I confess. "I'm a counselor at her school and I work for Search and Rescue, but she isn't one of my students and Search and Rescue isn't involved. But . . . I don't know. She reminds me of someone I used to know."

For a little while, he says nothing. Deciding whether I'm a crackpot, probably. "What can I tell you?" he asks at last.

"I was hoping she might have said something to you that might give me some kind of hint about where she went."

He makes a thoughtful sound. "I don't know if I can help. We spoke briefly. She said she had a story to tell, but she was pretty cagey on the details. All she would say is that she was in the woods, and she saw Jenny Red-Hands, but that she disappeared into the mist. She was being coy about it. I think she wanted me to work to get it out of her. It sounds terrible, but I think she was enjoying being in control. It made me think she was embellishing things for the sake of drama, so I cut things short. And—" He stops himself.

"And?"

He clears his throat. "She was being, uh, flirtatious. I'm pretty sure to make me uncomfortable. If that was the goal, it worked." I wince. I've known plenty of girls who acted like that—coquettish and provocative, looking for a reaction from older men. Frequently, they didn't want the attention. They wanted the power of making someone uncomfortable, or else they wanted the comfort of being turned down. It was proof that a guy was safe.

I remember suddenly Janie leaning across the counter at my dad's shop while he was working the register, showing off her cleavage. My dad's utter lack of reaction or attention had seemed to put her out, but later, as we were walking together, she said suddenly, "Your dad's pretty cool for an old dude." I was baffled by the comment then. Now I understand what she was looking for.

"Do you think she actually saw anything?" I ask.

"If you're asking if she saw the witch of Franklin, I have to say no, since she doesn't exist," he says with a light chuckle. "As to whether she saw someone or something—I couldn't tell you. She was definitely enjoying the attention, but I got the sense there was some kind of substance behind it."

"Did she say anything about what the person looked like?"

"The conversation didn't get that far," he says. "I couldn't even tell you if she knew it was a woman for sure. I'm sorry I can't be more helpful."

"No, that's okay," I say. I sigh, rubbing at the spot between my eyes. "I'm grasping at straws, mostly. Jenny Red-Hands seemed like as solid a lead as any. Which is pretty pathetic."

"At least you're looking for her." His voice is warm, understanding.

"I have always wondered if there's something going on in Franklin that led to the story," I say. "Girls do seem to go missing here a lot, I mean."

He sighs. "The thing about randomness is, most people expect that a random distribution is going to look pretty even. But true randomness results in clumping."

"I'm not sure I follow."

"It means that girls have disappeared in Franklin, yes. But absent evidence of a connection, it's probably true randomness that we see as a pattern," he tells me. "I looked through pretty much every violent crime and missing person report for the last four decades. Which isn't that hard, given how small your town is. I couldn't find anything. And for what it's worth, I can guarantee you that the Jenny Red-Hands story is just that. A story. It showed up right around 2000. Not a whisper of it before that. And this didn't come up until after the episode aired, but I think I know where it came from. I stumbled across a casting call for a Nolan Rustad movie."

"The horror director?" I say.

"Right, but this was before he actually made anything. He was in college at the time, and he's from Franklin originally. The casting call was for a character named Jenny, and the film was called *The Witch with Red Hands*."

"Terrible title," I say with a choked laugh.

"No kidding. The thing is, this was right after *Blair Witch*. I never heard back from Rustad's people, but I've wondered if it wasn't some kind of attempt at a viral marketing campaign. In any case, it pops up right in 2000, seemingly fully formed. It's become modern folklore, but it's absolutely not historical."

"At least I know I'm not going to run into a murderous witch while I'm hiking," I say with forced humor.

"There's the silver lining," he says. There's a pause in which he seems to be on the verge of saying something else, and I let the silence linger. "On the other hand . . ."

"Yes?" I prompt.

There's the sound of a chair leaning back. "Sometimes these things can take on a life of their own. The origin doesn't matter nearly as much as what happens once the story *does* exist. What people do with it."

"Like—say, if someone got inspired by the story of the witch and decided to off some cheaters," I say.

"Luckily, I don't think that's happening," he says.

"But it does give me an idea for a fun weekend activity," I quip. It's not that amusing, but he laughs obligingly. "I should let you go," I say.

"Hold on," he says. "You know, I'm looking through my notes and I just remembered something. I met Meghan in a coffee shop. I was a little late, and when I got there, she was writing in a diary."

"A diary?"

"Yeah. It definitely wasn't just a regular notebook—it was one of those ones with a strap and a latch," he says. "So I don't think it was schoolwork or anything. If you could find that . . ." He leaves the rest unspoken. Maybe I could figure out where she'd gone—or maybe I could just find confirmation that she left under her own power.

I thank him again. He promises to let me know if he thinks of anything else, and then we end the call. I sit drumming my fingers on the desk. And then I reach over to the desk phone and plug in the extension for the front desk. "Hey, Lisa. Quick favor—can you pull Theresa Abbott for me? No emergency, I just need to chat about her schedule. Thanks." I hang up, mouth dry.

Sorry, Len, I think. I can't let this go.

It's just before lunch when Theresa Abbott arrives in my office. Friend number two, as I've been thinking of her. She genuinely needs to swap class periods, so it's not like I'm pulling her out of class without reason, but my mind is on anything but her schedule.

"This should only take a few minutes," I tell her. She nods tightly. She's a round-faced girl, more likely to be called cute than pretty. Her grades, I can see, are decent but not stellar, which is par for the course among Meghan's friends. She's painted her nails black. The nail polish is chipped where she's chewed on the ends.

"Chloe said you asked her about Meghan," she says, looking at me intently. I straighten up, taking my attention from the computer screen.

"I did," I acknowledge. "I wanted to check in with her friends. Make sure you're all doing okay." I smile brightly.

"We weren't friends," she says flatly. My eyebrows crook in surprise. "I mean, she was my friend? But I wasn't hers? If that makes sense."

"Do you mean she was more attached to you than you were to her, or . . ."

"The other way around." She folds her arms. "Meghan didn't really *have* friends. I felt sorry for her. She was kind of weird and a loner, and I thought that was because other kids are awful, right? And I'm weird. All the best people are weird. So I figured, she can hang out with us. But I don't think she ever actually liked any of us."

"What makes you say that?" I ask, leaning forward a bit.

She blows out a breath. "So, like. I told her something once, about my mom, that was supposed to be—what's the word, *confident?*"

"In confidence?" I ask, and Theresa nods.

"She made a joke about it in front of everyone. She could be *mean*. So. You know. I'm good. I'm worried about her, but it's not like I miss her. I know that sounds awful."

It sounds familiar. I tap my pencil against the desk, biting the inside of my lip. "Did she ever talk about Jenny Red-Hands?"

She makes an angry noise. "All the time. But I'm the one who told *her* about it. There was this—okay, this isn't something you have to report, it was forever ago, like eight months? This guy grabbed me on the bus." She hovers her hands near her breasts to illustrate and rolls her eyes. "So I told Meghan I should sic Jenny Red-Hands on him, and she's like, who? So I told her, and then, all of a sudden, it becomes her, like, *thing*. And she won't stop going on about how awful guys are and how she's 'embracing female rage' and stuff. But nothing ever *happened* to her, okay?"

That you know of, I don't say. "Did she tell you that she'd seen Jenny?"

She laughs. "No? Because she's not real?"

"Right." What is it about teenage girls that can make you feel like the most pathetic, loathsome organism to ever walk the earth? A sheer embarrassment to the evolutionary line. "Well, you're swapped over to Mr. Robertson's section, so you're all set here."

"Thanks," she says, and flounces out. I drum the eraser against the tabletop, watching after her. So Meghan Vale was weird and standoffish and morbid and mean. And nothing happened to her, supposedly, and yet the behavior suggests otherwise.

I wish it didn't sound so much like Janie. And it's true, I don't know that Janie was ever hurt in a way you could pin down to one time, one story, one man. But there's a peculiar energy about certain girls—the ones who move through the world carelessly and then show off the bruises where they've banged into things. *I did this to myself*, they seem to be insisting, because if damage is self-inflicted, it means you chose it. It means you're in control.

An email alert pops up on my phone. It's from Tamara. *Appreciation Dinner*, the subject reads, and I let out a huff of dry amusement as I read through. Melinda Hill is hosting a dinner to celebrate the successful search for Bryson Lee, and I'm invited.

There's a knock on the door. "Come in," I say distractedly.

Dev enters, looking as dapper as ever. I blink at him, not quite processing his appearance. "You okay?" he asks.

"Dev. I—yes," I say, not sounding very convincing. I stretch a smile into place. "Just tired."

"Immensely relatable," he says. "So. About that second date. Still in?"

"I am," I say firmly, before I can chicken out. At least Len can't call me on that. I can do two things at once, I tell myself. "Later this week?"

"Just let me know. I have absolutely no life, which makes scheduling a breeze," he says with a self-deprecating chuckle.

"Actually—Saturday, there's this dinner I'm apparently supposed to go to," I say. "For the people who worked on the Bryson Lee search. It'll probably be terrible, but it does say there's an open bar."

"In that case, I'd love to," Dev says. Then he examines me. "Are you sure you're okay?"

"Yeah. Why?" I tuck my hair behind my ears. "Do I look like that much of a mess?"

"Mm. I don't know. You seem—you have that energy you get, right before you ditch us to go rescue wayward hikers," he says, bouncing his weight back on his heels a little. "Like you've got somewhere you need to be."

"I don't," I tell him. "Just tired, that's all."

"And four hours left before we can escape this cinder block palace," he says. "Well, I'll leave you to it. Just—text me?"

"I will," I promise, and then I'm alone again.

I stare at the door long after it closes. I should listen to Len. I should forget Meghan, and go out with Dev again, and sleep dreamlessly. In a few days, a week, my phone will chime with a text from Tamara—a wandering child, a rock climber at the bottom of a cliff, Grandma walking out the back door in her nightgown. People who exist and need to be found. People I'm *supposed* to be looking for.

Theresa's records are still up on the computer. I back out. Meghan isn't my student, but I still have access to her records. I call them up, and this time, I don't look at the notes or the grades or her schedule, but at the contact information.

I don't have a grid to search. All I have is Meghan's life. Theresa thinks nothing happened to her. But that doesn't mean it's true.

I jot down the address, and close out the window.

15

Above

I slink out of my office, muttering an excuse about a lunchtime appointment, promising I'll be back in an hour.

Franklin is divided into distinct rings—the smaller houses near downtown, like mine, built on the flat valley floor, and then houses getting larger the farther out you get, where developers had to tuck them in among woods and hills. The Vales live to the northwest, in a pocket of smaller houses on wooded lots, most of them a bit run-down. I park on the street. The lawn of the Vales' house is untrimmed, weeds outpacing the grass and the bushes encroaching on the walkway. The doorbell doesn't work when I press it, so I knock briskly, wait, knock again.

There's no answer. My hand strays toward the knob, but I stop myself. What am I thinking?

A clunk sounds from behind the house. I give a guilty jump and then square my shoulders. I walk around the side of the house, and there, emerging from a small, rotting shed, is a man who must be Meghan Vale's father. He's short but stocky, with red-blond hair mashed against his scalp like he's been wearing a hat. A thick sweater the color of oatmeal gives him more bulk, the sleeves shoved up above his elbows.

"Hello?" I say, more tentative than I'd like. He looks up from the old gas mower he's examining. His hands are dark with grease.

"Who are you?" he asks.

"My name is Audrey Dixon," I say, picking my way past the weeds. I stop a good fifteen feet back, not wanting to encroach too far. "I'm a counselor at Franklin High School. I was hoping to talk to you about your daughter."

"Meghan? What about her?" he asks, brow drawn down and eyes dark with suspicion.

What am I supposed to say? I'm not supposed to be here at all. "I've been thinking about her, that's all," I say. At least it's true. He doesn't reply, and the silence hangs awkwardly. "Is the investigation still active?"

"Don't know that there was ever much of an investigation in the first place," he says.

"I'm sorry. They should—that isn't right," I say.

"Isn't it?" he asks. He reaches into his pocket and pulls out a rag. He rubs grease from his palms methodically, not looking at me.

"They should be looking for her," I say.

He grunts. "I've never gotten far trying to get in that girl's way," he says.

"You don't want her back?" Maybe I shouldn't be surprised, but I am.

"If she doesn't want to be here, why should I bother?" he asks, an undercurrent of anger in the words.

I shift uncomfortably. I don't know what I thought this conversation would be like, but this isn't it. "I wondered," I begin. I stop and clear my throat, all too aware of how inappropriate this is. Len would be furious. I plow ahead. "Do you think I could look in her room?"

"Why?" He squints at me. I grope for an answer to the question, but he only grunts again. "You know what? Sure. Knock yourself out."

He strides abruptly forward, and I shy back before I realize he's angling for the back door. I follow at a distance, uncertain, as he throws the sliding glass door open and waves me toward it.

"Up the stairs. First door on your right. Don't go nosing around anything else," he says, and turns away, his interest in me apparently at an end. I mumble a thank-you and scurry in. I hesitate a moment, wondering if I should take off my shoes, but the way the carpet crunches under my steps, I'm guessing it doesn't matter much.

I head up. There are a few crooked pictures on the walls. A camping trip, a wedding photo—a much younger Mr. Vale looking somewhat stricken next to a woman with platinum blond hair done up in extravagant curls. At the top of the stairs is a photo of the same woman, sans updo, cradling a baby who can only be Meghan. There are no other photos of the mother, and in the most recent of Meghan, she looks about eight.

Her bedroom door is closed. A sign is taped to it, reading KNOCK FIRST OR BETTER YET GO AWAY. I can't help but smile a little. There were days I wanted a sign like that. But while my parents and I never got along, exactly—too different, too opaque to each other—they were always concerned and involved. Supportive of me even when they didn't get me.

The door is cheap hollow-core. Down near the bottom, it's cracked and caved in. Right about boot height. My imagination summons slammed doors, shouting. My parents disciplined us through long, disappointed lectures, but I remember being at Janie's house, and Len's later, and the soundtrack of bellowed words and stomping feet. I always felt like I had no right to be anything but happy, when my home was so peaceful in comparison. There wasn't anything wrong with my home life, just with me.

It makes me feel like even more of an intruder, passing into her room. It makes me feel like a fraud all too often, trying to convince my students that I understand what they're going through, when I really can't at all.

The room, though, reminds me a little of mine. I was never much for decorating. A few half-hearted objects planted on top of my dresser, but no posters on the wall, no color scheme, no character. Meghan's room is similarly plain. A bed with blue sheets, a dresser on which rests a single pink chunk of quartz and little figurine of a waving cat, and a desk. Her algebra textbook lies open next to a spiral-bound notebook. I flip through quickly, but there's nothing but numbers and formulas. It doesn't look like math was her strong suit. Another thing we have in common.

No diary. If it had been out in the open, surely the police would have taken it—surely they would have done that much. Len didn't mention one, so I'm assuming—hoping, maybe—they didn't find one.

I open her dresser drawers, rooting through. Her clothing is stuffed inside with only half-hearted attempts at folding. I find a thin, crumpled joint in a sandwich bag but nothing else of interest. Her desk drawers produce pens and a half-finished bag of Skittles.

On the wall above her desk, she's taped a handful of photographs. Photos of her feet, standing in various places—the rocky shore of a stream, a road, somewhere woodsy. I spot the photo of the beads, and near it one she didn't post to her Instagram—the handprint in the woods. Still no indication of whether she found it or made it herself. I flip the photos up to check the backs, in case she wrote on them, but no dice.

Diary. Where would she hide her diary? I was never much for hiding things. My life was too dull to have secrets I needed to keep. But I've seen enough movies to know the greatest hits. The floor here is carpet, so no loose floorboards to pry up. The vent proves empty, and I don't find anything tucked in the back of her closet. There's so little in here, it's not like there are many places to hide. Just the bed and the desk.

The bed it is, then. I glance over my shoulder, reassuring myself that I'm alone. At that moment, the lawn mower gutters briefly to life, and I relax. I'm not about to have company. I drop to my knees and then lie along the ground, peering under the bed. Dust bunnies, socks, and a discarded hoodie greet me. And there, tucked up between the mattress and the bed slats—a book.

I prize it out and sit up, sniffing at the influx of dust. It's just like Ethan described—a small diary with a purple cover and a latch holding it shut. I almost open it on the spot, but then I realize the lawn mower has gone silent. Footsteps sound, coming near the stairs.

I shove the diary into my bag and get to my feet quickly. As Mr. Vale's footsteps approach, I grab the textbook from the desk. He appears half a second later. He stands a moment, silent, examining me. I stare back at him, my heartbeat thudding in my throat. I feel like a thief. I suppose I am one.

"So," he says. "Did you find what you were looking for?"

I lift the textbook. "I can take this back to the school, if you'd like, and spare you the trip."

"More like the bill," he says. I dip my head in a quick nod.

"Do you mind if I take a couple of these photos?" I ask, pointing to the wall.

"I've got no use for them." He leans against the door as I pluck the two photos of the forest from among the others. I tuck them inside the textbook and turn to go, but he's still there, blocking the doorframe.

"I should go," I say.

His eyes are dark and hard. "Runs in the blood, you know," he says. "Leaving. Her mother left, too. Didn't care about anything except herself. Meghan's the same. Doesn't care how much I gave up for her. How hard it was, being on my own."

"I'm sorry."

"No, you're not." There's a sneer in his voice.

"I should really go."

"Then go," he says. He doesn't move. There's a bit of space next to him. I inch toward it. He shifts at last, opening a gap. I start through—and he grabs my arm. Not hard enough to hurt, but I freeze. "Why are you really here?" he asks. His breath smells stale, and sweat stink clings to his clothes, along with the tang of motor oil.

"Please," I whisper. He narrows his eyes at me and then grunts contemptuously and lets me go. I want to run, but I force myself to walk briskly past, trying not to feel his gaze on the back of my neck.

I clatter down the stairs and out the door, and by the time I reach my car, I almost *am* running, my pulse quick as a rabbit's.

I sling myself into the car and throw my purse on the seat next to me. Only when the doors are locked and the engine started does the welling panic start to subside.

"He didn't do anything to you," I scold myself, trying to calm my breathing. I glance over. The purple corner of the diary sticks out of my purse.

But did he do something to her?

I pull away from the curb. I watch in my rearview mirror all the way down the street, but Mr. Vale does not emerge again.

16

Below

The toilet lies on its side. So do I, my temple to the cold concrete as I work the bolt slowly. Each rotation makes my fingers hurt horribly, but I can't get a grip with anything but my bare hands. The threads have stripped my skin raw.

The bolt wobbles now. At last it rotates freely and comes loose in my hand. I don't have the energy to cry out in triumph. I only fold my hand around it, trying to measure the length by touch alone. If it's only a couple inches, I'll have done all of this for nothing.

But, no—it stretches the span of my hand. Five inches long, I'm guessing. Will it be enough? Two of them, straining in opposite directions—maybe. The chain isn't so thick. I think I can bend it.

I still need to unscrew the other one, but I'm exhausted. There's no time down here, only the internal rhythm of my body, and it's begging for sleep. My stomach cramps with hunger. A dull, pulsing headache has lodged behind me eye.

There isn't time.

I thought they might be gone for good, my gossamer girls, but here they are. They surround me. Their feet are bare and blistered. I can feel the sores on my own feet—too long in the cold and the damp. Too long pacing a rough floor in the same endless circuit.

The bones of their ankles gleam through their skin. I reach out and close my hand around the nearest of them. The skin is cool and moist. The girl bends down, peering at me. Her eyes are a cluster of moth wings, twitching. Her gums are black. I imagine maggots in her chest, and there they bloom, tumbling from between shadow-slashed ribs. She isn't the one who's spoken to me before, but that doesn't matter. I know now why they all look alike. Why they all look familiar. I've created them all, and they all have my face.

Keep going, the rotting girl says.

I pull myself across the floor to the remaining bolt. I have trouble getting any kind of grip. I didn't think I would get this weak, this quickly.

The screw turns. A fraction and a fraction and a fraction more. It all adds up. Every small thing piles up.

You think you have it bad, says one of the girls—the girl's voice, my father's words. He loved to make my suffering small by standing it up next to his. Like I should be grateful for the things he *could* have done to me and didn't. Well, let him see me now. My lips peel back from my teeth, a skeletal smile. Let him tell me now that nothing I've suffered has been so bad. That I'm being dramatic.

See? See? I want to say.

The bolt gives way, turning easily. Excitement leaps in me, slick as a fish, and then excitement turns to horror as it flicks into my palm. Not the whole bolt. An inch, maybe. The end of it jagged and dusty with what I know by touch must be rust. It's snapped off at the ground, the rest of it impossible to retrieve. Useless. It's useless.

My breath comes too fast, and then not at all, stuck in my throat.

The gossamer girls ring me, crouched down. They bend their heads together over the unseen remnant of the bolt in my palm. My light-starved eyes conjure the image of it, burnished orange at the end. The girls keen. They grab at their arms, at their hands. But then the one with moths in her eyes speaks:

One will have to be enough.

I will find a way. I have to. And I will return to the light and speak my name again.

17

Above

I'm still shaking when I get home. In the foyer, I sink down and wrap my arms around Barry's beefy neck, and I don't let go until he starts to wriggle and whine, licking at my face. His tongue is big enough to match the rest of him, which makes this a disgusting enough process to leave me laughing and shoving him away. The laughter teeters on the edge of tears, but there's a relief to that, too, and I'm finally able to pry myself up off the floor.

I pour myself an unadvisedly large glass of wine and sit at the kitchen table, Meghan's diary and the two photographs in front of me. I don't want to intrude, but what choice do I have? I've gone this far.

Part of me hopes that what I'll find is simply evidence of what everyone has assumed: a plan to leave, the execution of it. Another part hopes for something else, and it unsettles me that it exists. How can I be hoping that something else happened to this girl? Why? Just to prove myself right?

Because maybe then you can be the one to save her, I think. It isn't a kind thought.

I flip open the cover.

IF YOU ARE READING THIS STOP SNOOPING AND GO KILL YOURSELF, it reads in block text. I nearly snort wine out of my nose. Not exactly the most tactful message, but I'm starting to like this girl—and like her all the more for the ways she's drifting from Janie in my mind. Janie would never have been so blunt. She would have inscribed an ancient curse against spies, maybe, or jotted a passive-aggressive dig at the reader's moral character, but direct wasn't her deal.

I tell myself I'm only going to skim through, but I find myself reading more than I don't. It's a typical teen diary, a mix of banal recitation of things done that day with attempts to capture the overwhelming emotion of adolescence. Meghan's efforts range from the melodramatic and poetic to the terse and understated. None of it is exactly Shakespeare, but it's not meant to be; it oozes angst in a way that makes me feel like I'm sixteen and brokenhearted all over again. She writes poetry every once in a while—blank verse, dripping with adjectives. Black roses and blood and tears and angels with dark wings, that sort of thing.

Theresa's characterization of the friendship isn't exactly borne out by Meghan's writing. She's writing to make herself look like the aggrieved party, of course, and it might not be accurate, but balancing the two stories, I get the sense of a girl too wounded to know how to be a friend and a friend too sheltered to spot the pain behind Meghan's lashing out. She berates herself for making the joke about Theresa's mom, castigates herself for being flaky and moody. She was trying. It just wasn't good enough. And the less adequate she felt, the angrier she got.

No, this girl isn't like Janie at all.

Or maybe I'm wrong. Maybe, reading Janie's diary, I'd see things the same way—see the pain that shaped her actions, made them understandable.

It doesn't change the harm, though. It wouldn't take away the years I spent with her words echoing in my head. She was deft at plucking out my flaws (and telling me of course she didn't care) or inventing them to put me in my place. Always with a laugh.

Things change midway through the diary. The friendship with Theresa and the others has gotten strained by that point; Meghan writes about being done with them in a way that aches with loneliness. She doesn't talk about her father, not directly, but I see his shadow in the words as she lists her flaws and mistakes. She keeps an inventory of the things she's done wrong—bad grades, forgetting to do the laundry, staying out too late. She lists them bloodlessly in bullet points at the top of every page. And for everything she does write, I can sense a gap—a blank space.

There are things, I think, she did not put to paper even in this most private place. Her snippets of poetry and unskillful drawings are suggestive. There's nothing spelled out. But I've worked my job long enough to know the signs. I would bet anything there was abuse. What kind, I can't be sure.

Then comes the night she saw the witch.

Went to the stupid thing with the stupid jocks tonight because Theresa said we should go, but she ditched me as soon as we got there basically. It was all just a bunch of assholes drinking and throwing things in a fire, so I went on a walk. I followed a trail in the woods. It was dark, but I started to be able to see and it felt like the night wanted me there. I felt like a wild creature. FERAL. Like I belonged to the woods and to the moon.

I don't know how far I was walking. All of a sudden, I saw her.

The *her* is crossed out, replaced with *Her*.

She was like a ghost. A spirit. She moved gracefully among the trees. All I had was my phone flashlight, and I could barely see her. She had pale hair and her hands were dipped in blood. She was right at the edge of the light and then she was gone. I was so scared I couldn't even move. I swear it was Jenny Red-Hands. She's real.

I'm going to find her again.

After that, every entry is a spiral into an obsession. It's not pathological, I don't think—there's a manic edge to her interest, but it feels more like artistic passion and an outlet for her anguish than some kind of delusion or compulsion. She returns to the woods several times. She mentions the beads, and the mark on the tree. But she doesn't mention seeing the woman again—Jenny, according to Meghan, but I have my doubts.

Then the entries mostly stop. There's a gap of a week or so before another entry.

> *I don't think I'm going to be writing much. The things I've found shouldn't be written down. They're too important for that.*

All that's left are a few scattered lines of poetry. I trace my fingers over the final lines—words that have little grace or skill to them but thrum with the melancholy truth of an isolated girl.

> *I am voiceless, I am faceless.*
> *I am forgotten and unwanted.*
> *The mirror reflects an unfamiliar face.*
> *My friends don't know who I am.*
> *I don't know who I am.*
> *I am nothing. I am no one.*
> *My name is Stranger.*

18

Above

At two o'clock, my phone rings, and only then do I remember that I'm supposed to be at school. Stammered apologies and claims of a migraine buy me sympathy but not much patience. I get someone to cover my afternoon and take the rest of the day, but it sounds like I'm going to get a lecture when I return.

I can't believe I forgot I was supposed to go back. This is concerning. I should be concerned. But I've never done anything like this before. It was a lapse, that's all. And for a good cause. Because now I know something I didn't before. Meghan wasn't just making things up—at least, I don't think she was. Why would she invent a sighting only to hide it away in her journal? The podcast is from a year ago, and the entry is from before that. She was going out into those woods for a long time.

And I'm pretty sure I know who she found there. There's only one person who makes sense.

"You gotta stay here this time, buddy," I tell Barry. I promise him a walk when I get back, then gather my things and head out the door.

Only Emily's car sits in the driveway at the Hill house. I'm glad. I assume Andrew is still hanging around somewhere. He lives twenty minutes away, after all. But I don't feel like dealing with him right now. I want to get Emily alone.

This time, she answers the door quickly. She's enveloped in a soft gray sweater, oversized for her petite frame. She looks unsurprised to see me, but she always has that canny look about her. Her hair is up in a messy bun, the roots touched up again to perfect golden blond. "Audrey," she says simply.

"You lied to me." It's not what I meant to lead with, but I swallow down a stammering follow-up and let the words linger, demanding a response.

Instead, she stares at me a moment, and then lets her hand drop from the knob and turns. She drifts inside, leaving the door open. For a moment I stand on the doorstep uncertainly. Then, gritting my teeth, I follow.

Music is playing somewhere deeper in the house, the fuzzy edge of a woman's voice pushing through a thumping beat. Emily is in the kitchen, her back to me. She's pouring water from an electric kettle into an oversized mug.

"Can I get you anything? Tea?" she asks without turning around. "I don't keep anything alcoholic in the house, but there should be some Coke in the back of the fridge."

"I don't want anything," I say. "Except answers."

She turns, holding the mug with the string of the tea bag draped over the lip. She rotates it slowly in her hands, regarding me. "You're angry."

"I read Meghan Vale's journal," I tell her.

Her eyebrow raises slightly. "What did it say?"

"She saw you. In the woods. She saw you and thought you were the witch." It sounds less damning, spoken out loud.

"Really." She sounds genuinely curious.

"She said your hands were red, like they were covered in blood," I press on. "What were you doing out there?"

"What makes you think it was me?" she asks, again with that air of untroubled curiosity.

"You think there's some other woman wandering around on your property?" I ask.

"I don't know." She glances to the side, eyes focusing on nothing in particular. "She could have been making it up."

"She wasn't."

She makes a soft humming sound. "Are you sure you don't want anything?" She waits for an answer, but I don't supply it. She hums again and then walks back the way she came, leaving me to follow. She pads through the living room and down a hallway beyond to the back of the house, where a sunroom has been converted to a studio. Canvases lean against the walls, are slotted into shelves, hang haphazardly. There are so many my eye has trouble picking them apart from each other. The easel in the center of the room hosts a large canvas on which the beginnings of a portrait seem to be forming—rough, broad strokes carving out the planes of a face in flesh tones. You can see the angles of the cheeks and jaw, the line of the nose, the shadowed sockets where eyes will be painted, but nothing else has been added.

"Who is that?" I ask.

Emily sets her tea on a small table beside the canvas, cluttered with paints and jars of grayish water. "I don't know. I haven't found her yet," she says, turning emerald-bright eyes on me. An unfamiliar scent suffuses the air—paint and canvas, I suppose, and something astringent laid over it.

There are other portraits tucked among the paintings. Some of them look familiar, as if I've passed them on the street, and maybe I have. My eye catches on one—a man with tousled dark hair and high cheekbones and blue eyes to drown in. "Liam," I say.

She steps over to pull the piece out from behind one depicting a spray of fern leaves with a snake twining through them, and looks down at it with a critical eye. "It isn't him," she says.

"But it looks—"

"It's a version of him. That's all you can do. Images are nothing but light falling in a particular way, in a particular moment. And painting is trying to pin it into place, but it will always get away. This version of Liam doesn't exist, but I tried to preserve it anyway."

"I don't think I know what you mean," I say.

"It doesn't make much sense," she concedes. "Words aren't really my thing. Trying to explain it, it's like—" She opens a hand as if to grasp something from the air, closes it. Her eyes shut briefly. "When you spend enough time by yourself, you lose the trick of making sense to anyone else." It sounds like a self-deprecating joke, but she doesn't smile.

"Did you meet Meghan Vale or not?" I demand, impatient. She drifts past me, back to her working canvas. She picks up a brush but doesn't do anything with it yet.

"I met her."

"Did you talk?"

"Yes." She picks up a palette smeared with the colors of the portrait and begins to mix two patches together, darkening one to deeper shadow.

"Why didn't you tell me?" I ask. "You knew I was looking for her."

"The things she told me weren't for sharing," she says.

"But you let me come out here. You acted like—you pretended to help me," I say.

"Did I?" She looks over her shoulder at me, her eyes devoid of any hint of deceit. "You wanted to look for her. I brought you out to where she'd been. It was what you needed to do."

"You could have told me you spoke to her."

"It wouldn't have made a difference," she says. "The last time I saw her was well before she left. Nothing she told me would find her for you."

"You can't be sure of that. You could know something that might help me find her." Frustration is growing in my voice, but my anger can't find purchase. She seems so incredibly unbothered by all of it.

"Is she even who you're looking for?" Emily asks quietly, and then my eyes track past her, and I freeze.

"That's—you—why did you paint Janie?" I demand, because there she is, staring at me from a background of smoky gray.

"Is that who that is?" Emily asks, twisting to look. There's a little frown on her lips.

Suddenly I'm not so certain. It looks like Janie, yes. The red hair, the round face, the elegant nose she always hated. She had a list of the things she would change about herself someday. Her jaw (too weak), the skin under her chin (too loose), her boobs (too small, of course). She would laugh about how she would reinvent herself so thoroughly she could be someone else entirely. But now I can't hold the memory of her clearly enough in my mind to say for sure if the features in the painting belong to her, or if the sight of it has brushed aside memory, and suddenly there's a thudding fear in my chest that I've forgotten her, let go of her, and that this betrayal at last is the thing that will damn me.

I couldn't even hold on to her memory properly.

But, no—I do remember. The jangle of the bell and her hair whipping around as she burst in that first time we met, strands of copper. The crinkle of her nose when she didn't approve of a joke I made. The moss green of her eyes. The woman in this portrait has blue eyes, muted ones, and a narrower jaw; her hair falls in waves, and it's more golden, the red only a gleam where the light hits it just right. And she's older than Janie was when I knew her. Older than Janie ever got to be, in all likelihood.

Emily moves to a desk against the wall and retrieves a framed photograph from the drawer. She hands it to me, and I see my mistake.

The photograph is of the Hill family as I never knew them. Two adults stand to either side, each of them holding a pale-haired baby. Liam and Emily, the twins. Melinda and Andrew stand in between—Melinda with dark hair and serious eyes, wearing a bib dress a bit too young for her; Andrew in a soccer uniform, showing off the dimpled grin that would make him a darling of the school for more than just his athletic skills.

I don't know if I ever met the siblings' parents. I certainly don't recognize their father—dark-haired like Melinda, with a neatly trimmed beard and shaggy hair, grinning wide. The mother, though, looks familiar for obvious reasons.

"Classic psychosexual pattern," Emily says, and I stare at her blankly. "Andrew and Janie," she clarifies.

"You mean he dated someone who looked like his mother," I say. "And you." I remember how angry he was that night, when Janie joked that she and Emily could be sisters. She'd hit too close to an uncomfortable truth.

"Word of advice. Don't point out to Andrew that he has a type. It gets awkward fast," she says with an unpleasant twist to her lips.

She's beautiful in an ethereal way, and almost kind, but altogether strange. She unsettles me, and she seems to want me to call her on it. "Why were your hands red?" I ask.

"Because I was coming back from the slaughter," she says. Her smile is a slash like a knife. "You won't find her here, Audrey."

My lips part. I mean to ask her something about Meghan, but instead, I find myself saying, "What happened to you?"

She doesn't give me the mercy of looking away. "The classic tragedy. My mother died," she says in uninflected syllables. "Saintly Elizabeth." She tilts her head toward the portrait.

"She was beautiful."

"She was perfect," she says, like it's a correction. She puts on a voice, like she's quoting someone. "'And doesn't Emily look just like her? So she should be perfect, too.' Imagine putting that on a child. Imagine only ever hearing how wonderful a dead woman is and how you ought to be just the same. It only lasts so long, of course. Before you grow up and the gaps start to show. So maybe you aren't so much like her after all. Not so beautiful. Not so perfect. And the only other thing you know about her is she's dead. So."

"I'm sorry." I don't know what else I can say.

"After she died, my father became convinced that there was danger lurking behind every rock," she goes on, as if she hasn't heard. "Melinda and Andrew didn't get it so bad. They were older. Melinda was almost out already, and Andrew had football. But with me, it just got worse and worse, until he didn't want me leaving the house at all. He used to stand at the foot of the bed at night and weep. What a terrifying thing." Her gaze grows distant. She turns, frowning, and busies herself with shading the curve of an eyelid. "Anyway. Maybe I understand someone wanting to escape and not be found."

"But you stayed," I point out.

"He wasn't wrong. About the world out there," she says. "There are awful things in it."

"That's not all there is."

She doesn't answer. There's only the soft sound of her brush against the canvas.

"It was because of you, you know," she says softly. "Because of homecoming."

"What are you talking about?" I ask. "What was because of me?"

"I blamed you. Because you left me to walk home instead of taking me with you. Because I was where I wasn't supposed to be. He never let me leave again, not really," she says. Her voice is still distant, untroubled. "He pulled me out of school. Locked me away in my tower."

I grasp for words, but can't find them. She looks straight at me, and now it's my turn to dodge her gaze, turn away. I left her there, yes. But how could I have known? How could any of that be my fault? It isn't. Of course it isn't, and there's no anger in her eyes, but she speaks it like a fact.

My eye fixes on a set of paintings in the corner. More nature paintings—a fallen tree, its roots packed with earth; a scattering of leaves around a single speckled egg; a hole in the ground, rectangular, dropping into solid shadow.

The trunk of a tree carved with five lines.

"You knew it was there," I say, voice hoarse. "The hand. You painted it." The carving in the painting is just that—lines slashed into the bark. No red to mark it. Red palms—not blood but paint.

Did Emily make that mark, and then let me "discover" it?

"You knew about the hand. You saw Meghan Vale and you lied

about it. What else are you lying about?" I demand, stepping toward her.

Her hand moves. I flinch, but she only reaches as if to cup my cheek, her thumb barely brushing my skin. "You won't find her, Audrey. You should stop looking," she says. Her fingernails settle lightly against my neck.

"I won't," I say, hardly breathing.

"I know." She drops her hand. Turns away. She's done with me. She's blocking in the shape of an eye now, building it out of shadow and light. That's all any of us can see. The light and the shadow, and our mind fills in the rest.

With my heart hammering in my chest, not fully certain if I am afraid, I retreat.

19

Below

The light is dead. It was dying before, but now it's gone for good, and if I don't get out, I'll never see light again. I wish I knew it was the last time, when I switched the flashlight off, but I thought I was saving them—those final flickers of dim illumination, those final moments of sight before it all vanished.

What's next? the gossamer girl asks. The one with copper hair and eyes I almost recognize. I think she was the last—the last girl to breathe this stale air and wonder if she'll ever be free.

"How did you die?" I whisper. "Did it hurt?"

Less than I thought it would, the girl answers. She touches the end of the bolt—single, whole. *This isn't nothing.*

Not nothing. Not much better than that, though. I had the image in her mind of bracing the bolts against each other, using them as levers to prize apart one of the links of the chain. I can't do it with one.

I'm so thirsty. So tired. Not hungry anymore, but there's no comfort in that. It's as if my body knows it's nearly dead, is shutting off pieces of me in anticipation. I will go slowly, gasping. Did the others die this way? Is this how it ends? The door no longer opening, the girls like me left to wither?

I used to say things like *We're all dying. Some of us are just dying faster than others.* I thought it made me better than other people, being cynical.

I hate that girl now, that version of me who thought I knew what suffering was. I was proud, wasn't I? To be clever and cruel, as if one demanded the other.

I don't think I'll be mourned.

You deserve this, the gossamer girl says, matter-of-fact.

"No."

Then why are you sitting there?

I shake myself. I need to move. Gripping the bolt in one hand, I follow the length of the chain, feeling each link. One of them must be weaker than the others. How many girls have twisted and tugged and pulled at this thing? It's damp down here. I've seen the rust on the metal. It's weakened.

Link by link, I follow it, marking where I feel the rough texture of rust. Those links will be the most likely to break. But it's only at the end that I truly find hope, because the final link—the one attached to the metal ring sunk into the wall—is the most rusted of all. I grope along the wall, and notice for the first time what I never have before: the slightest whisper of moisture. I long to press my tongue against the liquid, but it isn't enough to wet my mouth with.

I pinch my fingers around the seam where the two ends of the link meet. The bubbling of metal tells me it's welded—but how well?

I slide the bolt through the link of chain. Here, I can brace it against the wall. Wrap my fingers around it.

I pull hard. All my strength, all my weight into it. Does it start to give? Or is it my flesh that's yielding?

All at once, the resistance is gone. The bolt slips. Flies free. My position puts my hand in line with my face, and without the tension of the bolt, it flies back, my knuckles striking my mouth. I cry out at the pain, grab at my face. My lips sting and ache. I taste blood and feel something shift in my mouth. A tooth already loosened by a fist so long ago (or not so long, maybe—I can't tell anymore). I spit it into my hand, a hard lump with a twist of gristle at its end. My mouth floods with the taste of blood.

I press my brow against the cold wall, gripping the tooth. *Five more,* I think. Isn't that the story? Six teeth on a string, and you can summon the witch. But what good would a witch's vengeance do me down here? There's no one left to punish except me. But there was another part of the story. The girls swallowed up and gone. I would like that, I think. A gentle vanishing with only this one price.

I set the tooth carefully on the bedpost and run my hands over the ground. The bolt. Where's the bolt? My movements become more frantic. I scrabble over the ground, patting at the concrete. Nothing, nothing, nothing. I thrust my upper body under the bed and run my fingers all the way to the seam of the wall. Nothing.

I'm panicking.

Stop.

Dead girls cluster. Have they always looked so hungry?

Breathe.

Have they always sounded so scornful?

I swallow another mouthful of blood and shut my eyes. It changes nothing. I open them again.

I stare at nothing for the space of a dozen heartbeats. I still taste nothing but blood.

I raise my palm and spit into it, once and then again. With my other hand, I spread it down each finger methodically, blood and saliva cooling quickly in the air.

Fingers splayed, I press my hand against the wall. I swear I can see it, gleaming in the dark. *I was here,* it says. *I was here, and I'm not dead yet.*

Begin again.

I shuffle to the limit of the chain and start my sweep once more.

20

Above

The night of the dinner, Dev picks me up, dressed in an impeccable blue suit that makes my off-the-rack black dress look frumpy by comparison. The event is in the school auditorium, so we're on familiar ground as we cross the parking lot.

"I'm impressed they pulled this together so quickly," Dev says.

"That's Melinda for you." Inside, tables have been arranged with white tablecloths. A display at the front of the auditorium bears a beaming picture of Bryson and his family. I spot Melinda right away, chatting with the mayor and Bryson's parents. Bryson himself squirms at his mother's side, clearly eager to explore. I doubt he's getting more than arm's length away anytime soon.

Tamara waves us down. "Paul's grabbing drinks," she reports. Her only nod to the glamour of the occasion is a blazer over her usual top and jeans. She looks me up and down approvingly. "Well, aren't you a tall drink of water. And the arm candy ain't half bad, either."

"Arm candy? I think I've been promoted," Dev says, and sticks out his hand to introduce himself. Paul returns with a gin and tonic for himself and a stiff whiskey for Tamara, who downs half of it in one slug.

"So what do you think? Campaign announcement tonight, or do you think it'll be another week?" she asks, eyeing the Hills.

"Subtle hints tonight. Announcement next month," Paul predicts. "But it'll be Andrew."

"He doesn't have the balls for politics," Tamara says disapprovingly. "Melinda is the one who knows how to get things done. If it weren't for the cancer, she'd be a senator by now."

"You're a fan, I take it?" Dev asks. My stomach feels pinched. The thing about this town is that you can't escape the Hills if you try.

Tamara grunts an affirmative. "Liked her before she ran, like her now. Hope's Hands is a hell of an organization, and we worked together on some DV stuff before she ran. That was my focus before I got roped into managing these chuckleheads." She jerks a thumb toward me and Paul.

"I did always think it was funny you went from helping people disappear to finding them," Paul says.

I twitch. "Disappear?" I say.

She waves a hand. "I spent a little time working with a group that helped women get new identities. When getting away from an abuser took more than a restraining order and a move. We'd empty their apartments out in the middle of the night."

"Can you even do that legally?" Dev asks curiously. "Change your identity?"

Tamara makes a considering noise. "Depends. The no-paperwork, no-crime version is keep a low profile. Work under the table, operate with cash, use free clinics. Giving people a fake name socially isn't a crime. Don't even have to do it forever necessarily, just until whoever's looking for you loses interest. There are legal avenues, but they're tough to navigate. We tried to connect our clients with folks who could help them with name changes and even petitioning for a new social security number, but most didn't have the time or resources."

"And then there are the illegal things you definitely never facilitated," Paul says, eyes sparkling.

"Only illegal thing I ever did involved a baseball bat and a strategic application of force to a vintage Camaro, and that was a matter of emergency deterrence," Tamara says, hands in her pockets and a smirk in the corner of her mouth.

I think of those first years after Janie left. She was basically a ghost. Using cash, crashing on couches. Maybe that's all that happened to her. She remade herself, the way she always talked about. But it takes an incredible amount of work, navigating those kinds of logistics long-term. Never drawing a proper paycheck, never signing a lease or having your credit run.

You only do something like that if you're running from something. Some*one*. And Janie wasn't—not that I know of.

"Can I grab you something?" Dev is asking. "I was going to hit up the bar."

I give myself a little shake. "I'll go," I say, suddenly needing the air.

"You sure?" he says, and at my nod asks for a scotch and soda.

"Coming right up," I tell him, and touch his arm lightly as I drift away.

I plant myself in the line at the open bar. All of the volunteers have been invited, and I spot the new kid, no longer limping. Tamara's brassy laugh sounds from somewhere behind me. I check for Len and Kenny, but they haven't arrived yet.

I finally reach the front of the line and place my order—a G&T for me, Dev's scotch and soda.

Hovering a few feet away, the new kid spots me and moves in with the laser-eyed focus of a social barnacle in need of a passing ship to attach to. I grab my drinks with a muttered thanks and turn quickly to make my escape—and nearly slop both of them over Andrew Hill's sports coat.

He catches me by both wrists, steadying me. His grip is tight, and he holds on a beat too long before he releases me, our eyes locked together. "Careful there," he says. His voice is baritone. It's always had a gravelly edge to it. Every local profile of him talks about how Andrew Hill is genial, a man of the people, open and humble all at once, but to me, he has always seemed to carry a fragility with him—the brittleness of thin ice over black water. He's too careful to make sure people like him, too precise in his efforts to be adored.

It makes me nervous about what he might do the day he stops caring what other people think.

"I'm so sorry," I say. I want to step around him, but he's squarely in my path, and the drinks line blocks my retreat.

"No harm done." He hasn't let go, looking at me like he's trying to see something in my eyes—or like he's on the verge of saying something.

"Did you want to get to the bar?" I ask.

"I don't drink," he says.

"Since when?" I ask, unthinking, and then my teeth click shut. His eyes narrow. I've seen Andrew Hill very drunk indeed. Not that I was sober at the time, either.

"That was a long time ago," he says, like a warning.

"Water under the bridge," I say. I start to step around him. He lets me, his grip breaking smoothly, but his voice stills me.

"Audrey." He swallows. He almost looks nervous. "It was a long time ago," he repeats.

"I know," I say. "I didn't—it wasn't my best day. You didn't do anything . . . ungentlemanly."

He chokes a little. "You have an odd standard for gentlemen."

"I just mean—"

"I know what you mean." He scrubs the back of his neck with one hand. "I was an idiot."

"Past tense?" I say, daring a bit of a teasing tone. His smile is rueful.

"I like to think I've improved."

Has he, though? Or is he saying what I want to hear? "What exactly do you want from me here, Andrew?" I ask.

"Nothing," he says. "I just want to make sure we're good."

"Why, is someone going to be asking? I don't think a drunken hookup in your twenties is going to disqualify you from office," I say.

He makes a face. "God, no, that's not it. I'm not running for anything."

Paul will be disappointed to lose that bet. "Then why bring it up now?"

He's still standing too close to me, giving me no easy way to exit. "No reason," he says.

I give him a skeptical look. "Like I said. Water under the bridge. It's forgotten. Now, if you'll excuse me . . ."

He looks as if he wants to say something more, maybe to extract a more thorough promise from me, but finally he nods. I walk away with my heart beating a little too fast, frowning. My *encounter* with Andrew was a mistake, but as far as I knew, he hadn't thought about it—or me—since. It's odd to think it still weighs on him.

"What was that about?" Paul asks as I rejoin the others.

"Oh. That?" I say lightly. Tamara's mouth is downturned, her eyes fixed on Andrew suspiciously. "I just almost spilled my drinks over the hometown hero, no big deal."

"He looked a little intense about it," Dev says, concerned. He takes his drink but doesn't sip.

I shrug, laugh. It sounds false. "We've never really gotten along."

"I didn't realize you two knew each other," Tamara says.

"We don't. Not anymore. It was ages ago. He dated my best friend," I say. *And a few years later,* I don't add, *I slept with him.*

Well. That's putting a nicer spin on it than it deserves. It glosses over the particulars—the grimy barstool that stuck to my thighs in my too-short dress, the glaze already on Andrew's eyes when he leaned against the bar next to me, my angry amusement when I realized he had no idea who I was. I was twenty-three and just another cute girl he expected to be bowled over by his almost-fame.

He dropped some low-effort pickup line, and I laughed. He thought I was charmed. I kept expecting him to figure it out. And for some reason, I decided to play along until he did.

What did Janie ever see in you? I remember thinking. I thought about his lips on hers and his hands on her body and the time he got that I didn't. I thought about how the last thing Janie ever did to me was ditch me for this man, and when he asked me my name, I just said, "Do you really need to know?"

I expected him to call me out, even as he whispered a suggestion in my ear. Even as I followed him out to the parking lot.

I still don't really know what I was thinking. We'd had several drinks on top of the ones I'd already downed, and he was worse off than I was. Every second I thought, *I should stop this*, and every second I didn't.

We didn't get far—just to the back seat of his car. He was at least sensible enough to have packed a condom, and I was sensible enough to remind him to use it. It was quick and unsatisfying and the whole time I was thinking, *This is what you left me for?*

Afterwards, I was pulling up my panties and he straightened the strap of my dress for me. "I didn't even get your name," he said, and it actually sounded like he cared.

"Audrey. We've met. I'm Janie's friend," I told him.

I expected him to be angry, and he was. What I didn't expect was the way he lost his footing. How he sank down onto the seat of the car and stared at me.

"Why?" he asked.

"I don't know," I said, and it was the truth. He offered me a cigarette. I hadn't smoked before and haven't since, but we stayed out there for one and then another. I can't remember what we talked about, other than a few fumbling attempts at questions that neither of us could really answer. He'd already asked the only one that mattered, and there was never a clear *why* when it came to Janie.

I'd always known she broke it off with him, not the other way around. What I hadn't known was how deeply it affected him. He didn't say as much, of course. But I could tell. Whatever happened to end things, it left a mark—even after only a few weeks together, even years later. Her name still hit him like a blow to the gut, and for the first time in my life, I had something in common with Andrew Hill.

What I can't imagine is why it bothers him so much. Parking lot sex is sleazy, sure, but it was entirely consensual. What else had he said that night? It's a blur now. Maybe it is for him, too. I do remember the abrupt way he left, as if he couldn't stand one moment longer of sitting still. He drove off, and I remember thinking he'd be lucky to make it home in one piece.

Across the room, Andrew is watching me. And next to him is Emily. She's wearing a silk blouse the color of moss, her hair twisted up on top of her head.

Has she told him I was at the house?

He keeps near her. All but interposing himself between her and everyone else, his stance protective but with a note of something else. She stares at me, unblinking. He notices and bends slightly to say something in her ear, his face turned away. The tiny sliver of expression I can see looks . . . unsettled.

She looks up at him and speaks. My eyes track her lips. I could swear she mouthed, *What do you think I'm going to do?*

I look away quickly. This is too much. Emily and the weirdness with Andrew and people flocking around to congratulate the volunteers. I'm suddenly remembering why I don't come to these things.

I grab Dev's sleeve. "Can we get out of here early?" I mutter to him.

"We just got here," Dev says. I give him a pleading look. "But I hate it and we should leave immediately," he corrects himself swiftly.

I slip over to Tamara, murmuring about a sudden headache. She gives me a knowing look; I know she'll cover my escape. I linger long enough to give Paul a hug and promise to be at next weekend's training, and then I'm gone.

Outside, people are still arriving. Dev and I give them stiff nods, smiles fixed in place, as we flee to the car. Inside, I bury my face in my hands and groan.

"Can I ask what that was about?" Dev ventures. "If it's none of my business—"

"It's complicated," I say.

"I'm good with complicated," Dev says sincerely. "Look, you

didn't get to finish your drink. Let me take you out, and you can tell me about it—or not."

I nod wordlessly. Dev starts up the car. I put my seat belt on and slump back against the seat, chewing on the corner of my lip.

It feels significant that Emily was there. She never shows up to these things. Why would she start now? Because she's getting involved before the big campaign launch?

Or maybe because they're keeping an eye on her.

Dev pulls into the lot of the Hopper, the semi-hip bar that replaced the dive that used to sit on this corner. It retains a selection of cheap beer for commuting college students and the regulars who refuse to acknowledge the change in management. We snag a booth near the back and order a couple pints.

"So," Dev says. "Does this sudden headache have anything to do with you getting sick in the middle of the day yesterday?" He raises his eyebrows, curious but carefully nonjudgmental.

"That was—I had something to deal with and I lost track of time," I say. "Just being flaky."

"That doesn't sound like you. I mean, not that we've known each other long, but *flaky* is not the word I would use to describe you," he says, worry darkening his eyes. "What's going on?"

I hunch over my drink protectively. I shouldn't be putting this on him, but I can't call Len. He's a cop, and while I haven't done anything illegal—well, apart from taking the journal—I've crossed lines I shouldn't have.

"I've been looking into Meghan Vale," I say. "Trying to figure out what happened to her." He listens as I tell him a bare-bones version of what I've been up to. Searching the woods with Emily, talking to Ethan, finding Meghan's journal. I tell him about Meghan seeing Emily. I leave out my history with Andrew.

"You got her address from school files and went to her house? Audrey, you could get in trouble for something like that," Dev says, leaning in. "Are you sure this is a good idea?"

I laugh bitterly. "Not even a little bit."

"I say this as your friend and just your friend—not the guy who would very much like to get a third date with you and is probably torpedoing his chances. But maybe you should talk to someone about this," Dev says.

"I thought that was what I was doing."

He winces. "Someone professional, I mean."

"You think I need therapy?"

"It's helped me a great deal," he says. "It's just . . . I know how it is. I've had students I wanted to rescue so badly. We watch these kids drowning and we're standing on shore throwing things at them we *hope* will float, we *hope* they'll grab, and all you want to do is dive in there with them. But there's too many of them, and you can get dragged under yourself." Dev's eyes shine with tender intensity, and in his voice, I hear the echo of the stories all of us have.

"There are kids you can't save," I say. "And kids you don't know how to save, and kids that will swim away from the life vest you're throwing for them. This is different. This is . . ." I don't know how to finish the sentence. I don't know how to explain. "She wasn't even my student. I probably couldn't have picked her out of a lineup. But I get this feeling when I'm on a search. I know when it's time to give up, and I know when it isn't. It isn't time to give up yet."

He drinks. The froth at the top of the glass sticks to his mustache. He clears it with a napkin, thinking. "So. Where do you go from here?" he asks.

"I'm not sure. This isn't what I do," I say with a helpless shrug.

"Maybe that's why it isn't working," he observes.

I shake my head. "What I do isn't helpful here. There isn't a grid to search, there isn't a trail to follow."

"Isn't there? You just said she was out there in those woods, right?" he asks.

"Months ago."

He scratches his chin thoughtfully. "Could a dog still find a scent after that much time?"

"Scent trails last hours, *maybe* days," I say. "We're talking about months of weather."

"I feel like I've seen dogs searching in areas where people have been missing longer than that," Dev says with the faint edge of a question.

"Sure, but in those cases they're not looking for someone who passed through eight weeks ago," I say. "They're looking for someone who's still there."

"As in . . ." he begins.

"As in a body," I say. "Cadaver dogs can find a corpse even years after someone dies in some cases."

"Is that a possibility?" he asks quietly. I look away. Of course it is. It's the first thing I thought of, isn't it? Meghan out beneath those beads, listening to them click in the wind. Not noticing the click of a gun being cocked.

"It's possible." I drain the last swallow of my drink. "I'm going to need another one of these." I cast around for our server, but there's no sign of her. From long experience, I know she's likely not going to be back for a while. I tell Dev to hang tight while I go up to the bar.

The bartender tonight is a skinny guy who desperately needs both a haircut and a sense of urgency. I manage to inconvenience him into pulling me a pint, and lean against the counter as I wait for the excruciatingly slow process to resolve. It's early in the evening yet, and the bar isn't exactly hopping. The only other person sitting at the bar is down at the end, head bent over a plate of fries that look like they went cold a while ago. It takes me a moment to recognize him, and then my stomach drops.

The gray-haired, flannel-wearing man is Bill. Neighbor Terry's gun-happy brother. He lifts his eyes like he can feel me looking, and his brow furrows briefly and then lifts, his own moment of recognition. "I know you," he says.

"You pointed a gun at me," I reply. The bartender shows his first glimmer of interest, his head coming up slow like a mildly startled tortoise.

"Yeah, I did," Bill says. He tugs at the brim of his battered baseball cap. "Sorry about that."

"Are you?" I ask.

"Guess I oughta be."

The bartender slides the pint onto the counter between us, slopping foam. I dry the side with a bar napkin, still watching Bill. "Do you get lots of trespassers out there?"

"Not really," he says. "I don't go out there much myself, though. Just since Terry's been in the hospital."

"How is he doing?" I ask casually.

Bill seems surprised that I'm still talking to him, but he straightens up and clears his throat. "He had surgery, but it didn't go so great," Bill says.

"Sorry to hear that."

A roll of his shoulders. "It's nothing new. Had his first heart attack five years ago," he says. "I didn't take it seriously then. He asked me to come around to help, but I was busy with my own life, and it took him going down last month for me to realize this might be my last chance to be a good brother. So I might have been a bit—what's the word—overzealous."

"That is the word for it," I say mildly. "So how well do you know Emily Hill, then?"

His brow creases at this line of questioning. "I know her brother a bit better. He's the one that's looked after things for Terry when I wasn't around."

My head cocks. "Andrew Hill has been taking care of your brother's land? I thought Terry didn't want anyone out there."

"He doesn't. But he doesn't have much choice," Bill says. "He doesn't get around like he used to, not after he got sick again last year. So Andrew offered to tend to things. Terry hates it, but what's he going to do?"

So Terry wouldn't—couldn't—have been wandering out in the woods while Meghan was exploring. Emily hadn't mentioned that little detail. Neither had Terry, for that matter, but it sounds like he wouldn't. Pride and resentment explained his omission, but why would Emily lie?

Unless Emily is the one hiding something.

Dev catches my eye from the booth and gives me a questioning look. I raise my fingers in a quick wave. "I hope your brother recovers quickly," I say, without conviction. He grunts and dips his head in what might be agreement or indigestion. I snag my beer and walk quickly back to the booth.

"Everything okay?" Dev asks. "That guy wasn't being a creep, was he? Because I'm a man of peace, but I have kind of always wanted to get into a chivalrous bar fight."

"Is that a thing?" I ask him.

"Probably not," he acknowledges.

I chew the side of my thumb. "That's the guy who almost shot me the other day. Turns out, that land where I found the beads? The Hills look after it for him. They're the only ones out there."

"I still don't totally get what the deal with that family is," Dev says. "They're like . . . Franklin royalty?"

I give a little laugh. "Side effect of being kind of a nowhere town—when people do make it big, we never shut up about them," I say. "Their mother, Elizabeth, was pretty beloved around here. She taught at the school, in fact. Melinda's the oldest, and she was in Congress for a couple terms. There's Liam, of course."

"Ah, yes. The heartthrob. My sister had a crush on him," Dev says. "Hell, I had a bit of a crush on him. Those soulful eyes? The leather jacket? He was the perfect bad boy. My sister sobbed for an embarrassingly long time after Kyle bit it in that drag race accident. You'd think someone had really died."

"He was actually really sweet," I say. "Liam, I mean, not Kyle. Obviously."

"You know him?"

"No. I mean, when we were kids, kind of," I say. I think of his hands cradling that box. How he let them lie limp in his lap afterwards, staring down at them. A gentle boy in an ungentle world.

"Then there's Andrew, obviously. Quarterback. A brief but glorious stint in the NFL before an injury took him out, which people will still tell you about like it's the worst twist of fate the town's ever seen. Jackass, don't ask me how I know. The point is, they've always been . . . not prominent, exactly? But notable." Except for Emily.

And that's striking, isn't it? The Hills were always around in one way or another—Melinda volunteering all over the place; Andrew at all the football events and constantly roaming with a pack of other student athletes; Liam starring in the school play, where he somehow made *Our Town* feel fresh the nineteenth straight year of its performance at Franklin High. But Emily was kept cloistered. She suggested that was her father's doing. That he was paranoid and controlling. She was the one who looked exactly like her beloved mother. So he built a tower to lock the princess into. But maybe it was more than that.

Emily is lying. She's hiding something—I'm certain of it.

And she and her older siblings are entirely occupied at the moment.

"What are you thinking?" Dev asks, sounding a touch nervous.

I run a finger along the rim of my glass. "I'm thinking of breaking some laws."

21

Above

Barry knows something's up the moment I get his working harness. He walks to me with a tight, wary gait and none of his usual bounding enthusiasm. "Good boy," I tell him. "We're going to do some work."

Dev is waiting in the car. Barry inspects him with a cursory snuffle across the ear before collapsing to cover the whole of the back bench. He pants at me in the rearview as I buckle up.

"You sure about this?" Dev asks.

I give him a look. "If you want to back out, I can drop you at home. You don't need to follow the crazy woman on her crusade."

"Following a crazy woman on a crusade might be exactly what my life needs right now," Dev says with a tight smile. "But if anyone catches us, I'm telling them I'm your hostage."

"Fair."

We drive in silence. When we get to the pull-off near the Hills' land, I direct Dev to park with trees between us and the road. The concealment will hold up to only the most casual inspection, but hopefully no one's going to get too curious. I open up the back for Barry. He waves his tail uncertainly as I clip his GPS tracker onto the rugged harness he's fitted with. It's a souvenir from our brief attempts at training him for SAR, but he seems to remember what it's for. He looks around as if searching for Matsuda and the others.

"Just us, Barry," I say. And maybe that means he'll be the least bit useful, with fewer people to distract him.

We take out flashlights. They're not the ones I'd normally use—much smaller, again to avoid detection. We'll be in and out, and if we don't get anything, tough luck. But that hum is a live wire in the air. We're going to find something. I know it.

"Stick close," I tell Dev, and tug Barry's leash to get him moving.

There's a thin path, little wider than a deer trail, cutting between the trees. I let Barry take a long lead. "Find 'em," I tell him, which is his cue to start tracking. He stares at me for a long moment. He's a far cry from Matsuda's border collies, with their foxlike noses and uncanny intelligence. But eventually, those few little drifting brain cells connect up, and he turns his back to me, sniffing enthusiastically.

After that, he circles around us, sharklike, nose working at a constant snuffle. I'm forced to let him off lead quickly, but thankfully he sticks close. Matsuda's dogs will zip off and vanish from sight, trackable only by the bells he keeps attached to their collars, but Barry's less adventurous. Plus, he has to take frequent breaks to check if Dev has snacks hidden in his pockets. At least it'll help him sort out Dev's scent from anything lingering out here.

Dev and I walk in wary silence. This is one of the most reckless things I've ever done—and this time, I'm dragging someone else along with me. But something is happening here. I can't just leave it alone.

"Here are the beads," I say. We've passed onto Terry's property. I don't think Bill is going to be out here with his gun tonight, at least. We left him drinking at the bar, and according to the server, he tends to stay there until closing. We've still got an hour before then. "The marked tree should be this way."

"I'm remembering, all of a sudden, how much this witch doesn't like men," Dev says with nervous humor, sweeping his flashlight around.

"Make sure to tell her you're a feminist. Maybe you won't get eviscerated," I say. Barry digs at the ground, then loses interest. We walk a little ways farther. I'm starting to worry that I've forgotten where the tree is when it appears, the red hand splashed vividly in the path of my light.

"Not creepy at all," Dev notes. Barry lopes in and freezes, body a comma as he catches a scent, makes a decision.

Suddenly he takes off at a gallop.

"Barry!" I say, too softly. It's been too long since we did this kind of training. He could be after a rabbit or just a shadow.

Just as suddenly as he took off, he's thundering back. He skids to a halt in front of me, drops his hindquarters, and lets out a low *boof*.

"What does that mean?" Dev asks.

I swallow. "Theoretically? It means he found something."

"What does *theoretically* mean, in this context?" Dev asks.

"It means it's been years since I did any scent training with him, and he might just have found a French fry," I say, but my heart is hammering. "Show me, boy."

Barry bounces back to his feet and takes off at a lope. We have to scramble to follow, Dev falling in a few steps behind me. A branch rakes across my cheek, drawing a sharp line of pain in its wake, and then we burst into a small clearing, where Barry stands panting. He dips his head, snuffles the ground, and looks up again. After a moment, he seems to remember what he's supposed to do, and lets out another bark—this one sharp and loud.

My stomach clenches, my mouth completely dry, as we draw close. Barry walks forward, putting his head under my hand for a congratulatory pat. I can barely move my fingers to scratch him.

"There's nothing here," Dev says. "So that means . . ."

Barry paws the ground, whines.

"He's scenting on human remains," I say dully. "Something buried."

"Oh. *Oh*," Dev says. We'd discussed the possibility, of course, but this is different. This is the ground we're standing on. He looks stricken. "It doesn't mean—it might not be her."

"It might not be anyone," I say. "Barry's not certified." But he was good, when he wasn't distracted. I've never seen him give a false positive. Accuracy was never his issue.

"We need to call the police," Dev says firmly.

"And tell them what?" I ask. "How are we even supposed to explain what we're doing out here?"

"So wait until tomorrow," Dev suggests. "We're right by the preserve, right? There are trails all through there. We'll take Barry on a walk, say he broke loose. Followed his old training."

I nod slowly. It's a decent plan. Dev puts his hands on my arms, soothing me.

"I should do it alone," I say. "Keep you out of it."

"Absolutely not," Dev says. "I am fully committed to my life of crime, and you won't take it from me."

I manage to crack a small smile. I'm about to respond when Barry suddenly tenses, nose testing the wind—and takes off again.

"What's he doing now?" Dev asks.

"I'm not sure," I say. "Barry!"

Barry doesn't respond. He's off like a rocket. Dev and I glance at each other, and then we break into a run.

I'm not sure what direction we're heading. I barely dodge rocks, roots, and grasping branches as we follow Barry's path, and then we're skidding to a halt as Barry trots back and forth at the base of a small hillock. He scratches at the side of the slope, whining, and there's something strange about the sound of his claws—he's scraping at something hard.

"Barry, back," I tell him, and he backs off, still whining anxiously. I swipe my hand over the ground, clearing leaf litter, and shine my flashlight at the metallic surface it reveals.

"Is that—" Dev starts.

"It's a door."

22

Below

Once, I wanted to die. I even made a plan. I couldn't see a way out. No light at the end of the tunnel. If only I could whisper to my past self, make a form of gossamer and tell that girl how accustomed to the dark I could truly become.

Once, I had friends. Better than that. Had a best friend. But for every ounce of love in my body, there was an equal measure of hate, because it hurt, standing at the edge of a life where love was not just expected but assumed. I would watch the way her family moved around each other with such casual affection and feel something sharp and broken lodged between my lungs.

Eventually, it hurt too much. So I ruined it, all of it. But it wasn't just my fault.

Couldn't you see? Couldn't you hear me asking for help? But I never had, of course. I lied and lied and waited to be called on it. For someone to swoop in and wrap their arms around me and tell me, *I know, I know, but it'll be all right.* They didn't. Just as well. I would have sunk my teeth into them if they tried.

I tried running away. I thought I could be someone else if I could be some*where* else, but the world doesn't work like that. It demands a name. It despises reinvention. I carried my failures with me, and eventually, I came limping home. But when I got back, things had changed. The people I knew turned away from me. Treated me like I was tainted.

So I made my plan.

I'd met lots of men and women, boys and girls, who'd tried and failed. I had a good grasp of the available methods. My approach was rational: the best chance of success balanced against the least chance of lasting effects if I failed. Lorraine, the woman I met in the shelter with her sunken skull and slack jaw, the curled-in fingers that failed to hold the gun steady as it leapt, would not be my future.

It was the best I'd felt in a long time, those days that were supposed to be my last. Everyone I spoke to said I was doing so much better, and I was. I was about to be free. A smile lodged itself at the corner of my mouth and wouldn't quit.

Six hours, more or less. Six hours more, and there would have been no girl to cage. I would have been gossamer, but instead, I was still locked in this net of sinew and bone, weak blood and dumb nerves, this dull thing of meat, when I was brought to this place.

It was going to be my choice. Mine. And maybe I don't know how to live, but I'm not going to die because of someone else.

Dad always said I was a contrary bitch.

I wedge the bolt, retrieved from a dusty corner, against the wall once again. I steady it. My efforts have chipped the concrete wall, giving me a pit that helps brace it. I position myself more carefully. Jenny doesn't need any more of my teeth today.

With all the meager strength I have left, I push the end of the bolt downward. This time, there is no doubt. The metal gives, a stiff surrender. I pause, adjust my weight, try again. Another easing, and I stop, feeling at the link with my fingers. The amateur welding has given way. There's a gap. Narrower than my finger. Wider than the links of the chain.

My hands shake as I ease the next link up and feed it through the gap, and then—

The chain is broken. One end in my hand, the other hanging from the wall. For an instant, I sit frozen, uncomprehending.

And then I scramble for the door.

I hit the table on the way, clipping it hard with my hip. I fall to one knee and give a bark of pain but shove right back up to my feet. One hand gropes ahead of me, the other holding the chain wrapped around my fist to keep it from dragging. There's the wall. And the doorway. I force myself to slow down as I reach the steps. The last thing I want is to fall.

I make my way up one at a time, fingers reaching ahead and above until they bump against the hard barrier of the door.

I know it's locked. It has to be. But still, I shove at it. It lifts a fraction and my heart leaps—but then it sticks.

I swallow down panic, but the darkness lights up with purples and yellows, and my knees go suddenly slack. I collapse onto the step, my breath thin, my limbs weak.

You knew it was locked, I chide myself. *Come on, come on, what's next?*

Light. I need light, and then I can see what I need to do next. I half crawl down the steps again, the retreat feeling all too much like failure. My mouth is uncomfortably dry. My limbs frighteningly weak.

The light switch is to the right of the stairs. I feel along, my palms scraping at the wall. There. A box sticking out, cords running from it. I find the switch and flip it.

Nothing.

I flick it again, up and down, but nothing happens.

No water. No electricity, either.

No light.

This time, when I sink to the ground, it isn't my knees going out but the whole of me.

I can't do this in the dark.

Even the exertion of walking these few steps has my heart hammering, my head spinning.

I was never going to get out.

I see that now. My dreams always ended at the bottom of the stairs. I could never see the door. Never quite picture it opening.

But I tried. Didn't I? I tried, and I got close, I really did, and that matters. It has to matter.

Of course it does, says the girl with copper hair. Her eyes are made of copper, too. Bright pennies for the dead.

She takes my hand. The chain sings behind me on the floor as I drag it. The bed is where I left it. The sharp stone, too. The gossamer girl holds it out to me (it's already in my hand).

It's time, she says.

Yes.

Time at last to add my name, my real name, to the list of the dead. They gather around me, moths in their eyes and lichen in their hair. Their footsteps bloom with mushroom caps.

Now, they say, and *here,* and *what is*—but they aren't speaking at all.

There are voices. Outside. Voices, and the sound of metal being struck.

Someone is here.

23

Above

"What the hell is this doing here?" Dev asks.

I barely hear him. I shove Barry aside, scraping the leaf litter from the door. It's a metal door set on sturdy hinges, locked with a chain and a padlock, both rusted but functional.

"Do you think it's a bomb shelter or something?" Dev asks. "Root cellar?"

"I don't know."

"Audrey, we should really head back now." He's more than unsettled. He's scared. I drop my pack and unzip it, clawing through. "What are you doing?"

"A couple years back, we had to haul an injured climber out of an area that was blocked off by a locked gate. Too high to hoist her over easily so we had to wait for bolt cutters," I say. "Can't exactly haul bolt cutters everywhere, but I learned a trick in case it ever happens again." I pull out two small wrenches.

"I think I've seen this on YouTube," Dev says, crouching down next to me. "But, Audrey, we are way beyond wandering off-trail here. How are we going to explain this?"

"If she's down there, it doesn't matter," I tell him. I set the wrenches inside the loop of the padlock. Positioned properly, they provide enough leverage to slowly break the lock. It takes muscle and three goes, but it springs open. I jerk it free of the chain and toss it aside, and then pull the chain rattling free from the handle.

Dev looks pale in the glow of the flashlights, but I feel calmer than I have this whole time. Clarity has settled over me. There is a feeling like weightlessness in my chest, and a cold fire burning between my shoulder blades.

"Last chance," I say. Last chance to turn back and not be part of this.

"Open it."

I haul on the door, standing up. The hinges shriek, echoing in the hollow space beyond, and the sound is somehow familiar. The space beyond drops sharply down, a pit of black interrupted by the pale teeth of stairs. The flashlight beam seems reluctant to pierce that dark.

"Hello?" I call. My voice leaps back at me, garbled. "Meghan?" I think I hear a noise, an exhalation with all the substance of a bruised petal. I surge forward. Dev grabs for me with a sound of alarm, but I'm half falling, half running down the stairs.

24

Below

The door opens with a tortured sound, and then the light streams in. I curl against the wall, trained fear taking me over. *The light is here the light means pain there is no salvation in the light—*

"Oh my god," says a voice, and it isn't one I know. Not the one with orders and recriminations, the one that saws between sweetness and rage, the one that belongs to the hands whose touch has marked my days down here.

I force my eyes open and find a woman staring at me.

"Melinda?" a voice calls from above. "What's down there?"

25

Above

"What's down there?" Dev asks from above. I don't answer at first, my flashlight sweeping around the abandoned room.

The room—*bunker,* my mind supplies—is a cold rectangle of concrete, filled with refuse and broken furniture. Milk crates are stacked in one corner. Broken chairs are heaped in another, along with a toppled table and a broken toilet. On the opposite wall stands a bed frame. The thin mattress, rotted and, from the looks of things, inhabited by any number of small creatures, leans up against the wall. The slats of the bed are broken, several of them scattered on the ground.

But what I stare at isn't the furniture. It's the wall before me. It's covered in red—red handprints, pressed onto the concrete in frenetic clusters.

"Holy shit," Dev says, coming down behind me. "Is that blood?"

"Paint, I think," I say distantly, drawing forward. I set my hand against one of the prints. It's nearly a match. I sweep the flashlight around the room.

"I don't think anyone's been down here in a long time," Dev says.

I walk toward the bed. A few links of rusted chain dangle from a metal ring on the wall. There are scratch marks by the metal plate that secures it. They look old.

"Audrey."

Barry's nails click on the stairs.

"We should get out of here," Dev says urgently. "Now, Audrey."

I crouch down. There's something on one of the bed slats. Scratch marks. No—writing. I draw it close, leaning in to make out the worn words.

Don't swear
Be polite
Don't cry
Save food
Toilet = water

A cold trickle goes down my spine. I reach for another board, flip it over.

NEVER SAY YOUR REAL NAME
NEVER SAY
NEVER SAY IT

The writing is frantic. And then, below it, in styles too disparate to have come from the same hand—

My name is Amanda.
My name is Madison.
My name is Stranger.

My breath catches between my teeth. I've seen that phrase before. Where have I seen it before?

"Audrey?"

"Someone was down here," I say. "More than one."

I stand, look back at Dev. He looks gray, queasy. He looks like I feel. "Where are they now?" he asks.

Barry sits in the middle of the room, staring at a place near the wall. Then he looks at me and gives a single bark.

The sound that means he scents death.

Part II

Before

After

26

Before

"Holy shit," says a man's voice, drawing up behind the woman. They stare at me, unmoving. And then comes another voice.

"Andrew? Melinda?"

Recognition jolts through me.

The light streams down behind them, turning them into solid silhouettes. I hold out a shaking hand to shade my eyes as a third body lopes down the stairs to join the others.

I watched taffy being made once. Machines stretching and folding a great length of gummy sugar. My thoughts feel like that now, round and round and pulled into strange shapes.

"Jesus," one of them says—I can't tell which.

Another speaks rapidly under his breath. "What the fuck. What—"

"The *fuck* is this?" Andrew roars, and I flinch back, pressing myself against the wall and screwing my eyes shut.

"Stop it!" says Melinda. "Jesus Christ, you're terrifying her. Hey. Can you hear me?"

I let my eyes crack open. The light against my closed eyelids is harsh enough, but opening them is agony. Still, I force myself to take in the scene. The two men standing back, Melinda creeping forward but still keeping her distance. As if I might bite.

Maybe I will.

"Do you think there's something wrong with her?" I can't tell which of them is speaking. The sound seems to come from far away.

Melinda glares at them. "Of course there's something fucking wrong with her, Liam, she's locked in a fucking bomb shelter."

"She's— How did she—" Liam begins. Melinda shushes him, turns back.

"What's your name?" she asks.

Panic courses through me. This is how it happens. The light opens, and the question comes. *What is your name?*

I answered with defiance at first. Then not at all. Both were met with a fist. I learned the right answer soon enough and it leaps to my lips now, but I force it back down like swallowing my own vomit, shake my head.

"Okay, that's okay," she says. Andrew steps forward, light falling across his face so that I can make out his features, and I nearly scream, because it's *him*, he's back, I was wrong, but at my half shriek, he flinches, blinks in baffled confusion, and I realize I'm mistaken. It's not him at all. Not the one at the top of the stairs. Not the fist, not the gentle hand that soothes.

Liam's voice is high and panicky. "Who is she? What is she doing down here?"

"She's— Terry must have—" Melinda begins. She rakes her hair back from her forehead.

"Melinda. Dad had the key," Andrew says quietly. "Terry's the one who told us—he said Dad kept some things in the old shelter. Why would he have said that if she was here? But that would mean . . ."

"Oh god. How long has she been . . . ?" Liam says. His eyes go to the spent packets of food, the empty water bottles. "What do we do?"

"We call 9-1-1, obviously," Andrew snaps. He pulls a phone out of his pocket, flips it open. "Shit. No signal."

He turns toward the stairs.

"Wait," Melinda says, and the world halts in sudden, terrible stillness. Her breath is quick and shallow, almost panting.

Andrew doesn't move. The phone sits in his hand, his thumb hovering over the buttons.

"Melinda?" Liam says, voice shaky. She looks at him. Looks at me again. Swallows.

I make myself small. My hair hangs in front of my face in stringy clumps. The light still burns my eyes, but it's becoming clearer now. Melinda, Andrew, Liam. It's strange seeing them here, in front of me. Like characters out of a play suddenly stepping off the stage.

"What do you mean, 'wait'?" Liam asks.

"No. I—I didn't—I just want to think about this," Melinda says, hands moving in helpless spasms.

My stomach twists painfully. Something isn't right.

"What is there to think about?" Liam asks. Andrew's eyes cut over to me. He lowers the phone.

"We need to think about what happens when we make that call," Melinda says. She swallows. "Look at this place. Look at her. Dad did this."

"What are you saying?" Liam asks.

Andrew stares at Melinda. His mouth presses into a thin line. "She's saying that once we call the police, people will know Dad was, what, a kidnapper? A serial killer? You don't keep a girl locked in a fucking bunker to play Monopoly."

Melinda wets her lips, doesn't speak. Andrew looks almost calm.

"She's *saying* that when this gets out, people aren't going to 'vote for Hill.'"

Melinda hisses between her teeth. "Don't act like I'm the only one. What do you think this is going to do to *your* career? And Liam? *City Rescue*'s been lagging in the numbers, but I bet killing off Kyle in time for May sweeps would boost them."

"What are you suggesting? That we kill her?" Andrew asks, dropping his voice to an angry whisper at the end.

"No! I don't know. Just—I just want us to think this through," Melinda says, making a slight retreat.

"This is fucked," Liam says, but he hasn't moved. Hasn't objected.

Melinda covers her face with her hand. "We'll get her help. Obviously. I just— We need a plan, that's all. A moment to *think*."

"Is it? Obvious, I mean?" Andrew says quietly.

Melinda's eyes swim with uncertainty. My breath stills. I can barely feel my heartbeat now. Maybe I'm already dead. But that would mean the gossamer girl was wrong, because I still hurt. Every part of me.

There's a sound. Soft and whimpering, an exhalation threaded with a single syllable of distress. The three siblings shift, turn, their movement parting them so I can see the young woman standing at the bottom of the stairs, her hands pressed over her mouth.

The girl with red-gold hair, freckles over her bare shoulders. For a moment, I think she's one of them—one of my ghosts.

"Emily," Andrew says. *Emily*. She looks like us. The girls below. She has her father's eyes, sharp and bright in that pretty face, but otherwise—

Otherwise, we could be sisters.

27

After

Dev all but drags me out of the bunker and back up the stairs. I can't hear what he's saying over the rushing sound in my ears. We close the door behind us, and the hinges make a plaintive sound.

I don't speak again until I'm in the car, doors locked and Barry in the back seat with his hair still bristling. Dev looks over at me, expression haggard. "Talk to me," he says.

I stare out at the dark road. "There were names."

"I saw."

"There were a lot of them." My voice is a croak. My thoughts wheel, spinning through the implications of what we found. There wasn't just one girl down there.

"Audrey. Those marks were old," Dev says.

It takes me a moment to piece together what he means, and I nod. Who knows how many girls were down there, but none of them was Meghan Vale. *My name is Stranger.* Those words, too, were worn, faded by years. Meghan didn't write them; she found them and wove their echo into her poem.

"We need to report this," Dev tells me. "We should call the police."

"Not yet," I say.

"Audrey, we—"

"I mean, yes. But carefully," I say. "Let's be smart about this. I know where to go." I start up the car before he can voice an objection, and pull away. I watch for headlights in the rearview until we're back on the main road, and even then I don't relax.

Red handprints. A woman with hands drenched in red. Meghan saw something, all right. More than she should have, maybe. And Emily knew—she had to. She knew what Meghan had found and she knew it was there in the first place.

I shut my eyes. The door opening, shutting, the hinges—that's the sound I heard, the day of the search. Not a child's cry of fear but the wail of metal on metal.

Emily was conveniently on hand to save us. She said it was because she followed Bill into the woods, but what if it was the other way around? She could have gone to a hidden place that Bill didn't know about, and he followed her, thinking there was an intruder on his land.

Could she have something to do with what happened there? With the names carved in that plank of wood, a desperate cry through time?

"They're dead," I say softly. At first, I don't think Dev heard me over the sound of the engine, and then he lets out a breath, kneading the skin under his eyes with his fingertips.

"They have to be, don't they?" he says. I nod. The chain, the bed, the words—they tell a very specific story, and it's not one that has a happy ending. "How old do you think that stuff was?"

"I don't know." But, oh, the answer changes everything, doesn't it? Fifty years or five—it changes who was here. And who had the strength, the viciousness, the hatred to put them there.

I drive into town. Dev doesn't ask where I'm going. I don't have the coherent thoughts to explain, and when I stop, Dev follows my lead, getting out without questioning me. I tell Barry to stay. He fogs the glass, watching us.

I walk up the steps of the house and I ring the doorbell, wait. Hammer out a knock. Finally lights go on, and Len peers bleary-eyed through the window by the door. He yanks it open, forgetting about the chain, fumbles it off.

"Audrey. What's wrong?" he asks, looking between Dev's ashen face and mine.

"Can we come in?" I ask, my voice steady but thin. "We need to talk."

While Len listens to our recounting of the night's events and stares at the photos on my phone, Kenny brews coffee. Both because we need it and because he needs an excuse to eavesdrop.

When we've explained everything, Len takes a deep breath. I brace for him to berate me, but he only lets it out. "Okay," he says. His gaze is fixed on the phone in his hand. "Okay. We'll . . . I'll talk to Chief Wagner first thing in the morning."

"In the morning? Can this wait?" Dev asks.

"If you want Wagner to listen, it'll have to," Len replies. "Look. This bunker is years old. No one knows you found it, right? So a few hours aren't going to make a difference."

"Meghan—" I begin, but I stop. There's no evidence that Meghan has been there recently. Whatever happened to her happened months ago, and she's not in that bunker now. Len is right. It's better to take this slow and do it right.

"Meet me at the station at nine thirty," Len says. "He'll be past his morning coffee by then. When you get there, follow my lead. The less you talk, the better. Go with the hiking story. You went for an evening hike, Barry got away. Don't mention breaking the lock, okay? It was like that when you found it."

"Are you . . . Can you lie like that?" Dev asks.

"Getting you in trouble doesn't change what you found, it just makes a bigger headache out of it," Len says. He doesn't sound happy. The hinge of his jaw is flared, his eyes dark. Kenny sets a cup of coffee down in front of him, and he takes it but doesn't drink. "This is bad," he says.

"I know," I reply. This is so much worse than I imagined.

"You two should get home," Len says. "Get some sleep. Make yourselves presentable. And don't tell anyone else about this." He hands my phone to me.

"We won't," I promise. I take Dev's hand as I rise from the table.

Kenny walks us to the door. Len stays sitting, gaze overshooting the table and fixed on nothing at all. Probably trying to think of what to say to his boss. How to make this all work out so we don't end up sitting in a jail cell.

Kenny murmurs a goodbye, his attention already drifting back toward his husband. Dev and I stagger back to the car. Barry wags his tail and shifts his weight rapidly from paw to paw in the back seat, whimpering with relief at our return. I bat away his attempts to snuffle the side of my face, scratch his neck, and start up the car.

"Can I take you home?" I ask Dev.

He rubs his palms against his knees, hunched forward slightly. He looks over at me, his expression bleak. "You know," he says, "I don't think I want to go home to an empty apartment right now."

Our eyes meet. Understanding passing between us—a decision—an agreement. I don't say another word as I back out of the drive.

We don't say anything when I park at my house, either. Nor when the door locks behind us, and I shed my coat, help him with his—and then his hands are on my neck, my cheek, his lips against mine. There's a desperation to it, and a relief—the release of feeling something other than fear and uncertainty, because this? This is sure, and safe, and wanted, and a bright good thing that the night can't touch.

We leave a trail of clothing all the way to the bedroom, and I have the momentary regret that I didn't think to tidy up before committing misdemeanors with a handsome man, but he doesn't seem to mind.

I'm down to my bra and jeans, Dev shirtless. I sit on the edge of the bed, and he stands between my parted knees, his hand trailing down my shoulder as he watches me, as I watch him. "Are you . . ." he says.

Am I sure. Do I want this. Is this a good idea. Questions we should ask and think about and answer carefully, but I'm past careful. Tonight is a night to be reckless.

"Yes," I say, and draw him toward me.

We are alive and not alone, and that's all I need in this moment, but that's not all there is—because there is also the scent of him, the sheen of sweat and the woods; there's the quiet strength of his hands and the revelation of his body and the way he whispers my name like it's beautiful, as beautiful as he is, and there is the way for a moment I have no name at all and the edges of me blur into his, and how, when we fall apart at last, it takes a slow moment for the boundaries of my being to return.

"Don't go," I tell him, threading my fingers with his in the dark.

"I won't," he promises. He kisses my bare shoulder, his breath warm against my chilled skin.

I don't make the same promise. I can't.

But for tonight, I can pretend.

28

Before

The door is open. I'm alive. At first, these are such strange and overwhelming thoughts that the words I can make out from above still provide no meaning at all. There's only the cruel light and the fear and promise it brings. And then there's the sensation like the whole world has tilted forty degrees to the left and my mind can't comprehend the new images it sees.

Get out get out get out, my mind has been screaming, the chorus that replaced the hundred more nuanced methods of survival: *Beg. Smile. Obey. Bide your time.*

They're still arguing. It's hard to tease apart their voices after so long hearing only the voices of the dead and the one who killed them. But now I'm picking them apart, stitching their names to their words.

I can't make out much of what they're saying, but it's enough. Now Andrew is the only one seriously arguing against calling the police, but all of them are reeling. All of them want the excuse to wait, to think, to wrap their minds around this sudden heaving shift in their reality.

To wrap their minds around me, just as I'm wrapping my mind around them.

I have spent the last—how long?—weeks and months clamping my jaw shut around any scrap of survival I could get my teeth into. I have been biddable and obedient, I have been sly, I have kept secrets, and I have bloodied my flesh against the cold confines of my prison. I can be many things, to stay alive. Now I need to be someone new to survive *them.*

The arguing hasn't flagged, but there's a new sound—the tentative scrape of a footstep on the stairs. A slim form creeps down, one step at a time, half hunched as if to make herself small. It's the younger girl. Emily. *Emmie.*

The one who looks like me.

"Hello?" she says. I shudder. The voices of ghosts don't so much as stir the air. I can feel the voice of this living girl like an impact on my skin.

I look up from where I sit against the wall, arms wrapped around my knees. She creeps forward, disgust and horror on her face. I wait and say nothing. I'm not sure I can speak at all.

"I brought you something," she says, so softly it's almost a whisper. She moves closer but stops a few feet away. Close enough that I could reach her without hitting the end of the chain. Even knowing that it's broken, it's hard to picture going farther than that.

I imagine the length of the thing looped around her neck, imagine calling her siblings down and offering a trade. But I'm too weak. Even this girl could overpower me.

I say nothing. She draws closer and takes something from her pocket. A granola bar in a foil wrapper.

I can't help myself. I lunge, snatching it from her hand. She lets out a muffled cry and stumbles back, nearly falling. I tear open the wrapper and cram the whole thing in my mouth, barely tasting it as I wolf it down in three bites.

"Careful," she says. "You'll make yourself sick. If you haven't eaten. You haven't, have you?" The look in her eyes is more curiosity than pity. She creeps closer. "I have another. But you can't eat it yet. You'll throw it up if you do."

My hands crab into claws. I force them to relax. She's right. Already my stomach is cramping. "Water," I say. It comes out a croak.

She considers, nods. "I'll bring some."

She looks so young. So beautiful, with those green eyes and pale skin. I have the urge to slice her open, see how easily that softness parts. I try not to imagine moth wings twitching in her eye sockets.

"How long have you been down here?" she asks.

My voice is a wreck, but I can speak. "What day is it?"

She blinks. "March thirteenth."

I try to do the math, but time is crumpled here. I can't smooth it out. "I think—it was before Christmas," I say. There were lights on the houses and the same five songs on the radio.

She nods slowly, like she, too, is running the numbers. Calculating the weight of that stretch of days and weeks, and imagining what might have filled them. "What's your name?"

I flinch. The words echo, again and again, a question and a demand and a trap. I can't answer her. Couldn't if I wanted to—I reach for the name, and in its place, I find a small, cold void, and a truer name within it.

"My name is Stranger," I say, and repeat it. It feels like a shield. I am not who I was. She couldn't survive this. I will.

"Stranger," she echoes, and if she thinks it's odd, she doesn't voice an objection. "My name is Emily."

I know that. But I nod, as if it's new information. "What are you going to do?" I ask her.

She looks to the side. The light makes her hair glow like fire. "Everyone's freaked out," she says, as if it's an answer to my question. "I mean. You understand, right? All of this—it's so awful. They don't understand how he could do it."

I stare at her, the cavity of my chest empty of any sensation. My heart must be beating because I'm still alive, but I don't feel it, or the breath stretching my ribs. *They don't understand.* But she does. There is no shock in her expression.

"Where is he?" I ask.

She looks startled. "You don't know? Of course, how could you know? He died. That's why we're here. We came home to clear out the house. There was a key we couldn't match to a lock, and Terry told us—he said he'd been letting Dad use this place for storage. Andrew thought there might be—I don't know. Something we needed to deal with."

Her shoulders rise, a convulsive shrug. If she keeps biting that lip, she's going to bloody it.

"How?" I ask, the word like the scrape of rocks.

"Heart attack. We think," she says. "The coroner said probably a heart attack, but it had been so long . . ." She swallows.

So that was why he stopped coming. He was dead. Decaying up there while I rotted down here.

"The door didn't open," I say. Confusion sketches faint lines on her face. "Sometimes it didn't. No light for a while. A few days. Hard to say. But it always came back. The light." Not the light. *Him. He* always came back. He's transforming. Becoming a person again, now that he's dead, and there's a danger in that because there are so many things that happened in the light that I can't think about, can't contain.

Mason Hill. A man, just a man, a man whose daughter looks so much like me, my echo-twin, but her skin is unbroken, her eyes bright and accustomed to the light.

"Did he hurt you?" she asks, as if there could be any answer but one.

I turn my face away. Dig my hands into my hair, nails against my scalp, and a sound comes out of me like a shriek.

"I'm sorry, I'm sorry," Emily says hurriedly. She draws forward, hand outreached, but she doesn't want to touch me. "Please stop, I'm sorry—*stop*." She hisses the last word, eyes wide as if in a panic, as footsteps descend rapidly.

"What the hell?" Andrew's at the bottom of the stairs. He strides forward and I think he's coming for me, but he grabs his sister by the shoulders and drags her back. He stands there, half shielding her, and looks over his shoulder at me. I hunch against the ground. I must look like an animal, a filthy beast.

Melinda is here, too. Liam stands three steps up the staircase, spine curved like a question mark. Melinda gathers Emily to her, back toward the far wall. Andrew remains. He straightens. Clears his throat. "Listen," he says. "We're not going to hurt you, but we need to figure out what to do. The person who did this is dead, so. No need to cause any more damage, right? Stay here for now. We'll bring you something to eat."

"This is fucked up," Liam mutters. No one responds.

"Don't," I say, but the sound is nothing but the whisper of insect wings.

Andrew turns. The others start up the stairs.

"Don't," I say again, and now the word is louder, but they keep going. My whole body is shaking, a juddering that reaches into the deepest part of me, and there is a horrible howling in my ears. They're up the stairs, they're leaving, and I cry out, and at last my body responds to my mind and I surge after them—

Don't leave don't the light don't I can't don't leave me in the dark—

My foot catches the loose length of chain. I sprawl, barely catching myself on my hands, and for an instant, I think they've stopped, that they've turned back, but there's only a pause, space enough for guilt to be felt and to be set aside. And then the door clangs shut.

I am in the dark once again.

29

After

By the time the sun is nudging against the horizon, I've been up for a couple hours. With Barry warming my feet, I hunch over my laptop, plugging in search terms. The notepad next to me is filled with half-legible scrawl.

Dev pads out of the back bedroom, wearing his boxers and undershirt and looking rumpled in a way that would normally be impossible to ignore. This morning, I barely glance at him. He leans over me, hand on the back of my chair. "You're looking for them," he says.

The names. They have to belong to someone, but without a sense of what time range I'm looking at, it's been hard. Still, a pattern has begun to emerge.

"I've found three that might match," I say. "Right name. Right general region. They all went missing in the same stretch of a few years." I show him. Amanda Dennis. Madison Sebold. Isabel Whipple.

"They're pretty common names," Dev says. "It might not be them."

"Right. But look at the pictures," I say, pulling up the photographs of the three girls, and he sucks in a little breath.

Three girls. All of them in their late teens or early twenties, all of them with pale skin and delicate noses. Isabel's hair is a deep strawberry blond, Amanda's auburn, Madison's pure ginger. They look like they could be sisters.

They look like Janie, I think, but I don't say it, and I won't. Because this is undeniable, objective. The moment I speak her name, though, I know how people will look at me. With pity. They won't hear reason; they'll only hear grief.

"Those dates," Dev says. "Andrew Hill would have been in his twenties, right?"

I nod. Old enough, Dev means, that he might have something to do with the disappearance of these girls. "Back then he was gone most of the year," I say. "The life of a pro football player isn't exactly conducive to keeping girls in a bunker."

"Then who?" Dev asks. "That guy who owns the land now?"

"Mason Hill was still alive then," I say. Wasn't he? I try to remember when he died, exactly, but it wasn't like it was particularly relevant news to me. I only remember that it happened sometime after Janie came to the house that last time.

Not long after, though. Was it?

"The father," Dev says. His grip on the back of the chair is tight. "That would be simplest, I suppose."

"Simplest?" I echo.

Dev slides over to sit in the chair next to me. "If the bad guy's dead already, I mean."

"Except that there's no one to confess," I say. "To give us the names. Tell us where they are."

Or what happened to them, before they died. Though maybe that much is a mercy. Knowing their suffering won't lessen it, and my imagination fills in the gaps readily as it is.

"We should eat," Dev says.

"Right, of course," I say, closing the laptop and getting up. "Let me see what I can rustle up."

"You sit," Dev says, gently pushing me back down. "I'll cook."

"After committing crimes with me last night? I think I owe you breakfast," I say.

"It wasn't the only thing we did," Dev reminds me. "And I'm a very, very good cook. This is part of me making sure you don't only keep me around for my criminal expertise." He opens the fridge. I brace myself, but I actually went grocery shopping this week, so it's not too embarrassing. Apart from the great wall of takeout in the back that I've been meaning to clear out. Dev plucks out eggs, cheese, various odds and ends. A few minutes later, he's humming while the smell of sautéing onions fills the small kitchen, and I might be in love. The way his shoulders fill out his white T-shirt don't hurt, either.

"Do you think they knew that was there?" Dev asks.

"The Hills?" I ask. "Emily did."

"How can you be sure?"

"Meghan saw a woman with red hands," I say. "Those red prints on the wall—Emily must have put them there."

"Which suggests?" Dev prompts. He pushes a mushroom, spinach, and sausage scramble onto two plates as he talks.

"Which suggests that she didn't just know about the bunker. She knew what happened there," I say.

"If you found out your father had done something like that, would you report it? If he was already dead?" Dev asks.

I don't like how quickly we're settling into this story. Mason Hill—someone no one in the town particularly knew, someone long dead—as the monster in the woods. Nothing to be done but shake our heads over it. No one to be punished, no one to be blamed who's still drawing breath. It gives me a bad feeling: the creeping sense that someone is going to get away with something. That they already have.

"Audrey?" Dev says. "What are you thinking?"

I take a bite of the food. The flavor bursts into my mouth with the first bite, exquisite, but I can't enjoy it. I have to force myself to swallow it down. "I just have a bad feeling about what happens next," I say.

"Whatever happens, our part of it is done," Dev says earnestly. "It's up to the police now."

"Right," I say, nodding. It's out of my hands.

I wish that thought held some comfort.

Len meets us in the lobby. He doesn't look like he got any sleep last night. "At least you're on time," he notes. He looks over at Dev, taking in the fact that he's wearing the same clothes he was last night. Thankfully, he decides not to comment.

"I did some research," I say. I hold out a folded sheet of paper—notes I made before we came over this morning. "I think I might have found some of the . . . the names." I don't know what to call them. *Girls, women, victims?* They still exist in a strange half-world, guessed at, not quite real.

"Me too," Len says. "I found four that fit."

"More than me."

"I have better resources." He looks at the list. "Yeah. I saw these ones."

"They look alike."

He nods. And in his eyes, I see that he knows the rest—the ghost who would stand among them and not look out of place. But he doesn't say her name, and neither do I.

I've wanted to find her for so long, but not like this. Not in that place. I wanted a life for her—or, if not, a gentler end. There was no gentleness in that shattered room. No mercy except the final mercy.

"Wagner's waiting," Len says. "Just let me do the talking."

I don't mind that at all. Chief Wagner is a man who reminds me uncomfortably of my father, minus a bit of hair and plus a few years. He's barrel-chested, with thick knuckles and a habit of rapping them against the table to punctuate his sentences. Like my father, he always looks vaguely disappointed when he's talking to me.

The three of us file into the room where Wagner is waiting. Dev and I hover in the back while Len steps forward, clearing his throat.

"You know Audrey Dixon, and this is Dev Khanna. He teaches at the high school," Len says. "They found something alarming yesterday, and I thought I should bring it to you immediately."

He's printed out the photos I took. He has them tucked into a manila file folder, looking almost official. He slides them across Wagner's desk. Wagner traps them under blunt fingertips and drags them in, looking down without comprehension.

"Audrey's—Ms. Dixon's—dog is trained in search and rescue," Len says. "While they were walking the trails in the preserve, the dog broke loose. He alerted—responded to a scent. When they investigated, they found this."

"What is this, some kind of art project?" Wagner says, looking at the photograph of the handprints.

"It's a bunker," I say. Len shoots me a look, but I step forward. "It looks like it was built as a bomb shelter or something. Barry—my dog—he alerted to the presence of human remains there, and one other spot in the woods nearby. And it looks to me like there was someone being held down there. The chain and—"

Wagner grunts, cutting me off. He looks through the photos again. "Where is this?"

"South of the preserve," Len says. Wagner fixes him with a hard look. Len swallows. "It's on Terry Butler's land."

Something passes over his expression, and my stomach sinks. "Right next to the Hills' land, then."

"I believe that's correct," Len says. He straightens up. "I'd like to get a warrant to search this bunker, and get some official cadaver dogs out there. I've already matched several of the names to potential missing person reports. Cold cases from over a decade ago. I think—"

"I think you need to slow down," Wagner says. He folds his hands on the table and looks at the three of us. His gaze lands on Dev. "What was your name again?"

"Uh, Dev? Dev Khanna. I teach social studies at Franklin High," Dev says, plainly nervous.

"And what were you doing trespassing on private property last night, Mr. Khanna?"

"Like he said, the dog . . ." Dev trails off, gesturing futilely at Len.

"It was my fault," I say. "I've been neglecting his training a bit. He saw a squirrel and took off, and by the time we caught up with him, we didn't even realize we were on private land."

"If he's so poorly trained, what makes you think he smelled anything at all?" Wagner asks.

I want to snap at him, but I catch Len's expression out of the corner of my eye and I glue my teeth together until the urge passes. "He's a reliable tracker. Just doesn't have focus. He wouldn't alert if he didn't smell something."

"According to you." Wagner sits back in his chair. "All I see here is some graffiti and somebody's idea of a joke. We've got this shit coming out our ears. There's this damn story, you see. The witch in the woods. It's mostly the girls that cause problems." He's talking to Dev, as if to inform him.

"Jenny Red-Hands," Dev says. "I'm familiar."

"Every few weeks, we get a call about a cult or Satanists or a ritualistic murder, and it's just paint and Spirit Halloween props," Wagner says. "And half the time they've painted 'Jenny Red-Hands' on the wall, like if she was real, she'd sign her name. And do it with spray paint."

"This isn't that," I say.

"It's not against the law to have a bomb shelter," Wagner says.

"The names—"

"I've got a niece named Madison," Wagner says. "Best friend's name is Isabel, and there's three more in their class. I'm not saying girls didn't carve their names down there, but there's nothing to suggest there's anything nefarious. And you *were* trespassing."

"Accidentally," Len says.

"And the Hills are a good family," Wagner goes on, as if he didn't hear him.

"The land doesn't belong to them," I say.

"No, but they've lived in those woods for decades. Which means they'd no doubt be dragged into this sorry business, and for what?" Wagner asks. "Andrew Hill is a good man. And Melinda—don't much like her politics, but you can't deny what she's done for this town. I'm not going to drag them through the mud because of, well, whatever the hell this is." He gestures dismissively at the file.

"It's not even their land," I say. "Look at these girls." I lean over the desk, jabbing my finger at the files Len has printed. "Look at them. They look alike."

"I don't see it," Wagner says. He narrows his eyes at me. "You realize I could charge you for trespassing."

"Please, just go out there," I say. "I work with Paul Matsuda. He has dogs—trained dogs, the best in the state. If there's a body out there, they'll find it."

"Len, escort Mr. Khanna and your friend out, will you?" Wagner says.

"Please just—" I begin, but Len puts a hand on my shoulder.

"Audrey. Come on."

One look at him, and I can see he doesn't think we're going to get anywhere. My instinct is to keep shouting until something gives, but that's why I trust Len to rein me in with these things. He's the sensible one. And then there's Dev. He looks angry, and about ready to puke from nerves. I'm guessing he's never had a brush with law enforcement.

I turn on my heel and stride out, letting the guys scramble to catch up. I don't stop until I reach the lobby, well out of sight of Wagner's office. There I whirl again, arms crossed, and glare down Len.

"I know," he says before I can lay into him. "But that's about what I expected."

"Then why bother?" I ask.

"So that we can say that we tried, and that I didn't hide this from him," Len says, dropping his voice. He puts a hand on my shoulder, squeezes it. "There is something here, we all know that. I'm going to ask around. See who I know who might be able to go over Wagner's head."

"State police?" I ask. He nods. I swipe a hand over my face. It's sensible, which means I hate it. "And if that doesn't work?"

"I'll figure it out," Len says, and I note the pronoun. He doesn't want me involved any more than I already am. And I'm not going to convince him otherwise.

"Okay," I say, deflating. "Do your thing, then."

Len looks relieved. And a touch suspicious. I'm giving in too easily, but what can he do?

"I should get you home," I tell Dev.

"Before I start to smell," he agrees. Then, with a grimace, "Smell any worse, I mean."

I nod a farewell to Len and turn to go. "Audrey?" he says. "Don't do anything stupid."

"Too late for that," I point out. He doesn't look amused.

"Don't escalate the stupid," he says.

"Cross my heart." We both know I'm lying, but he lets me go. Outside, the sun hits me like a needle to the eye. I rub the back of my neck and think, for the hundredth time, that I really should start doing yoga or something for all this tension.

"I'm sorry," Dev says.

I look at him in surprise. "For what?"

"I was completely useless in there," he says. "I think of myself as a pretty competent person, not to brag, but apparently, stick me in a room with an officer of the law and all my rational thoughts are drowned out by a radio play of my mother on the phone when she finds out I got myself arrested. I'm going to have to turn in my bad-boy card."

"Where did you get a bad-boy card?" I tease him.

"It was in the pocket of a coat I bought at a thrift shop," he says, and I laugh. I loop my hand through his elbow, tugging him toward the car. He seems surprised by the casual contact, and all of a sudden, I am, too.

All my relationships have been tumultuous in some way. Dramatic. Dev is just comfortable—not in a boring way, which is what I've always assumed "healthy" relationships must be. But this—I could get used to this.

I drop him off at his apartment building, our farewell stumbling in its particulars because neither of us is sure if we should hug or kiss or wave awkwardly. Dev settles for a kiss on the cheek, which seems regressive, given last night's activities, but correct at the same time.

I pull into my drive with a gnawing feeling in my gut. I told Len I was done, but I'm the furthest thing from it. That hum has become as real as my own heartbeat. Whether I'm looking for a fresh body or old bones or a living girl, my job's not yet finished, and every nerve in me knows it.

I'm fumbling my keys from my pocket when footsteps sound behind me, bringing me around in an alarmed rush. Andrew Hill strides up my driveway, a storm behind his eyes.

"Andrew," I say, stumbling back. I'm two feet from the door. Inside, I hear the *whump* of Barry getting down off the bed he's definitely not supposed to be sleeping on.

Andrew stops a little too close for comfort, just far enough for plausible deniability. He's got nearly a foot of height on me, and years out from his athletic career, he might have softened around the edges, but he's still got muscle packed onto that frame.

"You were on my land," he says without preamble.

"I don't know what you're talking about."

"Wagner called." Of course he did, the bastard. "He said you were trespassing. Making up wild stories."

"I didn't make up anything. And I wasn't on your land," I snap. "You don't own it."

"Technically, I do, actually," he says. "Terry wouldn't sell, but he couldn't turn the money down, so we made a deal. It's ours when he dies."

"But he—" I start.

"Died last night," he says. I can't even summon up a reaction. Andrew's tone is entirely factual. "The rest is a matter of paperwork. So this is my business and my problem. What do you think you're doing, exactly?"

"Did you know what was out there?" I ask him, searching his face. He wouldn't be so angry unless he knew something.

He keeps his gaze steady. "What exactly am I supposed to have known?"

Barry's at the door. I glance behind me, see his huge blocky head, his breath fogging up the glass beside the window. He's tense, but he's not growling yet.

"Did you know about the bunker?"

He stares at me a moment, and then wets his lips with a little dart of his tongue. "Butler's father built that thing in the '40s. The paranoia runs in the family. We used to play down there, before Terry chased us off. We called it the fort. There's nothing sinister about it. Just the project of a paranoid man. One who's been dead for half a century."

"Something happened in that place," I say. I can't tell what he knows. I've never been one of those people who can sight a lie on someone's face in an instant. Angry is just angry to me, and he's got plenty of reasons for his anger that have nothing to do with the truth of the bunker.

"I'd bet no one's been in there for decades," he says, shaking his head. "Unless some kids found it or something, but most of them know not to mess with Terry's land."

"Not even Emily?" I ask. His brows draw together, his frown deepening.

"Don't bring Emily into this," he says. "She's not—this is the last thing she needs."

"She's been going down there. Did you know that?"

"Even if she was, it's none of your business. None of this is," he says, stepping forward, and now Barry gives a low warning bark. It's about half volume for him, which means it rattles the windows. Andrew's eyes track past me to the dog. His fist, clenched at his side, relaxes, and the corner of his mouth twitches up in an almost-smile. "He's protective, isn't he?" he says mildly.

"That's why I got him," I say tightly. "He's a good guard dog."

"Best security system there is," he says. "I bet you feel really safe, with a beast like that." There's something in his tone I don't like. The quietest hint of mocking, as if to say, *But you shouldn't.*

"I'm going to find out what happened to those girls," I say.

"What girls?" he asks. "It's just an empty room, Audrey. And it always has been." He starts to turn away.

"They looked like Janie," I say. He stops, but doesn't turn to face me. "Did you see her, Andrew? When she came back, did she come to see you?"

"I barely knew Janie," he says, looking over his shoulder. "The last time I saw her, she threw a book at my head and told me to drown myself in a ditch. You know what I thought when she left town? Good riddance. And that's the last time I thought about her at all."

"We both know that's not true," I snap. "That night at the bar, you didn't act like someone who barely knew her and didn't care."

"I was drunk," he says dismissively.

"She came back to Franklin, you know," I say. "Just once."

"Well, she didn't bother to tell me," Andrew replies. "That girl was a psycho. I never saw her again and she doesn't have anything to do with this. Now, I'd appreciate it if you left my family alone."

He walks swiftly down to the street, getting into a car I hadn't noticed parked out front. Only then do I realize there's someone in the passenger seat. Emily. She's been there the whole time, watching our exchange. She stares at me with wide eyes as they pull away.

Janie isn't the only one who could fit right in with Isabel and Madison. A shiver goes down my back. It isn't a coincidence; it can't be.

A sick sense of dread curdles in my stomach. "What happened to you?" I whisper, watching the car turn out of sight at the end of the street. Then another thought comes, from a deeper recess of my mind.

What did you do?

30

Before

In the early days, after my initial panic receded but before this started to feel normal, I would count to try to keep track of the passage of time. One to one thousand, and then I'd place an almond on the ground as a marker. Any way to record the passage of hours and days. It didn't last long, but now I find myself counting again.

Seven hundred and sixty-three. Seven hundred and sixty-four. It's not just about knowing how long it's been. Even the voice in my head is better than the silence. I thought I was used to it, but I was wrong, because the gossamer girls have been here for so long.

They're gone now. They've abandoned me. Perhaps they escaped when the door opened, or maybe they simply lacked the substance to survive the onslaught of the light. They've always come back before.

It's different now. He's dead. Gone, truly gone, and I hope it hurt, but I think it didn't. At least not for long. A few gasping minutes at most. I hope it felt like drowning.

There should be more relief in the fact of his death than this. There should be more safety. But whatever Andrew said, whatever his promises not to hurt me, he's crossed a line. They all have. And they know it, even if they haven't said it out loud yet. If they had called for help right away, or even after the first few minutes, it would have been simple. Any initial reaction they had would have been put down to shock, if it even was mentioned at all. But now? They know that if I live, it will be known that they debated the alternative.

My survival would have damaged them before. Now it could destroy them. Unless I can convince them otherwise.

He talked about them a lot. My captor. *Mason Hill.* He told me all about them, his hopes, his disappointments, his thoughts on how they were lacking (and, oh, he found them lacking). Mason Hill locked me down here, but maybe, just maybe, he also gave me the key to my survival. Because it isn't this hole I need to escape now. It's *them.*

It's an hour before the door opens again. I shut my eyes as the light floods down but keep my face pointed toward it, letting my eyes adjust. The heavy tread tells me it's Andrew, and when I finally open my eyes a crack, I see that I'm right. This feels like a small victory. Maybe I'm just desperate for one.

He's brought a plastic grocery bag, from which he extracts a bottle of water and holds it out, wordless. I take it, but my fingers wrap around the cap without the strength to twist it. He makes a noise that might be irritation or simply surprise and crouches down to help me. I flinch, turn my head away on instinct, watching him out of the corner of my eye. He pauses, and a look flickers over his face almost like he's offended. He hands the opened water back and I hold it in trembling hands. I can't look him directly in the face.

He looks too much like his father. With the same anger in his eyes. I've complicated his life. I'm proof of his father's evil, and he would be happy if I disappeared entirely.

"Thank you," I whisper. Andrew sees me as a threat. I need to make myself small.

He grunts. "I brought you some food, too. Melinda says go slow. Melinda, that's my sister."

"I know," I say. It's the wrong thing to say; his gaze sharpens again, and his eyes narrow.

"We've been talking," he says.

"Are you going to let me go?" I ask.

"Of course," he says. He's still lying to himself. Still pretending that he isn't seriously considering an alternative. "But we want to do this in a way where everybody wins."

They're the words of a salesman or a politician—*We want a win-win, everybody goes home happy*—but there's no home for me here or anywhere else, and happy stopped being an available destination even before that door slammed shut. I've been on a road to ruin longer than Mason Hill's been my keeper, and maybe Andrew can see that.

I'm not the sort of girl who gets missed. I'm the sort of girl who people are relieved to see gone.

"It would be helpful if you told us your name," Andrew says.

"I told your sister."

"Stranger." He tilts his head. "That's not a name."

"It's what I have." I trace a circle on the floor, the tip of my finger damp with water. I keep my eyes downcast, my body bent inward. I am nothing. *No threat at all to you, Andrew Hill, and if you let me go, I'll vanish into the brush like a rabbit and it'll be the last you see of me.*

"How did you end up down here?" he asks. "I mean, how did he . . ."

"He offered me a ride," I say. I was easy prey. Stupid, trusting. Too drunk to stay smart, but that had been on purpose. I wanted to be stupid, because staying clever is so exhausting. Sometimes you just want to drop your hands and let the blows land because it's better than the constant ghost of anticipation.

"And then what?"

"Does it matter?"

"I want to know."

I wet my lips. "He pulled over. I knew something was wrong, but I was slow. He put his hands around my neck. I blacked out. He tied me up. Is that what you want to hear?"

"He brought you here."

My teeth grind together. They're loose in the sockets. My gums bleed easily these days. Lack of sunlight, the wrong kind of food—

whatever it is, it's stealing the things that hold my body together. I've started to decompose before I'm even dead.

"What do you want to hear?" I whisper.

"Everything."

"Why? Do you like it? Do you get off on hearing about girls getting hurt?" I snarl. It's a mistake.

"You think I'm some kind of pervert? You think because my father did those things, that I—I'm trying to understand. I need to know. I need to know what he *did* so I can . . ." He can't finish, because there's no reason, is there? He knows. He knows enough, at least. What happened is: the obvious. What happened is: of course he did, and I will not lay it out in grotesque detail for this man, who looks so much like his father, with the same divot in his chin and the same pale eyes and the same long-fingered hands.

Not for him and not for anyone. Inside me is a room like this one, and all those days I lock inside it, except what I need to keep. The words. The ways to stay alive. The things that man told me about his sons, about his daughters. He spoke in a language of sin and vice and failed virtue, and so I know their vanity and their cowardice and their compassion (weakness, he calls it, weakness) and their wrath.

I know you, Andrew Hill.

But he doesn't realize that. And I need to keep it that way. I need to keep *him* away from me, because he's the greatest threat to my survival, and I to his.

"I'm sorry," I say, simpering and weak. I curl against the wall. "I'm sorry. I just can't. Please don't make me."

He softens. Not much, but a little. I have a chance as long as he thinks I'm weak. "I shouldn't have asked. Maybe I don't want to know." His hand passes over his face. "None of this feels real." Because his is the reality that matters. "Dad was a bastard, but I can't believe he would do something like this." He's still hoping that somehow there's been a mistake. It was some other man, someone else's father. *You aren't stained after all, you won't carry this weight until you die, no.* "I don't know what to do."

His voice is raw and vulnerable, and I would almost believe it if I hadn't heard that voice before. Mason Hill used to weep. He used to say nearly those same words, as if it was some outside force compelling him. As if circumstances had simply created the situation we were in and he was powerless against them.

I don't know what to do.

In the beginning, it frightened me, and I would cram myself against the corner of the bed with the wall at my back, compressed as a pill bug. Then the sobbing would turn into rage. I learned better. The girls before had learned the lesson, too, and left me instructions, though it took me time to understand them.

I steel myself. Maybe there is kindness here I can't see. A chance. I reach out. I don't cover his hand with mine, but brush only the very edge of my fingertip against the side of his hand. He startles but doesn't pull away.

"This isn't your fault," I tell him, my voice like velvet. "You didn't do anything wrong. If you hadn't found me, I would have died down here."

He stays there a moment, perfectly still. His eyes search my face, and I brace myself, but he only frowns, looking almost puzzled. He stands. He towers over me, but I don't try to rise to match him, only look up from my position on the ground, on my knees.

"I'll be back soon," he says. He starts to turn, and I can't stop myself. I grab at his ankle. He pulls it away with an expression of distaste, and then guilt.

At least he has the humanity to feel bad for how much he despises me.

"Don't leave me in the dark," I croak.

His eyes flick around, taking in the lack of light sources for seemingly the first time.

"Shit," he mutters. He reaches into his pocket and pulls out a small penlight. "Here. I've just been using it to look around the basement and stuff. I'll bring something better later."

I take it from him with unfeigned gratitude and test it. It's far brighter than the failing flashlight that's been my only light source for weeks, and my eyes flood with tears as I twist it to turn it on and off and on again. "Thank you," I whisper. "Thank you." I cradle it in my hands as he looks down, uncomfortable.

"Right. You're welcome," he says, and then turns abruptly.

At the top of the stairs, he hesitates for a moment—just a moment. Then the door swings shut, a guillotine dropping to sever the rectangle of light that stretches almost to my feet. It clangs. A chain jangles. A lock clicks.

My body floods with relief. I bend over, brow nearly to the ground, my arms wrapped around my rib cage.

To Andrew, I'm a threat. I will always be a threat. The best I can hope for is to hide myself from him, to become so small he doesn't think I can hurt him. But the others—maybe there's still a chance.

A chance that I can convince each of them that I am exactly what they need me to be. And then I will be the only thing that matters—

Gone.

31

After

I've decided what to do before the door shuts behind me, but it's hours before I can put my plan into motion. Barry paces constantly, a whine at the back of his throat. He can tell something is wrong.

I prepare, and I wait until nightfall. At nearly midnight, still with no word from Len, I throw my gear in the back of my car and whistle for Barry.

I'm about to get in when headlights swamp me. A car has pulled onto the street, and my stomach tenses as it slows in front of my house. Parks.

My shoulders sag with relief when Dev gets out. He's wearing the same mud-streaked jacket he wore last night, a decidedly unrugged sweater underneath. He puts his hands in his pockets as I approach, looking slightly sheepish.

"Sorry to show up unannounced," he says.

"Why are you here, Dev?" I ask.

"Thing is." He scratches the end of his nose and looks off to the side. "I haven't known you that long. But I've got this gut feeling that you are absolutely planning on escalating the stupid."

"Really." I quirk an eyebrow at him. "And what do you think I'm going to do?"

"At a guess? You're going back out there," Dev says. "And you're not going to stop until you find something that Wagner and the police can't deny. Which means pretty much one thing, doesn't it?"

"What does it mean, Dev?" I ask softly, wanting him to say it.

"You're going to try to find a body," he says. "Barry alerted in that clearing. There's something there, and we both know it."

"So you came out here to stop me?" I ask.

"Actually, I came to offer my help," he says. "Because with two of us, it'll go twice as fast. Which means half the time for you to potentially get caught and sent to jail, which would definitely impact my third-date plans."

"Oh." I blink at him. "Seriously?"

"Brought a shovel and everything," he says, gesturing at his trunk. He smiles, though it's strained. "Let's go be criminals."

We pick a different entry point this time, just in case someone's looking out for us. The hike takes us in from the northeast, which means that at least we're not crossing the Hills' property. Though I suppose soon enough it'll all be theirs.

"You know, this is almost romantic," Dev quips as we walk. "The moonlight, the stroll through the woods, the overpowering sense of dread."

"I think your idea of romance might need recalibration."

"I remind you I was recently traumatized on that front." He dips his head. "Sorry. Bad jokes are the only coping mechanism I've developed that doesn't cause long-term health issues, so I've leaned into it."

"I don't mind." Except part of me does, I realize. Part of me knows, against all logic, that I'm meant to do this on my own. I'm drawing near to something, a place that has been calling to me and me alone. The place between the trees where all the lost are waiting—but that's a dream. There is no magic to this hum in the air; it's only my anticipation.

There will be no miracles to uncover tonight. Only bones, and only if we're lucky.

Barry finds the scent again then. He strains against the lead, but tonight I give him less ground. I need him close. I've already raised

Andrew Hill's suspicions. He might be out here, and I didn't like the way he looked at Barry.

Some men are only happy when they know they could hurt you, if they wanted to. They tell themselves, tell you, that they never would. But they want the option. And if you think you're safe, there's nothing they love more than stripping away that safety.

I know we've reached the spot before Barry's haunches hit the ground. He alerts softly, as if he knows we're trying for secrecy, and I praise him in a low tone, ruffling his ears.

"Let's hope it's not too deep," Dev says. *It.* We talk about the hole, the grave, the body, but we're both thinking one thing.

Let's hope she's *not too deep.*

I leash Barry to a nearby tree, and the two of us begin to dig.

It's hard work. At least the frost has loosened its grip. In winter, the frozen ground would be impossible to unlock without pickaxes or heavy machinery. As it is, the dirt is packed with rocks and pebbles, and our shovels are loud as they strike again and again.

We work a few feet apart from each other, just far enough that we don't get in each other's way. We dig a foot down and then widen out before going deeper. I haven't done this kind of body recovery—the remains we find are out in the open. People dead of exposure or natural causes, mostly.

My arms and back are starting to hurt before we get much farther down, and the ground is getting harder-packed. The only comfort I have is that if we're digging up a grave, someone else had to do this labor before us, and I doubt they were any more eager to go a full six feet deep.

Dev pauses, bracing himself on his shovel. He wipes sweat from his forehead. We've propped the flashlights nearby, leaving us strangely illuminated. I can see only the sliver of his cheek, but exhaustion radiates off him.

"We might not find anything," he says.

"I know."

"What are you going to do if we don't? We can't keep coming out here," he says.

"Len's got his contacts." Not that I put much faith in that.

"You don't let go of things, do you?" he asks.

I bend to dig, not answering him. He doesn't know about the list I keep in the back of my head. It's not long. Nearly all of our searches produce some kind of result, even if the ending isn't a happy one. But there are those few still waiting to be found, and I have never forgotten them. I have never stopped looking.

"These girls," I say, punctuating my words with the shovel striking dirt. "They look like my friend. The one who went missing."

"Janie."

"She wanted to be named January," I say. "She told me that was her name when we first met, and I called her that for ages before her dad overheard me and laughed at her. He said, 'She's just Janie. Just plain Janie.' She laughed at me, too. I thought for the longest time that she did it to fool me, and that she was making fun of me. But she wanted to be someone else. Someone with a name like January—a romantic name."

The look on her face when I turned to her with confusion and betrayal in my eyes—for a split second, that had been sadness. It twisted so quickly into contempt I hadn't even realized it until long after she was gone.

"She asked me to call her January one more time after that. I thought she was teasing me again." I throw aside another shovelful of dirt. "I don't know why I'm telling you this."

"You don't need a reason," he says.

"There are so many things I wanted to tell her. There are so many things I wanted to understand. And the one chance I had, I didn't even . . ."

I stop. There's a light in the distance. A flashlight, bobbing. I hiss through my teeth. "Damn it."

"We should go," Dev says urgently.

We can't. Not yet. I can't turn away again.

Oddity. Oddity, wake up.

It's like she's right behind me. I can hear her voice still. Hear the click of her fingernails against the glass. If only I'd turned around. She would have stayed. We would have talked. And maybe we would have fought again, and I would still be here with more than a decade between us, but she wouldn't have gone to meet whatever fate was waiting for her.

Why did you come back?

After so many years, why that night?

The flashlight is drawing closer. Barry's ears prick, and he growls faintly. "Shh," I tell him.

I turn back and keep digging, my movements frantic. Dev hesitates, then follows suit. We toss shallow shovelfuls of earth aside, barely denting the bottom of the hole. We're little more than two feet down.

"Audrey," Dev says warningly. It's time to go. Past time. But I can't stop. My shovel bites the dirt again and again and then—

Something pale shows at the bottom of the hole.

"Audrey, we need to *go*," Dev says, and grabs for my arm.

I drop to my knees, clawing away the hard dirt with both hands. The light bobs between the trees. Only yards away. It's too late to run now anyway.

A shape emerges. The curve of a brow, cracked by my shovel. Two empty orbits.

"Oh god," Dev breathes. Delicately I brush the dirt from that curving brow. *I'm sorry, I'm sorry,* I think, the pad of my finger against the crack I caused.

There's a figure at the edge of the clearing. The source of the approaching light: Emily Hill. She walks toward us slowly, drawing up to the edge of our excavation. She looks down, the beam of her flashlight pinned to the skull.

No one speaks. Barry stands silently at attention, at the limit of his leash. Slowly Emily crouches down, only inches from where I kneel.

"Who is this?" I ask her.

She looks at me, lips parted. I can't tell if she's about to answer, or merely confused at being asked.

A siren wails in the distance. She stands, stepping back from the hole. "Andrew called them. You should go," she says.

"I'm not going anywhere," I say.

"Okay," she says simply. She turns and walks away. I look at Dev, stunned, but he only shakes his head.

Together we wait for the police to arrive, kept company by a lost girl's bones.

32

Before

When Melinda arrives, she hesitates outside the door; a solid minute passes between when I hear the chain unlock and when the light floods down, but then she marches down the stairs at a determined gait. I'm sitting on the bed, cross-legged. I've had water and a bit of food. It's taken everything I have not to devour all of it, but I know they're right—I'll make myself ill, maybe dangerously so, if I indulge my hunger.

She stands at the bottom of the stairs and examines me. She's not a beautiful woman. Her features are too severe, the lines around her mouth aging her prematurely. She has the face of the sort of woman you want in charge of things, the kind who's never been given any slack because her smile was pretty.

"I brought you some light," she says. She unslings a backpack from her shoulder and strides over, setting it at the end of the bed. She takes out a camping lantern and puts it between us. "I think we have a couple more I can scrounge up, but they're in the storage shed somewhere."

"It's more than I've had for a long time," I say.

She nods. Her mouth is tight, the corners tucked in. Andrew stared; she seems to want to look at me only out of the corner of her eye. "I saw that you're hurt. I brought some medical supplies," she says stiffly. I make a puzzled noise and her head jerks up, her eyes meeting mine almost by accident. She seems transfixed for a moment, and then she gestures sharply to my ankle. It sticks out a little, an odd posture I've adopted unconsciously after so long with the chain as part of my everyday reality.

"Oh." The skin beneath the manacle at the end of the chain is raw. Sores have turned to scabs, scabs to scars, but others are open and weeping. "It's always like that."

"You're lucky it hasn't gotten infected," she says. She takes a closer look. "Any more infected. May I?"

I extend the leg. She sits at the edge of the bed and pulls out supplies—alcohol, wipes, bandages. She moves efficiently, shifting the chain out of the way so that she can dab the sores clean. I hiss in pain but keep my leg still. Melinda is a practical woman. She's focused. Which is a problem for me, because *I* am a problem.

It won't be enough to show her that there's a solution to this problem that lets me live. I need her to see that I'm a person, not just an issue in need of resolution.

"Do you think you could take the chain off?" I ask.

"I'm sure we can find some bolt cutters or something," she says. "Once . . ."

"Once you decide whether to let me go." At her silence, I stifle a hollow laugh. "What was it Andrew said? 'Vote for Hill'? Are you a politician?" I know she is, of course. I know so much about them.

"Trying to be," she says tightly.

"Are you going to be a senator, then?"

"Eventually," she answers without a trace of humility—or pride. It's just facts. "House first, though. The incumbent is a Republican, but the area's gotten a lot more blue lately. I've got a decent shot."

"But not if people find out about me," I say.

"It wouldn't exactly poll well," she says dryly. She secures the bandage around my ankle, giving it some extra padding to protect it from the manacle.

"I wouldn't have to tell anyone," I say. "You're saving my life. I wouldn't want to cause any trouble for you."

"How are you going to explain where you've been?" she asks.

I have to be careful now. Because the truth makes letting me go easier—but it also puts me in danger. "No one is looking for me," I say. It's a gamble. On the one hand, that means no one is around to question where the hell I've been, should I reappear. On the other hand, it means no one's going to cause problems if they decide to leave me down here for good.

"That can't be true," Melinda says. "Don't you have family? Parents?"

I draw my knees up to my chest. "Technically. But I took off years ago. They haven't wondered about me yet."

"Friends?"

"Not that kind," I say. Not the kind you keep. Who care where you've been when you vanish for months at a time. The only ones who might have, I drove away a long time ago. "If you let me go, I'll just . . . go. You'll never hear from me again."

She thinks about this as she gathers up her supplies, packing them meticulously back into her bag. "Andrew says Dad offered you a ride. Were you hitchhiking?" she asks.

"Does it matter?"

"It matters who might have seen you," she says.

I could lie. Tell her it was the middle of nowhere and no chance anyone could connect us. But I get the feeling that she's someone good at reading people. And then there's the fact that my brain is still half suffocated with hunger and exhaustion and the horrible sameness of months in this pit. I don't trust myself to keep track of a lie.

"I was staying at a shelter. I was stupid, showed up drunk. They turned me away. He was there, offered to take me to a motel."

"A shelter."

"Yeah. He volunteered there sometimes. That's why I thought I could trust him," I say. Stupid. "Hope's Hands."

She flinches, her whole body drawing back and her face contorting in something like disgust. "That's—I *run* Hope's Hands," Melinda says, stammering. "Andrew and Liam are on the board. He was—our *mother* started that place. Elizabeth Hill."

My mind is filled with terrible light.

Lizzie—

No. Leave the door shut. Leave that memory locked where it belongs.

She stands abruptly, grabbing the backpack. "I'll be back soon." The words are rushed. She won't meet my eyes. I've made a mistake. I shouldn't have told her.

A murderer for a father is one thing. But this? She's right. It would destroy them. It would destroy all of them, and so I'm a threat again.

She flees up the steps. At the last second, I come to my senses and lunge for the lamp, twisting the knob to turn it on just before the door slams shut. In its glow, I sit panting, the cold grasp of memory still like a hand gripping the back of my neck.

At the end of the bed, where Melinda perched a minute before, is the oil-slick shimmer of the gossamer girl. *It's not over yet,* she says. *But you have to get out of here. As long as you're in here, you're not real to them.*

I have to convince them to bring me up.

No.

I have to convince *one* of them. And I think I know which one.

33

After

Two hours later, Dev and I are enjoying the hospitality of the Franklin Police Department from the wrong side of its holding cell bars. At least we have the place to ourselves. No Sunday-night drunks to enliven our stay, though they've left some smells behind as a parting gift.

Dev sits on the floor, which might be slightly more comfortable than the metal bench I've chosen. He hasn't moved in a while, staring at nothing with his eyes unfocused. I saw between guilt and relief. They can't ignore this now. Surely they can't. They'll have to investigate, identify the body, actually look at the bunker. They'll have to question the Hills.

"That wasn't Meghan," Dev says suddenly. He looks over at me. "Right? It couldn't have been her."

"I don't think so," I say. "She's been gone a couple of months. Under the right conditions, a body can skeletonize that fast, but buried, in cool temperatures—I don't think so."

"One of the names, then," he says. "I keep thinking—someone's going to find out their daughter is dead. That's the ending of the story. Just someone's life imploding."

"It might be a relief," I say. "It's an answer, at least."

"Would it be for you? If it's Janie in that hole?" he asks. "Knowing everything that girl must have gone through, would you be *relieved?*"

"No." I swallow. He's right. It could be her. And if it is, all my fantasies of a life well lived out of sight are shattered—but they were false to begin with. I've never truly believed she could be alive.

She wasn't built to go unnoticed. Janie wanted to be known.

The door opens. Dev pushes himself to his feet, futilely smoothing the front of his shirt, which only succeeds in moving some of the dirt around. We look, and smell, exactly like we've spent the night digging up a grave.

To my surprise—and relief—it's Len who enters. He's not exactly happy with me. Last I saw him, he was loading Barry into the back of his squad car.

"Is Barry okay?" I ask.

Len gives me an *are you serious* look. "He's fine. Kenny's looking after him," he says. He rests his hands on his belt. "I can't believe you, Audrey."

"I just—"

"Don't," Dev says. I give him a questioning look. "Look, Len, you're a nice guy, I get that you're friends, but we're not saying anything without a lawyer."

"It's fine," I say.

Len rolls his eyes. "It's not fine, Audrey. Dev's right. Anything you tell me, I'm going to have to tell Wagner, and then it's going to be my fault you're in more trouble than you already are."

Echoing voices sound in the hallways behind him, and he glances over his shoulder. "Say. Nothing," he says in a low hiss, and then Wagner appears—Melinda Hill trailing him.

It's close to three in the morning, but Melinda looks as immaculate as ever, with her dark hair pulled back, her makeup understated and professional. She's gone for an upscale-casual look, a blazer over jeans. She's in full politician mode.

"Chief Wagner," Len says.

"Deputy Howard," he replies. "You know Ms. Hill."

"I don't think we've actually met," Len says, sticking out his hand. She takes it, smiling tightly.

"And these are the two who found it?" she says. We're avoiding specific nouns, I see. "You can release them."

"They're being charged with trespassing," Chief Wagner says.

She fixes him with a cold look. "They'd better not be."

Dev and I look at each other in surprise.

"Ma'am," Wagner begins.

She sighs. "Chief Wagner, Andrew and I have gone to a lot of trouble to buy that land. Now there's a *body* on it? We need to find out who it is and what happened to them, and we need to do it in the open. Which means *not* locking up the people who uncovered it."

"It's not your land yet," Wagner says.

"No. But Bill Butler is the executor of his brother's estate, and he'll tell you the same thing," she says with the kind of confidence that makes it clear she's made sure it's true.

Melinda and Wagner lock eyes. Wagner's jaw clenches. He doesn't want to be ordered around. And Melinda isn't an elected official, not anymore. It's not like she has real sway. But she's also got a reputation—one that says she's no one to be messed with. There's a reason she was reelected with a healthy margin in our barely blue district. She gets things done. With ruthless efficiency.

Wagner grumbles, but he pulls out his keys. Dev and I emerge, trying our best not to shamble. Looking respectable is a pipe dream, but we can at least stand up straight. Melinda eyes us, hand on her hip.

"Well. That's that," she says. "Chief Wagner, Deputy, could you give us a moment?"

Wagner clearly wants to object, but again, he decides it's not worth the fight. The guys slouch out, leaving us, dirt-spackled and bedraggled, squaring off against the former congressional shark.

"I want to make something clear," she says. "You won't have any more problems because of what you did tonight. But if you come near my family again, you are going to have a whole new set of problems. Do you understand?"

Dev mutters an affirmative, shoulders hunched. I meet her gaze. "You've always been good at cleaning up messes, haven't you?" I ask.

She doesn't dignify it with a response.

Take her home, I said that night she brought Janie to me. And Melinda looked at me, and I knew then that she'd figured out, like I had years ago, that *home* was far from a safe place for Janie.

You're her friend, aren't you? Melinda had asked. I hadn't been. Not for a long time. But I opened the door. Melinda knew how to get rid of a problem, all right.

"You knew what was out there," I say.

Her expression is unreadable, a practiced blank. "I don't make a habit of wandering around Butler's land. I certainly had no idea he had a skeleton out there," she says.

Terry's land. Terry's skeleton. And he's conveniently dead. The story has already written itself. "And Meghan Vale? She was there. She saw the bunker. What happened to her?" I ask, searching her face.

"I have no idea who that is," Melinda says. She crosses her arms. "Do yourself a favor. Back off. Let the police do their jobs."

"We'll do that," Dev says. He takes my arm. "Come on, let's get out of here." *Before they change their minds* goes unsaid.

I let him move me along. Melinda steps aside and watches us go. I can feel her gaze on me the whole way. Anger burns in my gut—senseless, without direction. I have no reason to be angry at Melinda Hill, not *really*. I can't be sure that she knew anything at all.

Yet she had to. They all did. They knew something was out there.

And the last person to stumble across it disappeared.

It's still dark outside when we finally leave the station. It seems like more time has passed, between the questioning and then the interminable waiting. On the sidewalk, we halt. My car is still sitting by the trail, as far as I know.

I rake my hair back, adjusting my ponytail. I desperately need a shower and a few hours of sleep, but for now, adrenaline is keeping me going. "Okay," I say. "I need to think."

"You need to slow down," Dev says. "It's over."

"It's not over," I say. "It's not even close to over."

"Your part is," he says. His face is creased with concern. "What more can you do, Audrey? Melinda's right. It's time to leave this to the professionals."

"I can't," I say.

Dev sighs. "We did something good tonight. Massively illegal but good, and we're lucky we might get away with not going to jail over it. It's time to take the win and let the police handle the rest."

"She's still out there," I say. My voice cracks.

Len is coming down the steps. "Hey. I'm off for the night, I can get you two home," he says.

"Thanks," Dev replies immediately.

"I'll walk," I say, voice tight. They give me identical looks of worry—Len's tinged with more than a bit of annoyance. "It's not far. I'll be fine."

"I am not letting you walk alone at three in the morning," Len says.

"It's Franklin," I say, rolling my eyes.

"And I just watched a body getting dug up, so let's not pretend nothing bad happens here," Len snaps. "Get in the damn car, Audrey."

He's not going to back down. And he's right. I'm being ridiculous. I nod, and we follow him like a couple of dogs that have been caught rolling in something unspeakable.

Dev takes the back seat. We don't talk on the drive to his apartment building, and when he gets out of the car, he only nods a farewell. When the door closes behind him, I rest my head on my hands.

"So. That thing about not screwing things up with the new relationship, how's that working out?" Len asks. The only humor in his voice is bitter all the way through.

"I shouldn't have dragged him into this."

"No shit," Len says. "I know you get obsessed, but this is absurd. You are damn lucky Melinda Hill is insisting that you don't face consequences."

"She's only doing that because it would make her look bad."

"And? A record would make you look pretty fucking bad, too," Len says. "You could lose your job. *Dev* could lose his job. Still might, actually, so if you could just not try to justify your shitty life choices for at least the rest of the night, I'd appreciate it."

He pulls away from the curb with too much gas, making the wheels squeal. I lean back against the seat, shutting my eyes.

"I know it was reckless."

His words grind out past clenched teeth. "I was doing what I could. You didn't even wait for me."

"It would have gotten back to the Hills. They would have gotten out ahead of it."

"You're acting like they're some shady crime family. As far as we know, they're completely innocent in all of this," he points out.

"Do you actually believe that?"

"It doesn't matter what I believe." His phone rings. He gives one-word answers to whoever's on the other end of the line, and when he hangs up, his face is tense.

"What is it?" I ask.

He pulls off onto my street. "They got cadaver dogs out there right after you left. They found another body."

"Old?" I ask.

He looks over at me. "It's not Meghan Vale. Just bones. They're both just bones."

"Len. You saw that list of names," I say. "It's not going to just be two of them."

"Yeah," he says quietly. He slows in front of my house. "I know you're not going to listen to me. But the state police are here, and at least one of those girls we found was from out of state, which means the FBI could get involved. This is going to be handled properly and it is going to be investigated thoroughly. You can stop. You really can stop."

I can hear the plea behind his words. He's right, of course. It's ridiculous to suppose that there's anything I could do that trained investigators can't.

I'm done. I need to let go.

Answers will come. But I won't be the one to find them.

"I'll stop," I say. This time, I mean it. Len can tell. Tension drains out of him. He reaches over, grabs my hand. He holds it tight, and I return the squeeze. "If it's her—Janie—"

"I'll tell you," he promises. "As soon as I know."

"Thank you," I whisper. If I say anything more, I'm going to burst into tears. I fumble with the door handle. Len leans over me to pop it open, and he doesn't move until I'm all the way inside the house with the dead bolt locked. I hold my hand up in a wave, and finally he pulls away.

I found one girl. The police will find the rest.

It will have to be enough.

34

Before

One by one, they've come, each of them waiting for their chance to peer and prod. One by one, and all of them have had their turn—except for Liam, and so I'm not surprised when he creeps down the stairs with an expression like an apology.

"Hello," he says, almost shyly. I saw his show, in that other life before this one, when I didn't yet know how badly I could be hurt. He plays a boy with a crooked smile and a wounded soul. The girls go wild for him. They love the idea of a man who's dangerous to everyone but them.

In real life, Liam is quiet. That swagger on the screen is as much a costume as the battered brown jacket.

"Hello," I say, soft and sweet and a little bit afraid. Andrew wants me to be afraid of him. Liam would say he doesn't want me afraid at all, but he'd be wrong.

He wants me scared so he can be the reason I'm not anymore.

I know his type. They're easy, for a little while. You let them rescue you, and it lasts right up until they figure out they can't fix things when what's broken is *you*. Then they've sliced their gentle fingers on your sharp edges and you try to tell them that you warned them, but that never stops them feeling betrayed.

I only need Liam for a little while, though.

Come closer, I think.

"My name's Liam," he says, like I don't know. "I'm not really supposed to be here, but I wanted to make sure—do you need anything?"

"Your brother brought me food and water. But eventually, I'm going to need a bucket," I say. He looks at me blankly, and I tip my head toward the toilet. He gets it then. His cheeks turn red.

"Oh. God, I'm sorry."

"Don't apologize. I'm the one that broke the toilet. I wasn't really expecting to live long enough for it to be a problem." I smile, careful not to show my teeth. They're not looking so hot these days.

"I'll see what I can do," he says. He rubs the back of his head. "I'm really, really sorry about all of this. We're not bad people."

"That might be more convincing if I wasn't locked in a bunker," I say, but I put the slightest hint of a laugh in it. The thing about a wounded bird is that it can't be so badly hurt you have to put it out of its misery. Just hurt enough that it can't fly away from you.

"I'm sorry," he says again. He draws closer. "They're just afraid."

"Are you?" I ask him. "You have a lot to lose, too."

"It doesn't matter. There are plenty of things where there isn't a right or wrong answer, but this isn't one of them."

"I don't think your siblings agree."

"It's just Andrew," he says, shaking his head. "And we've all got to make sure *Andrew's* happy. We have to make sure he feels *heard*. Melinda's freaked out, but she wouldn't—she's not a bad person."

I'm not so sure about that. "But Andrew is?"

He swallows. "Sometimes."

"Like your father?" It's a risky question. He looks away.

"If you'd asked me yesterday, I would have said they were a lot alike," he tells me. "But this . . ."

Andrew wouldn't kidnap women and keep them prisoner. He'd just, maybe, not let them go after. I suppose it's an upgrade. "Are you going to ask me about it?"

"No," he says quickly. "I mean. If you want to tell me, I'll listen. That's the least I can do. But I don't want . . . I know enough." His hands close into fists, the tendons standing out along their backs.

"Did he hurt you, Liam?" I ask quietly.

"Sometimes," he says again, and draws forward another step. I shift toward him. "Melinda and Andrew say he changed, after Mom died. He was different before. But I never really got to meet that version."

Lizzie, where did you go?

There's something broken in this boy. Broken, and beautiful. He's like the delicate cup that's dropped, and suddenly more precious for shattering.

I could have loved him in another life. I could have poured myself into him. He couldn't contain me, of course, but I would seep so slowly out between those cracks that neither of us would notice until I was gone.

I could be mourned by him, and really, what love is greater than that?

Isn't that what I wanted? Those nights in the shelter I lay on a stiff bed that didn't belong to me, listening to some other girl weeping down the line. I didn't want to *die*, or not *just* to die. I wanted to be mourned. To be precious at last because I was gone.

Then you'd see. Then you'd wish you'd answered when I called.

What an idiot I was. I've been dead all this while, and I doubt I've been more than a passing thought.

I can't dwell in self-pity. And I can't lose myself to those big blue eyes, those doll's lashes, that sadness turned into a smile. I don't need this boy to hold me. I need the sharp, broken edge of him—*and I'm sorry, Liam, but that means I've got to break you a bit more to get at it.*

"What about Andrew?" I ask.

His head twitches. "I know Dad was tough on him, but it wasn't as bad," he says. "He was big. Dad couldn't exactly pick on him like he could with me."

"No. I mean," I begin. I stop, as if this is difficult, as if I hesitate to even suggest it. "Has he ever hurt you, Liam?"

He looks quickly away, and that's more of an answer than what he says next. "He tried to protect me."

"What does that mean?" I press, cruel even as my voice is whisper soft, so honey sweet it nearly chokes me.

"I screwed up. A lot. Made Dad angry, and Andrew tried—he was trying to teach me the only way he knew how," he says. And then, defiantly, "He's a good person."

"Is he?" Still gentle, oh so gentle, because I can't let him see I'm not the sort of damsel who gets rescued. He's forgotten where he is—there's no princess in a tower here, only a witch cast in a pit.

"He is," Liam insists.

"Then why am I here?" I ask helplessly. "You know what happened down here. And you're still keeping me here, in the dark. Chained up like an animal. Worse than an animal. The only things you keep like this are the ones you're about to slaughter."

I let a hint of accusation into my voice, and turn my face away.

"We won't—he won't—" he stammers. He's a better actor than a liar, and he isn't a very good actor. His face flushes.

I turn my shoulder to him, blocking him out. "Just go," I say.

"I don't want to leave you down here."

"But that's what you're doing. All of you." For the first few words, my misery is an act, and I think that I can hold it back, the true wretched horror of the thing. I tell myself this is all a manipulation and I'm in control, but then my throat constricts and my body pinches inward and there is a howl in my chest waiting to loose. Not the sort of tidy suffering that Liam will want to soothe, but a wounded, rageful thing. A sound torn from deep inside the belly, a sound with talons, one to leave you bloody.

"I'm going to get you out," Liam says as I bite down on my tongue to keep the horrible sound contained. "I promise."

Oh, he means it, too, and tears flood my eyes—tears of hope, maybe, but mostly anger. *Where were you? Where were you? WHERE WERE YOU?* I want to scream at him.

YOU SHOULD HAVE KNOWN.

I can't speak. I don't dare turn to face him. I only hunch over on myself and hold back my howling, and after a minute, he finally leaves. He says something as he goes, but I don't hear it. I wait until the door at the top of the stairs closes and then as long as I can bear, and then I scream.

I know he can't hear me.

No one ever has.

35

After

I text Dev when I get home. He doesn't respond. It doesn't surprise me. I doubt he'll be swinging by my office anymore. I should never have let him get involved.

The first order of business is calling in sick. No one wants me dispensing advice to teens today. Maybe not ever. I can only hope that I get to keep my job. *Local school counselor fired for uncovering serial-killer plot,* I think. The podcasters will love it.

One long shower and a bowl of desultory Cheerios later, I'm draped on the couch in my living room, feeling a blend of sorry for myself and too numb to feel anything at all. There are bodies out there, and I found them, and there's more to do. The glade of the lost is waiting, and no amount of telling myself that it's foolish and irresponsible and irrational will stop me from feeling its presence.

The doorbell rings, followed by an eager *boof*. Barry's blocky head appears at the window, and Kenny leans in to wave. I scurry over to let them in, and then stand still to let Barry do a thorough and somewhat intrusive olfactory examination of me.

"Oh, my disaster child," Kenny says with a sigh, gathering me up in a hug. Kenny isn't tall, but he's big, and a hug from him is an enveloping and nourishing experience. He pats me gently on the top of my head as I rest it against his shoulder. "You beautiful little idiot."

"Hello to you, too, Kenny," I say. He releases me, but takes hold of my arms to give me a good once-over.

"Where are we on the spectrum of breakdowns?"

"Are you asking me if it's safe to leave me alone?" I ask wryly.

"Yes. Precisely." For all his joking tone, he's dead serious.

"I am not a danger to myself or others at the present moment," I say. "Though my dating life may be DOA. Dev is never calling me back, is he?"

"Probably not," he says delicately. And then, "Have you eaten?"

"Cereal."

"What are we going to do with you?" He wanders into the kitchen, and for the second time in a week, I have a man cooking breakfast for me. This time around, it's less fun.

We eat together, and I pretend I don't notice Kenny sneaking Barry bites of egg. "So. Len tells me you've promised to leave well enough alone."

"I have."

"Right, so you're either lying to him or yourself," Kenny says knowingly.

"I can't interfere with a police investigation," I say with a shrug. "I'm not going to go get myself arrested again." It's going to make my skin feel like it's crawling off my body, but I don't see how I have a choice other than to stay out of it.

"I'm not suggesting that you do. But you're going to do something, and so I feel it's better to direct your energy in a productive direction. Otherwise, that pressure is going to build up until you do something truly unwise." Kenny's look is a little too pointed for comfort. I shift in my seat. The cheap IKEA chair squeaks under me.

"What would you do?" I ask.

He considers the question as he eats. "Your problem is that you're looking for answers, but you don't have the right questions," he says. "So you're running headlong at the problem. Digging up *bodies*." He looks toward the ceiling with a *god help us* expression.

"I know what question I'm asking."

"What's that?" he asks.

I spread my hands. "What happened out there? Who are those girls? Who killed them? Where is Meghan Vale? Where's—" I stop myself.

"Where's Janie," he finishes for me. I nod, not meeting his eyes. He sits back in his chair. "Nope."

"What do you mean, 'nope'?"

"I mean, none of those are the question."

"Then what is?"

"I don't know. You figure it out," he says around a bite of breakfast sausage. He wipes his fingers on his napkin and rises. "It's not your job to find Meghan. And Janie—you're not looking for her, not really. She's not part of this as far as you know, so figure out what it is you're *actually* looking for."

"I don't know what that means," I say.

"Eh, maybe it's bullshit," he says with a dismissive wave. "But if you get arrested again, Len's going to kill you and then he's going to go to prison and I can't afford the rent on my own, so. Work it out. Find the part in this you're *supposed* to play. Hint: it does not involve sneaking *anywhere* at midnight."

He leaves me, offering Barry a final dollop of praise and pets before he heads out the door. I sit staring at the wall, my coffee going cold in the mug. Barry takes advantage of my inattention to snag the corner of a piece of bacon from Kenny's abandoned plate. He locks eyes with me as he slowly, delicately, gently pulls it off the plate and lowers himself out of view. With stealthy gobbling noises, he devours it.

I decide he's earned it.

I clear up the rest of breakfast, Kenny's words pinging around in my head. Am I asking the wrong questions? What other questions might there be? Missing girls, dead girls. They're at the heart of this, aren't they?

I need to get out of here. Clear my head.

I get dressed, whistle to Barry, and head for the car. Twenty minutes later, I'm parked at the bottom of Eden Crest. It's broad daylight, but with darkness gnawing at the edge of my mind, I still pull up my email and schedule my usual message to Len.

It's a clear day, so Barry forgoes his fetching jacket. Not many people are out on a weekday, and I get up to the viewing point without seeing a soul. The climb hasn't ordered my thoughts any better. I take a seat on the broad, flat boulder where hundreds of people have sat before me.

Rock band, I think. *International jewel heist. Australian sheep farm.* We imagined so many futures here, Janie and I. So many ways to vanish and be remade.

In her stories, we were always together. Sometimes, it felt like that was a promise and a pledge. Other times, it felt like a leash. *Come along, Oddity. Keep up. Not that way. We're such good friends. Prove it to me. Tell me all the ways we're friends.*

She loved nothing more than to be told how loved she was.

She needed someone to cling to. It's hard now to hate her for it, like I did once. She was only a child. A child who wanted to escape only slightly less than she wanted a reason to stay.

I couldn't be that reason for her. She made sure of it.

My pack sits on the boulder beside me. With Barry leaning his impossible weight against my shins, I rummage inside and pull out Meghan Vale's journal. I know I should give it to the police, but they aren't looking for her—not yet. Giving it up feels like giving up on it, and her.

I flip it open and page to the back, blank pages. It has an elastic loop through which a pen is stuck. I pull it free and uncap it.

Where is Meghan Vale? I write. Kenny says it's the wrong question, but I can't imagine a more worthy one.

Where is Janie?

They're the wrong questions because I can't answer them—not yet, at least. I don't exactly have the money to hire a PI, and I don't have the skills to track down a runaway on my own. Much less a victim of murder or abduction.

Saw Emily Hill, I write idly. The Hills are in the middle of all of this.

What did they know? I write. It's closer, I think.

I flip back to those final pages of writing. Once again, I read the entries about the witch in the woods, Meghan circling around the truth of what she saw and learned without ever writing it down. As if she knew it was too dangerous even for a private diary.

And once again, I read that poem. It's the sort of deeply felt mediocrity that makes teenage poetry truly precious. It's one thing to pour your heart out in verse when you have the skill to do it in a way that you know will be beautiful. The poems of adolescence are a machete hacking away at undergrowth in the dark, desperate and unlovely and glorious in their imperfection.

My name is Stranger. She's built the poem around those borrowed words. The kind of girl who'd write a thing like that is the kind whose self had been battered, obliterated.

It reminds me of the stories Janie used to tell. Her strange and half-real myths of terrifying fairies—fae, she'd call them, of course—and the power of names. How you had to keep them hidden. She claimed that was why she always used nicknames for people. Because otherwise, her words would be too powerful. *You wouldn't be able to resist me.*

After I'd refused to call her January, I'd only ever called her Janie.

Except.

Except.

My breath catches in my throat as a long-discarded memory bubbles to the surface. It was after that first disappearance. My summer alone, abandoned, confused. And then Janie sweeping in like the whole thing was a laugh.

I wanted her to think I was as cool as she was. So I'd feigned indifference at first. *Hey, stranger,* I'd said. *Where have you been?*

When she shrugged and laughed and told me what a fabulous summer she'd had, I knew I couldn't mope and complain. She'd only mock me for it. So I played along and hid my hurt. Except that it kept needling at me, so I kept needling at her.

Hey, stranger, I kept saying, every time I saw her. *Thought you might have disappeared again.* I said it so much it became more than a stock phrase. I started calling her that in conversation. *Where are you going today, Stranger?*

Oh, Stranger. I didn't see you there.

Where have you been, Stranger?

Each time, it was a jab. Each time, I saw the flicker of annoyance in her eyes, and that was why I kept doing it. If I had to be Oddity, she could be Stranger, because she'd left me, she'd gone away, she'd changed where I couldn't see her, and how could I be sure I knew her at all? I wanted her to hurt, like I had.

I kept waiting for her to snap and tell me to stop, but she never did. And eventually, the nickname dropped out of use. I can't remember now how long it was. A long time in my memory, but now that I try to fit events around it, probably a couple of weeks.

I trace my finger over those last words.

My name is Stranger.

"It was you," I whisper.

She was there. She had to be. And I know, I *know,* that means she never left.

I've mourned her a hundred times. I'll mourn her again, but not in this moment.

Because Meghan Vale saw Emily Hill in those woods. And Janie dated Andrew Hill. It's more than a coincidence.

I turn to the last page. Look at what I've written.

What did they know?

I cross it out and try again.

What are they hiding?

36

Before

It's a few hours before Liam returns. I'm hungry again. My food sits piled in front of me, but I don't eat yet. I don't know when I might need to ration again.

They might still decide to leave me down here. It's not hard to imagine it emerging as a solution: murder by passivity and feigned ignorance. But that possibility vanishes at Liam's appearance.

"Stranger?" he calls, as if I might have decided to nip out while he was gone. He comes down the stairs two at a time with a wild look and a pair of bolt cutters in one hand.

"Liam," I say, infusing his name with all the hope and relief I can muster.

"I told you. I'm going to get you out. Right now," he says, breathless.

"Where are the others?" I ask.

"Andrew and Melinda went into town. We've got a little while," he assures me, coming swiftly forward to examine the chain.

"An hour," Emily says. She descends the stairs more slowly and stands at the bottom, thin arms crossed over her chest. Her hair is back in a tight ponytail. It makes the angles of her face more severe. She looks between us, biting her lip. "I'm still not sure this is a good idea."

"We have to, Emmie," he says. He turns to me. "I figured you'd want that chain off properly."

My mouth is so dry I have to wet it twice before I can speak properly. "Thank you," I say. "Really." My heart hammers. This is it. They're going to let me go, and it won't matter what Andrew says—as long as I can get away.

Please. Please, I think, imagining with every breath the thunder of feet. In my mind, it isn't Andrew appearing at the top of the stairs to blot out the light. It's his father.

Dead, he's dead, I remind myself, and then I have to remind myself to breathe, too, because I've suddenly misplaced the habit.

"Okay. This should do it. Hold still, I don't want to hurt you," Liam says, and despite his words—because of them—I flinch.

I don't want to hurt you.

They meant something else when his father spoke them.

He doesn't notice my reaction, but Emily does, a faint frown dragging at her lips. Liam sets the bolt cutters carefully at the small padlock that secures the manacle. He braces himself and squeezes.

With a jolt, the jaws of the thing snap shut. The chain falls, snakes to the ground with a clatter. I grab at the manacle eagerly and pry it open—I'm loose. No more dragging this thing around. He's done what took me hours and days, blood and tears, done it better than me and with hardly a thought, and he stands there grinning like a hero.

I throw the manacle aside. It hits the wall with force and rebounds, clattering to the ground. My teeth are bared, my breath ragged. Liam's smile turns a touch uncertain.

"There," he says.

I seal my lips. Still my face. "Thank you," I whisper.

Emily steps forward. The manacle has landed nearly at her feet. She picks it up, staring down at it with a mix of fascination and disgust. She wraps the chain around the manacle slowly, and then sets the whole thing on the table.

"Emily?" Liam prompts.

She tears her eyes away, clears her throat. "Right," she says, and reaches into the small backpack she's carrying. "I brought you a few things." She pulls out a sweatshirt and a pair of flip-flops.

My heart sinks. If they were letting me go, they'd give me proper shoes. These were chosen because there's no way to run in them. They're as good as a hobble.

So I'm being moved, that's all.

But that's something. That could be *everything*. So I force myself to smile. "Thank you. I know I keep saying that. Thank you so much."

Emily doesn't meet my eyes. Her fingers twitch and leap on the backpack strap. She slinks back to the stairs, but Liam stays as I struggle to put on the sweatshirt and slide my feet into the sandals. He puts out a hand to help me stand.

I wish that I didn't actually need his help. I wish that I was faking how much I need to lean against him as I limp toward the stairs. The food has made me stronger, but I'm still so weak.

Liam puts an arm around me to help me up the stairs, one at a time. Emily watches with discomfort, leading the way by a few steps.

At the top, I have to stop, gasping, with a hand shielding my eyes from the direct glare of the sun.

"Are you okay?" Liam asks earnestly.

"Too bright," I manage. It's like a blade straight through my skull. I shut my eyes entirely, hand covering them, and still I think I might faint.

Liam waits. He hardly moves as the seconds drag on. Finally I drop my hand, and then carefully ease my eyes open. The light is still painfully bright, but the world comes into focus. It looks unreal at first—the sky above so open I'm gripped with the fleeting certainty that I'll fall up into it. It's terrible and beautiful, and part of me wants to fall, is hungry for it, to become untethered from the ground and wheel away on crooked wings.

"We should go," Emily says.

I nod. "Okay. We can go." I tear my eyes from the sky reluctantly, my gaze falling on other strange things—branches, trembling leaves, the bright bodies of birds.

Sticks and rocks jab at my feet as we walk, but the rough floor below has left them thick and callused. It's a long walk at my stilted gait, but at last a house comes into view. It's a single story, the exterior dark wood. They bring me around to the back door, which leads first into a garage where a car sits under a cloth cover, and then into a hallway carpeted in a yellow-green color like dry grass. My eyes settle again, adjusting to the gloom inside. It's a welcome middle ground.

"What now?" I ask. It comes out gravelly and demanding. Emily's jaw tightens.

"You can stay in my room," she says.

"Stay," I repeat.

Liam swallows. "We still need to convince Andrew and Melinda. But it'll be easier. Once you're here and cleaned up . . ."

"It'll be harder to kill me," I say. The blunt words make his cheeks flame.

I want to rake my nails down their faces and scream at them to let me go. My body shakes with the effort of containing my desperation and my rage. I can't let it out. I can't let them think I'm anything but grateful. I'm closer than I've ever been to free.

Hold on, I think, and bite down hard on the inside of my cheek. I let out a long, slow breath. "Okay," I say. It's the best I can do. I touch my hair. It's stiff with grease and grime. "Can I take a shower?"

Liam looks surprised. "Of course," he says, like this shouldn't be in question.

"I'll take care of it," Emily says, drawing forward. "Liam, you should make us some lunch or something."

"Yes. Okay," he says. He reaches out to touch my arm. "You'll be okay?"

Somehow, I manage to smile. "Better now," I whisper.

He leaves at last, and Emily ticks her head down the hall. "This way," she says. "And I'll, um—I'll get you some better clothes while you're getting cleaned up."

"I appreciate it."

"You don't have to keep thanking us," she says, shaking her head quickly.

"Don't I?" We stare at each other. I can't read those eyes. Wide and frightened and fascinated and maybe even angry. Her movements remind me of a bird deciding whether to take flight.

"Everything you need should be inside," she says abruptly, and steps back.

I step past her into a cramped bathroom. She shuts the door behind me. I hesitate, then push the button to lock it. It feels impossibly strange to be the one locking a door.

"Well," I say quietly to myself. "Here we are." I turn toward the sink, and I freeze.

The girl who stares back at me in the mirror is violent proof of the name I've claimed. I don't know her at all. Her hair is a wild thicket. Not matted—not much—but tangled and filthy and dulled to a dingy brown. Before I was alone with the gossamer girls, I washed regularly in the sink on the other side of the room, but it's been weeks. My skin is a gray patchwork of dirt scabbed over gaunt, jutting cheekbones and a sharp jaw—I always hated my rounded face, the kind of cheeks that get pinched when you're a kid, but now they've melted away and what's left is deprivation. It leaves my eyes too large for my face, and the color of them too intense. My hands claw at the sides of the sink. I look like a creature. Like the witch in the woods. I bare my teeth.

My ferocity pleases me.

I strip off my clothes. Borrowed sweatshirt, tank top. I had to keep my sweats and underwear on since I wasn't able to remove the chain to change, and I'm glad to peel those off. My nose has long since gotten used to the smell, but I'm sure to the others I reek. I stuff the clothes in the trash can. No point in even thinking about salvaging them.

Nude, I examine myself again. I can count my ribs easily, which once I would have considered an accomplishment. We try so hard to be *small* all our lives. Well, here I am. Like a doll made of sticks with shiny stones for eyes. I crook my elbows, tilt my head. I have a scarecrow look, twig-doll angles; I'm the thing stuck in the corner to scare you. I turn my back and flare my shoulder blades. They heave outward, spade-like, hard-edged. I pull down my lip to examine my blood-tinged gums and dig my broken fingernails into my hair to find its knots, and I think I'll never tire of looking at my monstrous self. I want to laugh and I don't understand it, how there is not one hint of horror in me at seeing myself this way.

I look half dead, and that's amazing, that's wonderful, because halfway dead isn't dead at all. The gossamer girls get to glimmer and shift. I'm not like them—not thin like onionskin, but like a knife blade. I'm solid. I'm dirt and puke and blood still pumping. I haven't faded at all. I've withered down. I've become something dangerous.

I draw the water. Even lukewarm, it's luxurious, and I let it dislodge the evidence of the pit. The dirt, the dust, the dried-up fluids of my own body. It should disgust me, but I watch it all swirl down the drain with triumph. Call it my chrysalis. I'm spreading my shoulders. I'm breaking free.

I comb my fingers with my hair and then a brush from the side of the sink. It takes me a long time and several rounds of shampoo and conditioner before I can run the brush through without catching. I clean every crevice of my body and let the cooling water run over my face with my eyes wide open.

Only when the water is ice-cold do I shut it off and step out. The startled animal in the mirror who blinks back at me wouldn't frighten anyone now, but she doesn't look tame. I open the medicine cabinet. I luck out: there's a toothbrush still in the package and half a tube of toothpaste. I brush gingerly. It makes my gums bleed profusely, but my teeth feel clean for the first time in god knows how long.

There. Most of the way back to human—and still I hardly recognize myself. Wet, my hair is too dark to show more than a slight reddish tone, and my new skin-and-bones look has completely transformed my face. My nose looks different, too. I think it must have been broken and I didn't realize it. If even I don't recognize myself, would anyone else?

I lean in close. I think I can still see myself somewhere around the eyes. She looks afraid.

There's a knock on the door. A towel wrapped around me, I open it, expecting the sister—but it's Liam, who blushes when he sees me as if he's fifteen and not a fully grown man, a TV star who's certainly seen plenty of girls naked.

"I brought you the clothes," he says. I wonder what happened to let him snag that responsibility from Emily.

"Great," I say. I take them from him unceremoniously and vanish back inside the room.

The clothes are not what I would have chosen. A cute peasant blouse in pastel blue and a pair of jeans with a heart sewn on the back pocket. The panties are plain cotton and pink. But they're clean, and that's absolute luxury right now. I dress in them, my feral self vanishing a few degrees more, and step out of the bathroom. Liam is waiting, head low and a hand rubbing the back of his neck. When I exit, he looks up and smiles.

"That's better," he says, with a hint of a question.

"Much." My smile is genuine, if perhaps a bit too wide for polite company.

Emily appears at the end of the hall. She keeps one arm close by her side, the other hand gripping it tight. Her pose is compressed, intended to make her small, but her eyes are wide and watching. "I'm glad they fit," she says. "You're a bit taller than me."

There's a beat of silence, and then she clears her throat.

"My room's all made up. Down here." She points past me, and I awkwardly lead the way to the door she indicates. There's a keyed lock on the door. I frown a little. I wouldn't have expected a man like their father to allow his children that kind of privacy.

The room is small. There's a twin bed with a metal frame against one wall, covered in old handmade quilts. A tiny desk is crammed into the corner next to the dresser. The closet is open, and seems to have been hastily emptied except for a few hangers and a laundry hamper.

Paintings and drawings hang on the walls. Landscapes, a twirling ballerina shown from behind, still life studies. "Yours?" I ask, turning in a slow circle to appreciate them.

Emily hums an affirmative. "She's in art school," Liam supplies. "She's really good."

"I used to want to be an artist," I say distantly. It feels like another lifetime. I suppose it is. "But then, I wanted to be everything. I guess what I really wanted was to be the best at something."

Emily leans against the doorway, arms crossed. "That's the thing about art school. You think you're good and then you get there and realize there are a dozen kids who are way more talented. It's kind of awful, actually."

"Really?"

She shrugs. "I'm thinking of dropping out."

"You didn't tell me that," Liam says, taken aback.

"We don't exactly talk much anymore, Liam," she says, her voice quiet and angry.

"You shouldn't," I say. She blinks at me. I've surprised myself by speaking, but I keep going. "Don't let them chase you off. Fuck them. Get better and rub it in their faces."

Emily regards me. There's something about her quiet, her watchfulness, that leaves me feeling like I've put a foot wrong. "I'll think about it." She straightens up and tugs her brother's sleeve. "Come on. She should rest and we should figure out what the hell we're going to tell Andrew and Melinda."

"I'll be back soon," Liam promises. They back out. Emily closes the door, reaching into her pocket as she does, and I realize a moment too late.

A key slides into the lock and turns. And I see what I missed before: There is no locking mechanism on the inside of the door. It only locks from the outside.

I'm trapped in here.

And so, I realize, was Emily.

37

After

I cancel the scheduled email as soon as I'm back at the car, thrumming with new purpose. Kenny was right. I've been thinking about the girls, but I need to be thinking about the Hills. Melinda, Andrew, Emily—Liam, too, I suppose.

They know more than they're saying. And if it's something worth hiding, it's something worth finding out. They'll wall themselves off with lawyers and carefully calibrated statements that make it clear they had no idea, that they're as horrified as the rest of us. Melinda's a politician, and a good one. She'll know how to protect them from the press and the police. But maybe I can find something, if they don't think to stop me.

It's back to searching through the thickets of the internet, then. I'm far less accustomed to this particular wilderness, but I pick up where I left off, wandering aimlessly through the articles and posts that have touched on the Hills. Melinda's political career is overwhelmingly the best documented and the least relevant. I like her politics—I'll give her that. Practical, with a progressive streak she knows how to camouflage when the crowd won't like it.

All politicians have to be liars. And she's good at it.

Then there's Andrew, and the foundation—and it bothers me that they're so tied to it, an organization for wayward young women. Men, too, I suppose, but it started with girls. They have teen shelters that work to mediate runaways' return to their parents, as well as shelters for older youth. They have extensive programs for foster kids who have aged out, which was why Hope's Hands started—their mother was in foster care.

The story is on the website. Elizabeth Hill—Elizabeth Sellick at the time—had been kicked out of her foster parents' house and was on the street when she met her husband. There's a photo of them on the website, early in their marriage. She's young, with strawberry blond hair and a big smile. Next to her, he's bearlike, with dark, curly hair and a thick beard; he has to be at least ten years her senior. There's something off about him. His pose is stiff, and there's a disconnect between the direction of his smile and his eyes, like he's not sure where he's supposed to look.

Maybe it's only that I'm aware that he might be—probably is—a killer, but his eyes seem dead to me, his grip on her waist too possessive. *He rescued me,* Elizabeth—Lizzie—said in interviews. *He took me in when I had nowhere to go.* It could read as romantic or predatory, depending on your leanings. I know which one gets my vote.

> *After Lizzie's death, Hope's Hands nearly shuttered. Its second life began when Lizzie's oldest children, Melinda and Andrew, worked together to revitalize and expand the program in her honor.*

I know all of this already. I skim through, but the PR pap isn't going to unveil any dark secrets. It's all Melinda and Andrew. Hardly any mention of the twins. I pull up another tab and plug in Liam's name. It takes some added search terms to even get him to surface. After *City Rescue,* playing race car–driving paramedic Kyle Barton, he was in one failed pilot and a few episodes of a hospital show. Then he dropped off the radar. Just another TV actor who couldn't make the leap from his first gig. After that, he popped up online only in relation to his rap sheet. I find one blog that's put together a sympathetic biography, but even that plays like a tragedy. Drug use on set even in the early days, sporadic arrests, his deteriorating performance on subsequent seasons.

I flip back to Hope's Hands. Buried in the news section is a photo of Liam, sitting on the hood of a vintage muscle car while he throws a thumbs-up. HOPE'S HANDS blazes across a banner behind him. Melinda and Andrew stand to the side, beaming photogenic smiles.

> *Liam Hill is photographed after donating a car driven by his character Kyle Barton on* City Rescue *to be auctioned in the Hope's Hands yearly fundraiser.*

Toward the edge of the frame, captured incidentally, is Mason Hill; behind him, in profile to the camera, you can just make out Emily. Mason almost seems to be blocking her from view.

She looks painfully young, even compared to her twin. She's dressed in a peasant blouse and jeans that look borrowed from a previous decade, her hair in pigtails. I stare at the image. Something is bothering me, but I can't place it.

Maybe it's only that I've never seen another photograph of her, I realize. Unlike her siblings, she never participated in anything through the schools that would have gotten her picture taken. She doesn't appear in Melinda's campaign photos; she's not standing with Andrew to celebrate his winning game; she isn't anywhere on the Hope's Hands website.

My stomach tightens, nausea creeping over me before I can quite articulate why.

She was hidden from the world. Not just now, of her own accord, but all her life. I look again at the way Mason Hill stands in front of her. The way he looks angrily toward the camera. He doesn't want her seen.

He wants her to himself, I think, and realize my heart is hammering in my chest.

She might not have been down in that bunker, but she was trapped all the same.

Why wouldn't you run far, far away from a home like that? Something kept her there. The same thing, maybe, that draws her again and again down into the dark, to leave handprints like blood on the walls of another girl's prison.

The road to the Hills' house—and Terry Butler's—is blocked off with a temporary wooden barrier. I'm guessing I'm not the first unwanted visitor. The police and investigators will be up by the Butler place, though, and I can only hope that Emily's house is still accessible. I park by the road and head up on foot, suppressing every sensible instinct I have.

I find myself walking along the side of the road, not wanting my footsteps to crunch on gravel. Emily's isn't the only car in the driveway. There are four—I recognize Melinda's and Andrew's, and alongside them is a Kia that looks like a rental.

Liam? I wonder. They've called the family home.

I stop short of the house, not sure I want to deal with the whole clan. Emily's not going to say anything in front of her siblings. Andrew will just slam the door in my face. Maybe coming here was a waste of time.

A burble of conversation comes from the house, voices tense but not yet shouting. The blinds are shut, blocking out whoever is inside—and blocking me from them. Curiosity wins out over caution. I creep closer, straining my ears to make out Melinda's clipped words.

"—unreliable. You know how he is."

"He looked good, I thought," Andrew replies. They're talking about Liam. Which makes me wonder where, exactly, he is.

"You mean he looked clean," Melinda says bluntly. I've sidled up all the way to the window now. If anyone spots me, there's no way to make this look like anything other than what it is.

"Well. Yeah," Andrew says.

Emily says something, too soft for me to hear.

"It isn't Liam I'm worried about," Andrew snaps, as if in response.

"We all made the same promises," Melinda says, and the hair

on my arms prickles. I'm holding my breath now, straining to hear every word.

Emily's voice comes again. I still can't make it out, but I think I catch the last couple words, tilted up into a question. "—find her?"

Or was it *there*? My skin is cold, my heart thumping.

"It's not going to happen," Melinda says, in a reassuring tone.

"You're sure?" Andrew asks, quieter now, and Melinda answers, her words comprehensible only sporadically.

"—made sure—nowhere near—no reason—" Then silence again, and she clears her throat. "Look—we're acting like this is complicated, but it's very simple. We're horrified, but it has nothing to do with us. We don't need to say anything more than that. Everyone already knows what kind of man Terry Butler is. Was."

"Hold on," Andrew says. "It's Wagner." A pause. "They're starting the search. I should go over there."

Search? He must mean they're searching Terry Butler's place, which means that there are dozens of cops just up the driveway from here, and I'm standing around eavesdropping.

"I'll stay here," Melinda says; if Emily answers, I don't hear, because I'm walking briskly and quietly away from the house, my pulse galloping. Whatever I just heard, I wasn't supposed to. None of it is specific. None of it damning.

But it obliterates my last doubt that there's something they're keeping quiet.

I relax a fraction when I get out of sight of the house, but all my fear and tension comes flooding back the instant I round the bend and spot my car.

A lanky man sits on the hood, dark bangs falling across his eyes and the last stub of a cigarette clamped between his fingers. Liam. My steps slow. He watches my approach placidly, letting out a long exhale of smoke-wreathed breath.

He doesn't look like the heartthrob paramedic from *City Rescue* anymore. Or the fragile teen I crossed paths with doing stage crew for the school play. The lines of his face are too craggy for his age, and he looks both too thin and too slack. But he smiles a little when he sees me, and in the spark of his eyes, I can see the hint of the young man he used to be.

"Liam," I say.

"That's me. You're Audrey, right?" he says. His fingers fidget with the cigarette. "I heard you've been coming around a lot. I recognize you, don't I?"

"I did a semester of drama. *Romeo and Juliet*," I say, as if this is a normal conversation, two old schoolmates catching up.

He taps the side of his index finger to his brow. "Right, right. I do remember you. Been a long time."

"What are you doing here, Liam?" I ask, trying to sound casual and unworried.

"Melinda sounded the trumpets. Called us all in," Liam says with a vague wave of his hand. "Wants to keep an eye on us in this *time of uncertainty*." He lets out a last smoke-plume breath and drops the cigarette, grinding it out.

"I kind of meant what are you doing sitting on my car," I say, squinting against the sunlight.

He laughs, tucks his hands in his jacket pockets. "Oh, sorry. I was just getting some air. My family aren't exactly the easiest people to be cooped up with. Then I saw your car and I wondered who was dropping by at a time like this." He gives me a considering look, that half a smile still pinned in place. "You came to talk to Emily, didn't you?"

"What is it to you?" I ask, crossing my arms protectively.

"Yeah. See, she'll do that to you," he says with a little laugh under the words.

"Do what?" I ask.

"Draw you in." He shrugs a little, sniffs, and stands, stepping clear of the car and closer to me. "As someone who's been there—keep your distance."

"People keep telling me that. None of them have told me why," I say. "No one in your family seems to like talking much at all."

"We were taught from an early age not to entertain the curiosity of outsiders," he says, enunciating each word with an almost jovial tone. He's standing within comfortable conversation range now, no closer, his stance casual. I can smell the layers of stale smoke clinging to him.

He pulls another cigarette from the pack, then tilts it toward me. I decline with a shake of the head. He shrugs and tucks it away. "I have kicked a lot of addictions, but never these," he says idly. "So what the hell are you doing here? I heard Andrew and Melinda told you to stay the hell away from us."

"Then why are you talking to me?" I ask him, eyebrows arched.

"I'm a grown adult. I can talk to who I want to," he says. He pulls out his lighter at last and flicks it open. The glow makes his face momentarily lovely before the shadows reclaim it. He settles his weight back on his heels. "I heard you found them. The bodies."

"Just the first one," I say. I watch him carefully. Liam was a sweet boy. That was a long time ago.

"It's fucked up," he says quietly, not quite looking at me. "I mean. They were there the whole time. They haven't stopped finding more. Do you think they'll be able to identify them all?"

"I don't know. Probably not," I say. I shiver. It's colder out here than I thought. "That many girls can't go missing unless nobody's looking too hard for them, right?"

"Well, that's fucking depressing," Liam says.

"Do you think Terry did it?" I ask carefully, watching his reaction.

He just looks back at me steadily. "It certainly looks that way, doesn't it?"

"It's convenient, isn't it? He's dead. He can't answer questions."

"He's been dying a long time," Liam replies with a shrug. "Not fast enough, if you ask me. No one's going to mourn Terry Butler."

"He and your father were friends."

"I wouldn't go that far," Liam says with a grimace. "They had common interests and a philosophy that overlapped. Though they did have one big disagreement."

"What's that?" I ask.

"Dad always believed the love of a good woman could save your soul," Liam says. "Terry didn't think there was any such thing."

"A soul?"

"A good woman," he corrects. "Harlots and jezebels, every one, according to Terry. Dad liked to think his girls were the exception, being born of the saintly loins of our mother." His voice has a scrape to it, damaged by cigarettes and who knows what else. The phrasing makes my stomach tighten with discomfort.

"Can I ask you a question?"

"Seems like you've been asking a lot of those already."

I huff a little; he smiles, and it's not unkind. "Emily said you used to be close, but you weren't anymore."

"That's certainly accurate," he says.

"What happened?"

He takes a long inhale and lets it all out before he answers. "I realized what kind of person she was, that's all."

"What kind is that?"

But he only shakes his head. "I should get back," he says. "It was good to see you again, Audrey."

"You too," I say automatically, and he smiles wryly, hearing the lie of it. "I'll see you around."

"Probably not," Liam says. He clears his throat. "Thanks, by the way."

"For what?"

"For finding them," he says simply, genuinely.

I give him a long look. "There's another girl missing, you know," I say. "Meghan Vale. She went missing in January."

He squints a little, thinking it through. "The cops said those bodies were old."

"Meghan was out there. In those woods. She knew about the bunker. She talked to Emily," I say. "And then she vanished."

I can't decide what I heard back there at the house. What was Emily saying? *What will they find there?* Or *What if they find her?*

A singular *her*. Who else could she be talking about but Meghan?

Liam runs the back of his thumbnail along his lower lip. "Meghan Vale," he repeats, and I'm certain he's never heard the name before.

"Can you ask Emily about her? She won't talk to me," I say, a note of pleading in my voice. "Please. No one else is looking for this girl."

"I'll ask," he promises.

"Do you think . . ." I hesitate. "Could Emily have hurt her?"

He lets out a sound that is not quite a laugh, and looks away from me. "You know, I stopped trying to guess what people are capable of a long time ago."

38

Before

It doesn't take me long to test the limits of my cage and determine that I'm nearly as trapped as I was before. The hinges are on the outside of the door—no hope of disassembling them. The window doesn't open. Emily and Liam have cleared out almost everything from the room—the desk drawers are empty, only a few clothes in the dresser.

At least this prison is far more comfortable than the last one.

Melinda comes back after an hour. I sit on the bed with my damp hair soaking into the sweatshirt as I listen to Liam and Emily intercept her. I hear muted voices, and then she looks in on me once. She only nods and then retreats again, locking the door behind her.

Andrew is gone for much longer. It's well after dark when he arrives. I hear the slam of the door first, and then footsteps, uneven in a way that's all too familiar. He's been drinking. I still myself.

Melinda talks to him. I can hear her plainly through the walls.

"Where the hell have you been?" she demands.

"Out," he says.

"Where are you going?"

"Out," he says again, and something clatters.

"You don't need a flashlight. She's not out there anymore," Melinda says evenly, and then her voice drops. Andrew's tone turns to confusion, and then anger—his voice rising to a furious shout.

"What the fuck were you thinking?" he demands, and his footsteps storm down the hall.

He reaches the door and there's a bang as he hits it, clearly expecting the knob to turn. I hide a smirk as he bellows for the key. It takes the drama out of him bursting in a few seconds later. I look up at him, demure, reminding myself I cannot appear defiant. He doesn't even look me in the face. I don't know if he can.

"Get up," he says. "You're going back."

"Don't be absurd," Melinda says, approaching behind him. She leans in enough to peer at me, her expression neutral and calculating. "It was bad enough leaving her in there for a few hours. We're sure as hell not forcing her back down there and *what?* You want to actually chain a girl to a wall, Andrew?"

His jaw works. "We didn't discuss this," he says. "We need to—"

"You don't need to do anything," I say. It's risky, interrupting him, but he's working himself up and it's going to get dangerous fast. I shift my gaze to Melinda. "Is anyone coming here?"

She shakes her head. "Just us."

"Then there's no rush, right?" I ask reasonably. "Whatever you're going to do, it doesn't need to be done today, or tomorrow." I'm so understanding. My voice so absent of blame. Give me a fucking Oscar for how accommodating I sound.

"She's right," Melinda says, and I feel like she's picking up the other side of a tricky load, both of us finding the balance of it. She puts a hand on Andrew's arm. "At least here we can take care of her. *And* keep an eye on her. We can talk, and think this through, and make a plan."

"You trust her under our roof?" Andrew asks.

Melinda's brow furrows slightly, like this train of thought is baffling. "Andrew, she's ninety pounds soaking wet, what do you think she's going to do? Not to mention—"

She stops. Looks at me with a burning anger in her eyes that I do not for a moment think is directed at me.

"Not to mention what?" Andrew prods.

She's doing the same thing I am. Navigating him. "We can't let her leave half starved with welts on her ankle if we don't want all of this to get out," she says quietly. Melinda might be on my side, she might not be, but at least she wants her options open.

"All right," Andrew says after a strained pause. "You'll stay here. In this room. Don't try to pull anything."

"What if I need to use the bathroom?" I ask.

"We'll get you a bucket," he says. Melinda gives him an appalled look.

"Just knock on the door," she says, glaring at him. "One of us will let you out."

She stands there, waiting with arms crossed. Liam lingers in the hall behind them, eyes downcast. He's so timid in the face of his siblings it's a wonder he had the guts to get me out of there.

"Dinner soon. Do you need anything else?" Melinda asks. I shake my head. I've asked for enough.

"My room's right on the other side of the wall," Liam pipes up. "You know. If you need anything."

Melinda cuts him a look—one that says she knows exactly what's happening in his tender heart. She steps away. Liam fades back as well, but Andrew remains. He's staring straight at me, his gaze intent.

"What?" I say, more challenge than is wise.

"What's your name?" he asks, insistent.

"You know my name," I say. I'll give him no more than that.

Of all his children, Mason liked Andrew the best. He tried the hardest to please his father, and Mason sounded the closest to proud when he was telling me all the things Andrew had accomplished.

Of all of them, I think, he did the best job convincing himself his father was a man worthy of love, admiration.

Imitation.

He sees what he wants to see. Believes what he wants to believe.

Andrew's expression shutters, as if he has come to some kind of decision. He shuts the door. I listen for the click of the lock, and when it comes, I let out a sigh of disappointment. I hadn't expected him to forget, but hope is a persistent creature.

Once I'm sure no one is lingering outside the door, I get up from the bed. I spread my feet, digging my toes into the carpet and finding my balance, filling the whole of my foot with my weight. Then I begin to walk. Back and forth. I used to do this, over and over, keeping up my strength as best I could. It feels strange now, without the chain dragging at me and tripping me up. It takes me a while of walking before I find the proper rhythm again.

When Melinda brings me dinner, I'm sitting exactly as she left me. She doesn't say anything. Just waits for me to eat and then removes the plate and cutlery. I suppose a fork is too dangerous to leave with me unsupervised.

That night, with the TV mumbling in the front room, I turn to the wall. I can hear Liam settling in on the other side. I reach out, and with my knuckles I give two gentle taps on the wall. For a moment, there's silence.

Then: two knocks, soft and secretive.

"Can you hear me?" Liam says, voice muffled and low.

"Kind of," I say.

"Are you okay?"

I roll my eyes, make my voice sweet. "I'm glad you're here. But we shouldn't talk much. They might notice."

"You're probably right."

"It's enough to know you're there," I say. And with that, I become his secret.

And he becomes the key to my escape.

39

After

The FBI wants to talk to me. I guess it's not exactly a surprise, but it's sure as hell intimidating. I ask Len if I need a lawyer. He says I should be fine without one, so I ask Kenny, who says that Len is a tool of the state even if he has a cute butt and calls in a favor. A few hours later, I'm sitting in the break room at the station with an FBI agent who looks like he could cut glass with his chin and my newly minted lawyer, an impossibly elegant fifty-something woman named Letty Ramos.

Len was probably right—the questions are straightforward, and the agent seems torn between impressed and exasperated with my harebrained schemes. Explaining the beads and Jenny Red-Hands proves a sticking point—I have to assure Agent Perry several times that no, I do not actually believe there is a witch involved, and no, no one else really does, either. He listens with patience as I talk about Meghan, about Janie, writing everything down in a way that makes me think he might actually be listening.

Ms. Ramos—*not,* she corrects Agent Perry, Mrs.—interrupts now and then, but at the end of it, she nods to me with a reassuring look. I don't think I'm in any real trouble here if the Hills don't make a stink. And I know they won't.

"Thank you for going through all of this with me," Perry says. "I can tell you that none of the bodies we've recovered have been recent, but we will take a fresh look at the file on Miss Vale, and I'll see what we can pull up about your friend. We've identified one of the bodies so far, but any leads on the others we will be sure to pursue."

They're up to five bodies. I saw it on the news this morning.

"Can you tell me who she was?" I ask. "The one you identified."

"Her family has been informed, and we're making a statement later today, so yes," he says. "Her name was Amanda Dennis."

"We were right, then."

He nods. "It seems so. And we're looking at the others you and Deputy Howard flagged as possible matches, but it's going to take time. We were lucky with Amanda—her family's been dogged in keeping the investigation going, and we already had her dental records on file."

"Will that be all?" Ms. Ramos asks.

"Should do it." Perry tidies his notes. "Will you be leaving town anytime in the next week or so?"

"No plans," I say.

"Good. We may want to speak with you again," he says, and that seems to be that. Ms. Ramos rises first, holding out a hand in a clear indication for me to do the same. I unfold myself from the seat, which I've been perched in with the kind of pretzel pose the teens in my office are always assuming, and walk out to the hall, waiting at any moment for this to have been a joke, and for Agent Perry to arrest me.

"That went well," Ms. Ramos says out in the hall. "I think yours may be one of the only circumstances where someone can fairly say that it's a lucky thing there was a serial killer in town." Her tone is dry and not at all amused. "I don't need to tell you not to get in any more trouble, do I?"

"Plenty of people already have," I say.

"And?"

"I won't?"

"Good girl." She looks down at her phone, sighs. "Call me before talking to anyone in law enforcement. That includes your friend Len."

"He wouldn't—"

She fixes me with a look. "You do not want to put him in that position."

My cheeks go hot. "Yes, ma'am."

"Well, then. I'll leave you to your own devices," she says, sounding like she's questioning the wisdom of this, but balancing her investment in me against the fact that she's not getting paid. "I'll be in touch."

She marches through the lobby, heels clicking. I turn aside—all the coffee I was swigging in that room has caught up to me.

The door opens while I'm in the stall, but I think nothing of it—until I step out and discover Emily Hill standing by the sink. She's wearing a loose flannel over a camisole, her hair up in its usual ponytail. Her roots are bleached now, the ponytail tidy; I wonder if Melinda had something to do with that. Must present the proper image. There are dark circles under her eyes, poorly concealed with makeup.

"Emily," I say, uncertain. My weight settles on my back heel like I'm ready to run, though I have no idea where I'd go.

"Audrey. I saw you come in. You were talking to the FBI," she says. I can't read her tone. Is she angry? Worried?

"Yeah, well. They've got a few questions," I say.

"They want to talk to me, too," she says absently, looking over her shoulder.

"I imagine they would." I wonder if I should try to edge around her. Instead, I stand my ground. "You knew. You all did. Liam, Melinda, Andrew—you know about the bodies in those woods."

Her lips part. She doesn't speak.

"You hid it. And the only reason I can come up with for why you would do that is if you knew who'd done it. It was your father, wasn't it?"

Emily blinks slowly. "Do you want to know what's going to happen?" she asks. She speaks almost in a whisper, and yet her voice presses into the corners of the room.

"What?" I ask.

"I'm going to sit down with the FBI and the lawyer my sister chose for me. And she and Andrew and Liam are going to do the same. And we're going to tell the FBI how shocked and horrified we are, and of course we are, who wouldn't be? And then they're going to ask us about Terry Butler. We're going to tell them he was violent, and reclusive, and misogynist. And no one will be surprised, because it's all true, and because yesterday the police found trophies from those poor girls in Terry Butler's attic."

My breath catches. "What?"

She smiles thinly. "They didn't tell you, then. Locks of hair, they said, that seem to match. Which means the man who did this is dead. There's no more blood to be gotten from him. So we'll tell them what a monster he was. We'll tell them we had no idea the extent of it. 'But, oh, part of me isn't surprised,' we'll say. Melinda will give such an incredible statement. She'll talk about 'centering the victims' and 'finding the truth,' and she'll write a big check to some appropriate cause and vow that every one of those bodies will be identified, and at the end of it, Audrey, at the end of it, everyone will think she's somehow the hero in all of this."

Her eyes are feverish. She's come forward as she talks, and now she stands uncomfortably close. She touches my jaw. I flinch; she keeps her finger there, like a punctuation mark on the end of her little speech.

"Melinda will probably even win her election," she says. "It's a hell of a story. You need those, in politics. Besides, the other guy is an idiot." She smiles without showing her teeth.

"There will be questions. You went down there. Over and over. Meghan—" I say.

Emily hums softly, cutting me off. "The thing about my family you have to understand, the thing about us, Audrey, is that we deal with our problems. We bury them deep." Her smile is a hook on one side of her mouth, mirthless and bitter.

"You don't seem happy about it," I say, my mouth dry.

"I'm not happy. Those girls are dead, why would I be happy?" she asks, head cocking to the side.

"Because you're getting away with it."

"What would I be getting away with?" she asks. She's not denying everything. She's daring me to say it.

"Where is Meghan Vale?" I ask.

She moves suddenly, so suddenly I don't have the chance to pull back as she holds my face in both her hands, staring into my eyes. "Stop looking for her," she whispers. "Please."

"Is she in one of those graves?" I ask. "Did you hurt her?"

The door slams open. Melinda, in her gray skirt suit, her makeup subdued. "Emily," she says, like a warning.

Emily drops her hands and steps back. "We were just catching up," she says.

Melinda's gaze flicks between us. She frowns. "They're ready for you," she says tersely.

Emily takes another loose step away before turning and walking out without another word. Melinda lingers a moment. She looks like she might be about to say something to me, and then she shakes her head and follows her sister out.

As soon as the door closes, I stagger against the wall. I'm shivering, I realize, and there is a strange taste at the back of my mouth.

"What the *hell* was that?" I ask my reflection. She looks as lost as me.

40

Before

The days congeal quickly into a routine. Food appears three times a day. The meals are fresh now. Emily's cooking, mostly. She's a good cook, though it's not like I had much of a basis of comparison before my diet shrank to a rotation of tuna, chicken, and dried fruit. I don't remember vegetables being such a delicacy, in any case.

When Melinda brings the food, she brings vitamins, too. I decide it's a good sign that she's worried about my health, but I can't get complacent.

Someone's always around. I try not to ask to use the bathroom too much—I don't want it to start to annoy them. I shower every day, with one of the girls guarding the door. Andrew stays away entirely, but I catch him staring from the end of the hall sometimes. Liam is eager to help—too eager, and they can all see it.

We have our ritual at night. Two knocks, two in return, a few words exchanged. I thought I was doing it to draw him in, but each night, I lie awake in buzzy anticipation of that small moment.

It's been over a week now. Over a week and no decision, but our time pretending that this can go on forever is officially at an end.

"I have to go," Liam says as I curl on my side, his voice muffled from the other side of the wall.

"Go where?" I ask.

"Back to work. I only had a couple weeks off," he says.

This is it. Because it's not just Liam who will need to go. Melinda has her work, Andrew has, well, whatever the hell Andrew does with his free time, and Emily will need to get back to school.

They haven't made a decision yet. I can't bring myself to believe that's a good thing. If they wanted to let me go, they could have by now.

"Don't leave," I say. "Don't go without me."

"I have to," Liam says, and I hear him draw away from the wall. His father thought Liam was weak. That only a weak man could want to make a living pretending to be other people. Mason Hill was a man who saw kindness and gentleness as weakness, of course, but he wasn't wrong. Liam *is* weak. I thought I could use that. Manipulate him into letting me go. But he isn't strong enough to do what I need him to.

He didn't promise to save me. He hasn't promised anything at all. He's surrendered already. Convinced himself there's nothing he can do.

I wonder if he thinks he's kind. If he thinks he's a good person. I think he knows he isn't. I see the way his pupils dilate, the way his hands shake. His words get slow, get tangled. I don't know what he's on. Probably any number of things. He's been taking more each day. Blunting the knowledge of who he is. What he's doing.

If any of them were good people, I wouldn't be here. But it hurts him that he isn't, and that still might be enough to save me.

The next morning, it's Emily who brings breakfast. Steaming pancakes, real maple syrup, a pat of butter starting to melt. She sits in the chair at the desk to watch me eat, as they always do. They aren't anywhere close to trusting me.

"We look alike," she says suddenly as I shovel pancakes into my mouth. I straighten up, made mute by the mouthful of food. She has her hands trapped between her knees, her shoulders drawn up near her jaw. "I didn't see it before. You were—you looked like an animal."

I blink. She's like this. Quiet one minute, then suddenly blunt. I swallow down my food. "Thanks? I guess?" I say. "I mean, you're very pretty. So I guess it's a good thing, looking like you." I try for a smile, but she doesn't return it.

"I look like my mother," she says.

Lizzie, Lizzie—

"I know." The pancakes are like glue on my back teeth. They stick in my throat.

"You look like her, too."

"Yeah." I look down at the plate. The butter is a greasy, malformed lump on top of the pitted pancakes. Syrup oozes down the side. Suddenly I'm not hungry. "Emily. Can I ask you something?"

She's silent. I look up. She shrugs one shoulder, which I take to be permission.

"The lock on the door. It only locks from the outside," I say. She doesn't move, doesn't respond. "How long has it been there?"

"I don't know. Always," she says, without particular inflection.

"Your father. Did he ever . . ." I don't want to ask her. If I'm allowed to keep my horrors locked within me, so is she. But I need to understand her.

She seems to consider for a moment. "After she died, he was destroyed. He loved her so much. She saved his life, you know. She said he saved her, but it was the other way around. She saved him from drink and despair, that's what he always said. She was his saint. His everything."

"Emily . . ."

"He used to stand at the end of my bed at night," she says. Her tone is steady, too controlled. "I'd wake up and he'd be there, crying. He'd beg me to forgive him and I didn't know what it was for, but he'd put his head in my lap and I'd run my fingers through his hair and tell him that he would be all right. He would say he loved me so much. That he would never hurt me. I knew it was true."

The back of my throat is sour with bile. He took us because we looked like his wife. Like his *daughter*.

I speak softly. "He called me Lizzie sometimes." *All the time.*

What is your name? Every time, it was a test. Defiance earned me black eyes, busted lips. I learned to answer with a laugh: *Lizzie, silly. It's your Lizzie, don't you recognize me?*

Oh, I was good at that. Good at *him*. He was simple. Easy to please, if only I let him devour every part of me that mattered. Growing up with a person like that . . . it's a terrifying thought. What would that do to a girl?

Emily rises. She reaches for the plate. "Are you done?" She doesn't meet my eyes.

"Yeah," I manage. I hold it out. "Sorry you have to wait on me hand and foot."

"That's all right," she says. She lifts her gaze, and her eyes lock with mine. "I mean, it's not like you're going to be here much longer."

She says it lightly. Not like a threat or a condemnation. Still, it makes my limbs go cold. She walks out, closing the door behind her, and I stare at the space where she was.

He would never hurt me, she said.

Suddenly I can't remember where the emphasis had been. *He'd* never *hurt me?* Or *He'd never hurt* me?

Living with someone like that—what would you have to become, to endure it?

The lock slides shut.

41

After

"My lawyer says I shouldn't talk to you," I tell Len, phone to my ear as I pour Barry his food.

"You called *me*," Len says.

"I know. I'm just saying. I'm going rogue out of love and respect for you, I want that clearly established."

Barry waits patiently, gobbets of saliva dripping to the floor. There's a reason I have a designated drool mop.

Len sighs. "What do you need?"

"Nothing. Exactly," I say. I adjust the phone and set down Barry's bowl, then step away quickly so the sound of him inhaling his kibble doesn't deafen Len. "It's just—I had the weirdest fucking conversation with Emily Hill today."

"You are supposed to be staying away from the Hills," he reminds me, irritation a burr in his voice.

"She cornered me in the bathroom. It was not my fault," I protest. I head over to the table, where my laptop is sitting. "I think she knows a lot more about Meghan than she's saying. What do you know about her?"

"Who? Meghan?"

"Emily. Obviously we didn't know her when we were kids, but I'm having trouble finding *anything*. She's not on social media. She said she sells her paintings, but it must not be under her name, because I've tried everything I can think of and they're not showing up anywhere online. I mean, maybe she just has them in a couple physical galleries, but . . ."

"I don't know what to tell you. There's really nothing there to find,"

Len says. "She barely exists as far as official records are concerned. Homeschooled most of high school, no job history, basically zero income. She files her taxes on time and she's got a driver's license. That's the Emily Hill biography. Oh, and she went to art school."

"Which one?"

"Savannah College of Art and Design," he says. "She was there for just under two years, looks like."

"That would mean she dropped out when her father died," I note.

"Yeah, I think that matches up. Listen, Audrey, I've got to go. I don't know how much I'll be able to share, or how long I'm even going to be in the loop, but I'll tell you what I can," Len says.

"Why? Don't you want me leaving this alone?" I ask.

"Yeah, but if I don't tell you, you're going to break into FBI headquarters or some dumb shit like that," Len says.

"Love you, too," I tell him, and he snorts as he hangs up the phone.

I let Barry out back for his customary post-dinner business and then pull up Facebook again. This time, I'm not looking for Emily. No one in this town really knows her, but she was at SCAD for two years—she must have had friends. An hour later, I've found a couple dozen of her contemporaries, and a few of them have even responded to my messages. I'm going for honest but vague:

> Hi! I'm reaching out because I'm looking for some info on a former classmate of yours, Emily Hill. I wonder if you remember her?

I've got mostly negatives, and one suggestion to talk to a woman named Marie Hiscock. To my surprise, she replies to my copy-and-paste message almost immediately.

> I knew Emily Hill. She was my roommate. Why do you want to ask about her?

I consider before I reply. I don't want to come across as a stalker, and I don't know whether this is going to get back to Emily.

I actually know her from when we were kids, and we recently reconnected. I feel like I can't really get a read on her, and so I guess I'm looking for a vibe check or something, haha.

Vague. Let her fill in the blanks. I watch the dots of a message being typed appear and vanish a few times before the response comes in.

I'm not sure how much help I can be. Hard to get a read on sums her up pretty well. But if she's anything like she was in college, I'd be careful.

Careful how? Why?

I don't really want to put this in writing. Can you do a call?

I agree quickly. A few minutes later, I get a link for a video call, and when I connect, I find myself looking at a woman with frizzy purple hair and thick cat's-eye glasses, sitting in a home office packed with succulents and crocheted animals.

"Hi," I say awkwardly. "Thanks for talking to me."

"I'm kind of curious why you're asking about her. It seems like a lot if you're just checking out a new friend," she says. She sounds suspicious, and I wonder if she really wanted to hop on the call so she could see my face, make sure I wasn't some guy stalking Emily.

"Can I be totally honest?" I say. She nods. "I met Emily again recently, like I said. We sort of—I don't know if *hit it off* is the right phrase, but we connected. But I can't tell if she's just a little bit odd or . . ."

"Or if you need to run the other way?" she says dryly.

"Pretty much. Normally I'd just go with my gut, but I was poking around and realized she's not online at *all*, and I think I got a bit carried away." I give a helpless shrug, impressed with my own improvisation.

She pushes up her glasses. "I haven't seen Emily since she left school. So all of this is way out of date, and I don't want to say that she's a certain way. I mean, people change, right?"

"Right," I say, nodding firmly. "I promise I'll take everything with the appropriate grain of salt."

She lets out a breath, like she still isn't convinced this is a good idea. "I was Emmie's roommate our sophomore year. I didn't really know her that well freshman year, but I had the impression she was kind of a loner? There was a weird rumor about her, but I didn't really believe it."

"What was the rumor?"

She looks uncomfortable. "Critiques can get pretty brutal in class. You put your heart and soul into something, and then your professor spends twenty minutes shredding it, you know? Some of the professors seemed to enjoy making you feel like shit, and Emmie was in the crosshairs on the same day that another girl got told she was the second coming of Michelangelo, her piece is perfect, that kind of thing. And then said perfect oil painting mysteriously got stored improperly before it was dry. Totally obliterated. No one copped to doing it, but a lot of people said it must have been Emmie."

"But you didn't believe it."

"She didn't strike me as that kind of mean girl," she says with a shrug.

"What did she strike you as?"

"She was homeschooled, right? She seemed like someone who had never learned how to talk to another human being. She was really smart and would know everything about a random subject and then she didn't know the US had a civil war. Or how to use a microwave. It was like all the normal patterns of just interacting and talking to a person never sank in, so there was always this weird stop-and-go feeling to all of our conversations. And I wouldn't say she was, like, *politically* conservative, but sex freaked her the fuck out. I let my boyfriend into the room in the middle of the day and we weren't even touching and she had a full-blown meltdown."

"Shit," I say. Some of it tracks—that not-quite-smooth pattern to conversation, the sense of a person who has been outside of society.

"Sometimes she scared me," Marie says plainly. "There was an edge to her. Like if she got set off the wrong way . . . I don't want to say she was angry or, I don't know, *malevolent*, but looking back, I think she had no idea how to deal with uncomfortable situations and emotions. To be honest, I was glad when she dropped out." She rubs the back of her neck, looking self-conscious at having shared so much.

"Do you know why she did?" I ask. "It was right around when her father died, right?"

"Yeah. I mean, I assume that *was* why," she says. "He died, she left school for a couple weeks, and she never came back. Her sister came to box up her things at one point and said she'd been in a car accident."

"An accident?" I repeat.

"Yeah. She was okay, but her sister said she couldn't make the trip. That's the last we heard from any of them. I sent her an email just to say hey, but she never responded."

I ask a few more questions, but she doesn't have much more to offer. I thank her and hang up, and then, without much hope, I plug in "Emily Hill car accident" and a date range into a search engine.

To my surprise, I get a result. A tiny entertainment outlet has the stub of an article about the accident—because Liam was driving. *Single-car accident,* I read. Slick road, middle of the night, lost control, sister in the passenger seat. Liam broke his arm. His sister was reported to have suffered serious injuries but was expected to recover. It sounds worse than Melinda let on to the roommate.

I look at the name of the road. I know it. It's not far from the Hills' place. It's barely more than a single-lane road, and it doesn't lead anywhere you'd be in a hurry to get in the middle of the night, which raises the question of what they were doing out there.

I know Liam was using by then. Wagner's name pops up in the article, saying drugs weren't believed to be a factor, but it wouldn't be the first time he bent over backwards for the Hills.

I tug on my lip. *Something* happened in those few weeks, obviously. The simplest explanation, of course, is also the least exciting: Going home made her realize she was unhappy. An unrelated accident made it so she'd have to miss more school anyway, and she realized she might as well drop out and call it quits.

Or there's something tucked between her father's death and that accident. A third factor, a hidden reason.

What happens when someone dies? The family converges. A funeral is arranged. The remains of a life are examined, divvied up, cleared out.

When my grandmother died, my mother spent a week with her siblings emptying her house. I remember her coming home with a box of letters—love letters, and not from my grandfather. *She had a whole life she never told us about*, she'd said, laying the letters out on the table.

There was more than a box of love letters for the Hills to find.

That year, Andrew was still playing professionally. Melinda's congressional campaign was gearing up, and Liam was getting buzz as an up-and-coming actor.

None of which would be impacted by having their next-door neighbor turn out to be a serial killer. But their father? That would have derailed everything.

I pull up the photo of Liam from the website again, looking not at Liam but at Emily—what little of her I can see. This keeps coming back to her. She's the one who never *really* left home. She's the one who stayed in that place, and who left those marks on the wall, on the trees.

They knew. They had to. Emily sank into isolation and her own strange mind. Liam numbed himself with drugs. Andrew and Melinda—they'd been older. Got out sooner. Emily said her father changed after her mother died.

On impulse, I send a quick message to Marie asking if she has any photos of Emily. A few minutes later, she comes through. Just one: Emily and Marie standing together in a college dorm room. Marie is smiling in a T-shirt sporting an 8-bit character I don't recognize. Emily looks like she's just remembered she should be smiling but hasn't gotten around to it. She has one arm across her body, gripping the opposite arm tightly. She looks like a deer in the headlights. She's strikingly young compared to the Emily I know, a softness to her features that has long since withered away.

I look between the two photos. There's less than a year between them. Stacked together, Emily's tense stance and stricken expression feel less like a bad photo and more like a bad omen. This was not a happy girl.

My phone chimes. It's a text from Len. *Check the news,* he says. *Making announcement now.*

I pull up the local news, and right on the front page of the website is a link to a livestream of a press conference. There's a man in a state police uniform talking. I recognize the FBI agent behind him, and Chief Wagner—and Melinda is standing off to the side, too.

I barely hear the words: "Believe Mr. Butler acted alone . . . no further threat to the community . . . work in the days and months ahead to identify the victims."

Melinda's expression is perfectly somber. Calm and in control, and why shouldn't it be? She's succeeded. No one is going to be looking for reasons it might not have been Terry Butler, not when the bodies are on his land, the trophies in his attic. How long ago did they plant those? I wonder. How long have they been planning for a contingency like this?

You did good, Len texts. *It's over.*

Next to the video, a live chat scrolls by, people adding comments.

There are a lot of people watching. I hadn't realized how much attention this was getting. God rest their souls, someone writes.

What is it about the PNW and serial killers????

FBI guy's hott

And then, flashing by so fast I barely see it: They're lying. Butler didn't do it.

I scroll back up, but the message is gone—like it was deleted as fast as it was posted. But I saw the username before it vanished. NoOneYouKnow.

Another way of saying *stranger*.

42

Before

It's the middle of the day when there's a knock at my door. I don't say anything, just wait for the lock to click open and Liam to slink in. He's carrying a bottle of wine by the neck, already open. His gait is unsteady as he turns and shuts the door, and when he approaches, his pupils are huge. He's on something. He almost always is, but this is different.

"Brought you a present," he says. His voice is slurred. For an instant, I freeze. It's always a gamble, dealing with people when they're wasted like this. You have to be able to sort the angry drunks from the weepers from the mischief-makers. Some people get easier to manipulate when they're under the influence. Plenty just get dangerous.

"Will you join me?" I ask, patting the bed beside me. Liam's not one for rage, I think. My guess is a weeper. The kind you end up talking off the edge of a bridge while he cries until snot runs down his face.

He sits and swigs. Only then does he remember to offer it to me. He sits facing out into the room with his back bent over, the slouch of a defeated man. Somehow, I have to talk him into fighting for me, but it isn't going to be easy.

"What's going on, Liam?" I ask him. I take a small sip of the wine. Enough to get the taste of it, not enough to hit my blood with any kind of power.

"What do you think? I have to leave," he says. He sounds miserable. I put a hand on his wrist. His skin is soft and smooth. It has a thinness to it.

"We can see each other again," I say with a smile. "We can meet up someday."

If he doesn't look at me, I'm out of luck. But if he does look—

He turns his sorrowful gaze on me, and my breath catches in my throat. He hasn't given up entirely, then. If he had, he wouldn't be able to look me in the face.

"What's going to happen to me, Liam?" I ask in a whisper.

He holds the bottle in both hands, staring down at it. "Melinda has this plan."

"What kind of plan?"

"She has resources. She works with women's shelters, and she has contacts who do this sort of thing. Getting someone a new life, I mean."

"So I can go be someone new," I say. My heart beats fast. Could it be that simple?

"Someone who's never met us," he says. He drinks in a quick, frustrated movement. "Sounds perfect, doesn't it?"

"Most of it," I say. *All of it.* Give me a ten-second head start and these people will never so much as glimpse my shadow again, but I trail a fingertip up the bone of his forearm, skating along the skin.

He looks toward me again, his eyes swimming with longing and with mourning, and then he looks away again quickly. "I don't think Andrew wants to let you go. He doesn't trust you not to tell."

"You can trust me. And I know you don't want to hurt me," I say at once, as if I'm not afraid at all.

"Of course not!" He grabs my hand. His grip is too tight; it makes my bones mash together. "I wouldn't. But Andrew—he's dangerous."

"I'm not afraid," I say. My lips tremble as I smile. "I've got you in my corner, don't I?"

"But I won't be here," he says.

"You're here now."

His eyes track away again. I'm losing him. He's going to walk out that door. He's going to go walk outside to puke up this wine and whatever other poison he's put in himself. He's going to spend the next thirty years thinking of these awful hours, and that's all I will be. Something to get out of his system, something to regret.

I don't want to touch him. I don't want to use the delicate pads of my fingertips to turn his face toward me, or to take the bottle from him and lift it to his lips and then mine. I don't want to slide myself into his lap and press my lips to his until the taste of me becomes indistinguishable from the taste of the wine.

"Liam," I whisper, as if I don't hate him. "Don't leave me. Not tonight. Please."

His touch is sandpaper against my skin, but, oh, I wish I could love him. I wish any of this was true. That this isn't a trick, that there isn't a knife to my throat and only this one hope.

I put the wine on the windowsill. His hands find the gap between my shirt and my jeans and steal their way against my skin, and I pretend.

I pretend that I want him.

That I love him.

That his cowardice is not every bit as monstrous as his brother's cruelty.

I push him down onto the bed. He sinks like a drowning man, and I am the siren with her hands in his hair. We descend together, but I belong to the deep; I'm not the one gasping for air.

I don't know what I expect, exactly, but this isn't it—this strange tangle of grief and guilt and hunger and claiming, a sharp and angry thicket of emotion that somehow translates into a slow and gentle movement between the two of us. Something tips, rebalances, and each of us is asking the other for something we cannot hope to give—some kind of healing, maybe, some kind of forgetting—and neither of us can grant it, and in our lack is a trembling hum of connection.

I expect to hate him in the moments after, but instead, I hear his heartbeat under my ear and my own heart stirs with only pity.

I curl against him. He lies still, staring at the ceiling. "Liam," I whisper. I wait for his touch, for his arm to tighten around me.

"I have to go," he says. "I'm sorry."

My breath seizes. No. After all of this, no. He stiffens, as if to rise. I brace myself on my elbow, looking down at him. My hair falls like a curtain closing the world off from the two of us. "Liam, please. If you leave me with Andrew—"

"I'm sorry," he says again, and shoves himself upward, sending me flopping back onto the bed unceremoniously. He grabs his boxers and his jeans, hiking them up to his slim hips. He doesn't bother to put on his shirt or buckle his belt, just heads for the door.

He yanks it open, and Emily is standing there. He freezes. She looks past him, her eyes locking onto me as I grab for the sheet to cover my nudity. "What are you doing?" she asks, her voice gravelly.

"Em—" Liam begins.

"You're disgusting," she grates out, face contorted in anger. "Get out of there." She keeps her voice low, but she might as well be screaming it.

"It's okay," I say quickly. "I was the one—"

"Get out," she snaps, ignoring me, and all but drags him out into the hall.

"Emily, wait," I say. She gives me one flat, empty look.

"He shouldn't have done that," she says. And then she slams the door shut.

The figure at the end of my bed looks toward me, her expression sorrowful. I haven't seen them in days, my gossamer girls. But maybe now I'm close enough to death for them to return to me.

It's over, she says.

It's over, and I lost.

43

After

The days tick by, one after the other. I take sick days, skip a training, leave a text from Dev unanswered. Another girl gets a name. Every article discusses Terry Butler as if proving his guilt is merely a formality. I take Barry up to Eden Crest most evenings, but I always turn back before dark.

"Does it matter?" I ask Barry as we stand at the peak. He seems to sense my unease, leaning his whole weight against me and looking up at me with big, earnest eyes. "They're both dead, Mason Hill and Terry Butler. Does it matter which of them gets the blame? Does it matter if the Hills get away with it?"

He whuffs at me anxiously.

"Maybe they didn't even know," I say. Or they suspected, but had no proof. Maybe I've made them into villains without any cause at all, except the crime of surviving their upbringing. The trophies were in Butler's attic, after all, and I have no evidence but my own gut instinct to say Mason Hill is the one truly to blame.

"Does it matter?" I ask again, but I know the answer, because the hum in my bones is an inescapable pressure now. This isn't done. *I'm* not done.

They're lying.

The comment had probably just been some random internet conspiracy theorist. There was no way to track them down, anyway, and the name could have been a coincidence. But I can't shake the connection. There are only a handful of people who know about the words carved down there.

My phone starts to ring. I don't recognize the number and I'm about to reject the call when I realize it's a Los Angeles area code. Liam.

"Hello?" I say. At first, I think the poor signal has already dropped the call, because there is a long, thick moment of silence before a raspy breath.

"Audrey Dixon," Liam says, and instantly I know he isn't sober. "You're not going to be a problem. Did you know that? Kind of nice, really. To not be a problem. I've never managed it."

His words are slurred, fading in and out. Alarm zings through me. "Where are you?" I ask.

He doesn't answer. "I did what you said."

Meghan. He means he asked about Meghan. "What did Emily say?"

He's quiet again, the silence syrupy. "Sometimes it's better not to know the answer. If you leave it shut, then you don't—it's Schrödinger's box, you know? Don't open it, and you didn't kill the cat, not really, it wasn't you, it might not have happened at all. She gets to be alive and dead at the same time. Open the box, and you're going to have to do something about it."

It's a struggle to make out what he's saying, and I don't like the sound of his breathing. "Meghan. Tell me about Meghan," I say.

"It's not my fault," Liam says. "It was too late. We couldn't stop now. Not after everything. It couldn't all be for nothing. We couldn't have done all that and then it doesn't even matter."

My heart is hammering. Barry gives a low, undirected growl, looking to me for direction, and I realize I have wrapped the leash tight around my fist. "What did you do?" I demand.

There's a pause, a hiccup of breath. "Nothing," he says distantly. "I never do anything. I'm not the one. Do you think I'm a bad person, Audrey?"

"No," I say, trying to sound soothing, not sure at all that it's true. "Liam, I don't think you're a bad person, but you need to tell me where you are."

"But that's it," Liam says. "Everything was going to be okay. It was going to work just like Melinda said, but she was so angry, she wouldn't listen, and I told . . ." He trails off.

"Liam?" I say. I repeat his name twice more. I can't tell if I can hear him breathing anymore. "Damn it, Liam, talk to me."

No answer. I jam the button to end the call and rake my hand through my hair. Calling 9-1-1 is useless when I have no idea where he is. I dig in my coat pocket again, and stab my finger on the crisp corner of Melinda's business card. I dial the number wrong twice before I get my fingers under control.

To my relief, she picks up. "Melinda Hill speaking," she says.

"Melinda, it's Audrey," I say, and I can practically hear her lips pressing together in annoyance.

"Audrey, let me be clear—"

"Liam just called me," I say, cutting her off. "He was on something. A *lot* of something."

"Liam's been clean for two years," Melinda says. And then, "Where is he?"

"I don't know. I couldn't get him to tell me, and I think he passed out," I say.

"Okay. I think I know where he might have gone," Melinda says. She hangs up without another word. I didn't ask her about Meghan. It would be useless anyway. There's only one person I need answers from on that front now.

I tug Barry's leash. "Come on."

Taking the downhill path at nearly a run, we reach the car in record time. Barry launches himself into the back seat, having decided we're on an adventure, and sticks his massive head over my shoulder as I buckle in. I bat him back and get a slobbery hand for my trouble.

We're only a few minutes from the Hills' place. The barrier is still there, and I park right in front of it. I leave Barry in the car. It's a cool day, and I don't want Andrew meeting us at the door with a gun.

I needn't have worried. There are no cars in the driveway when I arrive, no lights on inside. I pace around the house, but the place is empty. Emily isn't here, unless she's hiding in there.

With her family around, the house isn't a sanctuary right now. She'll be somewhere else, somewhere private. The only place I know about is the studio.

I scrub my hands on my jeans as I stride back to the car. The rational, logical part of me knows that my rush probably has no purpose. Whatever happened to Meghan, it happened months ago. But Liam called me now, broke his sobriety now. Something changed, and Emily was the cause.

The studio is tucked into the second story of a nondescript building. There's a laundromat around the back and a vacuum repair place at the front. I've never actually seen anyone go inside. Len and I used to joke that it must be a front for the Russian mob. The door Emily emerged from is unadorned and unlabeled—and locked.

There's an intercom button by the door. I hesitate, then press it. The harsh blat makes me jump, and Barry gives a half-hearted bark from the back seat.

It's a solid thirty seconds before an answer comes. "Hello?"

I tense. She's here. "It's Audrey," I say. "We need to talk. It's about—Liam."

Silence again, a long silence of considering. And then there's another buzz and the lock clicks.

I pull it open before she can change her mind. Barry watches me from the back seat, eyebrows twitching together with worry.

Just inside the door is a steep, narrow flight of stairs. At the top is a small landing and another door, this one unlocked. It opens onto a well-lit space; a skylight and large windows let the sun flood in. Several easels adorn the space—some clearly for display, and one in the center in active use. There's a half-finished painting propped on it: a girl's face interposed with the wings of a moth. Both girl and insect have a spectral quality to them, though maybe that's only that both are unfinished, devolving into blocks of color and a sharply contrasting underpainting in umber hues.

The paintings at the house were almost all still life and nature. Almost all of the paintings scattered around the room here are portraits.

I drift between them, taking in one face after another. You might be forgiven for thinking that she has painted the same portrait again and again and again. The red-haired girl—young woman—with pale skin and bright eyes. You might be excused for missing how her face shifts, changes. Narrowing, rounding. Eyes shifting toward green to blue to gray. Hair like wheat touched only lightly by strawberry tones deepening to copper, to auburn, to a bright ginger.

A dozen paintings. At least half a dozen girls. Some of them are shown only from the shoulders up, staring straight at the viewer. Others are painted from farther away, half turned. Their clothing is indistinct—white or dove gray, draping clothes like nightgowns. The sorts of clothes you imagine being worn by a ghost.

There's a soft footstep behind me. I turn, breath caught in my throat. Emily steps out from a back room carrying a jar of clear water, the rim streaked with mixed paints. She sets it on a stool next to the easel and regards me with eyes that might be calm—or merely empty.

"What is this?" I ask, my voice a croak. I gesture to the portraits.

"You know what they are," she says softly.

I look at the nearest painting. Like in all of them, the face is *almost* familiar. *Almost* the face of someone I've known. The slant of her mouth—that *could* be Janie, but isn't quite. The shape of her jaw—*almost* Emily.

There is a name at the bottom right-hand corner. At first, I assume it's an artist's signature, but then I look more closely.

Amanda.

I know what I'll see when I look at the others, but I check all the same. They're there. All the names—Madison, Amanda, Isabel.

"You didn't make these paintings in less than a week," I say. She shakes her head mutely. "You've known about them all along."

"Why are you here, Audrey?" she asks.

"Liam called me."

Her eyebrow raises in mild curiosity. "Oh?"

"He said that he'd asked you about Meghan. He was upset. He sounded like he was using. I think he was overdosing."

"Old habits die hard," Emily says quietly, looking down as she selects a paintbrush from a jar.

"You don't sound very upset."

She draws the paintbrush out slowly. "Liam doesn't like me very much. I think he might actually hate me."

I make a frustrated noise in the back of my throat. "He's your brother. Your twin. Shouldn't you care about him?"

She fans the brush against the palm of her hand. "I don't know if I can," she says. She sounds almost sad. Almost.

I shake my head in disgust. I take out my phone. One by one, I snap pictures of the paintings. The names repeat, I realize—and the portraits are inconsistent. As if she's trying to re-create the girls from memory, or from her imagination.

"What are you doing?" Emily asks.

"Getting proof," I say. I glare at her, but she only stares impassively back. "Why hide all of this? For Melinda's campaign? For Andrew's career? For Liam's show? Did Meghan find out? Did you do something to her?"

"You don't understand," Emily says simply, factually.

"Then explain it to me," I shout, my face hot and my heart pounding. Emily blanches, stumbles back a step, the first real reaction since I've walked in the door.

She looks to the side, breathing heavily. The quiver in her limbs is genuine fear, but I don't think it's me she's scared of. For a moment, I think she's going to speak, to explain—but she only wraps an arm around her waist. "There are more in the other room," she says.

"What?"

"If you want photos of all of them. There are more in the back," she says, eyes fixed on a portrait in the corner.

I wait, but she has nothing more to say. I walk with clipped, angry steps to the back room—a smaller space, the one window covered with a thick black curtain. There are paintings stacked against the walls and on shelves here. A chorus of dead girls, all different, all eerily alike.

In the back of the room is a large storage closet. The door stands open. Through it, I can see the concrete walls. The mattress against the back wall.

I walk slowly toward it, drawn forward by a feeling that thrums in my bones. Behind me comes the soft sound of a brush drawn over canvas. I reach inside and flick on the light.

Someone—Emily—has written on the walls. No, not written—carved. Scratched. Jagged, hasty letters spelling out messages I've seen before.

Do what you have to
Stay alive
Keep him happy
MY NAME IS MY NAME IS MY NAME IS MY NAME IS MY NAME IS MY NAME IS MY NAME IS MY NAME IS—

I suck in a sharp breath, my lungs burning—I had forgotten, for a moment, to breathe. It's all here. The words from below and more, blooming out like fungal spread. Words of warning and fear and frantic hope, an echo and a re-creation.

There's something on the bed. A book. A diary. It looks a lot like Meghan's, but this one is older, with a leather cover cracked and fraying at the edges. When I open it, the spine clicks.

Property of Emily Hill, reads the first page. The pages fan in my hands. I begin to read. And I can't stop. I flip frantically from page to page, drinking in the words, the confessions of the teenage Emily Hill.

And then I stop, staring at the final words of the diary.

We can't let her go.

I turn, knowing that she'll be there. She stands in the center of the room, hands empty, watching me intently.

"That bunker wasn't empty," I say hollowly.

"No. It wasn't."

"What did you do?" The words are almost a whisper.

"I did what I had to," she says. "We all did."

44

Before

If I knock at the wall tonight, there will be no response. I've lost Liam. I still can't say how much of that was me and how much was inevitable. Either way, he's failed me. He'll leave, and it will be the first domino. The rest will tumble one by one.

Andrew brings me my meal that night. Not good, but I knew that already. He looks me in the eye. I find no mercy there.

Melinda doesn't come at all. Her decision won't matter. Andrew's made his. He'll do it behind her back if he has to.

My ghosts keep me company. They faded for a time, like they couldn't figure out how to exist in this new place, but they've returned. They've rotted since I saw them last, holes in them like a moth-eaten sweater. Sometimes I think I see things moving in the gaps.

I'm glad they're here. I'll still be among them, one of them, in the end. I only wish I'd gotten the chance to leave my real name alongside theirs, for the next girl to find.

There won't be a next girl, she reminds me.

"There's always a next girl," I whisper. Doesn't matter that he's dead. There's always a hole in the ground waiting to swallow one of us up, and someone eager to put us there.

A tentative hand knocks on the door. As always, my visitor doesn't wait for a response before opening it. Emily stands there, a pile of laundry balanced in one arm. I sit cross-legged on the bed, holding a pillow against my torso. We stare at each other a moment.

"I got you some new clean clothes," she says. She steps in and shuts the door behind her. She goes to the dresser, putting her back to me. "Liam shouldn't have done that."

"It's not his fault," I say, not sure why I'm defending him. Of course he shouldn't have. I seduced him, but it shouldn't have been possible. Maybe it wouldn't have been, if it weren't for the drugs, the alcohol.

"We all make mistakes," she says, busying herself with putting clothes in the drawers. I don't bother to tell her that I won't need that many. I won't have time to need them. "The important thing is how we deal with them."

"What mistakes have you made?" I ask.

She looks back at me at last. Her eyes are doe-like. She isn't that much younger than me, but she seems childlike in so many ways. She moves like she's making herself small. "Melinda has to go back into the city tomorrow," she says, rather than answering me. "She's going to drive Liam to the airport, and then she's going to be gone all day."

My throat constricts. That's when he'll do it. He'll promise Melinda he's not going to do anything hasty, and then . . .

Or, hell. Maybe she knows. Maybe she just wants to be able to pretend she had no idea what he would do the minute her back was turned. And Emily? I don't believe for a moment that she's any protection against her brother.

"Do you know the story of Jenny Red-Hands?" Emily asks. I jolt.

"Yes," I say, throat dry, but she doesn't seem to hear me.

"They say she lived in the woods with her family, until something terrible happened. No one believed her. No one protected her. So she made herself into a monster. She did what she had to do," Emily says, not looking at me. "They say she's still out there. That if a girl brings her an offering, she'll come, and she'll have her knife with her. And sometimes, she'll hurt the people who deserve to be hurt. And sometimes, she'll make that girl disappear. So you don't go into the woods and call her name unless either version would be better than what you have now. I used to save my teeth."

She looks back at me, the abrupt shift startling me.

"I kept them in a box. Dad wanted me to leave them for the tooth fairy, but I wouldn't. When I heard the story, I finally knew why. Because that's her price. A string of teeth. But she didn't come." Her voice is matter-of-fact and distant, and I find myself sitting very still.

She moves a sweater from the top of the stack of laundry. Underneath, hidden by its bulk until now, are a pair of running shoes. She casually tucks the sweater into the top drawer, moves the shoes, and stows the remaining pairs of pants.

"Have a good night," she says simply, and steps out of the room. The door shuts behind her. I wait, holding my breath, ears straining.

The key scrapes into the lock. But it doesn't turn. She withdraws it, and then her footsteps move at a quick clip down the hall.

She's giving me a chance. A slim chance, but I have to take it.

I steal across the floor. The shoes are almost a perfect fit—a half size too small, but I'll take pinched toes gladly. I lace them up tight and tuck the ends in. Can't afford to trip.

I look outside. The bluish tint of near night casts the trees in somber shades. There will be enough light to see by, enough shadow to conceal me. If only I can get out undetected. Cut through the woods, and then across to the road. I've heard the sound of trucks; I know which direction to head. If only I can get past the others.

Down the hall in the living room, the sound of the TV starts up, the thumping bass of an action movie.

I won't get a better chance than this.

I creep to the door. Half of me expects that I misheard and the door will still be locked, but the knob turns under my hand. Every time one of them opens it, it creaks halfway, so I slot my body through the narrowest gap I can. The hall is hidden from the living room. To the left, I can reach the garage—and freedom.

I start toward it. And stop. Liam's door is open. The light is off, but the room is not empty—he's sitting on the bed, head in his hands, in the dark. As I hesitate there—for a second or two, no more—he looks up. His eyes reflect the light from the hall, but behind that glint I can't read anything at all.

Tentatively, I put a finger to my lips. And then I walk swiftly away. I have no choice but to hope.

The garage door is stiff but opens with hardly a sound. I have to restrain myself from sprinting. I can't afford a single squeak of my shoes giving me away.

I skirt the covered car, entertaining images of reversing it out of the garage in a squeal of tires and tearing down the road. Then the garage door is open—still no shout from behind me, no thundering feet—and I'm outside.

Outside, with a mist of rain against my skin and the cloud-draped sky dark velvet above me. I'm not free yet, but I can taste it.

My eyes aren't used to the dark anymore. I wade out into it, away from the persistent glow of the house lights. Not far now. Dead girls school like minnows around me, scale-flash shimmers, their movements quick and anxious. I pick up my pace. Branches crackle underfoot, eager to give me away, but muffled gunfire and percussion from the movie drown out their efforts.

The gossamer girls are all around me. I stumble. Nine days since I came to the house. Nine days of food and rest and warmth and wearing a track back and forth. I have the strength for this. I have swift feet and enough fear to keep me moving, and I will be free, I will run, I will find the road and a pair of headlights, and I will be found, I will live—

There is a girl in front of me. Copper hair and haunted eyes. My vision is so clotted with ghosts that for an instant I miss that this is no gossamer girl, that her flesh is solid and she's not one of us—

She was never one of us—

"I'm sorry," Emily says.

"Emily?" I manage, my voice small.

She looks at me with eyes so empty of life I understand why I thought she belonged to the gossamer girls. "You're already dead. This is better," she says.

"What are you doing?" I ask, backing away half a step.

"She didn't come. Jenny never came to take me away, but it was okay. He found a way to protect me," Emily says, drawing closer. The gossamer girls are flickers of light in my vision, harrying her. "You were bad girls. It's okay for bad girls to die if it means everyone else is safe."

I stare at her in dawning horror. "I'm no threat to you," I say.

"Yes, you are. I saw what you made my brother do," she says. "I'll tell them I tried to stop you and you attacked me. They'll see I had to do it. Then none of them have to feel bad."

She steps forward again, and I see the shape in her hand only as she brings it around in a brutal arc: a hammer.

The impact against my skull is an explosion of pain, a death of light. I feel myself falling, but I don't feel myself hit the ground. I am insubstantial; I am nothing; I am gossamer at last, and at last, in this darkness, I am free.

45

After

The door downstairs slams. Emily's gaze flicks toward it. "That will be Melinda, I imagine," she says.

Neither of us moves. Melinda appears in the other room, looking harried.

"Why aren't you answering your phone? I need to—" She stops when she sees me. Her braid has come loose, ragged strands of hair hanging around a face that is puffy from crying. Her eyes drop to the diary, and breath hisses between her teeth. Her hand darts into the large purse at her side, and before I have time to react, she draws a small silver pistol. "What the fuck is she doing with that?" Melinda asks. The gun points straight at me, but she's staring at Emily, who makes no move to intervene.

"'He's got another one already,'" I quote, feeling sick. I try not to look at the gun. My mouth is dry, but my voice steady "She knew. The whole time, she knew exactly what he was doing. She knew about every one of those girls. Did you?"

Melinda blanches. The gun trembles in her hand. Her finger isn't on the trigger, at least, lying alongside it instead. "It started after I moved out," she says. "Do you think we would have just left her there if we had any idea . . . ? If we knew what it was *doing* to her? What he'd turned her into?"

"It might not have been him that did it," Emily says mildly. "Some people are just born wrong."

Melinda shakes her head sharply. "I don't believe that."

Emily shifts her attention to me with a hum. "It was homecoming," she says.

I nod. It's all in there. The sweater, and walking home through the woods. He was supposed to have the place to himself. He wasn't as careful as he should have been, and so he didn't notice Emily coming home. Didn't notice her following him out to the old bomb shelter in the woods. But when she came down the steps, he saw.

He wrapped his arms around her that night, tight enough to bruise her ribs, and wept against her neck because of what he was going to have to do to keep his secret. But she soothed him. Whispered against his ear that she loved him. That she would keep the secret, too.

She convinced him. And she kept her promise. Day after day, year after year, she said nothing. She watched him go out to the woods. Even helped him with small things, sometimes. Burning clothes. Getting extra food and supplies.

He trusted her so much that when she asked to leave for college, he eventually said yes.

And she kept his secret even then, miles away from his influence.

She never told a soul.

"Meghan knew, didn't she?" I ask.

Melinda looks at Emily sharply. Emily only inclines her head. "Yes," she says.

Melinda lets out a soft moan. "Oh god," she says. The gun dips. Still pointing in my direction, but with less intent. I eye the distance to the door. No way to get past Melinda cleanly. "What did you do?"

Emily doesn't answer right away, but regards Melinda with a cautious expression. "What did Liam tell you?" Emily asks.

Melinda's breath hitches. "He didn't tell me anything. Liam's dead," she says. I suck in a startled breath.

"I see," Emily says carefully.

"Can't you show even a moment of compassion?" Melinda demands, expression contorted with grief and anger. I flinch as the gun jerks with the movement of her hand.

Emily's lip peels back in almost a snarl. "What do you want from me, Melinda? You want me to weep and beat my chest over a man who hasn't looked me in the eye once in the last ten years?"

"None of this was Liam's fault," Melinda says raggedly. "We did this to him." She presses the back of her free hand against her lips, holding in a sob. "He seemed—I thought he was okay. Everything was going to work out, I told him I had it under control . . ."

"When Liam called me, he was talking about Meghan," I say carefully, tracking the path of the gun's muzzle. "He felt guilty about something he'd found out after he went to you about her."

"I swear to you, I didn't hurt Meghan Vale." Emily's words are measured, her gaze intent.

"But you have killed someone before," I say softly.

Emily stares at me. There's something in her eyes, almost eager. "Yes. I killed someone," she says. There is a bitter twist to her lips, almost a smile. "Do you know her name, Audrey? The girl I killed?"

I match her gaze and nod. "Emily Hill."

46

Before

The hammer only clips my skull, but still, it's almost enough to end me.

It feels like an instant and an eternity that I lie on the ground, aware of my body but not in it. Pure black gives way to a seething mass of light, and reality returns just in time for me to roll to the side as another blow swings down. The hammer impacts the ground, throwing up bits of dirt.

"Emily!"

Emily whips around. It's Melinda's voice, but I can't see Melinda herself.

I pull myself away, but I'm too dizzy to push to my feet.

Run, run, run, my dead girls scream. Melinda calls again. Emily turns back toward me.

I shove to my feet and bolt. Instantly I stagger to the side, shoulder impacting a tree, but I use it to claw myself forward. There's blood in my eye, half blinding me. I used to be fast. I used to run until I couldn't breathe, until I collapsed laughing on the sun-soaked grass, but now I'm so slow, and she's right behind me.

My foot hits a slick patch of rotten leaves. Already off-balance, I can't correct. My shoe shoots out from under me and the rest of my body follows, sending me rolling down a short slope. I hit the bottom hard. I can't draw in a breath. Can't get my muscles to move.

Emily runs toward me, hammer in hand. I'm never going to get away.

I seize a fistful of rotten leaves and dirt and stones, and in the instant she swings, I fling it, twisting on the ground at the same time. The blow hits my shoulder, sending an instant burst of pain through my left arm. Emily staggers. I kick out with both feet, catching her in the shins. The slick ground gives her no purchase. She falls.

She lands awkwardly. I don't give her time to recover. She's never had to fight for her life before. It's all I've known for months.

My left arm isn't working. Dead weight. But I plant my knee on the hammer and slam my right fist into her face again and again. She gropes at the hammer, gives up, throws both hands up to protect herself.

It gives me half a second. I stop swinging. Shift my weight. Grab the hammer.

The rest is quick.

I sit kneeling beside her, the hammer, now slick, gripped in my good hand. The other drags in the dirt, the pain elemental, held at bay only by sheer adrenaline. Only then do I remember the voice. Only then do I turn and see Melinda behind me, holding the rifle.

"She knew," I say, my voice a croak. "She knew we were down there."

Melinda steps forward. The gun isn't pointing at me, but she keeps it at the ready, finger on the trigger. "I know," she says softly. "She told me. I called her after . . . She wasn't surprised. She already knew."

"Called her? Called her after what?" I ask.

Melinda's eyes are bright in the moonlight. A tear slips down her cheek. "I didn't realize he'd already found someone new. I swear."

"What are you talking about?" I demand.

She swallows. "I came home. I wasn't supposed to. He always wanted us to call first. He wasn't at the house, so I went out to look for him. He was . . . he was burying her. I've been thinking it through. I think I've figured it out. The ground had just thawed. I think when she died, the ground was too frozen to bury her, so he stored her all winter. And found you in the meantime." She says it like figuring it out means something. Like it's important.

Her father murdered a girl. And he kept her body all winter, and all the while he had me to keep him company.

"What did you do?" I ask.

She twitches, like she's forgotten I was there. "I know I should have called the police. But I called Emily. And she said—she said not to do anything. She tried to convince me it was better just to leave it alone, and I realized she'd known all along. She'd—" There's more that even now she can't say. She swallows it down. "If that got out . . . I had to stop him. But I had to protect her. So I killed him." She gives a little laugh, like she can't believe it. "I had a spare key to the neighbor's place. I took some of his heart medication and I put it in Dad's drink. I poisoned my own father and then I left and I let him rot here for *weeks*."

"He's not the only one you left to rot," I growl. My hand tightens on the hammer. I wonder whose reflexes would be quicker.

"I didn't *know*," she wails. "And then we found you and I panicked. I thought—they'd find out what I did, they'd find out about Emily, and I know I shouldn't have said anything, I put the idea in Andrew's head and then—I was going to get you out of here. I have the documents. I have a bus ticket in my purse. If I'd only had one more *day* . . ."

There are voices from the direction of the house. Liam and Andrew, calling for their sisters. "What are you going to do, Melinda?" I ask quietly. "Are you going to kill me, too?"

She doesn't want to. I can see it in her eyes. But she doesn't know how to get out of it.

"Melinda."

More shouts. The boys are getting closer.

"She was trying to kill you." Melinda lets out a shuddering breath and speaks to herself with cold logic. "She was trying to kill you. She knew about them all along. She was—there was something wrong with her."

She looks to me as if for confirmation. I nod once, and a shiver goes through her.

"Give me the hammer," she snaps. She walks toward me. I flinch back. She sticks out her hand impatiently, all her hesitation gone in an instant. "If the boys think it was you, you're dead. It has to be me."

I hesitate. But if she was going to kill me, she could have just shot me. "You killed her," I agree. I let her take the hammer. She grabs my hand, smearing her sister's blood over her own palms. She tosses the gun, as if it were dropped in a scuffle, and paws at her clothes and face quickly. It won't stand up to scrutiny, but maybe in the dark—

In the dark, she can say anything she wants. She can say she thought it was me when she swung the hammer. An accident. A mistake. We look so alike, after all, Emily and me.

She stares at me as the voices draw nearer, as if she's having the same thought. Because if Emily Hill is dead, there will be an investigation. All these secrets will come tumbling out, and all the things Andrew feared will come to pass, and worse, far worse.

But if Emily Hill is alive and well, there are no questions to be asked.

Which means there is one very good reason to keep me alive.

"Let me do the talking," Melinda says. She turns away from the body of her sister and walks toward the others.

Part III

Here

Now

47

Audrey

Emily—not Emily—watches me as I digest the information. Melinda says nothing. She hasn't lowered the gun.

I look down at the diary in my hand. The pages well thumbed, dog-eared, sections of it marked and notated so she could get the details right. I toss it onto the ground between us. "You studied this. You studied her. So you could become her."

"So I could understand her," she says softly.

"Who are you really, then?" I ask.

Something flashes in her eyes, deep and wounded. "My name is Stranger," she says. My heart seizes, but she only smiles faintly. "I found it carved down there. Some other girl's final gift to me."

Found it. Like Meghan had. *Not her. It isn't her.* And it couldn't be. I'd know Janie if I saw her again, no matter how long it had been, no matter how changed.

Wouldn't I?

I swallow. "You left the beads. You left those handprints on the walls," I say.

"For Jenny Red-Hands," Stranger says, her smile sharp. "She came for me, you know. She killed the man who hurt me and she helped me disappear." Melinda's breath hitches as Stranger tilts her head toward the older woman. "My Jenny. She's the one who talked Liam and Andrew into it. With logic and threats and promises and pity. She told them what Emily did. And took responsibility for killing her. She convinced them Emily's death was a problem—

a liability. But that I was the way out of it. They'd already gotten too deep to turn back, and it was such a neat solution."

"We didn't have a choice," Melinda says, but she doesn't believe it. It's just a lie she's told herself often enough she can't let it go.

With Stranger slotted into Emily's place, they could all hide their sins, and their father's.

"Andrew came around easily enough," Stranger says. "It was a deranged plan, but the only one we could all agree to. A way to protect everyone. At least those of us still breathing. I think he even got comfortable with it eventually. Not Liam, though. It broke his heart. But he went along with it. Even came up with the idea for the car accident."

That dark road. The car sliding out of control.

"Why?" I ask.

"We looked alike, but not *that* much alike," Stranger says. "He'd done some of his own stunts on *City Rescue*. He knew how to crash without actually hurting us. Andrew messed up my face beforehand, to be sure. Just enough to justify a bit of reconstructive surgery. We fixed my face, and I went blond—easier than trying to match the same hair color. I haven't seen my own face in the mirror in years."

"You still have a scar," I say. I touch the side of my nose. I noticed it one of the first times we met, but I didn't think anything of it.

She actually looks pleased that I noticed. "I asked for that special. In case anyone Emily knew thought I looked odd, it sold the injury story," Stranger says. She laughs a little. "But no one ever did. Not one person missed her. Another way we were so alike."

"Why stay so long? You could have left. You could have told someone," I say.

Stranger's gaze is distant, unfocused. "At first, I was afraid. But then I found . . . peace. A life, even if it wasn't my own. Melinda took care of me. She really did."

"We couldn't make it right. But I did what I could," Melinda says. The way they look at each other in that moment—whatever is between them, it might be twisted, but it's real.

Stranger continues. "And . . . I couldn't leave them. The girls before me. I felt like I was supposed to stay. I didn't know why, not for the longest time, but then I realized. They were all there to help me. I thought I was the last, but I wasn't. I was waiting for the last of us."

"Meghan," I say.

She looks at the woman who is not quite her sister. "I wanted to be like you, Melinda," she says. "I wanted to help someone. She reminded me so much of myself. And I thought I could help her get away. But she found the bunker, and she was so smart, and the questions she asked—she worked out so much of it."

"And you told her the rest," I say.

There is an aching loneliness in those eyes. She had been hidden for so long. And then this girl comes along—this girl who is seeking the witch in the woods Stranger once wished would save her. I wonder how it came out—bit by bit, or all at once, the lure of confession too powerful to resist.

"Not all of it," Stranger whispers. "But enough."

Melinda hisses. "How could you—Stranger, you can't—after all this time—" She sounds on the verge of tears, but Stranger hushes her. Reaches out. She brushes the hair from Melinda's face and presses her brow against hers.

"It's okay. She's gone. She stayed in the cabin a little while until I got her a new ID. Money. She's safe. She knows how to keep a secret," she says.

"No. Liam—before he died. He said, 'She came back,'" Melinda says. "I didn't know what he meant."

Stranger stiffens. She looks at me questioningly. "When he called you . . ."

My mouth is dry. I try futilely to draw some moisture into it. "He wasn't making much sense. I couldn't tell what he meant. He said that . . . that it was all going to work out. But 'she' was angry."

"She who? Meghan?" Melinda asks. The gun isn't pointing at me anymore. I try to take comfort in that.

"He said that she wouldn't listen, and so he told—told someone something. That's when he stopped talking," I say.

"Shit," Stranger swears. She shakes her head. "Meghan thought I should have turned you all in. I convinced her, but . . . that was before."

"Before Melinda got up on television to talk about how Terry Butler was a serial killer," I say blithely. Melinda flinches. There weren't many people who knew the name carved in that bunker. But Meghan was one of them. She'd left that comment. And then she'd decided to do something about it.

"Would she have gone by the house?" Melinda asks.

Stranger looks uncertain.

"If she was looking for you, would she go to the house?" Melinda repeats.

"Maybe," Stranger says, shrinking back.

"But you weren't there. Liam was," I guess. "If Meghan confronted him . . . He said he told. He didn't tell either of you."

"Andrew," Melinda says. She looks at Stranger, eyes wide. "Where is she? Where would she be? You said the cabin."

Stranger nods. Melinda swears.

"It's not going to take long for Andrew to figure that out if he hasn't already. We need to get there. Now."

I pull my phone out of my pocket. Melinda raises the gun.

Her voice is steady now. "No phones. No cops. And you're coming with us."

48

Audrey

"Let's go," Melinda says. She gestures with the gun.

"You don't need that," Stranger tells her, watching me. "Audrey will come with us."

I nod tightly. Melinda hesitates, then stows the gun in her purse. "My dog's in my car," I say. "I can't leave him here on his own."

Not when I don't know if I'll be coming back. Or maybe it would be better. Someone will find him here eventually.

"We can take your car," Melinda concedes.

She gestures for me to go out in front of her, Stranger trailing both of us. We reach the sidewalk. I chart escape routes. I could shout for help. Maybe someone would hear me before Melinda managed to get a shot off. I could run down the road—surely she wouldn't just take me out in broad daylight. Instead, my legs carry me right to my car. When she sees exactly what *my dog's in my car* entails, she pauses, her hand dipping toward her purse again.

"He's friendly?" she asks.

"He won't be a problem," I say quickly. I don't want her deciding he's a threat that needs to be dealt with.

"I'll ride in the back with him," Stranger suggests.

"Fine. You drive," Melinda says to me, and I walk stiff-legged around to the driver's side. I get in and quickly turn to reassure Barry, whose ears are pricked, his fur bristling at the nape of his neck. "It's okay, buddy. They're friends," I say as brightly as I can. Stranger slides in next to him, and he snuffles at her suspiciously before settling onto the bench with a groan, apparently unbothered. Melinda gets in more cautiously, keeping a wary eye on him. He looks uncertain, but thumps his tail. *Some guard dog*, I think, and I'm grateful. I can't let him get hurt.

If he does, it will be all my fault. I should have let this go. I should never have started down this road.

"Drive," Melinda tells me.

I am barely aware of starting the engine and pulling away from the curb. Melinda gives me directions. We head out past town, past Eden Crest. When Melinda gives the direction to turn, I almost miss the narrow dirt road.

I know exactly where we are, of course. I always do. Couldn't get lost even if I tried, and I know we're around the other side of Eden Crest, and that if I walked through those woods I'd get to Emily's house. And to the bunker.

A small log cabin sits tucked a good half mile back from the main road. Another car is already here.

"Andrew," Stranger says, voice tense. I throw the car into park. "Stay," I tell Barry firmly.

"Leave your phone," Melinda instructs. I toss it onto the seat. Barry whines as I shut the door. He stands on the back bench, clearly confused as to why I'm walking away and leaving him there.

Stranger is already starting for the house. And then she halts as a scream splits the air.

Meghan.

Stranger takes off running. I'm half a second behind her, Melinda lagging in her heels. Barry barks frantically behind us, nails scrabbling at the door, but I don't look back.

There's another yell. I put on a burst of speed, but I'm still five steps behind Stranger as we burst from the thick trees into a small clearing to find the source of the noise.

Andrew Hill stands in the middle of the clearing, his hand tangled in Meghan's hair. Meghan is on her knees, head wrenched back, grabbing at his arm. In his other hand, he holds a gun.

"Andrew!" Stranger shouts. I skid to a stop a few feet from her.

Meghan pants, holding on to Andrew's arm with both hands. "Stop. Put the gun down." She holds her hand out in a restraining gesture.

"Damn it," Andrew says. "What are you—why is she here?" He looks to me.

"Because she knows," Melinda says, approaching. Her own gun is in her hands again, small and gleaming, but she keeps it pointed at the ground.

Andrew laughs. "We're just telling everyone now?"

"Let Meghan go," Stranger says. I stay quiet, stay to the side, and watch Andrew's grip on Meghan's hair. I don't like how close to her his weapon is.

"She told Liam she was going to the police," Andrew says.

Stranger makes a noise in the back of her throat. "Meghan," she says softly. "You promised. You said you understood."

Meghan's face is streaked with tears. She thrashes in Andrew's unrelenting grip. "They can't get away with everything," she says. "What they did to you. You left the beads in the woods. You made the handprints. I thought you were the witch and you were supposed to help me, but it was the other way around." Her eyes are wide and wild.

"I didn't need help. I made my choices," Stranger says, shaking her head. But Meghan bares her teeth, her anger too righteous to be tamed.

"There's no way out this time," Melinda says softly. Her expression is almost one of relief. They might have skated by pleading ignorance of the bunker and all those bodies. But now? Meghan's disappearance might go unnoticed, but getting rid of me will only intensify the investigation. It's a strange knot, but not a hard one to untangle. They'll be found out. All of them.

But Andrew is shaking his head. His eyes well with tears. "After everything we did? We buried our sister in the woods, Melinda. We left all those girls out there to protect our family. And it worked. We paid the price, and we were happy. You were happy," he says to Stranger, almost pleading.

"Was I?" she asks, head tilting. "Is that what you thought, Andrew? Did you think we were friends, all this time? That we were family?"

His face goes hard. He lifts the gun. It points straight at Stranger's chest. "No. I guess not."

"Andrew," Melinda says warningly, but he doesn't falter.

"We don't have a choice," Andrew says. "You're the one who always talks about protecting our family."

"I don't want your protection," Melinda says. Her voice cracks. "And Liam doesn't need it. Not anymore."

"What are you talking about?" Andrew demands.

"He's dead," Stranger says bluntly. "He knew what he'd done and what you were going to do, and just like before, he was too much of a coward to do the right thing. He always thought feeling bad about it was enough."

Andrew's eyes swim with confusion. Melinda takes a breath. "He OD'd. After he told you, I guess, and he hadn't used in two years, maybe he couldn't handle the dose anymore . . ."

For a moment, I think Andrew is going to put the gun down. But then his expression shutters, hardens. I know that look. This possibility, his brother's death, has haunted him long enough that his grieving was done a long time ago.

He clenches his back teeth. "Here's an idea, Melinda. You're the expert, tell me what you think. The police find Audrey's body. We turn in that diary of Emily's—minus the final chapter. We're horrified to discover that it was Dad after all, and Emily followed in his footsteps. Liam found out. Couldn't handle it. And Emily's nowhere to be found, of course. We say she killed Audrey. The girl, too, if it even comes up. Not like anyone's looking for her. Maybe you don't get that Senate seat after all, but we move on."

"What do you do with me, then?" Stranger asks viciously. "I suppose you could always bury my body in the woods somewhere. Even if they run DNA, they'll think they're looking for Emily Hill, right? No match, no problem." There's a curl of a smile at the corner of her mouth. She's provoking him, can't she see that? But of course she can. She hasn't survived this long wearing his dead sister's name without knowing exactly how far she can push things.

"This is ridiculous. He's not killing anyone," Melinda says, stepping forward.

But Stranger isn't done. "Oh, but Melinda's a problem, isn't she? Can't trust her to keep her mouth shut. That's okay, you can always blame crazy Emily for killing her, too. Although at that point, they *would* look at you. That's a problem."

Andrew's face is empty now. There is no more grief there, no more rage, and my blood runs suddenly cold. Because that is the face of a man without hope, and without a future.

And there's nothing more dangerous.

"There's only ever been one problem, and we should have dealt with it years ago," Andrew says, and, gun still pointed at Stranger's chest, he squeezes the trigger.

I tense, caught between the instinct to leap toward him and to flee. Melinda is faster.

"No!" Stranger yells. I scream, an involuntary noise tearing from my throat as Melinda staggers, a circle of blood at her chest. One faltering step, and then she falls. Stranger half catches her, sinking to the ground with Melinda in her lap.

Andrew stares. His grip on Meghan falters.

"Meghan, run!" I shout. She doesn't take further urging. She scrambles away and is on her feet in a flash. Andrew doesn't seem to notice. He stares at his sister.

I should follow Meghan. Instead, I duck forward, pulling off the light jacket I'm wearing to press it against the wound.

"Help her," Stranger says, grabbing at my arm. "You know what to do. They train you."

They train me enough to know that nothing I can do is going to help. Melinda is trying to move. Or her body is. I've seen this strange, slow movement before, on an older man who'd fallen rock climbing. I've heard the labored, uneven breaths, the strange groan.

Agonal breathing. It isn't really breathing at all, just the last-ditch reflex of a brain deprived of oxygen. "I'm sorry," I say. "I can't—" But Melinda is already gone, blood-flecked face slack, eyes empty.

And I've lost my chance to run. Because Andrew still has the gun, hovering over us. And he has no way out at all.

He's got nothing but anger he's kept in check for years, and a life he did the unthinkable to protect dissolving with every dying breath in his sister's lungs.

Andrew Hill isn't going to let himself go to jail.

I think he and I realize it at the same time—the inevitability of what happens next. In that moment, we lock eyes. But the shock of what he's just done makes him slow. I move first.

I fling myself toward Andrew. He tries to track me with the gun, but I collide with his legs. We both go down. His weight lands on top of me. I twist under him, trying to see the gun, and then it's all I can see, filling my vision as he straddles me.

I have time to think the words clearly—*I am going to die*—before the gun goes off. It takes me another moment to realize that the ringing in my ears means a bullet hasn't hit me. Stranger has clamped her teeth onto Andrew's wrist, both hands gripping his arm. He bellows in pain and shoves her away, but she wraps herself around him, a howl tearing from her throat. Her fingers wrap around the butt of the pistol. She rips it free. I scramble for it.

Stranger makes a noise of pain, followed by a thump. My hand reaches for the gun—and something grabs me, yanks me away.

I flip onto my back. Then Andrew is on top of me, one huge hand around my throat, squeezing. A fist thuds into my side, quick jabs that make my whole body seize up with pain. I can barely see, have lost all sense of my body and his except for weight and pain and a horrible pressure against my throat. I can hear him breathing, ragged gasps. His spit strikes my face.

In my peripheral vision, I can see Stranger. She's moving, hand to her temple. Too slow, too weak to help. My vision fades to gray, to black.

They'll know, I think. *They'll find us. They'll find all of them. Every lost girl. Every ghost will have a name. At least there's that.*

There comes a faint clicking, clattering. Like beads rattling in the wind; like fingernails on a windowpane. *I need to tell you something,* a voice whispers in my ear.

And then I hear something else. A churning of gravel, and a terrible noise like the grinding of stones.

Andrew Hill begins to scream.

49

Stranger

I blink my vision clear with difficulty. Andrew's on top of Audrey, a hand around her throat. I reach toward them, but my hand claws ineffectually at the air.

Get up.

They've never entirely left. The girls before. I always knew they wouldn't until I was free, and I never was.

Get up.

But I can't. My limbs are too heavy, and Andrew is too strong.

He's killing her.

And Melinda is already dead. My savior, my jailer, my sister, my monster. I loved her. I don't think I realized until this moment how deeply I loved her and hated her and loved her still, and now she's gone.

Get up.

I push myself up on one elbow, but it's useless. I was never strong enough. Not strong enough to escape the bunker. Not strong enough to escape the Hills. I surrendered. To the dark and the deal we made and the fresh cage I built myself.

A dark form hurtles out of the edge of my vision, churning up the trail as it runs—Barry. His fur glitters, and my addled mind reads the glints as scattered stars until I realize it's glass. Safety glass, from the car window he must have broken through. I have only enough time to register his presence before his massive jaws clamp down on Andrew's leg.

Andrew screams. The dog gives a sharp yank, once and then twice and a third time, each one heaving Andrew off Audrey's limp body. He screams again and kicks out at Barry's muzzle. His boot connects. Barry snarls and whips his head side to side, dragging Andrew along with it.

Andrew flips over, hands scrabbling for purchase, for a weapon. His hand closes on a rock.

Audrey garbles something out, reaching as if to stop him.

Get UP.

Andrew brings the rock down. His aim is sloppy. It strikes Barry's shoulder. The dog lets out a horrible sound of pain and releases his jaws. Audrey twists, flipping herself over. Her hand scrabbles in the dirt, finds the gun, but she doesn't have the strength to lift it.

And then Barry bunches his hindquarters under him, launches forward, and closes his teeth around Andrew's throat. He shakes Andrew like a rag doll, snarling and growling. Andrew's limbs flail futilely.

Barry's going to kill him. I look at Audrey, the horror in her eyes. "Barry!" I yell. Barry freezes, sides heaving, Andrew hanging limply from his jaws. "Release!"

Barry drops Andrew instantly, springing back. He stands with his hackles up, a growl in his throat, head down. Blood coats his jaws, his chest. Andrew's throat and leg are pulped meat, but he's breathing wetly, one hand lifting, fluttering like a wounded bird.

Audrey is propped on one elbow, gun bobbing as she tries to point it at Andrew. Her eyes are wild, her hair matted with dirt and blood. I touch fingertips to my own temple and hiss with pain.

"Audrey. It's okay." I stagger to her, drop down on one knee. Her face turns toward me, but her gaze can't find me. I close my hand around the gun, easing it from her. There's no strength in her to stop me, even if she wanted to. I put an arm around her, pulling her in to plant a kiss on her forehead. "You're okay. You're going to be okay," I tell her.

I knew when I saw her at the witch tree that a moment like this was coming. She was never someone who would stop looking. And isn't that what I was waiting for? Isn't that why I confessed to

Meghan? I wanted to be known. I wanted my name remembered, added to the inventory of my ghosts. But it was a mistake.

That girl died in the dark. I am something else now.

I let Audrey go. Still dazed, she remains there as I limp to where Andrew lies and bend down over him. The growl is gone from Barry's throat. He pants, teeth still ready, but he looks at me without fear.

The damage is mostly to the sides of Andrew's neck. His eyes are glazed, but he's conscious. Still breathing, still bleeding. I set a palm against the side of his neck. Blood flows over my skin. My other hand is coated already in the blood of his sister. The panic in his face gives way for a split moment to hope—he thinks I'm trying to stop the bleeding.

Emily and Melinda and Liam and Andrew. They'd all have gone on if it weren't for me. To live their lives and claim their fates, and let my life be the price paid for it. It was always going to be this way. Them or me.

The swing of a hammer.

The ravages of regret.

The path of a bullet.

"I killed you all," I whisper, and I set the gun against Andrew's forehead.

When the gunshot fades, all I hear is a sound like the rustling of insect wings.

50

Audrey

"You're okay," Stranger tells me. She helps me up, pulling me over to a wide-trunked tree and propping me against it. Barry checks me over delicately, and I don't care that his muzzle leaves swipes of blood across my clothes. I run a hand over his shoulder, knocking loose bits of safety glass, and lean my head back. My whole body hurts.

"Why did you do that?" I ask. My voice is hoarse, throat bruised. She looks puzzled. "Why did you take the gun?"

Her expression clears, understanding. "You don't want to have killed someone," she says. "Trust me."

I blink. I can't seem to quite get a full breath, but I don't think my head hit the ground too hard. Mild concussion, maybe. I'm alive. More than I can say for the Hills. "I'm sorry," I say. Melinda's body lies where it fell, her head turned away from us.

"It's not your fault."

"I went looking."

"Not your fault there was something to find." She smiles a little and tucks my hair behind my ears. There is something in her eyes, a look half familiar and frightening. I seize her hand.

"Stay," I say, on instinct.

She stares at me, her expression strange. "Not this time," she says. "There's another cage waiting for me if I do."

"You didn't do anything wrong."

She laughs. "Maybe the justice system will agree. Eventually. But I'm not risking it."

"But where will you go?"

She looks to the side. Wind stirs her hair. The faintest trace of red roots shows under the blond. "I don't know. It feels like you can go just about anywhere from here, doesn't it? Maybe I'll even make it."

"You'd be surprised," I whisper, "how easy it is to disappear."

She puts a hand to my cheek. The blood in the creases of her palms is already drying. She starts to stand, but I grab her wrist, and she stills. I stare into her eyes. Green eyes. I almost recognized her, the day we met. Almost.

"Janie," I say, because I can't bear to form the full question. "I called her Stranger. When we were kids."

Her lips part ever so slightly.

"'My name is Stranger.' You wrote that," I say.

Silence. And then she shakes her head. "It was already written there," she says.

"Then she—"

"She's gone," Stranger says gently. "They'll be here soon. I have to go."

"Don't leave me here," I beg. Her head cocks to the side, almost as if she's listening to something, and she shuts her eyes. At the tree line, Meghan appears, hovering.

"You'll be okay, Audrey," Stranger says. She leans down. She presses her lips to mine. It is a soft, certain kiss—not fleeting, not lingering. A goodbye.

She stands. She walks toward Meghan. Her arm goes around the girl's shoulders, drawing her in. They confer a moment, and then, with one last glance toward me, they move away together.

I want to follow, but I'm too badly hurt. And maybe part of me doesn't want her caught. Not again.

In the distance, sirens blare. I wonder if they're for me. I wonder if she'll make it, where she could possibly go.

But somehow, I know she won't be found. She'll fade into the woods. Blood on her hands and the soft clinking of beads in her footsteps.

Barry climbs gingerly into my lap, weighing me down with his massive forequarters. His head bumps against my chest, and I wrap my arms around him. He whuffs against me.

You'll be okay, Audrey.

Except, I realize, my thoughts half a slurry with exhaustion, was that what she said?

Or did she say *Oddity?*

You'll be okay, Oddity.

I can't tell which one it is anymore. Can't tell which one I want it to be.

With Barry's steady breath matching mine, I wait to be found.

51

Audrey

They haven't found her. Stranger and Meghan have both vanished without a trace. They haven't uncovered any more bodies in days, but we know there are more to be found. Too many names, not enough bones.

Janie could still be buried out there.

You'll be okay, Audrey.

You'll be okay, Oddity.

I still can't remember which one I heard. It's like I have two memories, interposed over each other.

"I wish I could be sure," I say. Dev sits at the edge of the chair across from my spot on Len's couch, his elbows propped on his knees. Barry sleeps next to me, head on my lap, as he has for the last several days basically 24/7. We haven't been home much. I haven't been up for being alone, and Len and Kenny wouldn't have let me anyway. I have a splint on one wrist and the tail end of a prescription for some decent painkillers, as does Barry for his bruised shoulder, but otherwise my encounter with the Hills left more emotional damage than physical.

Dev showed up the first day. He came with flowers—for Barry, he insisted, the true hero of the hour—and didn't ask me for details. I wasn't ready to share them. Not yet. Not until now, nearly a week later.

"Could it be her?" Dev asks when I've told him all the parts of it I can bear to. "Wouldn't you have recognized her? Wouldn't they?"

"I don't know. I haven't seen her since she was a teenager, and she had surgery," I say. "Andrew and the others . . . They didn't know her as well as I did. It was years between when she left Franklin and when they found Stranger down there. She was in bad shape." Half starved, hardened, beastly—the diary said as much. "And maybe they did know," I add. I shake my head. There's no one left to ask.

But could Janie even have done what Stranger did? Lasted that long, pressing herself into the small shape that was required of her?

She was in that bunker. I'm certain of that much. I'm sure it was Janie who carved those words in the wood, but I don't know what happened to her after that—if she emerged, or if she died and left her chosen name as a talisman for the next girl to find.

I play with Barry's soft ear. He grumbles and snuggles nearer. He's been such a baby since we got home, begging for treats and sympathy and praise for his bravery. All of them have been in ready supply.

"I just have this feeling," I say at last. "Or, not a feeling. More like—quiet."

"What kind of quiet?"

"Like I'm done. Like I found her," I say. Like a small voice that has been whispering to me since the night Janie knocked on my window has finally fallen silent.

Like wherever Janie is, she's finally found some kind of peace.

Epilogue

Stranger

I have a new name. It isn't my own, of course, but it's starting to feel familiar. Melinda had things in place for years before she died. A trail Andrew wouldn't be able to follow, if we had to use it. It was not so much more work to give my new self a sister. We look so alike, after all. It's how I knew, that day in the woods; I knew she was one of us. We had merely been waiting for her.

"You could go back," I tell her. "You're eighteen. You didn't do anything wrong, not really."

But Meghan won't leave me. We belong with each other. All of us. They're quiet now, unseen, but I feel the pressure of them. They aren't real, of course, but then again, neither am I. Neither is this girl Meghan has become. We're all of us inventions.

I think about you sometimes. I wonder if you're well; I think you are, but I think you must still wonder. You'll work it out eventually. When they don't find my bones in the ground; when you put the dates together.

I shouldn't have gone to see you that night. Call it a moment of weakness, the fleeting delusion that I might somehow be able to steal back into my old life. But there was nothing to go back to. *I need to talk to you,* I said, but you never turned around. And then I caught a glimpse of myself reflected in your window, my face reshaped by first deprivation and then the scalpel, and I realized that even if you did see me, you wouldn't know me.

You deserved better than me. You always had. It was so long between that night and when you finally started looking that I don't blame you for forgetting when exactly it was. For not realizing that

Mason Hill had been dead for months already. That I had already shed my skin and taken on a new one.

Andrew told me once about the night he went into town to get drunk—the same day Liam and Emily brought me to the house. The two of you in the back of the car, and how, when you told him who you were, he suddenly knew—realized who I was, under all that grime. You thought he was upset because I left him, that I'd meant something to him in those few disastrous weeks we dated, but I was never anything to him. His shock was only because he'd suddenly realized that the creature in that bunker was a person after all. It made me real. It made him ashamed. That I knew him, and knew what his father had done. What *he* had done.

It should have inspired mercy. But Andrew felt only rage. I think if Liam hadn't brought me into the house, he would have killed me that night.

I owe Liam that much, at least.

Andrew didn't say my name for another year. He didn't want it to be true. I told him he was wrong. He pretended to believe me. It was easier that way. Liam never put it together. Melinda might have, but if she did, she never said anything. She needed me to just be Emily. The sister she could still save.

Oh, Oddity. I loved you. But I only knew how to love you cruelly.

I like to think that someday you will come and find me. That you will walk into the woods with a string of white beads and I will be there, and you will not mind my bloodied hands, the things I've done. You'll look into my face and know me, and you'll speak a name that's truly mine.

In the meantime—

You'll be okay, Oddity.

And so will I.

Acknowledgments

This is a story about complicated girls. Messy girls, angry girls, girls who are lost and who have no desire to be found. So first and foremost, I want to thank all the wild and wonderful women and girls in my life, especially my mother, Alice, my fierce and funny Bean, and my fabulous writerly flock. Let's all be bog witches together.

This book has been a quiet thrumming in my mind for a very long time, and for most of that time it consisted of only four words: *My name is Stranger*. I didn't know who those words belonged to or why they were stuck so thoroughly in my mind until one night I had a dream about a girl and a chain and a door opening and another string of words: *Wait. Let's think about this.*

I am immensely grateful to the people who helped me take hold of that image and turn it into an actual book, especially Susan and Rashida, who helped me grapple with it from its earliest stages; Sarah, Amelinda, and Maxine for their help wrangling twists and reveals; and my editor, Christine, and her assistant, Kate, for helping to shape a rough draft that didn't even have an ending into a real book. As always, a huge thanks to the team at Macmillan. From design to copyedits to publicity and more, they always knock it out of the park. And thanks to my author assistant, Martinique, whose powers of organization leave me baffled and deeply relieved.

Special thanks to Wilma Murray for her generous and detailed help with the Search and Rescue sections. Any remaining errors are entirely mine.

About the Author

Kate Alice Marshall is the author of *What Lies in the Woods, No One Can Know, A Killing Cold,* and multiple novels for younger readers. She lives in the Pacific Northwest with her family.